FOLLOW
YOU
HOME

ALSO BY MARK EDWARDS

The Magpies

Kissing Games

What You Wish For

Because She Loves Me

WITH LOUISE VOSS:

Forward Slash

Killing Cupid

Catch Your Death

All Fall Down

From the Cradle

MARK EDWARDS
FOLLOW
YOU
HOME

THOMAS & MERCER

Text copyright © 2015 Mark Edwards

Published by Thomas & Mercer, Seattle

www.apub.com

Amazon, the Amazon logo, and Thomas & Mercer are trademarks of Amazon.com, Inc., or its affiliates.

ISBN-13: 978-1503944374
ISBN-10: 1503944379

Cover design by Lisa Horton

Printed in the United States of America

In memory of Philip Davies, 1971–1990

Author's Note

Parts of this novel are set in Romania. I have taken some liberties with the geography of that country, including the route taken by the night train from Budapest to Sighisoara. The town of Breva is fictitious, as is Thornberry Bridge in London.

Part One

Hungary–Romania
August 2013

Chapter One

The overnight train to Sighisoara, due to leave Budapest at eleven, was running late. The station was quiet and unwelcoming, bars and shops shut for the night, figures lurking in the shadows around the edge of the building. We sat on the hard floor, tired after a day wandering around the city in the summer heat with our backpacks. A gang of teenagers hung about nearby, shouting and posturing and badgering passers-by for cigarettes. A middle-aged man approached us, asking if we needed a hot meal and somewhere to stay, his oily smile vanishing as we shooed him away. Armed police strolled about in pairs, scrutinising us suspiciously as they passed by.

So we were relieved when the train finally pulled into the platform and more travellers, though fewer than I expected, appeared as if from nowhere.

As we were about to board I pulled Laura against me and said, 'I love you.'

She kissed me. 'I love you too, Daniel. Even if you are a tightwad.'

'Hey—' I began, but she turned away, hauling her backpack onto the train and throwing a little smile over her shoulder that told me she wasn't really mad with me. I followed her.

Passing the cosy, private sleeper compartments, I wondered if I'd made a mistake. It had been my turn to buy tickets and instead of booking a private sleeper compartment I had, at the last moment, bought seats in standard accommodation because they were half the price.

Laura noticed me looking through the window of the sleeper and stopped to join me. 'It's a shame, really,' she said.

'What is?'

'Well, I was quite looking forward to having sex on a train. I've never done that before.'

I slapped myself on the forehead. 'Do you think it's too late to change the tickets?'

But she laughed and went through from the relative luxury of the sleeper carriages into standard class. Laura surveyed the empty carriage and chose a pair of seats at the far end. She took her Kindle and a bottle of water out of her bag and settled back on the double seat, upholstered a long time ago in grey velvet, trying to get comfortable. I sat by the window, hoping the train had air-con powerful enough to blast away the night's humidity. I took my glasses off to wipe the sweat from my face and put them back on in time to see a young couple running along the platform. They made it just before the train shuddered and lurched into motion. An announcement crackled over the speaker system and we were on our way.

The couple I'd seen running for the train almost fell into our carriage, panting, the man laughing while his female companion looked pissed off. They were carrying overnight bags, which they hefted into the baggage rack before taking the seats across the aisle from Laura and me. I smiled at them, then averted my eyes. Although we had befriended a number of couples on our trip around Europe in a transient way, exchanging email addresses and Twitter usernames, I preferred to observe someone first, make sure they weren't crazy before engaging in conversation.

Going purely by appearance, they were a curious, mismatched couple. They were both in their mid-twenties but I would never have put them together. He was short and stocky, with cropped blond hair, and was wearing a khaki T-shirt and cargo pants. An average-looking guy who clearly spent a lot of time at the gym. In contrast, the girl was dressed all in black, with a leather jacket over a Stranglers T-shirt, plus tight jeans and biker boots. Her hair was black to match her clothes, with streaks of crimson. Beneath hooded, heavily made-up lids, her eyes were the colour of *café noir*. A shade away from black. She was several inches taller than him, about five foot ten, so when standing she towered over him, reminding me of Olive Oyl and Popeye.

They talked to each other in their own language. Eastern European, obviously, though I was unable to tell if they were from Hungary, Romania or some other part of this half-continent.

As the train made its way out of the city, another passenger came into the carriage from the other end. He was about forty, stocky, with cropped hair and an acne-scarred face. He had no luggage. Even though most of the seats in the carriage were empty, he sat diagonally opposite Laura and me. He appraised us, apparently not liking what he saw, then closed his eyes and fanned himself with a newspaper.

I watched Budapest go by, the lights of the city blinking out as the journey progressed.

'I need a drink,' I said after a while. 'There should be a dining car open on the train somewhere.'

'Not till it crosses the border.'

I looked up. It was the guy across the aisle. He shrugged good-naturedly and said, 'The dining car doesn't open till we reach Romania. In'—he checked his watch—'around two and a half hours.'

'I knew we should have bought supplies in Budapest.'

'Don't worry,' he said, jumping to his feet. 'We have plenty.' He fished a heavy carrier bag out of his luggage and crossed the aisle to sit opposite us. After a pause, his companion followed, settling down beside him and crossing her legs. He cracked open two cans of Hungarian lager and passed them to us before we could protest.

'I'm Ion,' he said, opening two more cans and taking a sip from his. 'And this is Alina.'

Chapter Two

The train windows were matte-black, the darkness broken only by the occasional glimpse of lights in the distance. I glanced at my reflection, my face stretched like melted plastic by some kink in the glass. It was creepy. I looked away and turned my attention to our new companions.

Ion laid his free hand on Alina's knee, stroking it. So they *were* an item.

'What brings you to Romania?' he asked, grinning broadly. Beside him, Alina wore a more muted smile, seemingly bored.

Laura answered before I could. 'We're travelling round Europe. We've spent the last few weeks lying on beaches—'

'Nice.'

'—but we wanted to visit Eastern Europe, soak up some culture instead of rays.'

Ion nodded. 'Good choice. Romania is the most beautiful country. Of course, there are many problems—poverty, with the Romani gypsies and so on.' He waved a hand like this was a boring topic. 'But this is real Europe. Far more interesting than a Spanish beach.'

I noticed that Alina rolled her eyes almost imperceptibly.

'So you're from Romania?' Laura asked Alina, trying to draw her in.

'Yes.'

Laura waited but no more words were forthcoming.

'She's from Sibiu,' Ion said. 'That's where we're heading now, to see her folks. I can't wait to see if Alina's mom is as smoking hot as her daughter.'

I smiled. 'You speak excellent English. I hope that doesn't sound patronising . . .'

'No, not at all. That's where Alina and I met—at English classes.' He moved his hand further up his girlfriend's leg. She remained stony-faced. 'So where have you been on your journey round Europe?' he asked, looking from Laura to me.

I took a deep breath. 'We started off in Brussels, then travelled down through France, then Spain, a week in Ibiza, then into Italy—Rome and the Amalfi coast—then over to Greece, up through Croatia into Hungary.'

That was it. Two glorious months condensed into a shopping list. The details, the memories, were precious to Laura and me. The trip, our Grand Tour as we self-mockingly labelled it, had been transformational. Being typical tourists on the Eiffel Tower and round the Louvre, people-watching and feeling all the knots in our muscles untie themselves as we finally relaxed after what had been an intense period back home. Going wild in Spain, dancing and drinking at the Benicassim music festival, clubbing all night and sleeping all day in Ibiza. Shopping and hiring scooters and more shopping in Rome. Making love on a beach on the Amalfi coast, lying under the stars and talking about the children we'd have when we got back to England. Snorkelling among a rainbow of fish off Santorini. Posing for so many photos in the Plitvice Lakes National Park that I began to feel like my soul was being eroded.

This was life, really lived, really experienced, a passage of magic that would flash before our eyes when we died. And to share it, to live through these experiences together, meant that Laura and I were closer than ever.

Talking to Ion and Alina, giving them this bare-bones outline of our trip, made me miss my best friend back home, Jake. He was the one person, apart from Laura, with whom I could be fully open and honest. Whenever I got the chance I emailed him with long accounts of what Laura and I had been doing, like I was sending him pages from my diary. In return, he told me about all the exciting stuff that was happening with him back in London, as he continued to work on making it as a musician.

I paused, wondering how much more to tell these strangers, not wanting to go into the details of how, in the last few days, in Dubrovnik and Budapest, fatigue had caught up with us. Maybe we were feeling homesick, despite the great time we were having, or feeling the human urge to settle, to spend a period in one place. But our legs felt heavier and it was hard to gather much enthusiasm for these two magnificent cities. Laura suggested heading back to Italy or Spain, renting an apartment and staying put for a while, but I was insistent that we had to continue the Tour. Press on with the plans. After Romania we were going to head north again: Russia, Germany, then Scandinavia. The Tour was scheduled to end on my thirty-fifth birthday in Stockholm. Then we would fly home, back to London.

To get married. To start a family. Not necessarily in that order. Laura's own best friend, Erin, was pregnant, and I knew as soon as Laura met Erin's baby she'd be keen to get pregnant as soon as possible. And that was fine by me.

'And it's just you two?' Ion asked.

'That's right.'

'Sounds like you've had an awesome time.'

'It's been . . .'

'Too good for words, yes?'

'You got it.'

Before I could say any more, I noticed Ion frown in a surprised way at Laura, so I turned my head in her direction. She looked uncomfortable.

Ion said, 'Hey, I'm sorry if we're intruding. We can go back to our own seats . . .'

'No, no, it's not you.' She leaned forward, and both Ion and I echoed her so we dipped into a huddle. Alina remained sitting upright.

'Don't look,' Laura said. 'But that guy over there keeps staring at me.'

I couldn't help but look up. The man with cropped hair who had entered the carriage after Ion and Alina had his eyes open now and was reading a newspaper.

'Are you sure?' I asked.

'Yes,' she hissed. 'He was . . . staring at my legs. He's doing it now.'

I looked again and the man's gaze drifted upwards to meet my eye. His expression was inscrutable but he maintained eye contact in a way few people in England would do. Eventually, with a humourless smile on his lips, he returned to his newspaper.

'Let's swap,' I said to Laura, and she moved to the window seat so she was out of the stranger's direct line of vision. In a way, I understood why he was looking at her, with her strawberry-blonde hair, blue eyes and legs that were like the eighth wonder of the natural world. Tonight, she wore shorts, because it was hot, not because she enjoyed being stared at.

She should have been out of my league. Luckily for me, she was attracted to tall, geeky guys with glasses. My hair is an average brown colour, I'm too skinny and I look a little like the guy who gets sand kicked in his face in the old ads. But luckily, there are women out there who are attracted to guys like me rather than to the guys kicking the sand.

While Laura moved over, Alina turned round and frankly stared at the man, who was watching us again. Eventually, he looked away, a sneer on his face.

'You come across a lot of guys like that,' Ion said, 'who think it's OK to stare at women like they're in a shop window. Alina gets it all the time.'

She nodded once.

I took Laura's hand and gave it a quick squeeze. I knew she would be feeling embarrassed so I said, 'Let's change the subject.'

'Good idea,' Ion said. 'So what do you guys do? When you're not travelling?'

'Laura works in marketing,' I said. 'For a children's charity.'

'Interesting.'

'It's really not,' said my girlfriend.

'But you're doing something good.'

Laura sipped her beer. As the biggest lightweight I'd ever met, she would be tipsy by the time she'd finished. 'It's better than selling Coke,' she said.

Ion widened his eyes.

'I mean Coca-Cola.'

The three of us laughed. Alina was still flicking hostile looks at the guy opposite.

'I guess you two don't have kids?' Ion asked.

'No,' Laura said, at the same time that I replied, 'Not yet.'

He looked between us curiously.

'This is our last big trip before we start a family,' I said.

'*Try* to start a family,' said Laura. 'You can't take anything for granted. Not when you're my age.'

'You're only thirty-four.'

We'd had this conversation many times. This was one of the reasons why we had come on this trip now. Laura's biological clock was growing ever louder—she said she felt like the crocodile in *Peter Pan,* with a timepiece ticking inside her—and I was ready too. But after seeing our friends with children restricted to exhausting family holidays, I had suggested to Laura that we go on a big, final trip before we started nesting. And the trip was made possible by a stroke of good fortune—or rather, the result of a long period of intense work.

'What about you?' Ion asked me.

'I'm a developer,' I said. 'I created an app for iPhones and iPads and sold it to one of the big tech companies.' As ever, I was concerned about sounding modest, rather than boastful, when talking about this.

'Which is how we could afford to come on this trip,' added Laura.

'Which company?' Ion asked. 'Let me guess—Google? Facebook?'

'No, Skittle.' Skittle were one of the biggest of the new crop of tech companies that had sprung up over the last couple of years, specialising in mobile apps.

'Wow. That's beyond awesome. Did you hear that, Alina?'

She dragged her attention away from the window and nodded at me. 'Great.'

'So, are you famous in England?' Ion asked, eyes shining.

'No! I'm barely even famous in my own flat. What do you two do?' I wasn't allowed to talk about my app until it was officially announced; I had signed a confidentiality agreement. I deliberately aimed the question towards Alina, whose reticence was making me uncomfortable.

But Ion spoke up before his girlfriend had a chance. 'Alina's an illustrator.'

'Really? What kinds of things?'

'Comic books,' she said, meeting my eye. For the first time, I saw a spark of something other than boredom. Pride, plus a hint of defiance, as if she expected to be mocked.

'That's so cool,' I said, genuinely impressed.

'Yeah,' said Ion. 'We're going to collaborate on something, aren't we?' He rubbed her knee.

'So, what, you're a writer?' I asked.

Before he could open his mouth, Alina said, 'He does nothing.'

The volume was turned down on his smile. 'That's a little unfair.'

This was interesting: the sudden crackle of tension between them.

Ion turned his smile up again, but removed his hand from her knee. 'OK, so I am between jobs at the moment. But I'm writing a book. Along with the, you know, thing with Alina.'

'What's it about? The book?'

'Oh, just, like, my personal philosophy. Thoughts I've had about . . . stuff.'

Laura had gone to the toilet. I made a mental note to tell her about Ion's book, knowing she would find it amusing.

As Ion was about to elaborate on his work in progress, the train pulled into a station. It was almost deserted, just a man in his sixties with an enormous, boxy suitcase.

Alina, to my surprise, jumped up and slipped through the door, helping the man onto the train, carrying his case into the carriage. The old man, who looked strong and fit enough to be able to handle the suitcase himself, thanked her in his own language then headed off to a seat at the other end of the carriage.

The four of us chatted for the next hour. Ion wanted to know all about the app I'd developed and we talked about that for a while, while Laura and Alina, who had come out of her cocoon after

helping the older man, chatted about travel. Flattered by how interested and impressed Ion seemed—I was used to my friends' eyes
glazing over when I said anything at all about the app—I temporarily forgot all about my confidentiality agreement.

Towards the end of this conversation Hungarian border guards,
wearing blue jackets and yellow high-visibility vests, got on the
train and checked our passports. They studied Alina's passport for
a long time before finally passing on to the next passenger. Like the
police at the station, they had guns on their hips.

After they'd gone and I'd put our passports and tickets back in
my backpack, Laura whispered in my ear, 'That guy was staring at
me again.'

'What?'

'He's looking at my reflection in the window.'

'Are you sure you're not being paranoid?'

'Maybe. I don't know.' She flexed her shoulders and arched her
neck. 'I'm so tired.'

'I know. Me too.' I yawned.

'But this seat is too uncomfortable.'

Ion, who had just returned from the toilet, overheard. 'Hey,
there's an empty sleeper compartment just down the corridor. Why
don't you go and have a nap in there?' His voice was hushed, con-
spiratorial. 'It will be a couple of hours before the Romanian guards
come through and we can keep an eye out for you, come and wake
you just after we cross the border.'

'I don't know,' Laura said.

'It will be fine,' Ion said.

'I think it's a good idea,' I said to Laura.

She pulled a face, torn between her desire for sleep and her dis-
like of breaking rules.

'Go on, Laura,' Alina said. 'I promise we'll wake you.'

'I don't know.'

'Come on,' I said. 'I'll set an alarm on my phone too. What time are we due to cross the border?'

Ion checked his watch. 'We left Budapest forty minutes late, so it will be about three-ten. You've got just under two hours.'

'Oh, all right,' Laura said. 'Thank you.'

She glanced across the carriage and I saw what had made her mind up. The man was staring at her again, the tip of his tongue resting between his lips, one leg jiggling up and down. Slowly, he looked away, a smirk on his face.

Chapter Three

The sleeper compartment was tiny, containing two narrow bunks with a gap of around three feet between them. Outside the window: blackness. We were deep in the Hungarian countryside now. I could hardly even imagine what the landscape would look like outside the window. Forests? Plains? I pressed my face against the window. I couldn't even see any stars. If it wasn't for the occasional flicker from an isolated building, the train could be hurtling through space. We could be anywhere. We could be at the end of the world.

Laura kicked off her boots and flopped down on one of the bunks. I sat opposite her and took my phone out of the front pocket of my backpack. The battery was almost dead—the bloody thing was *always* almost dead—but I set the alarm anyway, hopeful that it would last.

'So what do you think of our two new friends?' I asked.

'I'm not sure. He is a little in love with himself. Can't wait to read his book.' She raised her eyes to the ceiling. 'But Alina's graphic novel sounds interesting. She was telling me it's about female power, a kind of feminist twist on the typical superhero story. She said she'd send me a copy.'

'Cool.' I moved over to her bunk and bent to kiss her. 'You said you'd always wanted to have sex on a train.'

'You're priceless. Now, if you'd booked a sleeper like this for the whole night it might have been different. But the point of coming in here was to have a nap.'

'Come on, it will be exciting. Could you'—I leaned forward to kiss her—'be persuaded?'

'Mmm. Maybe.' She kissed me back. I slid my hand up her smooth thigh and her breathing grew heavier; I could feel her heart fluttering as she pressed against me. 'Lock the door,' she said, breaking away. The flesh that covered her collar bone was flushed.

I stood up as best I could and tried the lock. 'Oh, for fuck's sake. It's broken. It won't lock.' That was probably why this compartment was empty.

'You'd better take a cold shower, then.'

She gave me another of the little smiles that I loved, turned away and faced the wall. I couldn't help but laugh. Foiled by a broken lock. I lay down on the opposite bunk and watched as her breathing changed. Within minutes, she was asleep.

I was determined to stay awake and took my phone out again to play a game, even though it was draining the battery. I had a plug converter somewhere in my backpack but was unable to gather the energy to heave myself off the bunk and find it. I was going to stay awake anyway, in case anyone tried to come through the unlocked door, so it didn't matter if my phone died soon. I'd charge it before we got to our destination, assuming I could find a socket.

I had dropped my phone in Italy, cracking the screen. I played the game for a while, peering through the spiderweb of cracks, aware of the growing heaviness of my eyelids. I told myself I would stop playing in a minute, move around, have a drink of water. The train rattled and rocked me on my bunk. I needed to stay awake.

Closing my eyes, deciding it would do no harm to rest them.

———⌣———

I sat bolt upright. I was cold and sweaty and my mouth felt like the inside of a grave. My phone dropped to the floor with a thud. I'd been dreaming I was in a coffin and someone was knocking on the lid.

BANG BANG BANG.

Laura rolled over and opened her eyes, just as the door was yanked open and a thickly accented voice said, 'Passports.'

Chapter Four

I blinked at the guards, my sleep-sodden brain refusing to function.

The one in front had his arm outstretched. 'Passports.'

Laura sprang into action before me, crouching on the floor and unzipping the front pocket of my backpack.

The guards watched her. The one in front was in his thirties, overweight with a bald head and patchy stubble on his chin. His colleague was a little younger, with a neatly trimmed beard and intense blue eyes. They both wore the same impatient, pissed-off expression, like they had just been told their wages were being cut. The guidebook said the Romanian border guards were welcoming and friendly, so I smiled at them and nodded. They didn't smile back.

Laura looked over her shoulder at me, an anxious expression on her face, then unzipped the front pocket on her own backpack. She rummaged inside, then turned back to me, her face pale.

'They're not here,' she said to me.

'What?'

The guards watched as I scooted onto the floor beside her, sticking my hand into the front pocket where I always kept our passports, tickets and money.

'They were in here,' I said quietly. 'Definitely. I put the passports back in here after the Hungarian guards checked them.'

'Are you sure?' Laura hissed.

'Yes.' I was aware that my voice was trembling slightly. 'Didn't you see me?'

'I don't know.' Her eyes were wide, panic creeping in. 'I wasn't really looking.'

'Come on,' the bald guard barked.

I held up my hands. 'Sorry, one moment.'

He tapped his foot metronomically, a hollow sound that echoed around the compartment, as I searched the side pockets of the backpack, finding nothing but some chewing gum and various screwed-up receipts and leaflets. As Laura searched her own backpack, I stuck my hand into the main compartment. My hand touched something that felt like a passport and my heart leaped for a moment, but it was just a pamphlet I'd picked up in a museum in Barcelona.

I thought hard. Had I definitely put the passports back? Perhaps I had absent-mindedly set them on the ledge where we'd been sitting with Alina and Ion. No. I remembered unzipping the backpack because the zip had got stuck and required some yanking before it would fasten. I had definitely put them back in the front pocket.

The guard's foot continued to tap. I glanced up at Laura. She had gone even paler.

'They're gone,' I said, the second word sticking in my throat.

The bald guard said something in Romanian to his colleague, his voice bear-deep and humourless.

I stood up. 'Our passports, our tickets . . . They've been stolen.'

The guard glared at me, then at Laura, who stood beside me. I reached out for her hand, squeezing it. The guard noticed this and sneered.

'We're British,' I said, as if this would make some sort of difference, and now they both wore sneers. A part of me was tempted to make my ludicrous comment into a joke, mention the Queen, Harry Potter, Manchester United. I bit my tongue.

'What are your names?' Bald Guard asked.

We told them. Daniel Sullivan, Laura Mackenzie.

I was confident this could be sorted out. They would be on our side. We were victims of a crime, and the thief must still be on the train. Had it stopped briefly to let the guards on? I hadn't noticed. Whatever, we were the ones who had been wronged and these men, these figures of authority, would be able to help us. OK, so we weren't supposed to be in the sleeper compartment, but it had been empty. In England, if you travel in the wrong part of the train or without a ticket, you are asked to pay the difference or get a penalty fare. This would all be OK.

'Someone must have come into the carriage while we were asleep,' I said. 'Stolen our things.'

I had no idea if the guards could understand me. They stared at me blankly. Then Bald Guard, who appeared to be more senior, said something to Bearded Guard, who left the compartment, stalking off down the corridor.

Bald Guard picked up my backpack and began to pull items out of it. My clean T-shirts, the *Europe by Rail* guidebook, my sunglasses. There was a carrier bag full of dirty laundry at the bottom of the bag. I saw him lift it out and open it, then grimace and recoil. He dropped it with the rest of the items he'd removed on the bunk and grunted, then picked up Laura's bag. He unzipped it and peered inside, throwing her make-up bag onto the floor.

'Hey,' I said. 'You can't do that.'

Ignoring me, he rifled through Laura's backpack, pulling out her carrier bag of dirty clothes and pushing it back in immediately.

Then he pulled out a clean black and pink bra, held it up and looked straight at Laura's chest. I stepped in front of her and he laughed, throwing the bra on to the small pile of our possessions, dropping the backpack beside mine.

Laura sat down on the bunk and began stuffing our things back into the two backpacks. She was shaking and all I wanted to do was comfort her, make it all better. Make this stop.

I felt the need to say something to the guard, to appeal to him, make him understand, but before I could think of anything useful to say the bearded guard returned. With him was another man, this one tall and thin with a grey face. He was wearing a rail company uniform. In his hand was a long sheet of paper containing what I assumed was a list of bookings. He ran his finger down the list and shook his head.

The railway guard and the two border guards exchanged sentences rapidly.

Bald Guard pointed at me, groping in his memory for the English words he required, and at that moment Alina arrived.

'Thank God,' I said. Someone who could speak Romanian. She would be able to explain everything to them. I had never felt so pleased to see someone.

'Alina, we've had our passports stolen, and our tickets and all our money. Can you explain to them? I don't think they understand.'

I wanted Alina to appear business-like, calm, but she seemed nervous, jittery. She spoke to the men in their mother tongue, the words fast and hard.

Bald Guard shook his head, pointing at us and then at the list that the railway guard held.

Alina listened, then turned to us. 'They say you're not supposed to be in here. That this compartment should be empty.'

Well, yes, I wanted to say to her. *Perhaps you could tell them it was your boyfriend's idea?* But where would that get me?

The man in the rail uniform spoke. His voice was thin, emphysemic.

'They're accusing you of being . . .' Alina groped for the word, came up with something she must have remembered from movies. 'Stowaways?'

'Fare dodgers,' I said. 'But we had tickets. Ordinary tickets. They were stolen. Please tell them we're sorry, we know we shouldn't have come into the sleeper carriage. But we bought tickets. We're the victims of a crime.'

She nodded and, I assumed, relayed this to the men.

The bald guard exclaimed a universal word: 'Hah!'

Alina spoke to him again, raising her voice, her nervousness giving way to anger. I could tell from the way they were looking at her—at the leather jacket, her boots, her hair and make-up—that they thought she was some kind of freak. Had she been dressed smartly, or been older, more conservative-looking, perhaps everything would have been different. Or perhaps it was her manner. Alina, I realised too late, was not the best ambassador, and soon they were arguing, she and the bald guard, both their voices increasing in volume, their words piling on top of one another, neither listening to the other.

A man in the adjacent compartment poked his head out and the bearded guard shouted at him, prompting him to shut the door quickly.

The argument between Alina and the guard escalated, firing harsh words at each other. Suddenly, the guard put up his hand and spat out a single syllable—'Stop' or 'Enough'?—and said something to the railway guard, who nodded and scurried away.

The bald guard pointed at Laura and me and said, 'Come.'

Alina protested and he pushed her, propelling her along the corridor. She kept trying to turn back, still arguing, but he put his hand between her shoulder blades and shoved her.

'What's happening?' I said, following behind. 'Alina?'

She didn't reply, just continued to pour forth a stream of Romanian.

'The train's slowing,' Laura said in a hushed voice.

She was right. We were slowing down as if we were coming into a station, the brakes squeaking. The guard yanked open the door that led into the area between the carriages, and pushed Alina through, ordering 'Come, come,' to Laura and me.

The train continued to slow, and the vast blackness outside was punctuated by a few weak lights. The train slowed and halted, brakes emitting a high-pitched whine, and I rocked back, banging my shoulder on the wall. The train came to a standstill and the doors hissed and slid open. I looked out past the guard and Alina at a small, open-air station, the platform a foot below where we stood.

It was only then that I realised what was happening. I said, 'No,' but the guard ignored me. He pushed Alina off the train, causing her to fall onto her knees on the dark platform, and then he yanked Laura's arm, propelling her off the train too. She made a gasping sound as she half-fell, half-jumped, landing on her feet and managing to stay upright. Finally, the guard shoved me off the train. I turned to shout at him, to plead, and he threw our backpacks off after us. They landed with a thump.

'You can't do this!' I shouted, but he just stood there, blocking the exit until the doors slid shut, his eyes cold and hard. Moments later, the train heaved into motion, and as we stood there, stunned, someone appeared at the window where we'd been sitting originally, before we made the idiotic decision to move: Ion, a shocked expression on his face.

The train pulled away, gathering speed, out of the station. I watched as it slid into the darkness, leaving us behind, standing in the half-light, on a platform in the middle of nowhere.

Chapter Five

I was frozen for a minute, barely able to process or believe what had just happened. I stared at the space where the train had been until the night swallowed it up and I couldn't even hear it anymore. The full moon came into view, bathing the spot where we stood with weak light. Stars were dotted here and there. With the train gone, everywhere was silent. No crickets throbbing in the grass. No traffic rushing on nearby roads. All I could hear was my own heavy breathing.

Slowly, my eyes adjusted to the darkness. We were in the middle of the countryside somewhere not too far, I assumed, from the Romanian border, though it was impossible to estimate how much ground the train had covered before the guards had expelled us. And I wasn't familiar with Romanian geography. All I knew was that it was an alien landscape, and that we were a very long way from home.

On my left (without a compass I had no way of knowing what direction I was facing), the ground rolled and swelled, an undulating landscape of hills and valleys, trees clinging to steep slopes, an expanse of water in the distance winking silver when the moon showed its face. Beyond, looking down on the hills like elders standing guard over their children, were mountains, jagged and foreboding. They reminded me of the Tolkien books I'd read as a teenager, the hobbits setting off on a treacherous journey in search of the Ring.

In the other direction the ground was flat and covered in thick forest which stretched for miles. In the far distance, beyond the forest, another row of jagged mountains formed the horizon. A number of silent birds, black in the dim light, rose from the trees on the forest's edge before swooping and vanishing again. During the day, with the sun shining, it would no doubt be beautiful. But not now. Not on a night like this.

The station was tiny, with just two platforms which were connected by a narrow footbridge. There were no lights; the station appeared to be out of use. There was a small, wooden building with weathered, flaking paintwork that would have once been the ticket office, I guessed. I turned in a slow circle. There were a few dark, similarly abandoned-looking buildings nearby. It looked like a village, a settlement really, that had died at some point in the not-too-distant past.

'Daniel?'

I turned slowly to face Laura, who stood hugging herself on the dimly lit platform.

'Daniel,' she said again, more urgently.

I stepped over to my girlfriend and pulled her into an embrace, feeling her soft hair against my face. The temperature had dropped significantly and she was shivering in her shorts and T-shirt. Goosebumps rippled on the flesh of her arms, her teeth chattered. I looked around for my backpack, which lay on the concrete, its contents spilling out like guts. I dug out a hoodie, which I passed to Laura. She stared at it like she didn't know what it was.

'Come on, sweetheart,' I said. 'Put it on.'

She looked at me with wide eyes, jerking her head round at a movement in a tree overhead. A bird, its silhouette just visible among the black branches.

'We're going to be OK,' I said, but I sounded like I was trying to reassure myself more than her.

In fact, she seemed to be recovering from the shock more quickly than me, as she cracked a weak joke: 'When I said I wanted to go off the beaten track, I didn't mean this far off it.'

Alina stood a few feet away, gazing along the tracks, seemingly in a trance.

'Do you know where we are?' I asked.

She didn't reply.

'Alina?' I went up to her and, finally, she snapped out of it. I repeated my question.

She looked around and shook her head.

'What the fuck just happened?' I asked. 'Where was Ion? And why didn't you wake us like you said you would?'

She rubbed her eyes, shook herself awake. 'I . . . I fell asleep.'

'And Ion?'

'He went to the dining car to get something to eat. I must . . . I guess I was only asleep for five minutes, maybe ten. When I saw the border guard and the ticket inspector heading towards you I jumped up straight away, came to help.'

'And that went really well.'

She hung her head. 'I'm so sorry.' Then her eyes lit up. 'That guard—what a fucker. If I ever see him again, I'm going to kick his ass so bad.'

'I'm cold.'

We both turned around. Laura was still hugging herself, her eyes as round and wide as the sun that had burned so brightly on the first part of our trip. The beaches of Italy and Spain seemed a very long way away now.

I tried to hug her again but this time she flinched away.

'If you'd booked us into a sleeper carriage in the first place, hadn't been so bloody tight.'

I protested. 'We might still have been robbed.'

'No. No, we wouldn't.' She raked her hands through her hair and sighed. 'I shouldn't have agreed to go into the sleeper carriage. I knew it was a bad idea.'

'I thought it would be OK . . .' I trailed off. 'I'm sorry.'

Alina turned away to give us privacy and produced a crumpled packet of cigarettes from her pocket. She lit one, sucked on it hungrily, then looked over her shoulder. 'At least you guys still have your stuff. All mine is still on the fucking train.'

'Have you got a phone?' I asked.

She checked her jeans pockets, pulling out her passport, glancing at it, and sighing. 'No. It was in my bag.'

'And mine is dead.' The battery had shed its last scraps of energy while I was asleep. 'Laura?'

'It's in my backpack.'

She knelt and rummaged through the backpack, then raised her face to the sky. 'It's not there. They must have stolen it along with the other stuff.'

I swore. 'Someone must have looked into the compartment, seen us asleep, decided to try their luck. Hey, maybe it was that guy. The one who kept staring at you. Did you see him, Alina? Did he leave the carriage?'

'I don't know. I didn't see.' She took a long drag on her cigarette.

'It doesn't matter, does it?' said Laura. 'It's all gone. We'll never know who it was.' She looked around. 'I don't like this place. It feels . . . haunted. In a bad way.'

Alina raised an eyebrow. 'Haunted? You believe in ghosts?'

'Yes.' To my relief, she didn't say anything else. I had long since accepted Laura's belief in the supernatural but felt slightly embarrassed when she mentioned it to other people. And I really didn't want to talk about ghosts, right here and now.

Alina must have seen me staring at her cigarette because she held it up and said, 'You want one?'

'No. Thanks.'

She shrugged and approached the ticket office, peered through the filthy glass.

'There's a map,' she said.

I stood beside her at the window. Laura came over to look too. An A2-sized map showing what I assumed to be the local area hung on the wall opposite the window. It was just possible to make out a red arrow, indicating where we were, but in the half-light I couldn't discern any of the place names.

'Can you read it?' I asked Alina.

'Kind of . . . I think that green area there is the Apuseni Natural Park. So we're in that area of forest just below it.'

She squinted. 'There's a town, not too far.'

I scrutinised the black dot she was referring to. The name was short but I couldn't read it. Not that it really mattered. All we needed to know was that it was a town. People. Civilisation.

'Did you notice if we went through a town on the train, before we got here?' I asked.

'I think so. Yes, I'm pretty sure we did.'

We all turned and looked at the tracks, leading back the way we'd travelled. Whoever had built the railway had cut a wide path through the trees, slicing the forest in two. It was wide enough for two tracks, with another two metres of clear ground either side of the rails. Only the first few metres of this path were visible. Beyond, pitch darkness.

'How far do you think it is?'

'Hmm. I don't know. Nine or ten kilometres.'

'So that's, what, six or seven miles?'

Laura put her hand on my arm. 'You're not thinking of trying to walk there, are you? Wouldn't we be better off heading out of the station, trying to find a road?'

'I don't know,' Alina said. 'You can see here, on the map: the train track runs straight to the town. The road also goes into the forest, but is much longer.'

As she said that, a noise came from the blackness at the far end of the platform. Laura's grip on my arm tightened, her fingertips digging into my flesh.

'What the fuck was that?' she said, her voice escalating a pitch.

Something growled.

Alina took a few tentative steps along the platform towards the noise.

'It's a dog,' she said quietly.

The growl came again and the dog came into view to our left, at the end of the platform, the mountains behind it. Then, as Alina backed away, another appeared. Two black dogs. They looked a little like Dobermanns, but slightly smaller and completely black. They stared at us, silent now, but with drawn-back lips that displayed two sets of sharp, yellowish teeth.

Laura stepped behind me. She has always been afraid of dogs. My parents have a black Labrador, a docile but boisterous creature, and whenever Laura visited, the dog would have to be locked in the kitchen because Laura found him frightening. It stemmed from her mother, who was attacked by a dog when she was a kid, passing on her lifelong fear to her own child.

Alina had moved slowly back to stand beside the window. Laura was gripping my arm so hard that I would have bruises the next day.

One of the dogs took a step forward and growled again, low and menacing. A word popped into my head. Rabies. With it

31

came images of foaming mouths, thrashing bodies, heat and pain and death.

'I think,' Alina whispered, 'I would rather walk to the nearest town than stay here with them. If we walk along the edge of the tracks it should only take a couple of hours.'

'What time is it?' Laura asked.

I checked my watch. 'Just after three.'

'Then we'll be there in time for breakfast,' Alina said.

I nodded. 'Laura, are you OK with this plan?'

She looked at the dogs, then turned her head to look along the tracks.

'It's too dark. How the hell are we supposed to find our way?'

'They're railroad tracks. We just follow them. And I have the torch, remember?'

I had slipped the skinny Maglite into my backpack at the last minute when packing back home, thinking it might come in handy. I had stopped short of bringing a Swiss Army knife, but only because I didn't own one.

Laura looked at the dogs, then at the tracks, then back at the dogs, both of which took another step forward, teeth on display.

'OK,' Laura said, her voice just audible above the growling of the two dogs.

We backed slowly away from the dogs, careful not to make any sudden movements. I bent and picked up the two backpacks, passing Laura's to her, and we slung them onto our backs, but not before I'd retrieved the torch, which I switched on, relieved to find that it worked. We walked to the end of the platform, passing beneath the footbridge. Someone had graffitied a crude image of a man with huge genitals which were pointed at a smaller female figure. Next to that was a drawing of a devil, its face contorted into a scream.

Averting my eyes, hoping my girlfriend hadn't seen the graffiti, I followed Alina down onto the tracks, taking care to stay away from the rails in case they were live. I held Laura's hand and we began to walk towards the trees, onto the track that cut through the forest.

Chapter Six

We walked along beside the rails, the forest to our left, tracks to our right. The trees formed a wall beside us, as still as sentries. In some places the taller trees bent forward to create a threadbare canopy, their tips touching the tops of their counterparts across the tracks, as if they were reaching out, trying to fill the gap that had been ripped through them. I tried not to look at them too much, concentrating on the ground beneath my feet, the few metres ahead that were illuminated by the torch. The flat space between the forest edge and the rails was dry and crunchy, seed pods and leaves scattered around, along with the occasional sign of human life: a rusted beer can or crisp packet that had been thrown from a passing train. Alina lit another cigarette which, when finished, she paused to tread out.

It was so quiet that I had started chatting almost as soon as we left the station behind, eager to fill the oppressive silence.

'I'm starving,' I said now. 'I wonder what we'll be able to get for breakfast in this town.'

'We haven't got any money,' Laura responded. She had changed out of her shorts into a pair of jeans and had stopped shivering.

'I've got a little in my pocket,' I said.

'I don't suppose you've got a bottle of gin in there too?'

'No, but I've got some water in my backpack. Hang on.'

I found the half-empty bottle of mineral water and passed it to her. She took a sip and offered it to Alina, who waved a hand to say no thanks.

I groped for something else to say.

'This is a bit like that film,' I said. 'You know, the one with River Phoenix, when those boys go walking through the woods along the train tracks.'

'*Stand by Me*,' Laura said. 'At the end they find a dead body.'

'This is nothing at all like that film with River Phoenix,' I said.

She laughed. As we went further along the path she seemed to relax a little, especially when the clouds above shifted to reveal a bright moon. It helped illuminate the path, so I was able to switch off the torch. I squeezed Laura's hand and she squeezed back.

'I bet Ion was shocked when he saw that you'd been kicked off the train,' I said to Alina.

'He was probably pleased.'

'Why do you say that?'

She looked at us sideways. 'We had an argument. That's why he went to the dining car. To get away.'

'Have you been together long?' Laura asked.

'Hmm.'

Laura and I exchanged a glance, but Alina didn't say any more.

'Have you ever been to England?' I asked, trying to keep the conversation going. Every time it fell silent I could hear noises from the forest: rustling, swishing, unseen things stirring in the darkness.

'No.'

'You should,' I said. 'I'm sure you'd like London, if you're an artist. My best friend is a musician, a singer. He reckons London is the most creative city in Europe.' I wondered what Jake would say when I told him about this escapade. It comforted me to think

35

I could turn this experience into an amusing anecdote, even though I knew that Jake would tell everyone we knew about it.

'I think next year Romanians will be free to come and work in the UK,' I kept on. 'The right-wingers have been banging on about it like we're going to be invaded.'

Alina made a non-committal noise, then said, 'So what do you think of Romania so far?'

Laura and I laughed. Laura said, 'Oh, I'm going to recommend it to all my friends. I particularly like the forests, and the border guards are just lovely. So welcoming.'

I couldn't see Alina's face well, and wasn't sure if her question had been sarcastic or sincere. The former, I thought, but didn't want to risk offending her so I said, 'I'm sure once we get everything sorted out, and get back to civilisation, we'll love it.'

'If I were you,' Alina said, 'after this I'd get on the first plane out of here.'

I was about to say something about how much I'd been looking forward to seeing Sighisoara when Laura grabbed my arm and said, 'Did you hear that?'

I froze. 'What?'

'A clicking noise. Like animal claws.' She made a spidery gesture with her fingers.

'Oh God,' I said. 'Maybe the dogs are following us?'

I switched the torch back on and shone it behind us. Just an expanse of rail track. I took a few steps forward but there was no sign of the dogs or anything else.

'It's fine,' Alina said as I rejoined them. 'I'm sure it's just the branches of the trees. It's natural to feel scared in places like this. Let's just keep walking in a straight line. OK?'

'OK,' I said.

Laura didn't respond.

'OK?' I said to her as gently as I could.

'Are there animals in the forest?' she said, addressing Alina.

'I guess . . .'

Laura's eyes widened. 'What kind of animals? Wolves? *Bears?*'

'I don't know.'

I interjected quickly. 'I think it said in my guidebook that all the wolves and bears have been hunted to extinction around here.'

Laura looked at me like I was the world's worst liar. 'I just want to get out of here as quickly as possible.' Her voice broke at the end of the sentence.

'We'll be in town soon,' I said. 'Eating breakfast. And when this is all over we'll look back and—'

She started walking, striding forward with a new purpose, as if the backpack on her back was filled with feathers. I looked warily towards the forest. I *had* lied about the bears. As far as I knew, there were still brown bears living wild in this part of Romania. Though, to be honest, I was more worried about Laura than I was about the local wildlife. Did she really blame me for what had happened? It was a fact that if I'd booked a sleeper compartment to start with, we would have been safely tucked up in our bunks with the door locked. Nobody would have stolen our stuff. We wouldn't have met Alina and got chucked off the train. Everything would be fine.

Whether or not Laura held me responsible, I regretted the decision I'd made. If I could turn back the clock . . . Unfortunately, real life has no erase button. There was nothing I could do about it now. We just had to get out of here and then, I truly believed, we would be able to laugh about it.

I increased my pace to catch up with Laura, and Alina followed suit.

I waited for Laura to speak, even though the silence was agonising. Finally, she said, 'I suppose I did want adventure.'

'Laura, I'm sorry I didn't book a sleeper. If I'd known—'

She held up a hand. 'Daniel, it's OK. I don't blame you. Of course you didn't know this would happen. You know I'm not the kind of person who sulks or bears grudges. I'm just cold and tired and hungry and *scared*, and I want to get out of here. All right?'

I nodded. 'All right.'

After another thirty minutes of walking mostly in silence, eyes fixed ahead, concentrating on putting one foot in front of the other, Alina said, 'Guys.'

We stopped.

'I need the toilet.'

'OK, sure. We'll turn our backs,' I said.

'I'm going to go behind the trees,' she said. 'I don't . . . I don't like people looking at me when I . . .'

It was strange to see this punky, confident woman come over all coy. I went to hand her the torch but she said, 'It's fine. I'm not going in far.'

I looked up at the sky as she walked between the trees, stepping between two thick trunks and slipping out of sight. I checked my watch. It was almost 4 a.m. now. It shouldn't be too long, I hoped, before it started to grow lighter.

'Are you OK?' I said to Laura, pulling her close. Her body was tense, her shoulder muscles rigid. I rubbed them through the cloth of the hoodie I'd given her.

'I don't want to be a drama queen . . .' Tears sprang into her eyes. 'But it's all fucked up, isn't it? Our big trip. What are we going to do without our passports? How are we going to get money out?'

'It will be fine. As soon as we get into town we'll be able to sort it all out.'

'I don't know. One of my friends at work lost her passport abroad and she had to fly home to get a new one. She couldn't cross any borders without it. The British consulate gave her a document to get home but that was it. We're going to have to go home.'

I attempted a smile. 'Maybe that wouldn't be such a bad thing.'

'But we planned this trip for so long, and we've still got so much to see.'

'Maybe we can go home, sort out our passports, then head back.'

'But not to Romania.'

'Well, I'm sure it's not—'

'Daniel.'

'OK. Not Romania.' I gave her another hug. 'Nice though it is.'

She didn't laugh. 'Please don't write about this on Facebook, try to turn it into a funny story, Daniel.'

I stepped back. 'Of course not.' Though a few minutes earlier I had been thinking just that: how at least I'd get an amusing status update out of this.

'Because it isn't funny,' Laura said. 'I don't want to be reminded of it. I don't want everyone to know about it. Please, Daniel, do you promise me?'

I tried to hide the disappointment in my voice as I promised.

'Thank you.'

Laura looked towards the forest, at the trees Alina had slipped between. 'She's taking a while.'

She took a few steps towards the line of trees. A couple of half-crushed beer cans lay at her feet.

'Alina?' she called. 'Are you OK?'

We waited for her to reply. But there was no response. Just silence.

Chapter Seven

'Alina?' I called her name this time. Then again.

Nothing.

Laura and I exchanged a look, and I stepped forward, laying a hand on the cool bark of the nearest tree and leaning into the dark space beyond.

'Alina?' I called. 'Are you all right?'

Laura stood behind me, breathing heavily, audibly. My own heart was thumping hard in my chest, a cold bubble of air spreading through my body.

'Where the hell is she?' I asked, unsure if I was asking my girl-friend or the forest itself.

Laura called her name too, and her trembling voice bounced back through the trees, echoing and unanswered.

'She can't have gone in that far to have a pee, surely?' I said.

Laura stared at me. 'What if she went in and tripped over something? Bumped her head. Or . . . who knows—fell into a ditch or something?'

'We need to take a look.'

Laura took a sharp breath. The edge of the tracks felt like a safe place now. But the forest . . . The black space beyond the line of trees. My whole body tensed up at the idea of going in there.

But we had no choice.

I switched on the torch and stepped between the trees, into the exact spot where Alina had entered. Laura followed, holding on to my arm.

Even here, just a few steps in, the atmosphere was very different from the relative safety of the tracks. The spiky lower branches of the trees reached out for us; shrubs seemed to grab at our feet. The torch picked out muted colours, dull greens and browns, among the black, jagged shapes of the trees. Every dark space felt threatening, as if it contained and concealed something horrifying. My imagination filled in the details that my eyes couldn't see, not just memories from a hundred horror movies and books, but something deeper in my brain, a line that stretched back thousands of years, fear of the dark woods hard-wired into me.

I shone the torch left and right, up and down, trying to penetrate the darkness, to kill it with light. I tried to take another step forward but my legs wouldn't move. Instead, I pulled Laura back out to the tracks.

'We can't leave her. We have to go and look for her,' Laura said.

I was sweating despite the chill in the air. I looked back at the forest. I didn't want to go in there. My lizard brain was screaming at me: *Flight, not fight. Don't go in there. Run away.*

'What if it was a bear?' I whispered. 'Maybe that's what's happened.'

'You told me they were extinct.'

'Not extinct exactly. But rare.' We both looked at the treeline.

'We would have heard something,' she said. 'A scream, growling . . .'

'How do you know what a bear attack sounds like? Or it might not be a bear—it could be . . .'

I couldn't say the word that popped into my head. *A monster.*

'Could be what?'

41

I was desperate not to go back into the forest, felt almost paralysed by a phobia I didn't know I had. I had never been camping in the woods. Had grown up in the city, raised among concrete and light.

But the way Laura was looking at me now was even worse than my fear of the forest. Disappointment.

'We should go and get help,' I said.

'Help? That will take hours. We need to do something now.'

'Or we should wait till it gets light.'

She looked up at the sky, the moon directly above us, casting lovely, reassuring light onto the tracks—light that would vanish the moment we entered the forest.

'How long will that be? She could be in there, unconscious, in need of urgent medical help. Or maybe she's trapped. She could have sprained her ankle. What if she trod in a trap, a snare?' Like mine, Laura's imagination was full of images from films.

'Then why doesn't she cry out?' I asked. 'Shout for help?'

'I don't know! But we have to try to find her. I couldn't live with myself if we just left her, Daniel. Give that to me.' She snatched the Maglite from my grasp. 'If you're too scared'—she spat the word—'then I'll go in on my own.'

'No, Laura.'

She strode off towards the trees.

'Come back.' I lurched after her, catching her by the shoulder. She whirled around. 'All right,' I said. 'I'm sorry. We'll go in together. Give me the torch.'

'Why should you—?'

'Please. Just give it to me.'

I couldn't bear the thought of not being in control of the light.

Holding the torch, with Laura grasping my free hand, I faced down my fears. I knew I was being stupid. In the daytime I would have happily run into the forest. We just needed to be careful, to watch where we were going. We would be fine. I repeated these words silently. *Fine, fine, fine.*

'There's a path,' Laura said as we pushed through the first line of shrubbery, following the beam of the torch. She was right: there was a natural path among the trees, about a metre across. Perhaps Alina had found it straight away and decided to walk a little way along it in search of a good place to answer the call of nature. Though why she had gone more than half a dozen steps along it was beyond me. Although I was worried about her, I couldn't help but feel angry too, for putting us in this predicament. Part of me wondered if she was trying to scare us. Or maybe she wanted to get rid of us, had decided that she didn't want to spend any more time in our company. She might have ducked along the line of trees and re-emerged further down the track. We didn't know her. Maybe she thought it would be funny to scare us, would be waiting for us in town with a wicked grin on her face.

'If we don't find her after ten minutes, we should go back, mark the place and go and get help. I don't want us to get lost here,' I said. 'Do you agree?'

Something rustled in the foliage to our left and Laura gasped and grabbed at me, almost knocking the torch from my grip.

'Laura!'

'Yes, I agree. Ten minutes.'

I pointed the torch along the path. We could see about ten metres ahead of us; beyond that, the unknown. Except, of course, my rational brain reminded me, it would just be more path, more forest. Nothing more. Imagine this is a summer day, I thought, that bright sunshine is streaming through the foliage, dancing on the path. Cute animals peek out from the branches, flowers prettily adorn the path. It's just a big wood. But it didn't work. Instead of dancing sunshine, I saw creeping shadows. There were no cute animals, only the yellow eyes of hungry predators. The pretty flowers were poisonous: deadly nightshade and foxglove. Fallen berries were dotted here and there on the path, and I imagined that they too were poisonous.

I took a deep breath, calming myself, and we walked on.

'Alina,' Laura called. I echoed her, feeling a little foolish, worrying too that if there were bears here, our voices would attract them.

Something dashed across the path in front of us, caught in the beam of light, and we both jumped.

'Jesus,' Laura breathed.

'A rat,' I said. 'I think.'

I looked behind me, swinging the torch, trying to memorise the point at which we'd joined the path. I turned my eyes skyward, hoping to see the moon, or the glow of a star, but the leaves above were too dense. As we walked, I could hear noises in the shadows, small animals and birds, the creak of an ancient tree as the wind stirred it. Laura's hand was warm and damp in mine, but my whole body was cold, mottled with goosebumps. I tried to speak but my mouth was too dry. My chest felt it was about to burst open.

'I think we've gone in a circle,' I said. 'We've been here before.'

'We can't have.'

But I was sure I recognised the spot on which we were standing, that the edge of the forest was very close. The urge to flee, to turn and abandon this crazy search, was almost impossible to resist. Maybe she had got lost, had found her way back to the track, was waiting for us there now.

I was about to suggest that we go back and check when Laura said, in an urgent whisper, 'Look!'

Something lay on the path ahead. It was immediately obvious what it was, but I had to stoop to make sure, picking it up and holding it out to Laura.

It was Alina's boot. Black, leather, the zip half undone.

'Oh my God.'

44

I swept the torchlight in a circle around us, searching for the other boot, but it was nowhere to be seen. I opened my mouth to say that we really needed to fetch help, when Laura gripped my hand and said, 'Did you hear that?'

'No—'

But then the sound came again, faint but unmistakable. A human cry.

'Oh fuck,' Laura said.

'We have to go back . . .' But Laura was already moving forward, jogging along the path, and I unstuck my feet and followed her, both of us speeding up as the cry came again, closer this time. As we ran, taking a new, more uneven path towards the source of the noise, the forest seemed to close in on us, and in my nightmares now, when I dream of this scene, I see faces in the trees, laughing mouths and cruel eyes etched in the bark, mocking and jeering at us as we ran slowly forward.

And, then without warning, the path ended and we emerged into a large clearing. The ground was flat, stretching the size of a football pitch, the odd tree dotted here and there. Each of these trees was bent, leafless. Dead. And at the centre of the clearing, making me blink and stare stupidly, half-convinced I was hallucinating, was a house.

'What the fuck?' I said. Laura and I turned to stare at each other.

The house had three storeys and a flat roof, dark windows and a wooden door. It was impossible to tell how old it was, but the word that sprang to mind was *ancient*. As old as the forest itself. And like the blackened trees that stood hunched in the clearing, the ground around the house seemed dead, the grass tinged grey in the weak moonlight.

Lights flickered in the windows. Candles, I realised. Like the light that glowed in the hollows of a jack-o'-lantern.

I knew, with every instinct, every scrap of learned and inherited knowledge, that this was a bad place. That we needed to turn around, right now, and get away. That we shouldn't take another step towards this building, should not pass through that door, must not go inside.

But then we heard another cry, a strangled sob from inside those stone walls, and as the silence descended again, Laura and I walked towards the house, towards the door, as if our legs had a will of their own.

Chapter Eight

Out we came, bursting from between the trees, back onto the path, stumbling in the half-light, almost falling, one of us catching the other, stopping only to scoop up our backpacks from the edge of the forest.

We ran all the way into town.

We didn't talk.

We didn't look back.

Part Two

London
November 2013

Chapter Nine

I sat on the chair in the corner of the bedroom and stared at the empty bed. The room was musty, stale, smelled of alcoholic sweat and dirty clothes which exploded from the overstuffed laundry basket. Used mugs and painkiller packets and unread books threatened to push each other off the bedside table.

Sometimes in the night I could hear something scratching and skittering in the walls. Rats, drawn to the spreading squalor? I needed to let some fresh air in, but the effort of doing this, of crossing the room and trying to find the key that unlocked the sash window, of forcing the frame open, was too much. Everything felt like too much effort.

All I wanted to do was sleep. I was exhausted, permanently jet-lagged, with scratchy eyes and the clumsiness that comes with over-tiredness. I was forever bumping into things, dropping my phone, smashing crockery. I hadn't been able to sleep, not properly, for three months.

The quilt was folded over so it appeared there was someone asleep in the bed. Not just *someone*. Laura. I could almost see and hear her soft breathing, the little snuffling sounds she made in her sleep. If I hauled myself out of this uncomfortable wooden chair and slipped my hand beneath the duvet I would be able to feel her warm skin, stroke her hair.

But the shape in the bed was not Laura. It was an empty space. A phantom.

Because Laura wasn't here anymore.

She left in mid-October, six weeks ago. The day she went, I had been at a meeting that I had been unable to avoid. I would never forget the way that Camilla and Damien from Skittle had looked at me, as if wondering if the real Daniel had been bodysnatched, whether the person sitting in front of them with the chewed nails and the inability to form a coherent sentence was an impostor. I told them I'd picked up a nasty virus on my travels, was still trying to shake it off, which was a warped version of the truth. I wanted to tell them that the old Daniel, the person they knew, hadn't returned from Romania. This was the new, diminished model.

Luckily, I wasn't expected to do much apart from co-operate with their PR efforts. I'd been interviewed by a couple of journalists from *Wired* and some other tech magazine, who asked me lots of questions about the app I'd created and the deal I'd done. My app, Heatseeker, was due to launch in the spring. Until then, I had little to do, though I kept telling myself I needed to start work on something else. I was waiting for inspiration to strike.

When I got home, Laura was standing beside a black cab, the driver heaving her suitcase off the pavement.

'What . . . what are you doing?' I asked.

Laura blinked at me and got into the cab.

'You all right, love?' the cabbie asked. She nodded and he climbed into the driver's seat.

'Where are you going?' I said, leaning through the window, fingers gripping the frame.

She took a long, deep breath. 'I'm going to stay with Erin and Rob.'

They were friends of ours who lived in Camden.

I could barely speak. 'Why?'

She shook her head sadly. 'You know why, Daniel.'

And then she had gone, the taxi accelerating through puddles, soaking an old woman on the other side of the road and vanishing around the corner.

I stood in the street for a long time, not aware of the rain until it dripped into my eyes and all I could see was a watery veil that at least, though it didn't really matter, hid my tears.

I hauled myself off the chair and drifted into the living room, almost tripping over the recycling box that I'd left by the door, all the empty wine bottles inside it rattling and clinking together. This reminded me that I needed to do an online grocery shop. I only had two bottles of alcohol left in the flat, one of which was a litre bottle of Ouzo that Jake had brought back from a holiday in Greece a year ago. Poor Jake had been forced to endure several nights sitting with me while I got drunk and openly mourned my relationship. It was particularly frustrating for him because I wouldn't tell him what had created the fracture that tore Laura and me apart.

'It doesn't make sense,' he kept saying. 'You guys were so good together.'

'I *know*.'

'Is she seeing someone else? Want me to kill the bastard for you? Or put him in a song?'

'There's no one else.'

'Then there's only one explanation. The two of you have gone stark raving mad.' He waited for me to respond. When I didn't, he said, 'Come on, you can tell me. I can keep a secret.'

'Hah. Come off it, Jake. You're the biggest gossip I've ever met. You can't resist sharing a good story.'

'I'm offended, Dan. If you tell me it's a secret, I'll keep it right here.' He laid a hand across his heart. 'I can keep secrets, you know.'

It had rained so much in the past few weeks that I had taken to glancing out the window expecting to see bodies floating past. While I'm not so egotistical as to think the weather is connected to my own life, it certainly felt appropriate. I had spent many days sitting in my flat watching the rain pummel the windows, people dashing from their cars in the street below, kids splashing in puddles while their soaked parents tried to drag them home. I wanted the rain to wash away the memory of what we'd seen and done. But all it did was cause the damp patch beneath the front window to bloom and spread, and give me a good excuse to stay indoors.

I entered the galley kitchen. One of the three light bulbs was dead but I hadn't got round to changing it. I had a feeling that when the last bulb finally died I would come to rely on the light from the fridge.

I looked at my phone to check the time. Quarter to twelve. Too early to open the remaining Merlot. But I could have a glass with lunch. One o'clock was a more civilised time to have lunch, but noon was acceptable. I occupied myself for fifteen minutes watching a daytime TV item about a woman who believed she'd had a sexual encounter with a ghost, then returned to the kitchen. I wasn't hungry and there was green fur on the bread. Could I have a glass of wine without food? I knew I shouldn't but I could taste it, anticipating its bloody thickness on my tongue.

I poured half a glass, hesitated, then topped it up. Took it over to the sofa and slumped in front of the TV. An item came on about

Center Parcs: a family walking through a forest. I snatched up the remote control and changed the channel.

If I could sleep, could get just one decent night's rest, I was certain I would feel better, that I would be able to function again. This was one of the excuses I made for drinking, because after two bottles I would pass out. But an hour or two later, I would jerk awake, feeling like a nuclear bomb had detonated in my skull. The rest of the night would pass in a series of shifting hallucinations, some invented, some remembered, and I would try desperately to hold the door shut on my memories.

Sometimes they snuck through, as if revealed by a camera flashing in the dark.

Flash. My hand on the warped wooden door.

Flash. A face as white as bone, twisted in torment.

Flash. Laura, stumbling on the crooked staircase.

I swallowed a mouthful of red wine. As it slipped down my throat I could see an image of my mum, shaking her head and saying, 'This won't do, will it, Daniel? This can't go on.'

I yelled and threw the glass across the room. It shattered against the fireplace, dark wine splattering the walls like blood-spray at a crime scene, glass splinters settling on the carpet.

This can't go on.

As I got to my feet, knowing that I needed to clean up the wine and the glass, a terrible weariness seizing my limbs as I contemplated it, my mobile rang.

The display read LAURA.

Eagerly, I pressed 'answer' and said, 'Hello?'

'Daniel? Are you OK? You sound . . . weird.'

'Yes. I just . . .' I laughed. 'I dropped a glass. Of orange juice.'

'Oh. Do you want me to call back later?'

'No! I mean, no, now's fine. Now's great. What's up?' It took all my acting skills to sound normal.

Why was she hesitating? Was she about to tell me that she wanted to come home? Hope flared in my chest.

'I've got something I need to tell you,' she said.

'What is it?'

Her voice wobbled. 'I need to tell you in person.'

Chapter Ten

Erin and Rob Tranham lived in a house in a leafy back street of Camden, one of the most expensive parts of North London, an area where Laura and I had spent many weekends at the start of our relationship. We used to stay out drinking and dancing half the night before crashing at our friends' place, then wander, hungover and dazed, through the crowds around the market before going home. Erin's gran had bought the house for the price of a Starbucks venti latte in the sixties, signing it over to her granddaughter when she retired and moved to France.

I rang the doorbell and wondered if I looked as horrible as I felt. I was on my third piece of chewing gum, trying to mask the smell of the Merlot I'd drunk at lunchtime.

Rob opened the door and gestured for me to come in. He would deny it, but he did a double-take when he saw me, giving me time to note how fit and healthy he was, triceps pumped like he'd just been to the gym, and then Erin appeared. Chopsticks held her hair in place and she stood in that pose heavily pregnant women often adopt: one hand on her back. I stared at her enormous bump as Rob put a proud and protective arm around her.

'Wow,' I said. 'It must be due soon.'

'Yeah, Erin's eight months gone. And *it* is a *he*,' she said. 'We're having a boy.'

'A mini Rob. Congrats, mate.' I shook Rob's hand. He let go quickly, backing away.

Erin was looking at me with either sympathy or pity. 'Laura's in the kitchen,' she said. 'Come through.'

I knew where the kitchen was, had cooked dinner there, mixed cocktails and cracked open beers before nights out as a foursome. But Erin was acting like I was, if not a stranger, then merely an acquaintance. Someone she used to know.

Maybe, I thought, that was true. Because she only knew the old me. Not this new version. I was the living embodiment of that expression: a shadow of his former self.

'Hi, Daniel.'

Laura sat at the solid oak table, clinging to a cup of tea like it was a lifebuoy. Seeing her sent a jolt through me. She was wearing a black jumper and her hair was tied back to expose her face. She was still Laura, still lovely. But these many weeks apart allowed me to see the changes in her. Like me, she was thinner, her face paler; there was a new translucent quality to her skin. Her cheekbones were visible, her jawline sharper. Her fingernails were bitten like mine, something she never did before, berating me for the bad habit that left my cuticles in a permanent state of ruin.

She had also developed a new habit in the days following our return, a habit of swiping and rubbing at her eyes, like there was something in them that bothered her. There was, she explained to me, a shape that lurked in the periphery of her vision. Like when you stare at a light and see its imprint on your retina after you look away. But this imprint wouldn't fade.

I sat down opposite her and she asked me if I wanted a tea or coffee. I shook my head and looked over my shoulder. Erin and Rob had gone into the living room, giving us privacy. I wasn't sure if that was a good sign or a bad one.

'How's it going?' Laura asked. Without waiting for me to reply, she said, 'You look ill.'

'Thanks.'

She shrugged with one shoulder. 'Sorry, but it's true. I look ill too.'

'No, you look . . . nice.'

Once upon a time, she would have laughed at that. 'I don't,' she said in a flat tone. She stared into her tea, groped for more words. I hated this awkwardness between us. It wasn't fair, wasn't right. I wanted to grab her and stare into her eyes, say, 'Laura, it's me, Daniel. I'm still me. And you're still you.'

But I didn't do that. I didn't say anything.

'So,' she said. 'What's happening with you? Are you working much?'

'I'm thinking,' I said.

She nodded, understanding. She had been struggling with work too.

'So what did you want to tell me?' I said.

She took a deep breath.

'I'm moving,' she said.

'Moving? Where?'

She couldn't meet my eye. 'Perth.'

For a moment, I wasn't sure if I'd heard correctly. 'You're moving to Scotland?'

She laughed, a flash of the old Laura appearing then vanishing again. 'No. Perth in Australia.'

I floundered, mouth opening, closing then opening again. *'Australia?'*

'You know my aunt lives out there?'

I had a vague memory of her mentioning this once. 'So you're going travelling?'

'No. Emigrating.'

I opened my mouth but she cut me off. 'I've already been to see an independent consultant who's helping me with the application, and she thinks I'll get enough points to be able to go, especially with my aunt sponsoring me.'

It was like being punched in the head. 'But . . . why?'

She looked at me. 'Do you really need me to explain?'

'Yes. I do.'

She hunched over the table, pushing her tea away. 'I need a completely fresh start, far away.'

'Well, you couldn't get much further away.'

'Exactly.'

'You can't go,' I said, standing up.

'Daniel, I'm only telling you out of . . .'

'What? Politeness?'

The temperature in the kitchen had dropped several degrees. Laura frowned, her gaze fixed on the tabletop. 'I just thought you should know.'

I took several deep breaths, counted to ten. 'How long does it take? The application?'

'A few months.'

'*Months?*' I had been hoping she'd say a year.

'Please be understanding,' she said. 'You know how unhappy I am. I need to do something to change things, and this is the best idea I've got. A completely new start. For the first time since . . .' She trailed off. 'For the first time in ages, I feel excited about something. I actually *feel* something—something that isn't dread, or regret, or fear.'

'But it's running away, Laura.'

'No, it's not.'

'It is. Just like you ran away from me.'

'Daniel, I'm not a child.'

An idea grabbed me and I scooted back into the chair opposite her, tried to grab her hand. 'Let me come with you. I could emigrate too. I've always wanted to go to Australia.'

She looked like I'd just suggested we have sex on Erin and Rob's kitchen table. 'No. I need to do this alone.'

'There's nothing to keep me here.'

'Yes there is. Your work—'

'Which I can do anywhere.'

'And your family. Your mum. And, Daniel, the whole point is that I need a break. A complete break.'

My hand, which had been drumming the tabletop, fell still. 'So it isn't the UK that you want to be thousands of miles from. It's me.'

She stood up. 'If I'd known you were going to get aggressive . . .'

'I'm not being aggressive!'

'I thought you'd be understanding. You're the only other person who knows what I went through.'

'What *we* went through.'

She got up and crossed the kitchen to the sink, filled a glass of water and took a big gulp. 'Please, I really don't want to argue about it, Daniel.'

It was my turn to stand up. 'Instead of running off to Australia, maybe you should do what I'm doing. Go to see a therapist.'

She almost dropped the glass. 'You're seeing a therapist?'

'Yes. A woman called Dr Sauvage.'

'And is it helping?'

'I'm not sure yet.'

'Have you . . . Have you told this woman exactly what happened?'

'Not all of it. No. She wants to hear about how I'm feeling now.'

She looked relieved. 'I don't want to see a therapist. I don't want to talk about any of what happened. I want to forget it, if it's at all possible for me to do so. That's why I'm moving to a new country, starting a new life.'

At that moment, Erin came into the kitchen, pausing awkwardly in the doorway. Had she been listening to us? Had we raised our voices? Erin had both hands on her ripe belly, as if she were trying to protect her unborn son from listening to these arguing adults. I had an urge to tell the baby to stay in the womb, where he was safe, sheltered. *It's fucked up out here*, I wanted to say. *It's fucked up and there are monsters. Don't believe people when they tell you there's no such thing.*

'Sorry, guys,' Erin said. 'I'm having a bit of a blood sugar crash and just need to get something to eat.'

Laura moved across the kitchen, pulled out a chair and ushered her friend into it. Seamlessly, she opened the fridge door and started pulling out fruit and cheese and meat wrapped in silver foil. 'What are you craving?'

Erin sat down and grinned at me. 'Don't worry, I'm not about to eat a pineapple and mayonnaise jelly. Just a ham sandwich would be lovely, Laura. Thanks, sweetie.'

I watched as Laura made the sandwich, passing it to Erin. Even in the midst of her blood sugar crash, Erin radiated good health and vitality. Eight months pregnant. That could have been Laura now. But instead of being closer to me than ever, she was moving to the other side of the fucking world.

'What do you think of Laura moving to Australia?' I asked.

Erin took a bite of her sandwich and chewed before answering. 'Of course I don't want her to go.' She shook her head. 'I don't understand any of this. What happened to you two? You seemed so happy. What did you do, Daniel? Laura won't tell me.'

'He didn't do anything!'

'But neither of you will tell me what blew you apart. Come on, Dan. You can tell me, can't you? Did you sleep with someone else?'

Laura shot me a beseeching look. *We will never speak about it,* she had said on the way back from Romania. *Promise me.*

I promise.

I didn't need to promise. I didn't want to talk about it either. All I wanted was to forget. If I didn't talk about it, I could pretend it had never happened. Any of it. That was the only way to cope.

'He didn't sleep with someone else,' Laura said.

Erin sighed heavily. 'All right. But I think the two of you need your heads knocking together.' She waved her sandwich in Laura's direction. 'Have you told him what happened to you yesterday?'

'No,' Laura said quickly, eyes darting nervously.

'What?' I said.

Erin's eyes were big and round. Her voice dropped to a whisper. 'Tell him, Laura.'

She stared at the kitchen table, chewing a thumbnail, unable to meet my eye. 'I think . . . I thought someone tried to kill me.'

'Oh my God. Where? How?'

'At Charing Cross Tube station. I was heading home from Australia House, you know, where you go to apply to emigrate, and . . .' She broke off, still staring at the table surface, then told me what had happened at the station the day before.

Chapter Eleven

Laura walked down the steps of Australia House, the paperwork neatly folded in her shoulder bag, feeling curiously
light. She pictured herself as a helium-filled balloon, set free
by a careless child's hand, alighting from the frosty city streets, up
past the windows of the imposing buildings here on the Strand,
floating towards the clouds. *Set free.* How wonderful that would feel.

As she walked towards Charing Cross she kept as close to the
buildings as possible, feeling reassured by the solid concrete, as if it
offered protection. A man emerged from one of the tiny snickets
between the buildings and Laura jumped, slapping her hand to her
breastbone. She put her head down and scurried on.

The last week or so she'd felt like she was being watched. She
kept seeing a figure flickering in her peripheral vision, but every
time she looked the figure was gone. She knew she was imagining
it, and as if to prove this she saw the figure again, on the other side
of the road, a glimpse of black clothes and white skin that vanished in the crowd. She forced herself to keep walking, eyes straight
ahead. She wanted to be home.

She knew she shouldn't really refer to Erin and Rob's place as
home. It was temporary. A temporary shelter. Which was exactly

what she needed at the moment. She felt guilty about imposing on her pregnant friend for so long, but Erin insisted it was fine.

'You were there for me when Rob and I went through our sticky patch,' Erin had said, referring to a period a couple of years ago when she had discovered Rob had come close to having an affair. Thankfully, they had worked it out. 'Besides, it will be handy to have a live-in babysitter when the little one arrives!'

Everybody was being helpful. Her manager, Simone, was letting her work from home. Simone had confided in Laura that she used to suffer from agoraphobia too, believing what Laura had told her, the day she'd found herself crying at her computer while her colleagues gawped at her. 'Take your time,' she had said in that soothing voice that made Laura want to cry again, from gratitude.

So, thanks to Erin and Simone, Laura had a place to hole up during this period. Her 'tarantula period', as she secretly thought of it.

Last week she had watched a documentary about these spiders. *The tarantula sheds her skin once a year*, the narrator explained, *then seals herself away behind a wall of silk until her new skin has hardened. Only then can she re-emerge and start to feed again.*

Laura never thought she would compare herself to a big, scary spider. But that was exactly how she felt. She was waiting for her new skin to grow, to harden.

Since Romania, the shell around her heart, like the spider's skin, had been ripped away, leaving it exposed. She was in constant pain, unable to bear the sight of others suffering. And she had realised that she was never going to heal here. That was why she had to get away.

She was dreading having to tell Daniel about her plans the next day, but knew she had to do it. She hadn't spoken to him for several weeks. Maybe he had a new girlfriend by now. He had never struggled to attract women. There was a certain type of girl, like her, who was attracted to the sexy geek type, who liked Clark Kent more when he was wearing his glasses than when he transformed into Superman. And Daniel hated being on his own, had barely spent a night alone in his life. There were times when she'd gone away on business and he'd told her he'd spent the week pacing the apartment, talking to himself and going bonkers. So no, she couldn't see him staying single for long.

It didn't matter that the thought of him with another woman was like a knife in her gut. She couldn't keep him trapped, hanging on waiting to see if she came back. That would be cruel. She wanted him to be happy, and the best way for *him* to heal was to find someone new, to throw himself into a new relationship. If she was his doctor, that's what she would prescribe. By moving to the other side of the world, she would make it easier for him.

She bit down on the urge to cry.

Moments later, she arrived at Charing Cross station. She stopped. All those people. It was even busier now than it had been earlier, when she'd taken the Tube from Camden. She tried not to look at anyone. Maybe she should get a cab. But she needed to hang on to every penny she could at the moment, would need it for her big move. As long as she didn't look at anybody, she should be OK. Plus it was stupid for her to be scared of crowds. It was the empty places that ought to scare her.

She descended the steps into the station, clinging to the handrail like an elderly lady. The people below her shuffled about like zombies. She had a flash of one of them twisting towards her, vacant eyes rolling, teeth bared, grabbing her and ripping her throat out . . . She shook the image away and counted to five beneath her breath.

Come on, she urged herself. *You can do this.*

She followed the signs to the platform, heading towards the far end. The display board showed there was a train due in four minutes. In that four minutes, more and more people entered the platform, many of them heading to where Laura stood. She was surrounded, bodies too close to her, the smell of the McDonalds fries the woman next to her clutched in her fist making Laura want to be sick.

For fuck's sake, she muttered, squinting at the board. Then she heard the rumbling of an approaching train, thank God, and looked down at the track. A tiny, malformed mouse darted between the rails.

She jerked her head up. It wasn't only the people that scared her about train travel. It was the sight of the track. The rails.

An image appeared in her mind: she and Daniel running along the tracks towards the town, stumbling and tripping but staying upright, the sun rising, her throat raw from screaming. And Daniel had caught hold of her arm and—

She lurched towards the edge of the platform, arms windmilling. She could see the mouse, frozen between the rails, and she was falling, falling, and a roaring noise came from the tunnel, air blasting along the platform, the train rocketing into the light . . .

Someone grabbed her from behind, almost went over with her, but fought them both back from the edge. A tall man, wearing a suit. He held her.

She couldn't catch her breath. The man held onto her, murmuring in her ear, telling her to calm down, it's OK, calm down, it's all OK . . .

She pulled free of his grip and looked around. Everyone was staring at her, but the Tube train was at the platform now and the doors were opening, so their attention quickly wandered.

'What happened?' the man who had caught her asked. 'Did you trip?'

She couldn't remember tripping, but said, 'I must have. I'm always tripping over my own feet.'

She thanked him and tried to give him money from her purse, which made him laugh. He got onto the train and she could feel him watching her as the doors beeped and slid shut.

Had she tripped—or had somebody pushed her? She was sure she could feel the imprint of hands on her spine.

She looked around. More people emerging into the station. If someone had pushed her, they were long gone by now. She closed her eyes and took a long, deep breath. She must have tripped. Lost in her reverie, she had walked into someone, probably stumbled over one of those annoying wheelie suitcases. That was all. It was ridiculous to think that anyone here might want to kill her.

She'd boarded the next train and found a seat, a memory coming back to her. As she'd clung to the man who saved her, she'd seen a figure pushing hurriedly through the crowd away from her. She couldn't tell if it was a man or woman. She couldn't . . .

She killed the thought, reminded herself that it was stupid to think like this.

By the time she'd reached her stop, she had convinced herself that she had imagined it.

Chapter Twelve

Dr Claudia Sauvage's office was on the top floor of her huge red-brick Victorian terrace in Crouch End. Sometimes, on my way up the stairs to the room at the back of the house where we had our weekly sessions, I would catch glimpses of her life outside the therapy room. The smell of soup wafting from the kitchen, photos of Dr Sauvage and her husband framed and hung in the hallway, a couple of pugs poking their squashed faces out of the living room. But I wasn't allowed to ask Claudia about herself: our sessions were dedicated wholly to talking about me.

The first session had been dedicated to filling Claudia in on my background. I wasn't sure how pertinent it was but Claudia said it was important to get as much detail as possible so she could understand and help me. So I told her that I grew up in Beckenham, on the outskirts of south London, and was an only child. My parents were divorced and we weren't particularly close. Claudia wanted to know a lot more about this but I was reluctant to talk about it. I didn't think it was important. But she scribbled notes as I told her that I only saw them now at Christmas and on the odd special occasion. They had both remarried and thrown themselves into new lives with new partners. They usually wanted to talk about what the other one was up to, as if they were competing to be happier. I didn't want to get drawn into it.

I spent much of my adolescence in my bedroom playing video games and learning how to code. I was a geek, until I discovered music and met Jake, who showed me that life outside my bedroom was a lot more interesting. From that point I spent a lot of time trying to work out who I was. I was naturally mathematical, scientific, but I yearned to be artistic, bohemian. I studied computer science at university but went out drinking a lot and had a series of short-term girlfriends, all of whom were studying one of the arts. I stopped reading science fiction and read the books these girls pressed on me: Donna Tartt, Douglas Coupland, lots of Penguin Classics. I experimented with soft drugs. I watched a lot of films with subtitles.

After college I moved to North London and worked for an internet start-up for a few years before getting into app development in my spare time. I met Laura, via Jake, and fell in love for the first and only time. Laura was everything I'd ever wanted: well-read, arty, passionate and principled. She encouraged me to embrace my true nature, to do the things I enjoyed without worrying about the image I projected. She helped me figure out who I am. I filled our flat with gadgets and she made it come to life with clutter and candles and bright colours.

'It's interesting,' Dr Sauvage said, 'how when I ask you to talk about yourself, you quickly start telling me about your girlfriend.'

I shrugged. 'My life is unremarkable.'

She smiled. 'No life is unremarkable.'

Dr Sauvage was in her mid-forties, thin and elegant, with slender wrists and legs that I found it hard not to stare at. She wore fashionable glasses and a dark grey jersey dress. During our sessions, she puffed on an electronic cigarette, sending clouds of water vapour into the air. She'd asked me if I minded, which I didn't at all. 'I'm more addicted to this than I ever was to real cigarettes,' she confided.

'So,' she said now. 'How are you feeling, Daniel?'

When I didn't answer, she said, 'How about your sleep? Any better?'

I adjusted my position in the armchair. 'No. I only got two hours last night, maybe three.'

She waited for me to continue.

'I've got something new to worry about,' I said.

'Oh?'

'Laura, my girlfriend, my *ex*-girlfriend . . .' I sighed. 'She's leaving the country. Going to Australia. Fucking Australia. Sorry.'

A tiny smile at my apology. 'You can swear if you need to, Daniel. And how do you feel about this?'

'How do I *feel*? I'm devastated. I don't want her to go. I can't let her go. She's just trying to run away, after what happened. It's insane. I really won't be able to bear it if she goes away.'

She raised a hand, seeing how agitated I was becoming. I took five deep, slow breaths, closed my eyes, tried to visualise something pleasant. But all I could see was Laura, and then worse . . . I wrenched my eyelids open.

'Do you think that Laura would be interested in coming to a session with you? It might be helpful to both of you. When a family experiences a trauma together, it's common to treat them as a unit. The same with couples.'

'She won't do it. I tried to talk to her about it but she's not interested. She won't even speak with me about what happened. She certainly won't talk to you.'

'And what about you?' she asked, her voice gentle. 'Will you speak with me about it?'

So far, all I had managed to talk about was what had happened leading up to the walk along the rail tracks. I had spent the first couple of sessions telling her about the good stuff: our first weeks travelling around Europe, the fun times. I had also told her about our plans, our reasons for going. All the things that had been lost. And last week, I had told her what happened on the train, about finding ourselves at the deserted station with the feral dogs.

Post-traumatic stress disorder. That's what the NHS psychologist had diagnosed me with, something that I associated with war vets or the firefighters who had tried to save people from the World Trade Center. But when they described the symptoms, I ticked pretty much every box. Intense, intrusive memories of the traumatic event. Nightmares. Loss of interest in life. Lack of motivation. Insomnia. A feeling of being on constant red alert. Being easily startled. Substance abuse—alcohol, in my case. The list went on for pages.

Dr Sauvage had told me that she wanted to try what she called 'trauma-focused cognitive behavioural therapy'.

'When you suffer from PTSD,' she had said during our first session, telling me she agreed with the NHS psychologist's assessment, 'you want to block out memories of the trauma. You will do anything to avoid confronting it, or anything that reminds you of it. PTSD is where your brain remains in psychological shock, unable to shake off or move on from what happened to you.'

'That makes sense.'

'To get better, to move on, you need to face the memories, deal with them, which will allow you to regain control and feel able to face the future. To do that, we need to carefully expose you to those memories, to peel away the barriers.'

I had shuddered visibly.

'The key word being "carefully", Daniel. You have nothing to be frightened of.'

'You don't get it. I *do*.'

She had cocked her head. 'Do?'

'Have something to be frightened of.'

Now, I looked over at her, sitting on her designer chair with her notepad on her lap, e-cigarette in her hand, and wondered if I'd ever be able to tell her everything.

'I can tell you what happened afterwards,' I said. 'That's all part of it, anyway.'

'All right,' she responded. 'That would be good. Take your time, go slowly. And if you start to feel distressed, stop talking, OK?'

'OK.'

I sat back and closed my eyes.

'I can't really remember much of the walk into town. We started off running but our backpacks were so heavy we had to slow down. I know we didn't talk much. I kept opening my mouth to speak but all I could think of to say were stupid questions like "Are you OK?" When of course I knew she was a very long way from OK. And all I could think about was getting as far away as possible.' I glanced up at Dr Sauvage. 'I was in shock. We both were. But I remember the same words looping through my head. *We need to get home.*'

I paused. 'Actually, I don't think it was that coherent, if there were fully formed words in my head. It was more like screaming. Like white noise. Also, Laura said afterwards that she remembered screaming as we ran out of the forest, but I don't remember that. In my memory, she didn't make a sound.'

It was quiet in the office, like it had been back in the forest. A fly crawled up the window and I thought I could hear its footsteps.

'The town at the end of the tracks was called Breva. When we got there it was just getting light, but nothing was open yet. Though walking through the town, it didn't seem like there was much of anything anyway. There was nobody around. We saw a man walking a dog, a huge thing, like a wolf, which made Laura grip my hand so hard I thought she'd break my fingers. We saw a young guy walking along with a baseball cap on, head down. A few cars went past. After everything that had happened, what we wanted to see was a city. Lights, life. Not this. The whole place had this bleak feel, full of boarded-up windows and cars that looked like they should be in a scrapyard. Lots of signs of a place that used to be prosperous and lively but that was now dying. I don't know . . . It just had this atmosphere. It felt like a ghost town.'

She waited for me to continue.

'After we'd walked for ten minutes or so we saw an old lady scrubbing the front step of her house. I said to her, "Police?" and she looked us up and down before coming over and giving us directions, pointing this way and that and babbling away like we could understand every word. But we got the gist anyway.'

I pictured the old lady now, her milky eyes, her strong arms clutching the wooden brush she'd been using to clean the step. 'Just before we walked off, she reached up and touched Laura's face, whispered something in Romanian. I thought Laura was going to start screaming and I had to pull her away.'

I left out a detail. The woman had also touched Laura's belly, laying the flat of her hand on my girlfriend's stomach and nodding to herself. Laura had jerked away like the woman had stabbed her.

'This is good,' Dr Sauvage said. 'How are you feeling?'

'OK.'

'Able to go on?'

'Yes. I . . . I want to get to the end.'

I also wanted a strong drink.

I told the rest of the story.

Chapter Thirteen

Laura and I found the police station about ten minutes after our encounter with the elderly woman, a little building with *Poliția* written above the door. I took a deep breath before trying the door.

A police officer sat at the desk in the tiny reception area, a smartphone in one hand, a mug in the other. He looked up at us and frowned at me, then smiled at Laura.

'Do you speak English?' I asked.

He shrugged apologetically.

I immediately switched into Englishman Abroad mode, speaking slowly and turning up the volume. 'Anyone here speak English?'

He eyed me before drifting to the back of the reception area and vanishing through a door. He returned a minute later with a large man with red cheeks and broken veins on his nose. He took in Laura's messy hair, the dirt and scratches on our skin. I hadn't looked in a mirror at this point so had no idea how beaten-up I looked, how the dash through the forest had marked me, how wild my eyes were.

'How can we help?'

I didn't know where to start. I gabbled, mixing the whole thing together non-sequentially—the train, the forest, Alina, the border guards . . .

The policeman held up two huge hands. 'OK. Slow, please. I don't understand.' He came out past the desk and gestured for us to follow him, saying something in his native tongue to his colleague, who gave us a dark look that I didn't understand.

The large policeman instructed us to leave our backpacks behind the desk then led us down a short corridor, seeing us into what I assumed to be an interview room, where we sat down on a pair of plastic chairs. Laura still hadn't spoken. She sat there shivering and staring into space.

The policeman kept glancing at her suspiciously.

'What are your names?' he asked.

I told him and watched him write them down.

'I am Constantin.' I wasn't sure if this was his first or second name. 'OK, tell me. From the start, OK?'

So I told him about what had happened on the train, that we had fallen asleep in the sleeper carriage, that we had woken up to find that our passports, tickets and money had been stolen. That we had been thrown off.

He looked up from his notes. 'Why were you . . . thrown off?'

'Because we had no tickets.'

'You had no ticket?'

The atmosphere in the room changed. He glanced at Laura again, who was shivering even harder now, her teeth chattering.

'I think she's in shock,' I said. 'Do you have a blanket? A hot, sweet drink?'

He ignored my request, going back to his previous question. 'So . . . you were on the train with no ticket.'

'No! We had tickets, but they were stolen.'

He shook his head, like this made no sense. I didn't want to tell him that we had been in a private compartment that we hadn't paid for, or even that Alina had intervened and angered the guards. I felt instinctively that this policeman would side with other men in uniform.

He pointed at Laura with his pencil. 'Your girlfriend. She is on drugs?'

'No! I told you, she's in shock. She needs medical attention. And I need to tell you about what we saw in the house in the forest.'

The pen he had been tapping on the desk went still. 'House in the forest?'

'Yes. That's what we're here to tell you about.'

He stared at me. 'Let me see your passport.'

'I told you that too. They were stolen.' Beside me, Laura made a whimpering noise. 'Listen, she really needs to see a doctor. Or, please, a sweet drink.'

He sighed heavily and made a great show of hefting himself to his feet. He left the room and came back a minute later with a tepid can of Coke, which he set before Laura. I cracked it open and passed it to her. She took a sip and winced.

'So,' the policeman said. 'You have no identity?'

I opened my mouth to reply but no words emerged.

'Does anybody know you are here?'

'No. But . . .' I produced my dead iPhone from my pocket. 'Can you let me charge my phone so I can call home? Or let me use yours?'

'Wait.'

He got up and left. Beside me, Laura's shivering had abated somewhat but she still appeared on the verge of passing out. I put my arm around her shoulders, tried to pull her closer. She could have been made of stone.

This was maddening. Constantin hadn't yet given us a chance to tell him what had happened in the house in the forest. The vision of it loomed up inside my head and I dug my fists into my eyes, as if I could rub the memory away. I had to tell him.

I paced the room for ten minutes, Laura sitting silently, before Constantin finally returned. He didn't have a phone with him. He had the demeanour of someone who'd just been asked to make a difficult decision.

Before he could sit down, I blurted, 'I need to tell you what happened . . . There's been a crime.'

'In the house in the forest.'

At that point, the policeman who had been on the front desk appeared in the doorway and said something to Constantin in Romanian. Constantin huffed impatiently.

'Wait here,' he said, placing his hands on his thighs and pushing himself to his feet. Before he left the room he turned back and said, 'You are sure . . . no one knows you are here?'

'No. I'm sure.'

He left the room and I heard their footsteps recede, their voices growing quieter.

'We have to go,' I said to Laura. Her expression was blank. I took hold of her arm and pulled her up. 'Come on. We need to go now.'

'But . . .'

'There's something not right here,' I said. 'Why does he keep asking if anyone knows we're here? I don't like it.' I went to the doorway and looked out. There was no one in sight and I couldn't hear either of the police officers any more. 'It's clear. Let's go.'

Laura staggered to her feet and I put my arm around her. I took another look down the corridor. I could see nothing but could hear shouting. Maybe Constantin had been called away to deal with a difficult prisoner. Whatever, we had to take our chance to get out of this place.

We hurried to the exit, reaching the reception desk, which was now empty.

'Our backpacks,' Laura said in a quiet voice. 'Where are they?'

'We'll have to leave them,' I said. I was so convinced that Constantin was not to be trusted that leaving the backpacks behind seemed like a necessary sacrifice. As we stepped out into what was now a warm, sunny morning, I felt a surge of relief. I took Laura's hand and pulled her along, asking someone for directions to the train station as we went. We cut across a field towards the station and, to my great relief, I had just enough cash in my pocket to pay for a train out of town.

'What happened after that?' Dr Sauvage asked, blowing a stream of water vapour into the air.

In the distance, I could hear cars, a man shouting, a door banging. But above this, I could hear my own heartbeat, the rushing in my ears, like I was underwater.

'Daniel?'

I turned towards her.

'Our tickets only took us to another small town, where we found a pawnbroker who was willing to buy my watch. I got just enough for the fare to Bucharest. Once we got there, we found the British Embassy and, after lots of phone calls, they gave us temporary travel documents and found us a flight.'

'Did you tell anyone else what had happened?'

'No. We haven't told anybody.'

'But—'

'We couldn't. We can't.'

Her voice was soothing. 'Daniel, I hope you will soon be able to tell me. Like I've already told you, only then will you be able to deal with the way you feel.'

There was a thinning patch on my jeans where the denim was almost worn through. I stared at it now, unable to meet Dr Sauvage's eye. 'You don't . . . I don't know if I can. Not yet. Maybe next time.' We had another appointment later that week.

'What are you seeing, Daniel? In your mind's eye.'

'A Polaroid exhibition of horror.'

'What?'

I lifted my eyes towards her. 'Polaroids,' I repeated.

Flash. A crouching man, a glint of metal.

Flash. Numbers scrawled in ink. 13.8.13.

Flash. Flash. Flash.

I stood up. 'I have to go.'

'Daniel . . .'

'I'm sorry.'

I left Dr Sauvage's office and headed down the road. I felt queasy, still reeling from telling even just the part of my tale I'd been able to share. I thought about my watch in the pawnbroker's shop in the little town in Romania, the name of which I couldn't remember now. That watch had been a present from Laura to celebrate my deal with Skittle. It had cost half a month's salary, but that wasn't what mattered. She'd had it engraved with a few simple words: *Till the end of time, Laura xxxx.*

———⌣———

I took the bus back to Angel and visited the supermarket—milk, bread, paracetamol, red wine, white wine—before heading back to my flat.

Even as I headed up the stairs I knew something was wrong. I lived in an old Victorian building that had been divided into flats. Laura and I had long been planning to move to somewhere bigger and better but, even with the windfall from the sale of my app, we couldn't afford it.

I hardly ever saw my neighbours. My main contact with them was when they pinned notices to the wall in the lobby, complaining about each other. Noisy parties, bicycles and buggies left in the hall, somebody failing to put their recycling in the correct bin, another miscreant parking in the wrong spot . . . But today, the atmosphere was quieter and emptier than ever.

I reached the second floor and saw that my door had splintered around the lock. It had been kicked in.

Tentatively, I pushed the door open.

Chapter Fourteen

In the living room, the bookshelves had been emptied, paper-backs scattered across the floor like bricks from a bombed building. Paperwork from the desk lay among the mess, the drawers half-open. In the bedroom, the chest of drawers had suffered the same fate; there were clothes everywhere, along with pills and condoms and random items from the bedside table. Boxes had been pulled from beneath the bed and emptied, and photographs tossed aside, Laura's face smiling up at me from the floor.

In the bathroom, the sink was full of pill bottles and a tube of toothpaste lay squashed on the lino, its contents squirted across the floor where someone had trodden on it. I went back into the living room and looked around, mouth dry, heart thudding.

My laptop, which had been charging on the desk, was gone.

My recent work—what there was of it—had been saved to the cloud, but there were other files, including most of my photos, that I hadn't backed up yet. Log-ins to my bank account, social media accounts, e-commerce sites, every website I used—it was all saved on there too, my computer set to automatically log in to nearly all of them. With that laptop, anyone could run riot through my life.

I looked around to see what else was missing. The PlayStation 4. My iPad. The Bluetooth speaker that I listened to music on. So they had only taken gadgets, as far as I could tell. Had they made a mess just for the hell of it? Or had they been looking for hidden jewellery and cash?

I called the police, then phoned my bank and asked them if they could temporarily freeze my account.

I needed to get to another computer so I could change all my passwords. And I didn't want to be alone here, among this mess, the rotten ambience of my violated home.

I went back into the bedroom, treading gingerly through the debris. I sat on the bed and picked up a photo of Laura. She was so beautiful. And soon she would be six thousand miles away.

———

Erin answered the door, looking even more pregnant than she had the day before.

'Hello again,' she said, kissing my cheek. 'Laura's not here.'

'Oh.'

'But you can come in and wait if you like. To be honest, I'm going completely out of my mind with boredom. Maternity leave is great at first, but there's only so much daytime TV a woman can take. Now I just want this little bugger to arrive.'

We sat at the kitchen table where I'd sat the day before. There was a giant cardboard box on the side, full of nappies and bottles and baby wipes.

'Laura's popped out to the shop, but I'm glad I've got a chance to talk to you on your own.' She laid her hand on mine. Hers was warm. 'She would kill me if she knew I was talking about her to you, but . . . well, I know how much you still care about her.'

'Is it to do with the thing at the Tube station?'

'Not really. I mean, she insists now that she tripped, that she can't have been pushed, and I believe her. In fact, the more I think about it, the more I think that when she initially told me she'd been pushed, she was doing it to get a reaction, like she wanted sympathy.' She met my eye. 'But I think Laura's starting to imagine things. Really weird things.'

'Like what?'

'Well . . . I often have to get up in the night because this baby's pressing on my bladder. About three times every night, actually. I'm sure it's nature's way of prepping me for all the sleepless nights ahead. Anyway, the other night I got up and heard a noise down here.'

'In the kitchen?'

'Yep. I came down and Laura was standing by the window. She was just wearing a pair of knickers, nothing else. Rob would've been delighted. And she was staring into the garden. I said her name and she didn't respond, and I thought, shit, she's sleepwalking.'

The fridge emitted a clunking noise that made me jump.

'I said her name again and she turned round. Her whole body was covered in goosebumps. I mean, like she was freezing, even though the heating was on in the house. I didn't know what to do. You're not supposed to wake sleepwalkers, are you?'

'I don't think so.'

'Anyway, that's when she spoke. She said, "Out there. In the trees." And she pointed towards the garden, down where the shed is.'

'Jesus.'

I looked past Erin into the garden, which appeared neglected, as if Erin and Rob had decided not to touch it till spring. There was a little copse of apple trees at the end of the lawn, their branches bare, surrounded by damp, mulchy leaves. I could imagine how they looked at night, creepy silhouettes reaching towards the house. I shivered.

'Then she walked past me, went up the stairs and back into her room. I woke Rob up to tell him and he was mainly pissed off that he'd missed the nude show.'

'Did you go out and take a look?'

'Yeah, Rob did. But there was nothing there. We didn't expect there to be.' She frowned. 'I'm really worried about her. Add to that the whole thing with her almost falling under a train . . . And now saying she's going to move to the other side of the world. I can't work out if that's the best thing for her, or the worst. Can you talk to her? Try to persuade her to see someone? She won't listen to me.'

'She won't listen to me either, Erin.'

She stood up, running a hand over her belly. The baby inside had no idea how lucky he was to have this capable, caring woman as his mother. 'Well, try again.'

Erin went to the loo and when she came back I told her about my break-in. She was shocked and asked why I hadn't told her straight away, and she let me use her laptop to go onto all the sites I use so I could change the passwords.

Two hours later, when I was about to give up waiting for Laura and go back to my flat, to begin the painful task of clearing up, the front door slammed and she came in to the kitchen. It was six o'clock.

'Oh,' she said when she saw me.

'Hiya.'

'What are you doing here?' She was carrying a couple of shopping bags, one of which, I was pleased to see, contained two bottles of red wine. She seemed a little spaced-out, distracted. I noticed that she was wearing her poppy hair scrunchie, which I thought of as her signature item. The number of times she'd lost it and we'd spent half an hour crawling around the flat searching for it.

'I've had a break-in at home. I came here to use the computer.'

'A break-in?'

I explained what had happened and she looked suitably horrified.

'It's as if we're cursed,' she said.

'Laura, don't be silly. You don't believe that, do you?'

'I guess not.' She unpacked the wine from the bag and immediately unscrewed one of the bottles, pouring herself a large glass.

'Aren't you going to offer me one?'

'Why, are you staying?'

'I want to talk to you, Laura.'

'Not about Australia. Please.'

'No. I just want to chat. We're still friends, aren't we? And I don't want to go back to the flat yet. I don't have the energy.'

She poured me a glass of wine and sat down at the big solid table and asked me more about the burglary, and for the next hour or so we talked. As the wine slipped down, she relaxed, her moodiness vanishing, and I made sure to stick to innocuous subjects. No reminiscing, no mention of our trip, nothing about our relationship or her plan to move abroad. We talked about mutual friends, and TV shows that we used to watch together, and music that we both liked. Erin and Rob came in and told us they were going to order an Indian takeaway if we wanted some, and the food came and we ate, opening and drinking our way through the second bottle of wine.

It was lovely. For two hours, I forgot about all the shit, all the stuff that I had to deal with. I felt like my old self. It was like we were a couple again, the couple we were before. The only negative was this niggle at the back of my head, that I needed to ask her about the sleepwalking incident. But I didn't want to spoil the mood. For the first time in three months, I felt happy.

'The wine's all gone,' Laura said with surprise.

'How did that happen?'

She laughed tipsily. 'I think we drank it.'

'Shall I pop out to get more?'

She looked up at me through her fringe, a look in her eye that made me tingle. For a while her leg had been pressed against mine beneath the table. I knew she must be aware of the contact, was thrilled that she hadn't pulled away. 'Actually, I've got a bottle of Jack Daniels in my room.'

'Do you want me to go and fetch it?'

'No, let's stop hogging Erin and Rob's kitchen. We can drink it up there.'

I tried my best not to look excited when she said this.

'Come on,' she said.

She led me up to the room where she was staying. I had slept here before, when Laura and I had stayed over together, and it was weird to think that Laura was living here now, her clothes filling the wardrobe, her essential possessions piled up against the walls. The room wasn't much bigger than the double bed that filled it and there was nowhere else to sit, so I perched awkwardly on the end of the bed while Laura sat cross-legged in the centre and opened the bottle of JD.

She only had one tumbler, so she poured in some whiskey, took a couple of sips, then passed it to me, jumping up to put some music on. She staggered and half-fell onto the bed, giggling and saying, 'Whoops.' She was wearing jeans and a jumper but I could see the shape of her body through the fabric and longed to touch her.

'It's a bit like being a student again, isn't it?' I said, passing the tumbler back to her.

'Yeah. Except I was a very boring student. I spent all my time in the library. Little Miss Boring.'

'You were never boring.'

'Oh, I was at uni. And I had a very boring boyfriend.'

'The chairman of the debating society?'

'Julian. He was never happier than when he was mass debating.'

She smiled, then giggled, then laughed, and I joined in, and soon there were tears pouring down Laura's cheeks and I was clutching my stomach. I couldn't breathe, couldn't stop laughing. The joke wasn't even funny, but it was a release of tension, or possibly a sign of how close we both were to hysteria.

Finally, we got control of ourselves and Laura wiped her face with the sleeve of her jumper.

'Oh God,' she said. 'My stomach hurts.'

I held up the bottle, said in a ridiculous attempt at an American accent, 'Rock and fucking roll, baby.'

'Please, don't set me off again.'

I remembered what Erin had asked me to. 'Laura, you know I'm seeing a therapist. I think it's helping. Erin told me—'

She held up a hand. 'I don't want to talk about it. Please.' She giggled. 'I've managed to drink myself into a state of not giving a fuck, OK?'

We were sitting very close together on the bed now. Laura still cross-legged, me with my legs stretched out before me. My head was woozy, my ribs sore; I was intoxicated and happy. I wanted to say something profound, something that would make Laura fall in love with me all over again, that would fix all our problems, make her change her mind about running away. But I couldn't think of anything sensible, let alone profound. As I groped through the fog in my head, a song came on that we both loved, a piano intro, a softly plucked guitar, a deep male voice, and Laura turned her eyes towards me and whispered, 'This song always reminds me of you, you know.'

And then we were kissing.

Shortly afterwards, when we were both naked, and I was inside her, I made a groaning noise and Laura shushed me, whispering, 'Erin and Rob,' and I was surprised to remember that they existed, that anyone else existed. Her skin against mine, her tongue on my lips, her fingers on my back, the heaviness of her breathing . . . these were the only things in the world. I'm sure I cried out when I came, and she did too, and then I was slipping into unconsciousness, her limbs wrapped around me, her sweat drying on my skin, and as sleep claimed me I felt happy, cured, alive.

Until I woke up.

Chapter Fifteen

It was still dark outside, and the bed was cold and smelled stale, the scent of sex and whiskey heavy in the air. I found my jeans on the floor beside the bed and checked my phone. Seven-thirty a.m. I waited for a minute in case Laura had got up to go to the loo, and when she didn't appear I got out of bed, retrieved my clothes, which were crumpled in a pile on the floor, and went downstairs.

There were a couple of coffee mugs on the side in the kitchen but no sign of Laura. I assumed Rob must have gone to work and that Erin was still in bed.

Where was Laura?

I left the house. I felt wretched. My head throbbed and the rest of my body ached. I felt about ninety years old. Before leaving the house I had found a little box of painkillers in the bathroom cabinet and swallowed a couple.

Camden was waking up, early birds heading to work, people queuing at bus stops. A couple of runners jogged by as I walked down towards the market. I had an idea of where Laura might have gone. I knew her favourite spot in this part of the city.

As I walked, I thought about the previous night. Though it had only been a few hours ago I could only remember glimpses of skin against skin, a sense memory. I so wanted it to mean something and for Laura to feel the same way. But what were the chances of that? She had been drunk, emotional. We both had been. Sex with your ex. It was textbook.

If my male friends could see inside my head, I thought, they would want to slap some sense into me, tell me to give up and move on. What they wouldn't understand, though, was that I felt like I was drowning and Laura was dry land. I didn't know how to get through this, through everything, without her. Why had we reacted to the aftermath of Romania in such different ways? One of us wanting to cling, the other needing to get away. A mutually impossible situation. Deep down I knew the answer.

And I didn't know what to do about it.

I was right about Laura's whereabouts.

Camden Lock was one of her favourite spots, but only when it was quiet, when the crowds—who flocked to the market, the bars and noodle stalls, the goth boutiques and remaining record shops— had gone home or not descended on the borough yet. Down by the still water of the canal it was quiet, especially at this hour, in this weather. A few degrees colder and the water would freeze over.

Laura was sitting on a low wall beside the narrow towpath, wrapped in her green parka. She stared at the water, not moving. I watched her from the market courtyard above, hesitant and unsure if I would be welcome. Perhaps, now I knew she was safe, I should sneak away, go back home and call her later. Or would I be better going down and talking to her now, telling her how I felt? I wrestled with the question. But before I could make a decision I saw something that overrode my dilemma.

Somebody was watching her.

I could see him standing beneath the bridge, half concealed by shadows. For a fleeting moment he came out into the dim morning light but he was wearing a hood so I couldn't see his face. He was slim, with an athletic build. He stared at Laura, who was oblivious to his presence.

'Hey!' I shouted.

Laura looked towards me, while the man retreated beneath the bridge into the darkness. I ran down the steps, ignoring Laura's cry of 'Daniel?' and accelerated along the towpath and under the bridge.

When I emerged on the other side, he was ascending the steps onto the main road. As if he'd hailed it, a bus glided to a stop and he jumped aboard. I ran as fast as I could, but as I reached the bus stop, panting and sweating, the bus set off. There was no sign of the man through the window.

Cursing, I jogged back down the steps and walked along the path to Laura.

'What the hell are you doing?' she said, her words harsh, breath pluming the frigid air.

'That guy was spying on you.'

'What are you talking about? *You* were spying on me.'

I stepped towards her, tried to put my hand on her arm, but she jerked away. 'Laura. I woke up and you were gone. I was worried about you.'

'Why?'

'I still care about you, Laura.'

Her long strawberry-blonde hair stirred in the breeze. Her nose was pink from the cold and two more spots of colour burned in her cheeks.

She exhaled another cloud of ice. 'Daniel. You need to stop this. Last night, we were drunk.' She looked directly at me. 'It didn't mean anything.'

'You don't mean that.'

She wouldn't meet my eye. 'I do.'

Before I could respond she turned away and marched up the steps.

I ran after her. 'Laura, for God's sake. This isn't you.'

'Please, Daniel. Don't beg. It's not you.'

'I wasn't going to beg! For fuck's sake, why are you being so cold? *That* isn't *you*.'

'Maybe this is what I'm like now. This is the new me.'

I shook my head. 'I refuse to believe that.'

I could sense the market traders, who were setting up their stalls, watching us. I reached out to her and she shrank away. 'You need to forget me. We shouldn't have slept together last night. It was a mistake. I know you must've seen it as a sign that we were going to get back together. But we can't be together anymore, Daniel. Ever. Nothing will change that. I'm moving away and you'll never see me again.' She put her hand on my forearm. 'You need to forget about me and move on.'

I opened my mouth to argue but thought better of it. She was right. I was coming close to begging, or at least verging on harassment. Her words hurt me but made me frustrated and angry too. The best thing I could do now was retreat, go home and give her the space she wanted. But before I went there was one more thing I needed to say.

'Laura, that man *was* watching you.'

She looked down at the bridge and shook her head. 'No. He was just some random guy. You probably frightened the life out of him.'

I hesitated. Was she right? 'No . . . He was watching you. Specifically you.'

Doubt crossed her face but then she shook her head again. 'No. He wasn't.' She strode away again and I hurried to keep up.

'Where are you going?' I asked.

'Back to Erin's.'

She broke contact with me and walked away quickly, out of the courtyard and onto the High Street, which was teeming with people now. I stood there, frozen to the spot, for what felt like a long time. It wasn't just the crushing realisation that she really meant it, that our relationship was actually over. It was more than that. *Worse* than that. I was certain the man under the bridge had been there specifically to watch Laura. And now I had to go back to my ransacked flat. As I trudged back to the main road, I felt a prickle on the back of my neck like I, too, was being watched.

Chapter Sixteen

I spent the whole day clearing up the flat, taking the opportunity to reorganise my possessions: re-shelving books by colour-coding the spines, arranging DVDs by genre, folding and neatly arranging my clothes. I filled three bin bags with rubbish, got rid of everything in my drawers and cupboards that I didn't use or need any more, put my loose photographs into albums. I changed the bedsheets, vacuumed and cleaned every surface. When I was done the flat looked better than it had at any time since Laura had left, and I felt exhausted but calm. I found a chilled beer at the back of the fridge, sweaty with condensation, and sank into the sofa with it, trying not to think about anything at all.

The intercom buzzed. Laura? I jumped up, lifted the handset. 'Yes?'

'Hey, it's me.'

'Oh. Jake.'

I buzzed him up. As he walked in, throwing his coat onto the back of a chair, he said, 'Thrilled to see you too, Dan.'

'Sorry. I thought—'

'Holy shit.' He was spinning in a circle, his mouth agape. 'Have you had a team of cleaners in?'

'Actually, a team of burglars.'

'You what?'

I explained while I made him a coffee. Jake didn't drink alcohol, mostly because his mum was an alcoholic who had ripped their family apart with her drinking. He drank a hell of a lot of coffee though, ten or twelve cups a day, though he claimed he was naturally full of vim and energy, that his unflagging hyperactivity was not caffeine induced.

Jake was disgustingly good-looking, so much so that going out with him could be a depressing experience, girls' eyes sliding over me and fixing on him, this wiry, mixed-race guy with the boundless energy and charisma. His mum was a former model from Manchester, his dad a musician from Trinidad, and Jake had inherited her looks and his dad's talent.

'Fuck,' Jake said, eyes wide, after I'd finished telling him about the burglary. I decided not to tell him about all the other stuff that had been going on, including sleeping with Laura. I knew he'd think I was an idiot. Jake had introduced Laura and me, spent the next few years telling us that we owed him and that we had better name our first son after him. When Laura left he had been shocked and disappointed, but although he wanted us to get back together he had also taken on the role of cheerleader, telling me I needed to stop moping and start living again.

'So what's happening with you?' I asked, finishing my beer.

'What do you mean? I told you about my gig tonight. We discussed it the other day. Don't tell me you've forgotten.'

'I . . .' The truth was that I couldn't remember. I had the vaguest memory of having a conversation with Jake earlier in the week but had no recollection of what it was about.

'Anyway, you're coming. You can't sit around licking your wounds for the rest of your life. I'm worried about you, man.'

'Where's the gig?'

'I can't believe you've forgotten . . .' He told me again. It was a large pub near Euston. 'Going to be some A&R people there. This guy contacted me after checking out my YouTube channel and wants to see me live.'

I pictured myself in the crowd at the gig, all the people and noise.

'I don't think—'

'Don't say no, Dan. I don't want to sound like a ponce but I could really do with your support. Come on, you really can't sit around here festering forever. Come out, have fun. There will be girls there and everything. Tell them you know me and . . .' He winked and made a *click-click* sound with his tongue.

I sighed. 'OK. I'll come. But I'm really not interesting in meeting another woman.'

He grinned and raised his mug. 'Cheers. By the way, you really need to get some decent coffee. This stuff tastes like Nescafé.'

'It is Nescafé.'

'You know they murder babies, don't you?'

I zoned out for a moment.

'Nestlé,' he prodded. 'They –'

'Yes, yes, I know. The baby milk thing.' I got up and went over to the cupboard, retrieved the jar of coffee and dropped it in the bin. 'Happy now?'

He stared at me. 'You really do need to get out more, Dan. You look awful. And you're acting kinda crazy. Getting forgetful.'

'Maybe I am,' I said.

'Maybe you are what?'

'Crazy.'

～

The pub was rammed, even though it was a frosty Thursday night in November. I sat with Jake in a tiny room behind the bar where he was getting ready, tuning his guitar and hyping himself up, getting into the zone. For years he had sung in a series of bands that had got nowhere, never quite being what record companies were looking for, frustratedly watching lesser rival bands get signed and, sometimes, have hits. There was a guy called Zack Love—not his real name— who had at one point been in a band with Jake. Zack had left the band to go on *The X Factor*, reaching the live finals and having a few big hits. Word was that he was on the verge of breaking America.

Zack's success sent Jake into a tailspin of self-doubt and misery, but he had picked himself up and, propelled by rivalry with his former friend, started writing much better songs, working on his image and generally transforming himself. His YouTube channel had gained huge numbers of new subscriptions recently after one of his home-made videos went viral. As I left the backstage area, after giving him a good-luck hug, I could feel it. He was on the verge of a breakthrough.

As I pushed my way through the crowd I overhead a pair of girls talking about Jake.

'Did you see the new video he posted yesterday?'

'God, yeah. Those biceps.' She groaned. 'Do you think he's got a girlfriend?'

'No, Tara said he's single. But don't get your hopes up . . . He's mine.'

'He's probably gay anyway . . .'

I smiled as I passed them, tempted to give them some inside info. At the bar, I bought two bottles of beer so I wouldn't have to queue again for a while, and found a spot close to the stage, behind another group of excited young women. There were a lot of guys here too, but many of them appeared to have been dragged along by their girlfriends.

I wondered if Jake would still talk to me if he became properly famous. Or if he'd trade me in for a new bunch of rock-star-actor-model mates. Then I'd be properly alone, with my girlfriend living in Australia and my best mate not wanting to know me.

I sank my first beer, drowning the encroaching self-pity.

A hush came over the crowd as the MC announced Jake, and then the girls in the crowd, and some of the guys, were whooping and grabbing each other as he came on with his guitar and, with a little smile, started to play. He was great. I'd heard tons of his songs over the years, as he encouraged me to listen to his demos and go to his gigs, but there was no doubt this latest crop was a league above his earlier efforts. Envy had worked. Barring a severe dose of bad luck, he was going to be a star.

As he played, I noticed a young woman with blonde hair standing near me. She was wearing tight black jeans and a purple top, very little make-up. She was stunning. The second time I glanced at her, she smiled at me and, before I knew it, she was standing beside me.

'I love this guy,' she said, her lips close to my ear, though the music wasn't so loud that we couldn't have a conversation. She had an Eastern European accent. I was immediately reminded of Alina and shuddered.

'Are you OK?' the blonde woman said. 'You look like you saw a ghost.'

I wanted to get away but the crowd around us was too dense. I was temporarily trapped. I made a conscious decision to relax. This woman was gorgeous, and maybe I needed to heed Jake's advice, stop being such a recluse.

I was about to tell her that Jake was my best mate but changed my mind. I could see how the conversation would go. She would be surprised, and I would try to impress her, but all she would want to know was if I could introduce her to Jake. Was this the way my life would go now? I would be known as Jake's friend, a way to meet the big rock star.

'He's great,' I said. 'I love this song.'

She stuck out her hand. 'I'm Camelia.'

'Daniel. Where are you from?'

She grinned and said, 'Belsize Park. I like your name, Daniel. Makes me think of someone escaping the lion's den.'

'Yeah, that's my job. I'm a lion tamer. I ran away to join the circus when I was ten and I've got two pet lions in my shed.'

She smiled generously and laid her hand on my arm.

I swallowed. 'So where are you from really?'

'Romania. But don't worry, I'm not a vampire.'

'Oh.'

She tilted her head. 'You want me to be a vampire?'

'No. Sorry, I was just . . . It doesn't matter.' I paused. Her being from Romania had flustered me. It was stupid. London was full of people of every nationality and Romania was part of the European Union so its citizens could come work here whenever they liked. I could hardly go into a meltdown every time I met someone from the country where my life had changed. 'Your English is excellent. Oh, sorry. Did that sound condescending?'

'No, it was a compliment. So thank you. I've lived here for ages. Ah, I love this one.'

She turned towards the stage, nodded her head and swayed her hips to the music. Her eyes were half-closed, a little smile on her pretty face. I noticed other men in the crowd watching her greedily and felt strangely protective towards her, and flattered that she had chosen to talk to me.

I lifted my beer to my lips and found that the bottle was empty. 'Do you want a drink, Camelia?'

'Sure. I'll have what you're having.'

I struggled through the crowd to the bar, Jake's voice loud in my ears, a small pocket of the audience singing along. My blood was thrumming. After a long wait, I bought our drinks and headed back to where Camelia had been standing.

She wasn't there. I looked around, craning my neck, but there was no sign of her. Great. I told myself it was stupid to feel so disappointed, but I couldn't help it. There was something about her: not just her looks, but her playful tone, the energy she gave off . . . .

Oh God. Laura. I was hit by a wave of guilt, but then remembered how Laura had been that morning, the tone of her voice as she told me it was over.

'Hey.'

I turned, flooded with relief, at the same time chiding myself for feeling so relieved.

'Sorry, I had to use the bathroom and the line was *un*believable. I think there was a couple having sex in one of the stalls.' She rolled her eyes. 'So tacky. Though I guess I understand people getting carried away.'

I definitely wasn't imagining the way she looked at me then. I was momentarily speechless.

'It's so hot, isn't it?' she said, shrugging off her jacket. Something fell out of her jacket pocket and she stooped to pick it up. It was her phone. She slipped it back into the pocket.

From the stage, Jake said, 'Thank you. See you soon.'

'I'd better get backstage,' I said.

'You *know* him?'

Damn. 'Yes. We're old friends.'

'Wow. That's . . . interesting.'

I wasn't sure what she meant, but before I could ask, she said, 'So are you going to introduce me?'

I sighed inwardly. When Jake introduced me to Laura I assumed she was one of his former conquests, but she found this idea hilarious. She said he simply wasn't her type. 'Yeah, he's good-looking and charismatic and cool. But I'm not interested in those things . . .'

'Thanks!' I'd laughed.

Why was I thinking about competing with Jake? I wasn't looking for a new girlfriend. I didn't even want a one-night stand. My ego felt sore, though. Camelia had lifted my spirits, and now she was about to shift her attention to my best friend.

'Come on then,' I said, and she followed me behind the bar and through to the back room where Jake sat, sweating and smiling, the guitar propped against the wall. His manager, Robin, was in the room, talking about how he'd been standing with the A&R guy, who'd been 'creaming his pants'.

'That was fantastic,' I enthused. After lavishing him with praise I gestured towards my companion, whom Jake had been watching since we'd entered the room, and said, 'This is Camelia.'

'You were pretty good,' she said in a cool, disinterested voice. Then she turned to me. 'Thanks for introducing us, Daniel. Can we go now, though, do you think?'

Once again I was speechless as she took my hand and pulled me through the door. I glanced back at the open-mouthed Jake and shrugged an apology. He waved it off, a big smile on his face.

Camelia led me through the back door and out into the street. It was freezing outside, but I didn't care. Camelia was still carrying her jacket. The cold clearly didn't bother her. I was about to say something about this when she pulled me into a shop doorway and kissed me.

Her lips were soft. It felt good, but strange, the unfamiliar shape of her lips and the taste of her mouth, a faint trace of cigarettes. I hadn't kissed anyone apart from Laura in years. I was so busy marvelling at the fact that Camelia was kissing me, and trying to push Laura's image out of my head, that I was unable to relax and enjoy it.

I broke away. She stared at me, confused, then moved her lips back towards mine.

I turned my face away. 'I'm sorry.'

'What's the matter?' She looked hurt, pissed off.

'I can't. I've got a girlfriend.'

She made a little snorting noise.

'I have to go,' I said. Passers-by were looking at us, this couple having what looked like a break-up conversation in a doorway.

'What? Come on.' She moved towards me but I stepped away. She looked stunned, as if no man had ever rejected her before. Perhaps they hadn't. I could sense her searching her head for something to say. It made me think of a robot shuffling through possible responses before finding one, and this image made the chance that I'd give in to her advances vanish completely.

'Daniel, I like you a lot,' she said. 'I thought we had a connection.'

This was awkward. 'Camelia, you're gorgeous, but—'

'You have a girlfriend.' She took another step towards me. 'I won't tell her.' She leaned in for another kiss but I turned my face away like a shy virgin. Again, she looked shocked.

'Do you have something against Romanian women?' she asked, tilting her head. 'When I told you where I come from you seemed . . . upset.'

There wasn't enough air in my lungs for me to reply.

'Oh my God,' she said, stepping back. 'You really do have a problem with Romanians? You're not one of those people who hate immigrants, are you?'

'God, no!' I said.

She didn't appear convinced. 'Well, you certainly have a problem with *some*thing,' she said. 'Just me, maybe.'

I tried to laugh it off. 'How could I have a problem with someone who looks like you?'

She softened just a bit. 'So it's just Romania in general, then.' A little playful now. 'You should visit, maybe. Give us a chance. It's a beautiful country.'

'Oh I know. I've been.'

'Oh yes? How long ago?'

Again, I had trouble speaking.

'What is it? You had a bad experience?'

'No, I . . .' I couldn't form a sentence.

'Do you want to tell me about it?' she said, looking into my eyes.

'I . . . No. I don't.' I hastily added, 'There's nothing to tell.'

'Are you sure?' She laid a hand on my arm and for a moment I was tempted to take her home, to bed, to lose myself in her, to tell her everything. But that moment passed quickly and I shook my head.

'I'm sure.'

'Fine.'

Before I could say anything else, she spun round and dashed into the traffic, her jacket flapping in her grip. I yelled out as a car swerved around her, a bus swayed, the driver leaning on his horn. Traffic in both lanes screeched to a halt; someone on the pavement screamed. I dashed to the kerb, expecting to see her dead, flattened in the road. But she had gone.

In my peripheral vision, I had seen something drop from her jacket as she'd moved away from me. It was her phone, fallen from her pocket again. I held it in my palm for a moment, then slipped it into my pocket.

Chapter Seventeen

I needed to go home but didn't feel up to using public transport. I checked my wallet and found that I had no cash left so walked down the busy street to a cashpoint. A homeless man lay by the wall at the front of the bank, shivering inside a ragged sleeping bag, his eyes shut tight against the bitter cold. I slotted my card into the machine and keyed in my pin, choosing to withdraw £50.

The machine beeped and told me the transaction was denied.

Maybe the machine was running low on cash. I tried £30. Again, it was rejected.

Irritated, I pressed another couple of buttons to check my balance, waiting while the ATM contacted my bank before returning with the answer. But the number on the screen made no sense. No sense at all.

£2998 OD.

Overdrawn. £2 away from my overdraft limit.

This was my current account. Most of my remaining money from the deal with Skittle—a sum that was diminishing fast—was in my business account. But there should have been some money, a few hundred pounds at least, in my current account. I wasn't great at keeping up to date with my balance, but it wasn't possible that I was almost £3000 overdrawn.

The cashpoint machine spat my card out and I wandered, stunned, to the nearest bus stop. I tried to work out how much money I'd spent in the last week, if there had been any large transactions that I'd forgotten about.

A bus pulled up. Luckily, I had a few quid on my Oyster so I jumped on and headed up the stairs, almost losing my footing as the bus jerked and swayed. There was a seat free at the back and I sat there, behind the drunks, a thrumming in my ears, trying to process what had just happened.

My stolen laptop. Whoever had burgled my flat and taken my laptop must have got into my bank account. I had alerted the bank as soon as I'd returned to the flat to find it burgled, but clearly, I hadn't been quick enough.

Then a new, horrible thought struck me. What if they'd emptied my business account too? Was that possible? I took my phone out of my pocket. As usual, the battery was almost dead. With fumbling hands, I attempted to log in to my bank account on my phone, pressing the wrong digits, getting the password wrong twice, but eventually logging in. Thank God, my business account appeared untouched. I tried to check the list of recent transactions but the screen filled with the swirling circle of death before going blank.

My mind followed suit. As the bus bumped and rattled, I pressed my forehead against the greasy window and watched the streets of London go past, trying not to think. Trying not to feel.

A fox had been in the bins outside my flat. One of my neighbours had left what had clearly been a stuffed black bin liner on the pavement and it was torn open, segments of pizza and old nappies strewn across the path. This would no doubt lead to a poster in the lobby. I stepped over it and unlocked the door, dragging myself up the stairs to my flat.

As soon as I went inside I knew something else was wrong. I had tidied it and sorted out the chaos before going out with Jake, righting everything the burglar had messed up, and it was still clean and tidy. The cups and glasses I'd used earlier sat beside the sink. So what was different?

I was so shocked by what I saw that I actually rubbed my eyes with my fists, like a cartoon character.

My laptop was sitting on the desk, plugged in to its charger. Beside it lay the iPad that had been stolen. The Bluetooth speaker, iPad and PlayStation 4 were back in their usual spots too.

I picked up the laptop, turning it over in my hands. There was the tiny dent that I'd caused when I'd dropped it a few months before. There was the scratch on the back. I was sure that if I checked the serial number, it would match.

This was my computer. The computer that had been stolen two days ago.

What the hell was it doing back here?

I opened it and logged on. It seemed to be untouched. The same programs were open that I'd been using the other day. I had a habit of leaving my computer switched on all the time, having heard that Macs prefer to stay awake, with whatever programs or documents I'm using remaining open. My memory was a little hazy but these appeared to be the same programs I'd been using two days ago when I left to go to see Claudia Sauvage, my therapist.

To be safe, I opened my virus-checking software and started a scan of the machine.

All of a sudden, I felt sick. My skin went cold, all the way to my scalp, and a wave of nausea crashed over me. I made it to the bathroom just in time, leaning over the toilet, retching and feeling everything I'd eaten and drunk that day violently exit my body.

I sat on the bathroom floor. I couldn't think straight. I really couldn't deal with this tonight. After checking the results of the virus scan—all clear—I went into my bedroom.

As I undressed, I found Camelia's phone in my pocket. She would probably call it when she realised it was missing, but tonight I needed to sleep undisturbed so I switched it off and put it into the bedside drawer.

Sometime during the night I dreamed that Camelia was kissing me, except she had sharp teeth and kept biting my lips.

'Sorry,' she murmured, as blood dripped from my mouth. 'But tell me . . . Tell me about the terrible things you've seen.'

She was naked, but her body didn't look as it should. Her shoulder blades protruded, her ribs stuck out like the grill on a vintage car, and deep, pink scars encircled her wrists and ankles. Blood continued to drip from my lips as the dream Camelia dropped to her hands and knees and crawled across the floor towards me and I backed away until I was against the wall. Something small and square stuck to my back, and I when I tried to pull it off I felt it pulling my skin off like it was superglued to me.

I woke up gasping for air.

⌣

The next morning, after showering and drinking three pints of water, and taking what was becoming a daily dose of painkillers, I called the bank. I was transferred to a member of the fraud team, a young woman with a north-eastern accent.

'We've been trying to contact you,' she said. 'Did you get our messages?'

'No. Did you leave a voicemail? Sometimes it takes a day or two for them to come through.'

She didn't sound like she believed me. Had I heard the messages and forgotten about them, just as I'd forgotten my conversation with Jake?

'There were a couple of large transactions on your debit card yesterday. Five hundred pounds was withdrawn from a cashpoint machine in East London. There was also a transaction of sixteen hundred pounds at the Apple Store in Regent Street.'

Sixteen hundred pounds. I glanced at my laptop. That was how much I'd paid for my MacBook Pro.

'Why didn't you stop them?' I asked. 'I thought the bank automatically blocked unusual transactions like that? How on earth were two made without being stopped?'

She sounded annoyed. 'Both of these transactions were made at exactly the same time. They were picked up immediately afterwards and your account was frozen. That was when we tried to contact you.'

'But I didn't get the message. What number did you call?'

She read out a mobile number.

'That's not my number!'

'Are you sure?'

'Yes, of course I'm sure.'

'Please hold.'

I paced up and down the room while I waited for her to come back on the line. I looked out of the window. The fox that had ripped open the bins was standing on the front path, eating. I banged on the glass and it trotted away up the road, a slice of pizza clenched between its jaws.

The woman from the fraud team said, 'You changed your contact details two days ago, on the twenty-third.'

'I didn't. I . . . Oh.' The person who had stolen my computer must have logged in to my account and changed my phone number.

I explained this to the woman, who took the correct number. Then I thought of something.

'I was robbed when I was in Romania last summer. Could someone have used my old card?'

'Not if it was cancelled. Which, according to my records, it was. These transactions went through on your current card. I expect it was cloned—it's a common occurrence, unfortunately. When you were burgled, was your debit card in the house?'

I tried to remember.

'Yes. I think so.'

'Then it was probably cloned by your burglar. They use these machines—they swipe the card and download the information from the magnetic strip to create new ones. I have already cancelled your card and you'll be sent a new one. You will get the money back, Mr Sullivan, but it may take up to a week. In the meantime, if you need cash you should go to your local branch.'

After I'd ended the call, I went over to my desk and picked up the laptop. I had half-expected to find it missing again when I'd woken up, to discover that its reappearance had been part of a dream. But it was still here. I had been . . . how could I put it? *Un*-burgled.

I called the police.

Chapter Eighteen

'So let me get this straight, Mr Sullivan. Somebody broke in, stole your laptop and some other gadgets. Then brought it all back.'

The police constable's name was, confusingly, Sargent. PC Sargent. I hoped he never got promoted. He was six foot two and had that weird Fred Flintstone-like grey stubble on his face. He looked around my flat, taking in the neatness, everything in its place, looking more like a team of cleaners had broken in than burglars.

'Maybe they had an attack of conscience,' Sargent said. 'I read about this guy who stole a hundred quid from a pub, then twenty years later sent it back with a note of apology. But your repentant burglar got an attack of the guilts much quicker.'

'I feel like you're not taking this seriously,' I said. 'I reported this when it happened two days ago. An officer gave me a crime number for my insurance company.'

Sargent prodded a key on my laptop, making the screen flicker into life. 'Does your computer appear to have been tampered with in any way?'

'No. I scanned it for viruses and there's nothing there. I checked the browser history too and there's no recorded activity since I last used it.'

I had already told him about the fraudulent use of my bank card and how the woman at the bank had said it had probably been cloned by the burglar.

'What are you going to do?' I asked.

Sargent set down the cup of tea I'd made him when he arrived. 'There's very little we can do. Your bank is dealing with the card fraud. And as for the burglary, you should think yourself lucky.'

'Lucky?'

'Don't forget to contact your insurance company and cancel your claim.' He moved towards the door.

I stepped into his path.

'I don't think you understand. Someone is trying to mess with my head.'

'A practical joke, you mean?'

A pain was blooming in my skull, a sharp, white stabbing sensation like fat needles penetrating the soft flesh of my brain. 'No. More . . . sinister than that.'

'Sinister?'

I opened my mouth. But what was I supposed to say? As well as this apparently phantom burglary, someone *might* have attempted to push Laura under a Tube train, and I *thought* I'd seen someone watching her. It all sounded very weak, and Sargent was already looking at me like I was unhinged. The only concrete part was the fraudulent use of my card, but as Sargent had pointed out, the bank were dealing with that and the police would deal directly with them. I could imagine what Sargent would say if I told him my card had been used to buy a new laptop, of all things. The same model, going by the price, as the one I owned.

'Listen, Mr Sullivan, it seems to me like you're under a lot of strain,' Sargent said. 'Maybe you're working too hard. Either that or a friend played a practical joke on you.' He pushed the front door open and went out into the hallway. 'Take care.'

Follow You Home

'But . . .'

He descended the stairs. Seconds after hearing the outer door shutting I heard another door shut: the woman downstairs, stepping back into her flat after coming out to see what was going on.

I filled a glass with cold water and sat down. I needed to get everything straight in my head. There was a simple explanation for almost everything. Laura had imagined being pushed at the Tube station, and it was indeed a random person watching her in Camden. My card had been cloned and used here in London. It was a common occurrence, had happened to Jake once.

So one question remained: why had the thief brought my laptop back?

And would they come back again?

If they did, I wanted to be prepared. I went onto Google and searched for home security, finding what I was looking for. A simple CCTV system. I ordered it and wondered if it was possible to buy a mantrap or a device that shot poison darts. I smiled to myself. That was crazy thinking. And besides, if I bought a trap I'd probably walk into it myself.

Chapter Nineteen

Daniel—trying to get hold of you. It's URGENT!! Call me.
The police had been gone for a few hours, and I'd been napping on the sofa when my phone pinged. It was a message from Erin. I groped for the phone, which lay on the carpet by the sofa, and the moment I read it a shot of adrenalin jerked me awake. My clothes were damp with sweat and there was a patch of drool on the cushion my head had been resting on.

I rang her immediately.

'Daniel,' she said, picking up after a single ring. 'Oh God.' Her voice was hoarse.

I sucked in a breath, dreading the worst.

'What is it?'

'It's Laura. She . . . oh fuck.' She was crying. My stomach lurched like I'd gone over a bump in the road. 'She's in hospital. UCL. I need you to come. *Now.*'

Erin was leaning against the wall in the ward that Laura had been admitted to, a plastic cup of water in her hand. Her bump was huge—I could barely imagine how she could stand up straight. I rushed up to her.

'Where is she? Is she all right?'

Erin sniffed and grabbed hold of my hand. I wondered where Rob was. At work, I assumed.

'She's OK. She's recovering. They pumped her stomach and the doctor I just spoke to said she's lucky. If I hadn't found her almost as soon as she took the overdose . . .' She trailed off.

'I can't believe . . . What did she take?'

'A mix of sleeping pills and anti-depressants. Something called Zopiclone and . . . Trazodone, which is apparently prescribed for anxiety.' She held up her phone. 'I looked it up.'

I stared at her. 'Where did she get them?'

'From her doctor, I guess.'

I knew Laura had suffered from insomnia ever since we'd returned from Europe, but she hadn't been taking anything for it, not while we were together, anyway. Had she started taking pills after she left me? I hadn't seen her take a tablet the other night, after we'd had sex, though that didn't mean much. She'd been so drunk that she wouldn't have needed one.

'Oh, Laura,' I said, my eyes stinging. 'I want to see her.'

Erin and I had taken seats outside the ward. 'You can't at the moment. She's asleep. The doctor said they're going to keep her in for a couple of days for observation. He asked me *loads* of questions.'

'Like what?'

'Like, had she attempted suicide before? Does she drink excessively or take illegal drugs? He wanted to know about her support network too.'

'And what did you tell him?'

'Well, I told him that her family live at the other end of the country but that she has friends here. I've called her mum already, but they can't make it till tomorrow.'

'Typical.'

'But . . . Daniel, I need to talk to you about what she was like when I found her.' Her voice dropped to a near-whisper. 'I heard her shouting, so went up to her room and knocked. When I went in she was sitting on the bed, staring at the window. I didn't notice the empty pill packets at first. They were on the other side of her.'

I waited for her to continue, heart thudding.

'She kept staring at the window. And then she started . . . jabbering, muttering and pointing towards the garden. It was really hard to work out what she was saying. Something about being followed, about a ghost. That's what she kept saying. And she said something weird about her skin, something about tarantulas and how her skin wouldn't grow back. Her eyes were blank, kind of . . . cloudy. It was really scary. And then she crumpled, just fell sideways on to the bed. That's when I saw the pill boxes and called an ambulance.'

Erin turned her head towards me. Her hands rested on her belly as if she were trying to protect her unborn child from all the horror and pain in the world.

'Daniel. What the hell happened to you and Laura on that trip?'

116

Chapter Twenty

Laura lay in that grey space between waking and sleeping, lingering voices from her dreams merging with sounds from the real world: somebody coughing, something beeping, a wheel squeaking across a hard floor. She thought she could hear babies crying too, which made her bury her head beneath the pillow.

As she emerged from sleep she could hear two women talking, but she couldn't make out their words and it took her a minute or two to work out who they might be. Nurses, that was the answer. Because she was in hospital. And with that memory came the jolting realisation of what she'd done.

Her insides felt poisoned, her stomach and throat sore from where they'd stuck the tubes inside her. The doctor who'd talked to her when she'd woken up, after the drugs had been pumped from her body, had been soft spoken but behind his soft words she could sense reproach: there are hundreds of genuinely sick people in this hospital, people who want to live. *You are wasting our time.*

'If it wasn't for your friend . . .' the doctor had said.

Erin had saved her. Good old Erin. Her best friend, the friend she could count on, the person who'd given her somewhere to stay without asking too many questions, who was gentle and kind and compassionate.

The bitch.

Why had she interfered? If she'd left Laura alone, it would all be over now. She'd be free. It had come to her yesterday—in a flash, not of light, but of darkness—that her idea about going to Australia was foolish. Because the other side of the world wasn't far enough away. Sunshine and distance couldn't heal her, protect her or make her hate herself any less. Nor, she realised, could time. The skin she had shed was never going to grow back. She had lain on her bed in her tiny room and stared at the wall, and as she listened to her heart pounding in her chest, the darkness creeping through her veins, cold and shivering and not aware she was crying until she felt the wetness on her face, she knew what she had to do.

She must have been sobbing when she took the pills. That was her big mistake because the noise had brought Erin to her room, and there was still time for her to be saved. Though saved wasn't the right word. No, Erin had condemned Laura to more suffering.

She had seen Daniel here earlier. He had come onto the ward, sat beside her bed. As soon as she saw him coming she had shut her eyes, pretending to be asleep. She knew exactly what he would say and she didn't want to hear it. Seeing him reminded her of why she felt like this. She wished she hadn't encouraged him by getting drunk and sleeping with him the other night. When he had leaned over her bed this afternoon and whispered that he loved her, and she could hear the thickness of tears in his voice, she had expected to feel the urge to cry herself. But she'd felt nothing. At least that part of her had gone numb.

All she wanted to do was sleep. But it was no use: she was as wide awake as if she'd ingested a bag of speed. It wasn't helped by the conversation between two nurses she'd overheard after darkness fell: an old man had been spotted hanging around the maternity unit, hovering around the sick babies who were kept apart from their mothers. When staff challenged him, he strode off. The images this conjured up, of somebody stealing babies, harming them, made Laura's insides churn with dread.

She opened her eyes and squinted at the clock on the bedside cabinet. It was 2.20 a.m. All the other women in the ward were asleep, one of them tossing and turning, another snoring. Laura tried to sit up and recoiled from the flare of pain in her head, like she'd been struck by a hammer, falling back again. She pulled the sheet up over her face.

As she lay there, listening to the faint snoring from the other end of the ward, she became aware of a presence close to her bed.

Strange—she hadn't heard anyone enter the ward. Nor had she heard any of the other patients get out of their beds. But what other explanation could there be? As a tendril of cold crept beneath the hospital sheets it felt like someone had opened a window and let the frigid February air enter the room. Goosebumps rippled across her flesh. She was about to get up and find the window so she could close it, when she heard the voice.

'*Laura.*'

She went rigid beneath the thin sheet. The voice was soft, close to a whisper.

'*It's me.*'

She knew exactly who it was. It was a voice she would never forget, a voice she had last heard rising in a scream, then abruptly falling silent. It was the voice of a dead woman. And she realised, in that moment, that the glimpses of black clothes and white skin that she'd seen following her, that she thought she'd imagined, must be real. The presence she'd sensed in the central London streets and among the trees at the end of Erin and Rob's garden. It wasn't her imagination. It was real. It was a ghost.

'*You mustn't do it*,' the dead woman whispered. She was standing right by the bed now. Laura kept her eyes shut tight, the thin sheet forming a barrier in case the ghost turned hostile. '*You mustn't kill yourself yet.*'

Laura was crying now. Crying from the memory of a decision that had changed everything.

'*I need you*,' the ghost said. '*I need you to stay alive*,' and Laura threw the sheet forward, jerking upright, the pain in her skull gone.

The ghost was gone too.

Chapter Twenty-One

I trudged home through the freezing London streets, reeling from seeing Laura in her hospital bed, so pale and fragile, with dark circles around her eyes. She had been asleep during visiting hour, despite the chatter around us in the ward. Erin went home, angry with me for refusing to answer all her questions and needing to rest.

After murmuring to Laura, and fighting back tears, I sat and waited for a while in case she woke up. Tomorrow, her mum and dad would arrive in a cloud of self-importance. Erin had phoned them and, knowing them as I did, I was less than shocked to learn that they weren't planning to rush straight to London from their home in Cornwall. They had an important dinner, something to do with work. I had warned Erin not to tell them that Laura had talked about ghosts.

'What happened to you on that trip?'

I didn't—couldn't—answer. I tried to make sense of what Erin had recounted. Skin, tarantulas, ghosts . . . I looked back at Erin.

'Do you know about Laura and her ghost?' I asked, keeping my voice low so the other people in the waiting room wouldn't hear.

I waggled my fingers as I said ghost, putting the word in inverted commas.

'A *ghost*?'

I took a deep breath. I had to tell her this much. 'Yeah. I know. When I first went down to visit Laura's parents, after we'd been together for a few months, Laura's mum made a sneering joke about Laura believing in nonsense. When I asked Laura what her mum meant, Laura completely clammed up. But I eventually got it out of her.'

'Go on.'

'When she was twelve, Laura started to believe that there was a ghost living in her house—the ghost of another pre-teen girl, one who had apparently died there. This ghost—her name was Beatrice—would come into Laura's room at night and talk to her. Laura told me that she was terrified at first but then realised the girl didn't mean her any harm, that she was sad and lost and that she wanted Laura to be her friend. I think Laura's mum eventually heard Laura having conversations in her room and that's when Laura told her matter-of-factly about Beatrice.

'Laura's parents took her to the doctor who said it was all connected to the onset of puberty, that they shouldn't worry. But Laura's mum then took her to see a psychiatrist who, according to Laura, was pretty harsh . . .' Laura had refused to give me all the details, but I was sure this was one of the reasons why she refused to see a therapist now. 'In the end, Laura pretended that she knew the ghost wasn't real, that Beatrice had stopped visiting her.'

'But she still believed Beatrice *was* real?'

'Yeah. And get this—she went to the local library and found out that a twelve-year-old girl had died in her house thirty years before. Was murdered, actually, by her dad.'

'My God.'

'I know. Laura said she was convinced for a while that her own parents were going to murder *her*. You've met them, haven't you?'

'Unfortunately.'

'Well, then you have at least some idea. They were horrible to her when she was a kid. Just before this whole Beatrice thing happened, they took her out of the school she loved, where all her friends went, and made her start going to this awful, strict girls' school. They made her break contact with her best friend, because they thought she was "common". It was all pretty traumatic for Laura. That's why I think she started to believe in Beatrice. A kind of imaginary friend. Something her parents couldn't take away from her, no matter how hard they tried.'

'I guess that makes sense.'

'Yeah. Eventually Beatrice stopped visiting. Laura was fourteen by then—I mean, this went on for a long time—and she says that Beatrice told her that she was going to "the next place". And that was it. Laura's parents thought their daughter had stopped believing long before. But Laura still believes now that Beatrice was real. She still believes in ghosts.'

Erin exhaled. 'So what, you think she's seeing Beatrice again?'

'I don't know.' A chill ran through me as I thought about the trauma Laura had suffered recently. 'I think she's probably imagining a different ghost.'

Erin took out her phone again. 'One of the drugs she was on, Trazodone—apparently it can cause hallucinations.'

I shook my head. Had Laura been warned about these possible side effects? Hopefully after her overdose she would stop taking them. I resolved to talk to her about it.

The situation with Laura had made me temporarily forget the mystery I was grappling with, but it came back soon as I stepped into the relative warmth of my flat and saw my laptop. I poured myself a drink and was shocked to see how much my hand shook as I raised the glass to my lips. The inside of my head felt like a hive in which the bees were at war. My next session with Dr Sauvage was scheduled for tomorrow, thank God. I am by nature a reticent person, but right now I badly needed to talk to someone.

I was too wired to go to bed, so I switched the TV on and sank into the sofa with my MacBook on my lap. A horror film was starting on Channel 4, one in which a group of teenagers go into the woods and meet a grisly end. I quickly turned it off but it was too late, the memories were triggered.

A thin pink gown wrapped around a bundle of bones.

Tears sliding down a hollowed-out cheek.

Blood-stained fur and two pairs of glassy eyes . . .

I stood up and paced the room. When I was coding, working on an app, I would do this to work through problems. Moving helped me to focus, to dislodge the blockages and untangle the knots in my head. I picked up a DVD case, a rom-com, forced myself to remember the plot, the funny scenes, sunshine and beaches and kisses. Finally, the real memories were displaced, shoved back in their box, the lid slammed shut.

I put the DVD back on the shelf and returned to the present moment, sitting back down with my laptop.

Why had my burglar returned it?

Was it possible that I had imagined the break-in, in the same way that Laura thought she was seeing ghosts? No one else had seen evidence of the burglary because I had cleaned up before my only visitors, Jake and the police, had come round. I hadn't even taken any photographs. Was it a fantasy brought on by too much alcohol and too little sleep? Did I damage the door myself then forget I'd done it? When I thought back across the past few weeks, there were holes there, black spaces in my memory, pockets of time that I couldn't account for. I paced back across the room.

No, it had to be real. Somebody else had damaged the front door. My bank account *had* been defrauded, and that was because my burglar had cloned my card.

Unless it was me who used the cards.

I shook my head. No, that was impossible. I hadn't withdrawn that cash, or gone to the Apple Store. Unless I was losing my mind . . . When I closed my eyes, I saw a flash of myself surrounded by iPads and computers and speakers. Could I really have gone to the Apple Store and spent £1600 on a new laptop without remembering? And where was that laptop? Because the one sitting here now was definitely my old one, with the exact same scratches and marks.

Tomorrow, I decided, I would tell Dr Sauvage the rest of what had happened in Romania. I had to take the memories out of their box, expose them to sunlight, get them out of my head. I had to share them with someone who wouldn't be driven crazy by them before they drove *me* crazy. Only then would I be able to move on with my life.

Chapter Twenty-Two

After an hour of thrashing about in bed, my brain whirring like a helicopter, waking dreams in which I alternately ran through a forest and wandered through the glass temple of the Apple Store, I got up and opened a bottle of red wine. I craved oblivion.

I set the glass of wine—full to the brim, the liquid thick and dark as blood—on my desk and sat down. I opened Spotify and put on one of my favourite albums, drowning out the ticking clock and the rumbling voices of the couple who lived upstairs, who often stayed up late into the night, alternately arguing and having noisy sex, and decided to try to catch up with some emails. Most of them were junk. I deleted these and moved the numerous messages from Skittle into a folder to deal with when I felt more alert.

The last time I had sat up in the middle of the night with my laptop was when I was working on my app, Heatseeker. Skittle were confident it was going to be the next big dating app. Some acquaintances thought I had lucked out when I'd done the deal, but although there might have been some luck involved, I had worked hard to achieve my good fortune, sitting up through the night while Laura slept in the other room. I had poured hundreds, perhaps thousands, of hours into creating what I thought of as my baby.

I gulped down wine and carried on working through my emails until I spotted one from Laura that had arrived earlier that day, a few hours before her suicide attempt.

I thought you might want to see this. Laura x.

Attached to the email was a photograph. I double-clicked on it and the iPhoto software, which was set to automatically start when I clicked on a picture file, opened up and displayed the picture. It was a photo of a pair of kittens, wrestling each other. I sat back. Why had Laura sent me a photo of kittens? That was weird. But if she'd done it just before trying to kill herself, she clearly hadn't been acting normally. I scrutinised the photo for a few moments, trying to figure out if there was some kind of secret message hidden in the picture. But it was just a pair of cats.

Now that iPhoto was open I did something I didn't normally allow myself to do, not wanting to torture myself, and began to flick through old photos. Here was the record of my and Laura's time together.

When Laura and I were first together, we took photos of each other all the time. There she was lying back on the grass in the park, sunglasses on, a huge grin lighting up her face. Here we were with our cheeks pressed together on our trip to Alton Towers, the camera held at arm's length. There were dozens of pictures of us just hanging around at home.

As time went on, there were fewer spontaneous, everyday shots, but there were still hundreds taken at parties and friends' weddings and on days out. With changing hairstyles and clothes, lines spreading on our faces, an inch or two added to our waists, I watched us grow a little older together over the five years of our relationship. Of course it hadn't always been idyllic. No one photographs the bad times—the arguments, the periods of boredom, the blips when we took each other for granted or I neglected her for work. But this was our life together . . . the life that we hadn't been able to maintain.

There were very few pictures from our European trip because our camera had been in one of the backpacks we left behind in Breva.

The only photos from the trip that remained were those I'd taken with my phone. These had been automatically synced to my computer when we got home and my laptop and phone started talking to each other. I had never dared look at these photos, but now I felt my finger drift across the computer's trackpad until I was looking at the first photo I'd taken: a selfie with both of us on the Eurostar to Brussels. We had been so happy that day, setting off on our amazing journey, free from worries and responsibility. I flicked through the photos, smiling at the memories of France and Spain and Italy. I emptied my wine glass and fetched the bottle.

I reached a picture of Laura in the café near Budapest Station where we had eaten before taking the train. I had snapped a picture of her when she wasn't looking. Her face was in profile and she was brushing a strand of hair away from her eye, pensive, pretty. I stared at the photo for a long time, taking another swallow of wine to deaden the pain. This was the last picture of her before the calamity.

Or it should have been. For when I tapped the cursor key, expecting it to take me back to the first picture in the album, a new photograph of Laura appeared.

As soon as I saw this new picture I dropped my wine glass, the shattering sound distant beneath the thrumming in my ears, oblivious to the red stain that spread across the carpet by my feet.

In the photo, Laura was lying on a bunk, asleep, her arms wrapped around her chest, knees drawn up. The photo had been taken in the sleeper compartment of the Romanian train.

Hand trembling, I clicked.

In the next picture, I was asleep in the other bunk, mouth ajar.

I snatched my hand away from the laptop like it was on fire. The headache from earlier had returned. Out of the corner of my eye I could see the fresh red wine stain on the carpet, the colour of dried blood.

I thought back to that night. I had fallen asleep holding my phone. It had been dead when I woke up but there had still been a few per cent of battery life left when I fell asleep.

The person who snuck into the carriage and stole our passports and tickets must have used my phone to take photos of us sleeping.

Hand trembling, I clicked back to the first photo, and found myself looking at the picture of Laura at Budapest Station. Confused, I clicked again. Back to the first photo, of us on Eurostar. I went back to the album, scoured the thumbnail photos.

The two pictures from our night on the train weren't there anymore. They had vanished.

I thought I would never feel as scared as I had been that night in the forest. But now I started shivering, unable to move, my mind shutting down into pure instinct mode, aware of the shadows around me, the darkness outside.

I stood up, and the room spun around me. I was drunk, so drunk, more than I had realised. So pissed that I was hallucinating photographs.

Drunk and crazy, a little voice in my head said. *Or just fucking crazy.*

Something thumped above me and a woman cried out. I clutched my chest. But it was just my neighbours, fucking noisily again. I staggered across the room, my heart skittering crazily. I picked up my phone and called Laura's mobile, hanging up after two rings when I remembered what time it was and that Laura was in hospital. She was seeing ghosts and I was imagining phantom photographs. I started to laugh. We really were the perfect couple.

Chapter Twenty-Three

An elderly woman with a face that looked like it had been in the tumble-drier too long stood outside the hospital entrance in her dressing gown, attached to a drip that hung from a metal stand on wheels, smoking a cigarette down to the butt. I kept a wide berth; the smell of smoke was liable to turn my stomach after the night I'd had. I felt wretched, poisoned by alcohol and lack of sleep, but visiting hours were 10 a.m. to 11 a.m. and I needed to see Laura. Even the cloudless ice-blue sky and the wintry sunshine couldn't make me feel better.

I walked through the hospital quickly. I carried a bunch of yellow and apricot tulips: her favourite. I was eager to see her, though I had decided not to tell her about my weird episode in the night.

My eagerness waned as I approached her bed, which had a thin curtain drawn around it, and heard voices. The hectoring boom of her mother, Sandra, and the reedy whine of her dad, Frank. My heart sank. I had hoped I would miss them.

I took a deep breath and ducked through the curtain. Both of Laura's parents turned, frowns etched on their faces. Laura was propped up in the bed, a pillow behind her back, her skin as white as the bedsheets. She stared into the middle distance, her face blank.

Seeing her like that made me want to put my arms around her and, somehow, make it all better. An instinct that should have been even stronger in her mother.

'Daniel,' said Sandra, a hint of reproach in her voice. She air-kissed me—she had the faint scent of lavender talc; I hoped I didn't still stink of alcohol—and I nodded hello to Frank, who appeared to be dressed for a winter's day on the golf course.

'My daughter's been a very silly girl, hasn't she?' Sandra said. She tutted and looked at Laura like she'd been called into the headmaster's office to be told that her daughter had been caught snogging a boy behind the bike shed.

I went over to Laura and leaned over to kiss her cheek but she flinched away, refusing to meet my eye.

'I thought you'd come last night,' I said, addressing Sandra.

'Frank had a very important dinner meeting. We simply couldn't get out of it.'

I swallowed. While Laura and I had been a couple, I had bitten my tongue in her parents' presence, practised deep breathing exercises and made as many excuses as I could to avoid their company. When I first met them I could scarcely believe they were for real, had thought Laura's stories about how they cared more about money and status than they did about her must be exaggerated. They weren't. The Mackenzies had got lucky buying a couple of cheap houses in London in the eighties before selling them on for a ridiculous profit at the peak of the property boom. Since then they had moved to Cornwall and set up a 'lifestyle consultancy' business, advising rich people how to maximise their work–life balance.

They'd never hidden their disappointment in Laura. 'Working for a charity is all very . . . noble,' Sandra had said on that first meeting, her nose wrinkling. 'But don't you think charity should start at home, Laura? That you should look after your own needs first? What do you think, Daniel?'

'I think it's great that Laura is doing something she's passionate about. There's more to life than earning loads of money.'

Sandra had looked at me with disgust.

'They've always been the same,' Laura had once told me. 'If I came home from school and told them I'd got eighty per cent in an exam, my dad would ask me what went wrong with the other twenty. Mum was always pointing out my physical flaws—if I bumped into something it would be "typical clumsy Laura" or if I had a spot on my face she would point it out to all her awful friends. I couldn't wait to escape.' A big sigh. 'They're still my parents though.'

So there were the bi-annual trips down to Cornwall to stay at their huge, tasteless house, filled with expensive ornaments and horrible modern art. Frank was usually at the golf course or at work while Sandra endlessly recounted the exploits of the next-door neighbours, two gay black men who were, outrageously, going through the process of adopting a baby.

'I've heard they might get a white one,' she'd said, in a hushed, horrified voice.

It was beautiful there, though, the rugged coast and sandy beaches a short stroll away. One of my favourite memories was a time when Laura ran shrieking along the beach, listing at the top of her voice all the things her mum was appalled by: 'The gays, the blacks, the Arabs, single mums, the state of the NHS, the *Guardian*, trade unions, Russell Brand, next door's cat, the cost of parking in town . . .' Afterwards, she had flopped exhausted on the sand and yelled, 'Fuck you, Mother!', much to the amusement of a passing surfer.

I felt like saying 'fuck you' to Sandra right now, and I guess it would have been easy to vent my frustrations on this aggravating woman and her husband. Instead, I said, 'So how long are you staying?'

'We have to get back today. Cassie'—that was their dog, a cocker spaniel—'is with the neighbours . . .'

'Not the gay black neighbours?' I gasped.

'Peter and Laurence. Yes. They're very nice, actually, even though they are . . .' She trailed off, looking around, suddenly aware that many of the nurses and other patients were black.

'We're not in Cornwall anymore, Toto,' I muttered under my breath.

'Laura understands we must get back, don't you, poppet?' Frank said.

His daughter nodded, staring towards her knees beneath the sheet.

'Laura's friend, Erin, the unmarried pregnant one, was here earlier,' Sandra said. 'She asked if Laura could come and stay at ours for a while.' She tutted.

'Can't she?' I asked.

'No! It's impossible. We've got the builders in at the moment. And I'm so busy.'

With what, bitching about the neighbours and counting your money? I wanted to ask.

'Laura will be fine with Erin. She seems like a decent young woman, I suppose.'

'But she's about to have a baby,' I said.

'Maybe Laura could stay with you, then.' Sandra clucked her tongue. 'I don't know why you two ever split up. Weren't you supposed to be getting married? Young people today don't stick at anything. The first sign of a bump in the road and they abandon ship.'

'I think that's a mixed metaphor, my sweet.'

'Oh, shut up, Frank.'

I was still concentrating on the first thing she'd said, about Laura coming to stay with me. What was I supposed to say? It was what I wanted more than anything, not for her to come and *stay* with me but to come back, to move in again.

I glanced at Laura, whose eyes remained fixed on the bedsheet. Suddenly, she looked up at us. 'I want you to go,' she said.

I was about to smirk at Sandra and Frank when Laura added, 'All of you.'

'Poppet,' said Frank. 'We just got here.'

'We haven't had a chance to talk some sense into you yet,' said Sandra.

Laura picked up the bunch of tulips I'd laid on her bedside table and chucked it at her mother. As Sandra groped for something to say, Laura picked up an empty water glass and pulled her arm back. I grabbed her wrist to stop her from flinging it, too.

Sandra and Frank stood there, mouths flapping.

'Go home,' Laura said, apparently drained by the exertion. 'I don't need you. And you don't need to worry about paying for a funeral—I'm not going to kill myself.' Her voice grew even quieter. 'Not now.'

Sandra and Frank exchanged a look and gathered their things. Unbelievable: they would rather take this excuse to make an exit than argue. Before they went, Sandra produced a paper bag and handed it to Laura.

'I bought you this, thought it might . . . help.'

After they'd gone, Laura pushed the paper bag towards me and I took out a paperback book. It was called *Finding Your Happy Place: 21 Practical Ways to Beat Depression and Keep Smiling*!

I put it in the bin.

'Do you really want me to go too?' I asked softly.

She closed her eyes and nodded. 'I'm sorry, Danny. But I'm so tired. I didn't get much sleep.'

'OK.' I hesitated. 'I'm so worried about you, Laura.'

There was a long silence before she said, 'I'm not going to kill myself. OK?'

'Please don't. I couldn't bear to live in a world that you're not in.'

A smile flickered. 'God, you're so corny sometimes.'

'Are you still going to take the drugs you were prescribed?'

She cast her eyes downwards and shook her head.

I stood there a moment longer then said, 'All right. I'll come back later, if that's OK? I've got a meeting with my therapist now anyway.'

She nodded again, the blankness in her eyes creeping back.

'You should come with me to see her. She said it would help us. Especially . . .' *Especially now*, I was going to say. *Now that you've tried to commit suicide.* 'It wouldn't be like the therapist you saw when you were a kid, I promise.'

'I'm fine,' she said. 'I'm feeling a lot better. I'll see you later, OK?'

I took the bus to Crouch End, sitting on the top deck. I could still feel the alcohol sloshing about in my system, and maybe it was this trace of drunkenness that made me feel a spark of optimism. Laura had called me Danny. She hadn't called me Danny since we'd split up. Maybe, I thought, her brush with death would make her decide we were better together. That she needed me.

If she came back to me, if we were united again, I was convinced we would be able to recover from our experiences and fight anything else the world threw at us. We were a hundred times stronger together. In the days and weeks following our return to England, when everything at home had seemed so dismal, the two of us trapped in our own dark spaces inside our heads, barely communicating, I had lost sight of that. Laura had taken it further.

She said that looking at me reminded her of what had happened, that every time she saw my face she was jolted back in time. She could never hope to recover when she saw me every day.

'But do you still love me?' I had asked, in one of the final days before she left.

There had been a long silence. 'Do you still love *me*?'

135

She looked at me searchingly and maybe I took a moment too long to say, 'Of course. Always.'

I should have done everything I could to make her stay, to make it work. I should have convinced her that we were better together, that we could get through it if we were united. Instead, I had watched her walk out the door, barely protesting.

Now I allowed myself to hope, and as the bus rattled along the streets I tried to work out how best to play it. I decided I needed to give her time and space. I mustn't pressure her. But if I could persuade her to come and see Dr Sauvage, either with me or on her own . . . I resolved to talk to Erin about it. Perhaps Laura would finally listen to her, now that Erin had saved her life.

Dr Sauvage's house was a few streets from the bus stop. The brightness had faded and the sky above the terraced houses was colourless, like a picture in which the artist had forgotten to paint the sky. A child on a micro-scooter almost collided with me as I turned the corner onto Dr Sauvage's street, making my heart jump.

As I approached her house, which was halfway along, it gradually dawned on me that something was wrong. At first, I thought the house looked a little strange, darker than usual, with someone in a yellow coat standing outside. As I got closer, my mouth fell open.

A dark grey blemish stretched across the facade of the house from the top windows, which had been boarded up, down to the front door. The windows on the ground floor were cracked and coated with some kind of black substance. A broken chair lay in the front garden and tiles had fallen from the roof. Yellow tape was strung around the whole house. The person in the yellow coat was a police officer, standing guard in a waterproof jacket.

He looked up as I approached.

'What . . . happened?'

'Can I ask who you are, sir?'

'I'm one of Claudia Sauvage's patients. I have an appointment now.'

The policeman, who was younger than me and looked cold and miserable, said, 'I'm sorry to have to tell you this but there was a fire here yesterday.' He cleared his throat.

'Oh my God.' I forced out the words. 'What caused it?'

The policeman looked up and down the street. 'I'm very sorry, sir, but I can't discuss that.'

'Terrible business.'

I whirled round. An elderly man had strolled across the road and stood looking up at the house, shaking his head.

'I live across the street,' he said. 'Can't believe it—that poor couple. They'll be missed dreadfully.'

It took a moment for this to register.

'Missed?' I said quietly.

The old man stared up at the burnt-out house. 'Yes, both the Sauvages are dead. They were trapped upstairs. Nothing the fire brigade could do.' He walked away, muttering, 'Terrible business. Terrible.'

Chapter Twenty-Four

I stopped off at my flat, grabbed my laptop and went out. I didn't want to be on my own at home. I needed to be around people, around the living. There was a coffee shop at the end of the road that also served greasy all-day breakfasts. Just what my body craved.

The first item on my list was to look up more information about what had happened to Dr Sauvage and her husband. My relationship with my therapist had been purely professional but that didn't make her death any less shocking. She was only in her forties . . . and what a horrific and terrifying way to die. I wondered if her dogs, those snuffling pugs, had perished too?

The story was on the *Evening Standard* website, with a photo of the burnt-out house plus a snapshot of the smiling Sauvages, Claudia and Patrick, taken a few years ago. They had no children, which was something. There was no mention of the dogs.

Then I read the line at the end of the article.

Police are trying to ascertain whether the Sauvages were victims of arson and are expected to release more information in the coming days.

Arson? My God. Why would someone do that? I wondered if Dr Sauvage had made enemies. It was truly dreadful. And, feeling guilty for the selfish thought, I wondered who I was going to talk to now. Laura was too fragile and my therapist was gone. That only left one candidate: my best friend.

———

Jake and I arranged to meet the next day at Friends House, the Quaker place on Euston Road. He had a meeting at the offices of a record company who were based in a glittering new office block beside the station.

'This is it,' he told me on the phone. 'I'm pretty certain they're going to offer me a deal.'

'That's amazing.'

As soon as he gave me this news I almost cancelled. He was so excited and I didn't want to bring him down. But I suspected that the moment he agreed to the deal he would go into orbit for a while. It was best to talk to him now while he was still within Earth's gravitational field.

My CCTV equipment had arrived at lunchtime and I'd spent the early afternoon setting it up. The camera was positioned above the entrance to the front door of the flat. It was connected to an app on my phone and was triggered by movement. If anyone entered the flat the camera would start recording.

As I left the flat I looked up at the camera and smiled.

———

Friends House is the Quakers' London base, with a café and meeting area that is open to the public. It was one of Jake's favourite places to meet because of the relaxed vibe.

I arrived first, bought a coffee and carrot cake and took them to the back of the meeting area, where it was quiet and secluded. A few brave souls shivered outside in the courtyard, where a light dusting of snow that had fallen during the afternoon coated the tables and gathered on window sills.

While I waited, I texted Laura and asked how she was. I hesitated then sent another message before she replied, telling her I was going to talk to Jake about what happened. *My therapist is dead,* I typed. *And I need to talk to someone. I hope you understand x.*

Jake arrived wrapped in a chunky military-style coat, a long scarf wrapped around his neck. I had been right about him being ready for lift-off. Energy radiated off him as if he was a human microwave. He could barely keep still. He grabbed a large coffee and chatted up the Quaker girl at the counter.

'Got her number,' he grinned when he got back to the table. He sat down, his leg jerking back and forth, the worst case of restless leg syndrome I'd ever seen. 'Hey, who was that Eastern European girl you were with the other night? She was well rude. Hot though. Don't tell me you pulled her.'

'She wasn't *that* rude to you.'

He waved a hand. 'Sorry, I'm turning into an egomaniac, aren't I? I need you to tell me when I'm acting like a wanker, Dan.'

'Keep you grounded, you mean. Down here where the mortals live.'

'Hey, you're a supersonic business dude. Apps sell a lot more than music these days. It should be *me* keeping *you* grounded. Instead, you're still acting like the world is a funeral procession. Even though you're pulling hot women like that . . . where was she from?'

'Romania,' I said.

He slapped the table. 'Really? So is she your new girlfriend? Have you given up on Laura? That would break my heart. I'm still convinced the two of you are going to get back together at any moment. Remember, you promised I could be your best man. I've already got some great jokes lined up.'

I sipped my coffee. It had gone cold. I was tempted to ask Jake to hold the mug, thinking that the heat coming off him would make it drinkable again.

'No, she's not my girlfriend. But Romania . . . well, that's what I want to talk to you about.'

He sat forward. 'Surely you're not finally going to tell me what went down with you and Laura in Europe?'

'I don't know. But . . . I want to tell you about everything that's happened since.'

His phone rang. 'Sorry,' he said. 'Got to answer this.'

He wandered out into the frosty courtyard and I watched him talking animatedly. I was envious of him. Everything was going brilliantly, nothing tainted, no shadows clawing at the edges of his life. This moment—about to sign a record deal, with everything ahead of him, the promise of greatness—was probably as good as it would ever get. As he had said, I should be feeling like that too, had indeed felt like it when Laura and I set off on our trip. I wished I was back in that place, the magical garden where Jake stood now.

Seeing him striding about the courtyard, chatting away, a big smile on his handsome face, I realised that I couldn't be envious of him. He'd worked so hard for this. I was proud of him.

He came back inside, his hair glistening with snowflakes. 'That was my manager. Universal and Sony want to meet me now too. So that's three of the big four.' He rubbed his hands together.

'You deserve it,' I said.

'Thanks, man. Though I haven't signed anything yet.'

'You will. You're going to be a star. Soon the only glimpse of you I'll get will be when you're in the paper, hanging out with Taylor Swift and Rihanna.'

'Hmm, I think I'd prefer Beyoncé. Anyway, you're gonna be a big techie superstar. We'll be going to the same parties. We'll be . . . Shit, Dan, your face . . . You look like I just reminded you that you've got cancer or something. I'm sorry. You have my undivided attention.'

'Thanks.'

'Come on, then. Hit me with it. What's going on?'

So I told him about the burglar returning my stuff and the fraudulent use of my debit card. I told him how my therapist's house had burned down, leaving me halfway through my course of treatment with no one to talk to. I filled him in on the details of Laura's suicide attempt, which made his mouth drop open, and how she'd apparently been seeing ghosts again.

'I'm sure I saw someone watching her, too . . . and someone might have tried to push her under a Tube train. All this weird shit.'

'Fucking hell,' he said when I'd finished. 'Have you been to the police?'

'They think I either hallucinated the break-in, that I'm crazy, or that I'm a liar and a time-waster. Sometimes I think I *am* going crazy . . .' I trailed off. I decided not to tell him about hallucinating the photos from the train. 'It's ever since Romania.'

I looked at him, my eyes stinging.

He didn't say anything for a few moments, just stared at me. 'And are you going to tell me what happened?'

'I want to. I really need to talk to someone. That's what I intended to do. But now, when it comes to it . . .'

'Daniel. It's me. You can talk to me about anything. I'm not going to go and blab to anyone about it. I promise. I know you think I'm a major gossip but I swear, hand on heart, I won't tell. Whatever it is.'

I tore an empty sugar sachet to shreds, unable to meet his eye. 'It's so hard to talk about. Just getting the words out . . . Plus I'm afraid of burdening you with it.'

'Burdening me? Come on. It can't be *that* bad.'

I looked up him. 'But it is.'

I started by telling him about the train journey, meeting Alina and Ion, the guards throwing us off, the creepy station in the middle of nowhere. He listened, enrapt, as I told him about the walk along the tracks, Alina going into the forest and disappearing. Laura and I going to look for her.

'And then we found a house. In the middle of the forest.'

He stared at me, eyes wide, as I told him what happened next.

Chapter Twenty-Five

As we moved closer to the house, I could see grey shadows flickering in the upstairs windows, those jack-o'-lantern lights. Candles. Somebody was home.

There was a little boy inside me yelling at my adult self as we approached the place. *This is a witch's house, a witch who lures and eats the lost, who'll fatten you and devour you, make bread from your bones. Run. Run as fast and far as you can, find a bed, get under the covers and hide there.*

Laura touched my hand.

'Daniel. Look.'

Laura was pointing at something and at first I thought my heart had leaped from my body and was lying there, twitching in the dead grass, but I somehow got hold of myself, forced my eyes to focus.

'Alina's other boot.'

I stooped and picked it up, turned back to Laura, cradling the boot like it was a kitten.

'We should go, get help,' I said.

My girlfriend set her jaw and, not answering me, walked up the path towards the house. I wavered. What was I—a boy or a man? Perhaps if I'd been here on my own I would have run, gone to seek help. But the need to stay with Laura, to not look like a coward, was even stronger.

The door was solid, fashioned from the oak trees that surrounded the house. I could sense those trees behind us, like they were watching, daring us to go inside. All the hair on the back of my neck stood to attention; ripples ran the length of my spine. Why was this house here, deep in the forest? I guessed it must have been the home of—what? A huntsman? A woodcutter? Some kind of ranger?

A witch?

The house had an ancient air about it, centuries old. It probably pre-dated the railway line we had walked along. The door had no number, no letterbox. I suppressed a hysterical giggle at the thought of a postman traipsing through the forest to deliver junk mail and fliers from pizza places.

Laura raised a fist to knock but I caught her wrist.

I somehow knew, as if I'd seen it in a dream, that the door would open if I pushed it. It did. It was stiff, heavy, but it swung open slowly, revealing a large open space.

I stepped inside, Laura following, holding on to my shirt.

The room reminded me of the entrance hall of a stately home. It was dark, lit only by the moonlight that penetrated from outside. No candles here. I waited for my eyes to adjust and soon saw that the darkness concealed very little. A couple of chests, a coat stand with a black jacket hanging from it. Doors stood closed in both corners and, directly in front of us, a stairway stretched up into more darkness.

Laura and I looked at each other. She looked more afraid now we were inside the house. If I had sensed a sickness about this place before we came inside, I felt it more keenly now. Terrible things had happened here. I knew that as clearly as I knew my own name. Laura had taken a few steps into the room but now moved back towards the exit, like she'd had second thoughts. Maybe it was the smell that did it: the room had a musty, damp odour, the cloying reek of mildew and rot. But there was another smell, a top note, that was worse. Years ago I had lived in a bedsit that had a vile stink. Eventually I found the source: the previous tenant had left glue traps beneath the cooker and the fridge, and dead rats had been left rotting for weeks. That's what this place smelled like. Rotting flesh. Death.

'You want to go?' I whispered to Laura.

She stared at me, the fear evident in her eyes now. A look that said this was a mistake. A look that asked what the fuck we were doing here. The door had drifted shut behind us and I had a horrible feeling that it was locked now, that we were trapped. That we would be trapped here forever.

Maybe we would have gone then, done what we should have in the first place: gone back through the trees, kept going along the railway tracks, sought help in town.

But then we heard the noise.

Jake's mobile rang, jerking me back to the present moment.

'Fuck, sorry,' he said. 'It's the guy from the record company.' He clearly felt anxious about answering the call.

'It's all right. Take it.'

'I'm sorry, man. I'll be right back.'

He stood up and walked away, saying 'Uh-huh' and 'Right' as he went.

I had torn a dozen more sugar sachets to shreds while talking and now I picked at the pieces; grains of white sugar were scattered across the tabletop.

I felt sick, wondering if I'd have the guts to tell Jake the rest of the story. If I would be able to tell him the truth about what had happened.

He reappeared at the table. He wore a sheepish expression. 'Daniel, man, I'm really sorry. They've moved the meeting forward so the Executive VP of A&R can sit in.' Seeing my blank expression he added, 'He's, like, the top dog.'

'You have to go.'

'Daniel, I really want to hear the rest of what happened. Why don't we have a drink later? After my meeting.'

'OK. Maybe.'

He bounced from foot to foot, agitated.

'Go on,' I said, forcing a smile. 'I'll call you later. Knock 'em dead.'

'Thanks, Dan.'

He ran around the corner. I heard him bump into someone and apologise. Then he was gone.

———————

By the time I got back to my street the sky was dark and starless and the snow had given way to icy rain. Cold drops ran down the back of my neck as I entered my building and ran a hand through my hair. There was a new poster on the wall, the words printed by a trembling hand. TO WHOEVER PUT THEIR FOOD WASTE IN THE GREEN BIN—THIS BIN IS FOR RECYCLING ONLY!!! This was followed by a threat to REPORT this IRRESPONSIBLE PERSON to THE RESIDENTS' ASSOCIATION. I rolled my eyes. I was surprised there was no mention of the pizza-munching fox.

I trotted up the stairs and put my key in the lock, keen to get into the sanctuary of my flat, despite the recent intrusions. I felt jittery and uneasy in my skin and had already decided that I didn't have the mental energy to meet up with Jake after his meeting and tell him the rest of the story. Another day.

I flicked on the light. Nothing happened.

The light in the communal hallway behind me was working so it couldn't be a power cut. I left the heavy door propped open with my bag, which was just sturdy enough to hold it, and went into the kitchen to test the light there, flicking the switch. Again, nothing happened. The flat was in darkness.

The fuse box was in a cupboard beneath the kitchen worktop. On the rare occasions when the power had gone out before—in fact, I could only remember it happening once—I had simply needed to push the fuse switch back down. Kneeling on the floor, trying to see the fuse box in the nearly non-existent light, I heard the front door shut, plunging me into complete darkness. Fuck—the bag must have been too light to hold the door for long. But I was able to feel the fuse switches now, running my finger along to find out which one had tripped.

None of them had. I took my phone out of my pocket and used it as a torch to double-check. No, the fuse switches were all in position. Without removing the fuse cartridges I couldn't see if the fuse wires were intact, and I couldn't remember whether the switch would trip if the fuse blew. In normal circumstances none of this would have made me feel nervous, but recent events made me wonder . . .

Had somebody been in here again? Had they disabled the lights? Were they still here, hiding?

I went back to the front door, feeling my way along the wall, stumbling over the vacuum cleaner and almost falling. I looked up at the CCTV camera above the door, wondering if it had captured anyone. Maybe someone had spotted it and turned the lights out so they could move about without being filmed.

I fumbled for my phone so I could check the app that was connected to the camera, and promptly dropped it. It bounced and skidded under the furniture. I hesitated. My fear that someone was in the flat now overrode my desire to find the phone so I went back out into the communal hallway. The light, which switched itself off after a short while, had gone out now. I turned it back on and stood in the hallway, trying to decide what to do. I could knock on one of my neighbours' doors, ask them if they had a torch.

I looked at my nearest neighbour's door. I never spoke to the woman who lived here, suspected that she was responsible for the crazy signs that were always appearing. I didn't want to get her involved, especially as the likelihood was that this was a failed fuse.

I made a decision: I would go back in, recover my phone and check the app to see if someone had been in the flat.

I went back inside and, this time, used the vacuum cleaner to prop the door open. I got down on all fours and felt under the sofa and the coffee table, feeling for my phone. Where the hell was it? I swore out loud and thumped the floor with my fist.

A scrabbling sound came from the bedroom.

I jerked upright.

There was someone in my bedroom. Oh Jesus, I needed my phone. I needed to call the police. But then came another bang, then another. I jumped to my feet, headed to the front door, then thought *no*. This was my chance to find out who had burgled my flat, to catch them and get some answers out of them myself. The police would probably take forever to get here. And I was pissed off. Sick of my world being violated.

I crept into the kitchen and took a large knife from the block on the worktop. Then, trembling with fear and fury, I tiptoed to the bedroom door and, holding the knife aloft with my right hand, used the left to quickly push the door open.

For a moment, I could see nothing. And then something hit me, knocking the breath from my body as I fell to the floor, forcing the knife from my grasp. It spun away across the carpet.

Chapter Twenty-Six

I was pinned to the floor on my back, foul, meaty breath in my face. A growl came from deep inside my attacker's body and I pushed as hard as I could, but my attacker was on top of me, a blur in the darkness. Teeth and saliva and wet lips grazed my throat and, as adrenalin surged into my system, I found strength I didn't know I had, shoving and twisting on to my side. A second later and the dog—the black dog that had leaped out of the darkness—would have torn out my throat.

As soon as I twisted on to my side I saw the knife, just within reach. I grabbed it and swung it at the dog, which wriggled away as I tried to slash it. Instead, the blade nicked the side of its nose, and it let out a whimper of pain. As quickly as it had leaped onto me, it bounded away. I was free.

It shot out through the front door, growling and barking, as I pushed myself up, coughing and feeling my neck. Just stinking saliva, no blood. If I hadn't been able to twist away, if I hadn't been carrying the knife . . . I didn't want to think about it. The dog had had a Rottweiler's face but was completely black and the size of a pit bull. A dog bred to guard, to fight. To kill.

I staggered to my feet and went out into the hallway. The dog had run down the stairs and was dashing to and fro in the lower hallway, frantic, thumping into the door, bouncing off the walls. I stood at the top of the stairs, looking over the handrail so I had a full view of the hallway, coiled and ready to rush back into my flat if the animal showed any sign of coming back up the stairs.

At that moment, the door of my downstairs neighbour opened and she appeared in the doorway. She was in her thirties, frizzy hair, glasses, wearing a thick pink jumper. She pointed a finger at me. 'Hey, you're not allowed dogs in this building.'

The dog leaped towards her. She screamed and slammed the door shut with surprising reaction speed; the animal hit the wood mid-jump, crashed and fell to the floor, stunned for a moment before getting back on its feet. It turned to look up at me, baring two rows of teeth like knives.

I dashed back into my flat, shutting the door, plunged into darkness again. Once more, I crawled across the living room floor, and my hand made contact almost immediately with my phone. I said a silent prayer and hit 999, listening as the dog rushed around downstairs, emitting a series of harsh, low barks.

The police came and summoned a dog warden, who captured the animal using a loop on a stick and dragged it into the back of his van. After he'd taken it away, the young police officer helped me examine the fuse box, finding that two of the fuse wires needed replacing. Fortunately, one of the neighbours, most of whom had come out to see what was going on, had some spares, so my lights were soon working again.

'Bad luck for two to blow at once,' the officer said. His name was Sadler. 'So, sir, what happened?'

I hesitated. On impulse, perhaps because I didn't want him to start looking at me in the way PC Sargent had, I said, 'I don't know. It must have followed me in when I got home, snuck in through the door behind me. When I found the lights weren't working I left my flat door open and it came in and attacked me.'

He tutted. 'Lots of strays around here. Most of them come from the estate.' He shook his head at the state of the city he policed. 'Do you need a doctor?'

'No, I'm fine. It didn't bite me. I'm just a bit . . . shocked.'

'Understandable, sir.' He smiled. 'You don't have any sausages in your bag, do you?'

I had temporarily lost my sense of humour.

He said goodbye and went off to take a statement from the woman downstairs.

After taking a moment to gather myself, I stood up, my legs unsteady, and went into the bedroom. It looked like a tornado had ripped through it. The bedside lamp lay broken on the floor, along with books, papers and framed photographs of Laura and me; the bedding was trampled and one pillow had been chewed, pieces of foam scattered around. I wondered why I hadn't heard it as soon as I came in and guessed it must have fallen asleep after destroying my room and been awakened by the sound of my punching the floor.

There was a terrible stench in the air, the source of which I found quickly: a huge turd curled on the little rug in front of the chest of drawers. I rolled the rug up and stuffed it into a black bin liner, taking it and dumping it in the bin outside. I sensed a presence nearby and looked up to see the scavenging fox standing nearby. It turned and slunk away, tail dragging on the pavement.

Needing to calm my jangling nerves, I poured a shot of vodka and walked over to look out at the dark, empty street. Icy rain streaked the glass. I wondered what had happened to the dog. Would it be put down or would they attempt to rehome it? I waited until the warm bloom of the alcohol had slowed my heartbeat, quelled the tremor in my hands, then took out my phone and opened the app that had come with the camera.

Immediately, I could see that a video file had been created and stored on the cloud. The camera had captured whoever had come into my flat. The room was silent, and I found myself holding my breath, aware of my pulse thrumming in my ears.

The video started to play.

Because the camera was triggered by motion, as soon as the video started I found myself looking at the top of someone's head and shoulders. They stood a few feet in front of my front door. The image was grainy and slightly blurred, presumably because it wasn't very well lit, but there was still natural light in the room. It got dark about 4.30 p.m. That meant they must have been in here late afternoon, probably while I was with Jake.

I willed the person to step further into the room so I could see them better. All I could make out at the moment was that they were wearing a black top and a hat. I assumed it was a man. He took a couple of steps forward into my living room, the room where I sat now, so that he was visible down to his waist and then turned around. I leaned forward eagerly.

At the exact moment that he turned, somebody else walked into shot, obscuring his face. There were two of them! And as they both walked further into the living room, I saw that the second person had the black dog who'd tried to kill me, on a short leash.

The second person was also wearing a hat. The two of them stood still, apparently looking around, though maddeningly

I could only see the backs of their heads. I could see their bodies now, though. They were both dressed in black long-sleeved tops and black trousers. But as I squinted at the screen, at the shape of their bodies, I suddenly realised I had been wrong to assume their gender. One of them, the one holding the dog, was a woman. And as they turned to talk to each other I saw that they were wearing masks, those plastic masks that you attach to your head with a piece of elastic. But both masks were blank, plain white with two eye holes and a small circle to breathe through. Looking at the blank masks sent a shudder through me. It was like looking at two phantoms, faceless creatures who had invaded my home.

The woman yanked at the dog's leash and her mask slipped a little. Frustratingly, she caught it and pushed it back into place. Then she walked out of shot towards my bedroom with the dog. While she did this, the man walked around the room, opening drawers and cupboards, carefully shutting them again.

After a while, the woman came back with the dog and shook her head. I wished I'd bought a camera with an audio recorder, as they had another conversation. The man gesticulated angrily, pointed at the dog and then towards my bedroom. The woman nodded.

Then the man went over to the kitchen, disappearing from sight. The woman was facing the camera so I had a perfect view of her. She was slim with small breasts and narrow hips. The dog pulled at the lead and she jerked it back, causing it to jump up onto its hind legs. Poor thing. Whoever she was, she was strong.

The man returned and they both walked out of shot, towards my bedroom. And that was it. The video captured another minute of still life and then ended.

They had come in, cut the fuse wire—presumably so when I arrived home in the dark it would be harder for me to avoid the dog attack—then shut the animal in my bedroom, leaving just before it got dark.

I shut the laptop and stared at the space where they had stood. I could feel their presence imprinted on the air.

Chapter Twenty-Seven

It was unusually quiet on the South Bank, the bad weather keeping the day-trippers away; there were just a few Londoners scurrying beneath the snow-pregnant sky, hurrying to their homes and offices. The London Eye seemed to be turning more slowly this afternoon; the boats that drifted by on the grey, churning Thames looked like they should be carrying the dead across the Styx.

I browsed around Foyles for a while, then grabbed a coffee from Starbucks and took it to a bench that overlooked the river and the grand buildings on the Embankment opposite. I checked my watch. She should be here soon.

I felt strangely nervous, as if we were meeting for a first date, which was ridiculous. We knew each other intimately, inside and out . . . At least, I'd thought I'd known everything about her. Recently, she had been a different person, an alien that had wrapped itself in Laura's body, only occasionally showing me a glimpse of the person she used to be. But Jake said I was like that too. I hadn't contacted him since the previous afternoon, when he'd had to rush off. I resolved to call him later. I needed to tell him the rest of the story.

'Daniel.'

I turned around. 'You came.'

'Of course.'

Laura looked thinner and paler than ever, even more so than when I'd seen her in the hospital. She had her black coat wrapped around her, a coat which used to fit her perfectly, hugging the contours of her body, but which now seemed two sizes too big. She was wearing a woollen hat too, and make-up—a little mascara and a dash of pink lipstick. It was the first time I'd seen her wearing make-up in ages. She sat down beside me and clasped her gloved hands together. Her knees bounced up and down. She smiled but it slipped from her face almost immediately.

'You look . . . better,' I said.

She raised an eyebrow. 'Hmm.'

'No, really. It was so horrible seeing you in that hospital bed.'

'It wasn't much fun being there.' Her knees continued to bounce up and down. 'I do feel better now, though. Much better. My skin's grown back.'

'Huh?'

'But it's . . . different. New skin.'

I stared at her. 'Laura, I have no idea what you're talking about. Did you get my message yesterday morning?'

She stared at me, her eyes wide and blank. Her voice dropped to a whisper, just audible above the wind that whipped across the Thames. 'Message?'

Before I could say anything, she said, 'I've got some news for you. I've quit my job.'

'Oh, Laura, but you loved that job. You always said it was your calling.'

'It was.' She stared out at the river. 'But not now. I just can't . . . do it anymore. I could try but I'd be letting everyone down. Letting the children down, the ones I'm supposed to help.'

'I'm sure you wouldn't let anyone down.' I touched her arm lightly. 'But maybe it is for the best. You need to get well, and then I'm sure you could go back to it. Although,' I swallowed, 'you won't be here anymore, will you? You'll be in Australia.'

She hugged her knees, which at least stopped them from bouncing. 'I'm not going.'

I hardly dared speak, in case I'd misheard. 'Say that again.'

'I've decided not to go. I'm going to stay in London.'

'Oh! That's amazing.' I moved to hug her but she shrank away. I gathered myself. 'What made you change your mind?'

She opened her mouth to reply, then stopped. I could see that she was trying to decide how much to tell me. 'Like you said, it would be running away. I don't want to run anymore. I don't want to be a coward. I want to start again.' She spoke slowly, a spaced-out expression on her face. Had the doctors put her on more medication?

'But,' she continued, 'you said you have some stuff you need to tell me. When you texted me this morning.'

'Laura, are you *really* all right?'

A smile, a little more like the old Laura. 'Yes. Of course. I'm fine. Come on, tell me what it was you brought me here for.'

'OK.' I wasn't convinced, but what could I do? 'Can we walk and talk? I'm freezing.'

'Sure.'

We stood up and she gave me another little smile, the kind of smile she used to bless me with, and I was gripped by an urge to tell her, again, that I still loved her, that I wanted her to come home. But I knew if I did it would scare her away. So I swallowed the words and we walked along by the railing in the direction of the Millennium Bridge.

As we walked, I told her about everything that had happened so far: the fraudulent use of my bank card, the return of my laptop after the burglary, my therapist's death. Laura listened intently, nodding but not saying much. She flinched when I told her about the fire. Finally, as we drew parallel with the Tate Modern, I brought her up to date by telling her what had happened the previous day.

She stopped walking. Her smile had vanished. 'A dog? What did it look like?'

I described it.

'Like the dogs we saw at the station,' she said, nodding to herself as if this confirmed something.

I didn't think it would be possible for her to look any paler but all the remaining colour had drained from her face. The sky shifted and all the light was sucked from it, like the moment before a storm breaks.

Laura spoke. 'Maybe you should talk to her. It might help you.'

'Who?'

'Alina. She's here.'

So she *had* been imagining ghosts again.

'Laura, Alina is dead.'

'I know. But she's come to find me.' She leaned even closer, her eyes stretched wide. She looked left then right, checked behind her. Her voice dropped to a harsh whisper. 'I know what's following us, Daniel. It's *evil*. The evil from that house . . . It followed us home. You need to be careful, to stop telling people about what happened. Because every time you tell someone, you prise open the crack a little more and let the evil through.'

The way she was talking, the intensity of her gaze, the darkening sky and the echo of everything that had happened . . . For a second, I believed her. This was it, the explanation. Evil. The supernatural.

'The black dog—it wasn't real,' she said. 'It was . . . a symbol. Or maybe, maybe a physical manifestation of the darkness that followed us out of the forest. The evil.'

I tried to keep my voice even. 'It was very real, Laura. It jumped on top of me, tried to tear my throat out.'

She looked at me sadly. 'Oh, Daniel. I'm not saying it was a . . . phantom. Like I said, it was a physical mani—'

'No, this is crazy.'

Something soft touched my face and I realised it was snowing again. But this time it was fat, substantial, the kind that settles, closing schools and shutting down train lines. Heavy snow, this early in the season . . . It added to my feeling that the weather was somehow echoing my emotions. No doubt Laura would say we had caused it—that it was coming through this crack she talked about, brought forth by evil spirits.

The snow swirled around us, the air suddenly so dark and thick that the Tate Modern became a shimmering silhouette, and it felt like Laura and I were the only people in the world. When she took my hand I wanted more than anything for it to be the way it used to be. I wanted to kiss her, to put my arms around her and just cling to her, to hold on and hope that all of the madness would go away, leave us alone. Let us be.

'It's OK,' Laura whispered. The snow was settling already. It clung to her hat and coat and her face was wet. She blinked snowflakes from her eyelashes. 'Alina will help us.'

'But Alina is dead! Laura, I know you believe in ghosts, I understand everything that happened when you were a kid, but this is in your head. Caused by . . . what happened and the drugs you were taking. And all this stuff about growing a new skin.' I spoke gently. 'You need to get help.'

'No, Danny. No. Don't you see? She's come back to guide us.'

'Laura . . .'

She tilted her head. She hardly seemed to be aware of the snow. She should never have been discharged from the hospital, I thought.

'Laura, I think you should see a doctor.'

She smiled sadly. 'Another one? See if they'll give me more drugs?'

'Not that kind of doctor.' I groped for something to say to per-suade her. The weather was getting worse. Eventually, I said, 'Let's get inside before this snow buries us.'

She appeared to come to her senses, and I took her hand and ran with her towards the gallery. We took shelter in the vast entrance hall, shaking the snow from our clothes, the security staff glaring as we dripped all over the floor. She went into the Ladies and I went into the Gents, which was empty. I stuck my wet head beneath the drier then studied my face in the mirror. I dried my glasses on my T-shirt and tried to trap the thoughts that were running wildly around my head, to save them for later.

I waited for Laura outside the Ladies. Several women came out, but no Laura. When a woman around my age came out five minutes later, I asked her if she would check if my 'wife' was in there. She strode away, leaving me open-mouthed, shocked by her rudeness. I stuck my head in the door, calling Laura's name. All the cubicles stood open. She had gone.

I hurried back towards the entrance and approached the secu-rity man.

'The woman I came in with—have you seen her?'

He shook his head. 'You'd have to be mad to go out there,' he said. 'It's a blizzard.'

I went over to the door and peered out. The air was opaque, the snow so heavy that it seemed possible that it might bury the city. Through the curtain of snow, I saw a dark figure in the distance. I ran outside, calling, 'Laura!'

If it was her, she was swallowed up by the snowstorm. I went back inside, brushing the snowflakes from my coat, and considered looking around the gallery. Maybe she was in the café or the shop. Perhaps she had gone upstairs to look at the art. But before I could decide what to do, my mobile rang.

It was my friend Barney, someone Jake and I hung around with sometimes. He had moved out of London and started having kids. I hadn't heard from him for ages.

'Barney! Sorry, it's not a great—'

'Have you seen the news?'

His tone of voice scared me. 'No, I'm out. Why, what's happened?'

'It's Jake. I think . . . I assume you can get online on your phone? I'll send you the link now.'

It felt like the snow was falling directly into my bloodstream. 'What about Jake? Come on, you have to tell me.'

He hesitated and I knew this wasn't going to be news about Jake getting a big record deal.

'I think you should read it yourself,' he said. 'But ring me after, yeah?' His voice cracked and he hung up before I could say anything else. A text arrived from him containing a link to BBC News. I hesitated, happy to be ignorant for another second, then clicked. I found myself looking at one of Jake's publicity shots, his eyes downcast, looking sensitive and brooding. Above this was the headline:

Tragic suicide of musician on the brink of the big time
Police have confirmed that they are treating the death of
Jake Turner, whose body was found beneath Thornberry
Bridge last night, as a suicide.
Turner, 32, was on the verge of signing a deal with a major
record company, his manager said.

Then there was a section about famous musicians who had killed themselves. I stared at my phone, unable to take it in. Jake— *dead? Last night?* He had left me at around 4 p.m. and gone straight to the meeting with the record company. And *suicide?* Jake was the least likely person to kill himself I had ever met, and when I saw him he had been on a dizzying high, about to achieve all his dreams. Had the record company let him down, crushed those dreams? Surely he wouldn't commit suicide because of that. And he had told me he had two other companies interested. Even if the first meeting had gone badly, he would still have had hope.

I knew Robin, his manager, and called him, facing away from the security guy, who was watching me curiously. My hand was shaking and I was sure I was going to throw up. But at the same time I was sure this was all a mistake. Jake couldn't be dead. He couldn't. My eyes filled with tears as I heard the 'user busy' tone.

I called Barney instead.

'It doesn't make sense,' I said.

'I know.'

'Jake wouldn't do that. He wasn't depressed. Everything was going fucking amazingly for him.'

'That's what I thought.'

'Do you know how he's supposed to have done it?' I asked.

He hesitated.

'Come on, Barney.' I raised my voice. 'If you know, just tell me.'

'He jumped off a bridge. Thornberry Lane.'

'In Archway?' I knew the bridge well. It was a ten-minute walk from Jake's flat.

'Yeah. You know, the three of us have walked over that bridge loads of times.'

We both fell quiet for a moment.

'And did he . . . Do you know if he left a note?'

'I don't know.'

We ended the call with Barney muttering something about seeing me at the funeral. I wandered outside and sat on a wet bench, oblivious to the snow swirling around me and the cold moisture soaking through the seat of my jeans.

I couldn't believe it. Jake, committing suicide. When I saw him yesterday he had been so happy and excited. He had been horrified by what I had told him about Romania but . . .

It struck me.

I had spoken to two people about what had happened to Laura and me, both within the last few days. I'd told Dr Sauvage part of the story, and more to Jake.

And now they were both dead.

Chapter Twenty-Eight

As predicted, public transport was in chaos, buses and trains grinding to a halt, taxis stranded. I joined the crowds of people leaving their offices early and battled through the streets. All I could think about was Jake, unable to shake my disbelief that he had killed himself. Struggling through the blizzard, my face and hands so cold I thought my skin might crack and fall from my bones, I remembered a conversation with Jake a year or so before, when he was at his lowest point, unable to get anyone interested in his music, while his biggest rival was at the peak of his success. We'd sat in a crowded pub in Angel, Jake wearing a bleak expression, devoid of his usual spark and bounce.

'Sometimes,' he said, sipping his coffee, 'I think I should jack all this in and do something useful. I mean, Christ, the world needs more singer-songwriters like it needs another hole in the ozone layer. I'm thirty-two now. I'm too old for this.'

'Officially, you're twenty-six though, aren't you? That's what it says on your profile on YouTube.'

He grinned. 'Yeah. Well, I can just about get away with that. My dad told me I should train as a plumber.' He blew air through his nose. 'My dad lives next door to a plumber. Apparently he's just bought a brand new Audi.'

'The plumber or your dad?'

'Ha! My dad has a pushbike. Actually, not even that. He goes everywhere on Boris bikes.'

'You're not going to give up though, are you?' I said, lifting my pint to my lips. 'This is the thing you've always wanted.'

He rubbed his face. 'I don't know. I can picture myself in ten years, going on *The X Factor* and telling the judges this is my *last chance*, that it means *everything to me*.'

He looked up at me.

'I'm not going to give up though, Dan. Never. I'm still going to be doing this when I'm ninety. I'm not going to become a fucking plumber.'

'Not that there's anything wrong with being a plumber.'

He laughed. 'Very true, mate. It's just not very me, is it?'

And that was Jake all over. He was not a quitter. Of course, none of us ever fully knows other people; we can't see inside their heads. But time and again, since I'd known him, Jake had demonstrated that he was determined, unswerving. Even if something had gone wrong at the last moment, I was sure he wouldn't commit suicide. He had even told me that if he didn't get a deal it wouldn't matter.

'I'll release the music myself,' he said. 'Cut out the middle man. Loads of people do that these days.'

I stopped and leaned against a wall as the tears came, the realisation that I would never see him again, never hear his voice, his laugh, smell the aroma of coffee that clung to him. To everyone else, the people who didn't know him, the world had lost a talent, a singer. They had lost his songs. But I had lost my best friend, the person who knew more about me than anyone else. I had lost Laura. I hardly ever saw my parents. I had no siblings. And now I had lost my only real friend.

'What the fuck am I going to do without you?' I whispered into the snow.

As I got closer to home, I realised I was only a street away from the local police station. I needed to do something. I headed towards it.

The heating was cranked up so high that as soon as I stepped into the police station the snow began to melt and drip from my clothes, my flesh thawing as a puddle spread around me on the floor. A middle-aged man was arguing with the woman at the reception desk, something about his neighbour's Range Rover. I tuned out and studied the posters on the wall. Missing teenagers. Crimestoppers. An appeal for information about a knife attack in a kebab shop.

The irate man eventually left, heading out into the slackening snowstorm. The receptionist eyed me, soggy and shivering, with distaste. I remembered the last police station I'd been in and felt even colder.

'Can I help you?'

I approached the desk. 'Yes, I need to talk to about the death of Jake Turner.'

She cocked her head.

'He apparently committed suicide last night. But I was with him a few hours before he died. There's no way he would have killed himself. He was my best friend.'

She studied my face, then said, 'Please take a seat and I'll find someone for you to talk to.'

Five minutes later, a female police officer appeared, the third member of the police I'd spoken to in the last week. I wondered if they had my name on a database now, with an alert next to it: nutter.

'I'm PC Coates. How can I help you?' she asked.

I told her what I'd already said to the receptionist. 'I know that bridge is renowned for suicides. But Jake would never have jumped.' I stared into her blue eyes, willing her to take me seriously. 'He must have been pushed. Murdered.'

Coates looked at me sympathetically. 'I understand it can be difficult to believe it when a close friend chooses to take their own life.'

'But how do you know he killed himself?'

'Wait here.'

She disappeared behind the desk and came back later holding a sheet of paper.

'Mr Turner sent a text to his sister. I'm afraid I can't tell you the exact contents of his message at the moment but it was clear that he was intending to commit suicide. The text was sent just before a passing motorist spotted the body.' She grimaced. 'I'm very sorry. If you know Mr Turner's sister, perhaps you should talk to her. It might offer you some comfort to talk to another person who was close to him.'

She explained that the body had been referred to the coroner, who would need to complete a report before the body could be released for the funeral.

'It's not the first death,' I said, aware of the sceptical look that appeared on her face. 'My therapist, Dr Claudia Sauvage—her house burned down and it said in the paper it was arson.' I wanted to grab her hand, make her believe me. 'I think they're connected.'

'Wait here,' she said.

I was going to have to tell the police about Romania. When she came back, I would tell her the story, make her see. Although that might put her in danger . . . No, she was police. She'd be fine.

I was deep in thought when she returned.

'Dr Claudia Sauvage of Grosvenor Road in Crouch End?' she said, sitting down.

'Yes! If it was arson, it must—'

She held up a hand. 'It wasn't arson, Mr Sullivan. The report from the fire scene investigator came back yesterday. It was her e-cigarette.'

'What?'

'She left it charging in her kitchen overnight and the battery exploded and started the fire. This isn't the first incident of this. Those things are a menace.'

I was stunned. I remembered Dr Sauvage sitting there, sending plumes of water vapour into the air between us.

'If you were seeing a therapist, I guess you've been under a lot of strain,' the policewoman said. 'Seeing connections where there aren't any.'

I nodded, feeling a mixture of relief, foolishness and confusion.

'You're not thinking of doing anything like your friend, are you?' said DS Coates.

I shook my head dumbly, then got up and walked away.

It was still snowing outside. I stood there for a moment, lost, unable to remember the way home. Eventually, my legs carried me automatically in the right direction. All I could see in my head was Jake's body, broken and bent on the road beneath the bridge. I have never cried in public before, but hopefully the people who passed me in the bitter weather would have thought it was snow glistening on my cheeks, not tears.

⌣

As I entered my flat, I could hear a phone ringing. I had my mobile in my pocket, and this wasn't the strident tone of the landline. It stopped, then started again a minute later, while I was pouring myself a shot of vodka. I followed the ringing sound into the bedroom. It was coming from the bedside drawer. The phone dropped by the Romanian girl at Jake's gig. For a moment I couldn't recall her name. Camelia, that was it. Hurriedly, I opened the drawer and answered the phone before it stopped ringing, noticing there were loads of missed calls listed on the screen. I had turned it off the night I met her because I didn't want to be disturbed during the night. Weirdly, I didn't remember switching the phone back on, but it wasn't the only thing I had no memory of recently.

'Who's that?' It was the voice of a young woman.

'Is that Camelia? This is Daniel, from the gig.'

She laughed, a low, slightly dirty chuckle. 'Daniel? So you found my phone? That's wonderful. I've been ringing it for days. I thought it must be lost forever.'

'I switched it off.'

'Because you were angry with me? After I kissed you?' Before I could think of what to say, she said, 'Anyway, this is great news. My phone is not lost. Where can we meet?'

I glanced towards the window. I really didn't want to go outside again.

'Can you wait until tomorrow?' I asked.

'No. How about I come to you? I really need it. Where do you live?'

I explained that I was in Islington.

'That's great. I'm not far.'

I hesitated, not sure if I wanted her to come round. But I felt bad for turning the phone off so I gave her my address. I had another motive too. She knew who Jake was, had met him, and I wanted to talk about him. Not with someone who knew him well. Not right now. I thought Camelia would be the perfect person. It didn't sound like she bore a grudge over my rejection of her anymore.

'What about the snow?' I asked. 'Do you really want to go out in it?'

She laughed again, throaty and, yes, dirty. 'I'm from Romania,' she said. 'I'm used to it.'

She hung up.

Chapter Twenty-Nine

An hour later, my door buzzer sounded. By this point, I had downed four, possibly five, shots of vodka in an attempt to deaden my grief, but I still felt sober. Sober enough to walk across the room in a straight line. Sober enough to feel pain.

I went downstairs, wondering if my neighbour would be listening. I hadn't seen her since the incident with the dog.

Camelia stood on the doorstep in a black coat and hat, soaked through and pink-faced, but smiling. Snow clung to her clothes. God's dandruff, we used to call it when we were kids. Even in this state, she was beautiful, with her vivid blue eyes, sharp cheekbones and plump lips that some women would pay a lot of money to attain. Something about her reminded me of Laura when we had first met, though this woman seemed far more sure of herself. I handed her the phone. She glanced at it and stuck it in her pocket.

'Thanks, Daniel. Um, do you mind if I come in and use your loo?'

'Of course, come in. I was going to ask if you wanted to come in anyway . . .'

She raised an eyebrow, a little smile on her lips that made me wonder if this was a good idea. 'Really?'

I waited while she used the bathroom and, when she came out, said 'Do you want a drink?'

She looked me up and down. 'You seem like you've already had a few.'

'I've had a bad day.'

'You want to tell me?' She had taken her hat off to reveal her blonde hair, which she combed down with her fingers as she spoke. I noticed details I'd missed when we'd first met: her long fingernails that looked fake and the chunky silver rings on her left hand.

'Maybe.'

'Make it a double and I'll happily listen,' she said. I poured a drink for both of us and she downed hers in two gulps, exhaling with pleasure. 'Ah, that's what the doctor ordered. Cheers.'

I smiled at her use of English idioms. 'Another?'

I refilled her glass, and this time she took a smaller sip. 'Good vodka.' She looked around the room. 'And you have a very nice flat. Do you live here alone?'

'At the moment.'

'What about the girlfriend you told me about?'

Shit. 'We're not . . . together right now.'

Another smile. 'Oh. Really?'

I swallowed. The vodka was definitely having an effect now. I felt woozy, the pain in my chest less acute, and brave enough to suggest that Camelia take off her coat and sit down.

'Don't worry,' she said. 'I won't stay too long.' She hung her coat on the back of a chair. She was wearing a tight-fitting sweater and equally tight jeans. I imagined what Jake would have said about her. 'Hot, Danny. Extremely fucking hot.' It wasn't just how she looked, but the air of confidence and ironic humour that radiated from her. She had a feline way of moving. She licked her lips before taking another sip of her drink. I took a big gulp of mine.

'It's fine. Stay as long as you want. I'm glad of the company.'

'Because of your shitty day?'

My eyes prickled. Now it came to it, I found I couldn't talk about Jake and what had happened. The words wouldn't squeeze past the obstruction in my throat.

She didn't speak, just looked at me, waiting.

'Let's just say that it's nice not to be on my own.'

She raised her drink. 'OK. Here's to the end of a shitty day.'

We clinked glasses.

'I'll stay until the snow eases off, yes?' she said.

We both looked towards the window. The street light outside the flat illuminated the snow as it fell. There was no sign of it stopping.

'That might be tomorrow morning,' I said.

She lifted her glass to her lips and took another sip. 'Then I hope you have plenty of vodka.' She paused. 'Don't worry, I'm not going to jump on you.'

The atmosphere in the room shifted, something crackling in the space between us. I felt nervous and excited. Camelia stood up and moved over to the bookcase, hips swaying as she walked. She examined the spines of the books, pulling out a guidebook that I'd bought before my and Laura's trip. *The Rough Guide to Eastern Europe.* She flicked through it.

'So tell me what happened to you in Romania. You had a bad experience?' She came back towards me, leaning against the fireplace, the light catching the liquid in her glass. I was sitting on the sofa, looking up at her.

'I can't tell you,' I said.

'Can't?'

I really felt drunk now, my head tight, the room tilting slightly. 'It might be too dangerous,' I said. 'For you, I mean.' In my drunken state, there was part of me that believed this. The police had told me Dr Sauvage hadn't been murdered, but I felt uncharacteristically superstitious, Laura's words from earlier haunting me. What if there was something supernatural going on? A curse that meant that bad things happened to anyone I talked to about Romania? The moment I thought it, I dismissed it. A curse! It was ridiculous.

'That sounds intriguing,' Camelia said.

'Ignore me. I'm just kidding.'

'It didn't sound like you were joking. What was it?' Her tone was light, playful, but there was a serious look in her eye.

'Honestly, it doesn't matter. I wasn't being serious.'

'OK . . . if you say so.' She went over to the window. 'This weather. Did you go to Bucharest? I was there two years ago, when we had so much snow it buried houses. I hope that doesn't happen here.' She turned and there was a wicked glint in her eye. 'We'd be stranded—stuck here together.'

The breath felt thick in my lungs. 'That would be terrible.'

'As long as we have enough vodka.'

I laughed. 'I think we're going to run out soon, the rate we're going.'

'Too bad, Daniel.'

'And what would we eat?' I asked.

She crossed the room, putting her almost-empty glass down on the side table with a soft clunk. She stopped for a moment and then climbed onto the sofa. Her eyes searched my face and, drunk and craving human warmth, I reached out for her. She straddled me, kissing me, her tongue slipping between my lips, her hands holding my face. I kissed her back. Like before, there was the faintest trace of cigarettes in her mouth, plus the smell of perfume lingering on her skin. I slipped my hands up the back of her sweater and pulled her closer, her breasts pressing against my chest through the fabric of our clothes. She felt warm now, heated from the inside by alcohol. I was so drunk that I didn't stop to think about how surreal this was.

'Hmmm,' she said, smiling into my mouth.

I felt breathless. 'Bedroom?'

'No, here is good.'

She pulled her sweater off over her head, revealing a red push-up bra and a tattoo on her upper arm. She unbuttoned my shirt and I shrugged it off, then took off my T-shirt. My erection strained against my underwear. She reached down into my lap and unbuttoned my jeans, shuffling back slightly and freeing my cock, wrapping her fist around it. She leaned forward and kissed me deeply, raking my chest with the fingernails of her free hand. I closed my eyes, and found myself imagining that she was Laura. We had made love on this sofa many times. Lost in the drunken moment, lips against mine, I could believe that Laura had come back to me.

'Tell me your secrets, Daniel,' she whispered into my mouth.

I tried to keep kissing her but she pulled back so our lips were barely touching.

'Have you ever broken the law?'

'What?'

Her hand still stroked my cock. I was close to coming already. She must have sensed this, taking her hand away and wriggling closer, the fabric of her jeans pressing against my naked flesh.

'I want you to talk to me, Daniel. Tell me. Something illegal. It excites me.'

She kissed me again, quickly, then broke away. I opened my eyes to find her peering at me intently, a smile on her lips.

'I don't understand,' I said.

'Come on. Don't be shy.' She pulled back, examining my face. She pressed her crotch against my cock. I could feel how warm she was through the denim. She stroked my chest and leaned forward again.

'You must have done something to break the law,' she said, breathing into my ear.

175

Was this really what turned her on? I wanted to comply so she wouldn't stop but I couldn't think of anything. I had stolen a pencil once from Argos but I doubted that would turn her on.

She rubbed against me and kissed my neck, raked her fingernails across my chest again. 'Come on. Something illegal. You must have broken the law, Daniel.'

'No.'

'I don't believe you. Come on, tell me.'

I could feel Jake's presence in the room, laughing, telling me to make something up. But I felt so pissed, so confused. All I wanted was oblivion, for this woman to keep kissing me and touching me. I wanted to lose myself in her, in my fantasy that she was Laura. But suddenly I felt cold, my erection waning. She felt this and reached down, touching me again.

'Come on,' she said, sounding impatient now. 'Tell me something bad . . . maybe something you and your girlfriend did together. Or maybe something you haven't done yet.'

I was thoroughly confused now.

'Camelia, I don't think . . .'

She looked into my eyes intently, like she was trying to search my brain. Then she sighed and climbed off me, standing up and peering down at me.

'I'm sorry,' I said.

'Whatever.'

She picked up her sweater and put it back on. She looked at me with contempt. I hurriedly buttoned up my jeans, looked for my T-shirt. I was freezing now, and felt sick.

'Where did I put the phone?' she said to herself, scouring the room.

Outside, a car alarm went off, and the noise shook me out of the almost-fugue state I was in. I stared at her. There was something familiar about her, something I'd seen since our first encounter. 'What was all that about?'

She shrugged.

'Have you been here before? In my flat?'

She rolled her eyes. 'I think you're paranoid, Daniel. Of course I haven't been here before.' She found the phone and tucked it away in her jeans pocket. She headed towards the door. Before she went, she turned towards the window and took in the snow that continued to pummel the city.

'Fuck this country,' she said, and left.

Chapter Thirty

Laura noticed the man watching her on her second circuit of the park, but as soon she looked towards him he turned his attention to a woman walking her greyhound.

She had needed to get out of the house, to get some air. Not only were the walls of her room closing in on her but the inside of her head itched like there were hundreds of baby spiders crawling about in her skull, feathery legs tickling her brain. She couldn't sit still. She went into the garden to look for Alina but she wasn't there. Since that night at the hospital, Alina had visited her here several times, shimmering between the bare trees. But she only came at night, it seemed.

Although the path around the park was mostly clear of snow, patches of black ice lurked like land mines, and Laura had watched a fellow walker thump to the ground before her, eliciting a chorus of laughter from a group of children having a snowball fight nearby. Laura had paused to help the fallen man to his feet before pushing on, feeling his eyes on her back.

On her third circuit, she tried not to look directly at the man. He was a pensioner, in his sixties, or perhaps a fit-looking seventy. He was broad and ruddy, wrapped in a wool coat and wearing a black hat and gloves. And he was definitely watching her, but in the same way she was watching him, surreptitiously, pretending to be looking past her.

She stole another glance at the man. The air around him appeared to waver, like he was giving off heat, and something struck her like a punch in the chest, making her gasp. He wasn't a man. He was a *devil*.

She entered a thicket of trees and he was obscured from view. She stopped and caught her breath.

'Are you OK?'

She looked up. A young woman in a black woollen hat was regarding her with concern. 'You were talking out loud. I just wanted to check you're OK.' She had an accent—German, Laura thought. A native Londoner would never have asked if she was all right. They would have assumed she was a nutcase or a drunk and given her a wide berth.

She beckoned to the German woman. *Follow me.* The woman hesitated but followed Laura to the edge of the thicket.

'Over there,' she said, as they emerged from between the trees. 'There's a devil sitting over there.' She pointed over to the bench. The German gawped at her with alarm.

There was no one there.

'You need me to call someone?' the woman asked.

Laura couldn't react. She stared at the empty space where the devil had been sitting, tuning out the woman's questions. She felt dizzy.

What if he was another ghost? Only yesterday, on her way home from the Tate Modern, when she had felt the need to get away from Daniel, she thought she'd glimpsed Beatrice again for the first time in twenty years. She had been standing beneath a lamppost in the snow, and Laura had stopped dead. Beatrice looked so unhappy, her face accusatory. It was the expression of someone who had been betrayed. But when Laura stepped towards her, she vanished.

Was this what was going to happen now? She had unlocked the doors of perception; was she going to start seeing ghosts and devils everywhere? Was she going to become a magnet for the unliving?

She scuttled away from the thicket of trees, leaving the German woman standing open-mouthed, and hurried towards the park gates. She needed to get to the safety of her room before any other ghosts came looking for her.

As soon as Laura unlocked the door of Rob and Erin's home, Erin called out, 'Rob?'

'No, it's me.'

'Oh.'

Laura went into the kitchen, casting a glance over her friend's shoulder, hoping that Alina would be waiting for her at the end of the garden so she could tell her about the devil in the park. Her attention snapped to Erin, who was pacing up and down alongside the table, blowing out breaths like a two-year-old attacking the candles on a birthday cake. Laura wanted to go to bed, to wait until dark so she could talk to Alina. Wanted to pull the covers over her head and block the world out.

'I'm in labour,' Erin said. 'I've been trying to call Rob but he's not answering.' She gasped. 'Fuck. I knew this baby was going to come early.'

Erin's words seemed to come from a great distance away.

'Laura? Wake up! Did you hear me?'

'I . . .' Laura tried to stay calm. 'Have you called the hospital? Are they going to send an ambulance?'

Erin's laugh was cut short by a contraction. 'Ah. No, they don't do that . . . unless it's an emergency.'

'Isn't this an emergency?'

'Not yet. Oh, shit, I've been waiting for Rob. He wants to be the one to take me to the hospital. But I can't wait any longer. I called a cab but they said it would take an hour because of the fucking *inclement* weather.' She grimaced and blew out air. 'I'm assuming you don't want to be the one to deliver the baby.'

'No! God, no!'

Erin studied her curiously. 'My God, you should see your face. It's all right . . . But you're going to have to drive me.'

'I . . . But I don't have a car.' Laura felt like she was being dive-bombed by black birds. They swooped about her, screeching, drowning out Erin's words.

'Well, duh.' Erin snatched her own car key from the hook on the wall. 'We'll take mine.'

Laura stared at her.

'Come on. My bag's in the hallway.'

Still, Laura hesitated.

'For fuck's sake, Laura. If we don't get a move on, you *are* going to have to deliver the baby.'

Erin ushered her out the door and they headed for Erin's Golf. The front and back windows were covered with snow, but the road was clear. Erin handed Laura a scraper and a can of de-icer before getting into the back of the car. As Laura removed the snow and ice, she told herself repeatedly not to panic, to ignore the birds that flapped about her head. They weren't real. This was real. She needed to help her friend and her baby. OK, she hadn't driven a car for over a year. The streets would be liable to bear the same patches of black ice as the path in the park. And snow had begun to fall lightly again, the sky dimming like someone had thrown a muslin square over the sun.

What if they crashed? What if Laura killed Erin and, even worse, the baby inside her? She thought of her bed, the cosy darkness. That's where she wanted to be. Where she needed to be.

She opened the door to tell Erin she couldn't do it. Erin was lying on the back seat, her face scrunched up, timing the gaps between contractions on her iPhone.

'I can't—' Laura began.

Erin glared at her. 'Just. Fucking. Drive.'

Laura got behind the wheel and started the engine.

Chapter Thirty-One

*B*aby arrived at 10.15 last night! Oscar James Tranham, 8 lb 4 oz. Erin was brilliant! Oscar is amazing! The text from Rob was accompanied of a picture of a tiny, pink-faced infant in a transparent plastic cot, wearing a crocheted white hat. Then a separate text arrived a few seconds later. *Mate, Laura was a hero. She drove Erin to the hospital through the snow. Got there just in time.*

So while I'd almost been having sex with a Romanian woman, Laura had been pacing up and down outside the maternity ward, waiting for Erin to give birth. It added to my sense of shame. What had I been thinking?

But layered over the shame was something worse: fear. The questions she had asked, wanting me to tell her my secrets. Was it just sex play, or something more? And if it was something more, what was she trying to get from me?

She was Romanian. Was there any way she could know what had happened in the forest?

Or was she trying to find out?

I wanted badly to cling to the belief that Camelia's words had been part of a game, the equivalent to asking someone to talk dirty, and that her being Romanian was a coincidence. But as soon as she had left I had checked the CCTV video of the intruders with the dog, studying the shape of the female intruder's body. Slim, small breasts, a hint of blonde hair beneath the hood she wore. The more I studied the video and replayed our encounter in my mind, the more convinced I became.

Camelia was the female intruder. And that probably—almost certainly—meant she was one of the burglars who had taken then returned my laptop. I paced the flat as I thought it through. She had followed me to Jake's gig, tried to seduce me then, for whatever reason. She must have dropped her phone deliberately, knowing I would take it home, not realising I would switch it off. I had no memory of turning it back on—probably because *she* had done so when she came into my flat with the dog.

I felt cold and shaken. Why was she following me? Why had she broken in? Had she been trying to kill me? Was it connected to what had happened to Laura and me in Romania, and if so, how?

I felt sober now, as sober as if I'd never touched a drop of alcohol in my life. I could still feel the echo of Camelia's body against mine, could still taste her on my lips. But who was she? And what the hell did she want?

⌣

The next morning I went out for a long walk, then decided to take the bus home. There was a man my age on the top deck with three small children who were acting like they were full of E numbers and sugar. Every time he got one of them under control, another would run off shrieking down the bus, or start banging on the windows. I watched him as he eventually gave up, letting them do what they liked as he stared at his phone, pretending they weren't his, probably wondering how his life had got like this. I empathised, except my toddlers were in my head. Every time I felt like I'd got a grip on

one problem, another—Jake, Laura, the break-ins and Camelia—
would run screaming into the forefront of my mind. Like the dad
on this bus, all I wanted to do was sit and stare at something uncon-
nected to my problems, to hide from everything, switch my brain off.

But I forced myself to stay switched on. I remembered something Laura used to do when she was overwhelmed at work. She
would sit and write everything that was bothering her on a sheet of
paper, get everything out. Then she would put it into priority order,
bearing in mind the consequences if she didn't tackle each particular
issue. A common technique, but one I seldom used. Now was the
perfect time to start.

I didn't have any paper with me, so used my phone, tapping
words in a stream of consciousness into the Notes app:

Laura left me, crazy, ghosts, want her back.
Jake—suicide??
Who is Camelia? What does she want?
Health, sleep, alcohol. PTSD.

This was it. The total of my problems on a single phone
screen. Studying the list, it struck me that it could be displayed in
a different way, as a mind map. Romania would be in a circle in the
centre, with lines leading to all the other problems. Unless Jake's
death shortly after I'd started telling him about my experiences was
a coincidence, everything stemmed from that night.

The thought of somebody pushing Jake from the bridge made
me clench my fists, a red mist swirling around me. The anger must
have been evident on my face because one of the errant pre-schoolers
saw me and ran off crying to his dad, saying something about 'the
scary man'.

So far, ever since getting back from Romania, I had allowed
things to happen to me, a passive victim. Even my attempts to win

Laura back had been ineffectual. Installing the security cameras had only led to more questions.

It was time to change. To be active. I needed to find out exactly what was going on. But how? The first step, surely, was to find Camelia. I didn't know exactly how I was going to do that, but if I could track her down, I could make her tell me what she knew. There had to be a way to find her. But I didn't know anything about her: her surname, where she lived, what she did. What was I supposed to do, wander around London looking for her?

I could, I supposed, sit and wait for her to make her next move. Surely there would be one. But I wasn't going to do that. I needed to get the upper hand.

As I approached my flat, I saw the fox, tearing into a bin bag that, yet again, one of my neighbours had left on the pavement. It had crept out beneath the cover of twilight and dug out a KFC box, scattering chicken bones and half-chewed corn-on-the-cobs across the entrance of the building. Sick of the mess, I shouted, 'Hey!' and broke into a run, chasing it up the street until it vanished into a garden and shot round the back of somebody else's house.

Indoors, I went straight to my laptop and onto Google.

I typed in 'private detective London'. There were over one million results, although of course the vast majority of these would be junk. I skimmed through the listings. Most of the private detectives listed specialised in finding out if your partner was cheating, checking up on employees or tracking down debtors. Grim stuff. I was looking for someone who had experience finding people. Clicking onto the various private detective sites, most of which looked like they were designed in 1998, made my sense of determination leak away. I could just pick one at random and hope they were competent, but there had to be a better way of finding the right person to help me, especially as I felt the need to find Camelia quickly.

Trying a different tactic, I filtered the results so they showed only news stories, expanding my search to 'private detective London missing'. I wanted to find a news story about an investigator who'd been successful finding a missing person. Again, most of the results were completely unhelpful, but after clicking through a dozen pages I found a news story from the summer, something that had taken place while Laura and I were on our Grand Tour.

I read through the story. A young Eastern European woman, from Belarus, had been reported missing by her employer. A private detective, based in Kentish Town, not far from here, had discovered what happened to her. It was a dark tale involving London's immigrant population, illegal employment practices and rough sex gone wrong. The investigator had discovered the truth before handing the case over to the police. His name was Edward Rooney and his website consisted of a single page, filled with basic information and a couple of glowing testimonials, and a contact form.

I completed the form and hit 'send' before I could change my mind.

Chapter Thirty-Two

Edward Rooney's office was on the second floor of a dirty white building in a Kentish Town side street. The street was half-scuzzy, half-gentrified; there was a betting shop next to a trendy coffee place. The snow here had been cleared from the roads and pavements and it was warmer today, rain in the forecast. By the end of the day the snow would all be gone.

Erin and Rob lived a ten-minute walk from here. I knew from looking at Rob's Facebook page that they were home from the hospital and Rob had already shared a dozen photos of little Oscar and an exhausted but happy-looking Erin. Laura was in one of the photos too, holding the baby in her arms. I tried to read the expression in her eyes, saw sadness behind her smile. If everything had gone to plan, she'd be heavily pregnant now. We'd be spending our weekends shopping for pushchairs and decorating the nursery.

I tried to push this from my mind as I rang the buzzer. Maybe after this I would call round to see them. The baby gave me the perfect excuse. Of course, I was keen to meet Oscar, wanted to congratulate the proud parents, but really I wanted to see Laura, whom I hadn't contacted since losing her at the gallery. I had vowed to give her time, deal with everything else first, get answers, before trying again to win her back. But when it came to Laura, I was an addict. I couldn't help myself.

I was buzzed in and went up a narrow staircase that smelled of mildew and years of cigarette smoke. A young, punkish woman waited for me, holding the office door open. She reminded me a little of Alina, the way she dressed, the spiky attitude. The big difference was that this woman was still alive.

'I'm Sophie Carpenter, Edward's assistant,' she said, looking me up and down. 'He's with another client at the moment but you can wait here.'

I sat on an uncomfortable chair and Sophie offered me coffee. When I said no, it was OK, she sat back down behind her computer, chin cupped in her hand, tapping at the keyboard with one long black fingernail. The desk was open underneath, giving me a clear view of her rather wicked-looking black leather boots, the toe of one of them tapping along with her typing as though keeping time.

I fidgeted on the chair. Ten minutes passed. I needed the loo and asked Sophie where it was. When I came back, a man I assumed to be Edward Rooney was seeing another man out of the office. Another client, I guessed, one with white hair, though I could only see his back.

The older man went down the stairs and Edward Rooney turned around. 'Daniel Sullivan?' He introduced himself. He was tall, in his early forties, I guessed, with black hair that contained a number of grey streaks and bags under his eyes. He was tall, over six foot, and was dressed in a suit that had probably once been smart but that was now shiny at the elbows and knees.

'Sophie, have you offered this gentleman coffee?'

'Yeah,' she said, not looking up from her screen. 'He didn't want any.'

'How about tea? Did you offer him tea?'

She rolled her eyes.

'It's fine,' I said. 'I don't want anything. Just your help.'

He nodded, his expression serious, and gestured for me to follow him into his tiny office. Once we were both sitting down, either side of his desk, I saw that the room was full. There was a tiny window with pigeon-deterrent spikes visible on the sill. His desk was piled high with paperwork. He pulled a laptop out from beneath this pile and flipped it open.

'I looked you up,' he said, 'after you called yesterday. You're an app developer.'

I was keen to skip the preamble. 'I need you to find somebody for me.'

He looked at me over the lid of the laptop, shoved it aside and grabbed a notepad. 'I was about to go through my introductory spiel but you seem like a man on a mission. Why don't you start from the beginning.'

I sighed. 'I don't know if I can do that. Do I *need* to do that? Can't I just tell you what I know about this person I'm looking for, and then have you find her?'

'Mr Sullivan—'

'Please call me Daniel.'

'Daniel, the more information you give me, the more chance I have of being able to help you.'

Even if Camelia was connected to what had happened to Laura and me in Romania, I didn't see the need to tell Edward Rooney about it, couldn't see how it could help. In fact, it would probably confuse matters.

'The woman I need you to find is called Camelia. She's Romanian, in her mid-twenties, possibly a bit older. Blonde, very attractive. Speaks excellent English and told me she's been in London for a couple of years. She uses a Blackberry phone, has a tattoo and wears false fingernails and chunky silver rings. Um, on her left hand.'

He looked up at me from his notes.

'Is that all?'

'Yeah. I met her in a pub, at a gig, and . . .'

'Hang on. I need to know why you need to find her.'

'Why?'

'Yes. Daniel, I only take on missing persons cases where I know my client doesn't intend to cause the person he's looking for any harm. I also need to know whether there are any legal ramifications. I've had men here asking me to look for their ex-wives who left them because they were being battered. I've had gangsters looking for women they've trafficked who escaped. I don't take cases like that.'

'I don't mean her any harm,' I said. 'I want to stop her from doing *me* harm.'

'OK. So . . . tell me what you know. You met her in a pub . . .'

There was nothing for it but to give him at least some information. I spent the next fifteen minutes telling him the story of what had happened over the last week, starting with the break-in. I felt myself turning pink as I told him about my encounter with Camelia the evening before last.

'She kept asking me if I'd done anything illegal. When I couldn't come up with anything, she got angry and left.'

'Any idea what she wanted you to tell her?'

'None at all.'

He laid his pen down. 'Daniel, if we can figure out the connection between you, it will make it easier to find her. Are you sure you have no idea?'

I hesitated. I genuinely didn't know what Camelia had wanted me to say, and still thought it might simply be her equivalent of talking dirty. The only possible connection I could think of was Romania, but I really didn't want to tell this person I'd just met about that. I hadn't even been able to tell my therapist. The only person I'd felt able to tell, after a huge internal struggle, was Jake, and he'd died before I could finish the story. Thinking about Jake

191

made my eyes sting and I looked up to see Edward looking at me curiously.

'I honestly have no idea.'

He leaned across the desk, elbows resting on scattered paperwork. 'I'm sorry, but I don't believe you.'

'What?'

He sat back. 'I can't take your case, Daniel. Not unless you're completely open with me. There's no point. You might as well go.'

I opened my mouth, shut it again, aware that I must look like a stranded goldfish. There was a voice in my head screaming 'Tell him, just tell him!' but when I opened my mouth again no words came out. I simply couldn't do it. My frustration with myself transformed into anger with Edward Rooney. There were plenty more private detectives out there. Hundreds of them in London. I'd find someone who didn't need to know everything, who would just take my money and do what I asked.

I stood up. 'Fine. I'll find someone else.'

'Good luck.'

I pulled open the door and stomped out into the reception area until I stood behind Sophie's desk. She swivelled her chair, the wheels squeaking, and, seeing my thunderous expression, asked, 'Everything all right?'

'No. Your boss is a—'

At that moment, the front door of the office opened. A man stood there, framed by the doorway. It took me a moment to realise he was wearing a balaclava. The other details only came back to me afterwards: in his hand he held a bottle, three-quarters filled with a clear liquid, a rag attached to the neck of the bottle. There was a cigarette lighter in his other hand.

Chapter Thirty-Three

Get down!' I yelled, leaping at Sophie and pulling her off her chair onto the floor just as the man threw the now-flaming bottle into the room and slammed the door shut. The bottle shattered on the floor in the centre of the office and exploded with an immense, deafening blast of heat and light.

I'd piled in next to Sophie behind a tall filing cabinet beside her desk. When I peered around it, I found the centre of the small room engulfed in a ball of flame. I have played enough video games in my life to recognise a Molotov cocktail. Within seconds the room was filled with fire and thick black smoke. I could barely open my eyes, couldn't breathe, was choking on a lungful of smoke. Almost blind, I figured the door was only ten feet away, her desk between it and us. Remembering seeing Sophie's spiky, knee-high black boots from the other side, I knew the desk was open underneath. The quickest and safest route out had to be under it. Squinting from behind the cabinet, I could see the flames spreading, engulfing the two-seater sofa and the bookcase, licking at the edge of the desk. The heat in the room was indescribable. I felt like my insides were cooking. We had to get out. Now.

'Go!' I managed to gasp, pulling Sophie out from behind the cabinet and shoving her forward. 'The desk,' I said. 'Go *under.*' Coughing, guarding her face with a forearm, she crawled like a three-legged dog to the desk and disappeared beneath it. I followed her, though I could hardly see her. It was hot as a blast furnace under there and I thought *This is it. I'm going to die.* But then I was out the other side and the door was open and someone was shouting, pulling Sophie through first, then me.

I fell onto the carpet in the corridor, which was full of people, yelling and gesticulating. Looking back into the office, I watched as through the wall of smoke a shape appeared: Edward standing in the doorway of his inner office, grappling with a fire extinguisher which didn't appear to work. The flames, which had reached the desk now, consuming the papers that lay beside the computer, were blocking Edward's exit. More people, from other offices in the building, had appeared in the corridor. Sophie lay on the floor beside me, gasping for breath.

'Is there another way out?' I asked, my throat burning, eyes stinging. The only window I'd seen in Edward's office was tiny.

'I've called the fire brigade,' said a black woman with an air of competence. She shouted at Edward: 'Get back in your office, shut the door, find something to block the bottom of the door. Not paper!'

Edward stared at us over the flames then retreated into his office, slamming the door.

'Who the fuck was it?' Sophie said, pushing herself into a sitting position. Her voice was hoarse, her eyes pink and watery.

Everybody in the corridor was staring at us. I pushed myself to my feet, surprised to find I felt OK, apart from my desperate anxiety about Edward, trapped in his office, the flames beating against the door, hoping he'd managed to find something to block the space beneath it to stop smoke pouring through. And a question pulsated in my head: was this my fault? In his line of work,

I assumed Edward must upset numerous people. Husbands who'd been exposed as cheats. Employees caught with their hands in the till. But so much disaster had followed me lately—

The evil from that house . . . It followed us home.

—that I couldn't help but think this was down to me. That someone was trying to stop me from telling Edward my story.

But who? Camelia? No, the person who threw the Molotov was definitely male. Camelia's companion, assuming it was her, from the CCTV video? As Sophie sat and sobbed beside me, black mascara streaking her face, I hugged myself, shivering despite the heat that emanated from the burning room.

A minute later, I heard the blessed sound of sirens and the fire brigade arrived, several of them running up the stairs, clearing us out of the building. I stood on the street and watched as they did their work, putting out the fire. The police were there too, and an ambulance which Sophie was sitting in the back of now, an oxygen mask clamped to her face. I felt fine, had somehow breathed in less smoke than her. *Please God*, I prayed silently, *let Edward be OK. I can't be responsible for another death. Please.*

My prayer was answered quickly. Within moments, he was escorted through the front door of the building by a firefighter. He sat down on a low wall and I hurried over to him.

'I'm all right,' he said, waving away my concern. 'The fire didn't get through the door and I had a towel in my gym bag that I used to block out the smoke.' His face darkened. 'But what I want to know is who the fuck just tried to burn down my office.'

He looked at me as if I could tell him the answer.

The three of us were taken to the nearest hospital where we were checked over. None of us had been burned, and although I still felt a little wheezy, the doctor told me I could go home. They wanted to keep Sophie in for the night for observation. As I came out of the room where I was checked by the doctor, I saw Edward talking to a police officer, shaking his head. The policeman walked off and Edward spotted me and came over.

'Have they got any idea who did it?' I asked.

'No. They wanted to know if I did. They want to interview me tomorrow.' He rubbed his face. 'I've been doing this for fifteen years and nothing like this has ever happened before. The worst I've had is an abusive phone call and some dog shit shoved through the door by a woman who I caught shagging her yoga teacher.'

'Maybe they were after me,' I said quietly.

He studied me. 'I think we should talk, Daniel. If they were after you, or were trying to stop you talking to me, this is my problem now too. Sophie could have been killed. *I* could have been killed. And let's not even mention the state of my office and the fact that everyone else in the building is now in fear of their life.'

I nodded.

'I'm going to go and say goodbye to Sophie, see if she needs anything. Then we should go.' He licked his lips. 'I don't know about you but I could bloody well do with a drink.'

We took a taxi to the Lord Palmerston pub near Dartmouth Park. It was quiet at this time on a weekday afternoon. Full-time drinkers perched at the bar and condensation clung to the windows. Edward led me over to a corner seat and fetched two pints of lager. He produced his notepad from his pocket.

'I need you to tell me everything,' he said. 'I need to know what kind of people you're mixed up with. And if you don't tell me, then I'm going to have to talk to the police.'

'It's OK,' I said. 'I want to tell you.' I took a big gulp of lager, soothing my throat.

'Come on then. I'm waiting.'

I started with the first strange incident back home: the time when somebody might or might not have tried to push Laura under a Tube train. 'That's my girlfriend. I mean my ex-girlfriend. She insists she tripped,' I said. 'So that might not be relevant.'

'It might be,' he said, making a note.

'OK, so the first concrete thing that happened was when I had a break-in.'

I went on to tell him everything that had happened since then: meeting Camelia at Jake's gig; my bank card being used fraudulently; the return of my laptop; Dr Sauvage's death, though that now seemed to be unrelated; seeing somebody watching Laura in Camden, not far from where we sat now. I brought him up to date by telling him about the dog and Jake's supposed suicide.

For now, I left out the part about Laura seeing ghosts, and the disappearing photos. I didn't want him to think that Laura or I were crazy.

'I've got a surveillance camera in my flat,' I said. 'It's motion-triggered.'

He nodded.

'The video of the intruders and the dog are here, on my phone.'

I opened the app and leaned across the table, angling the screen towards Edward. He took a pair of glasses out of his pocket and put them on, instantly making himself look ten years older. He took the phone from me and watched the video.

'I think that's her,' I said. 'Camelia. It looks like her body shape.'

He raised his eyebrows. 'Any idea who the man might be?'

'No. But . . . he could be the person who firebombed your office. I wonder if he's Romanian too . . .'

Edward tapped his notepad. 'There's a huge chunk that you're still not telling me, isn't there? Like, what has Camelia's nationality got to do with it? What's your connection to Romania?' When

I didn't reply straight away he glanced down at his pad. 'You haven't told me anything at all about why you think Camelia is interested in you. What she's after?'

I gave myself another second by sipping my pint. 'OK. So . . . last summer Laura and I went travelling around Europe. We ended up in Romania on a night train to a place called Sighisoara. Something . . . happened. That's why I think Camelia's nationality is important.'

'All right,' he said. 'Now we're getting somewhere.'

I told him about meeting Alina and Ion, getting robbed in the sleeper carriage, how we were thrown off the train. He jotted down more notes, occasionally butting in with questions. Once or twice he gave me an incredulous look. I reached the point where we tried to find Alina in the forest. There was a man at the slot machine near our table and I was paranoid that he might overhear. I waited until he wandered back to the bar.

'After that,' I said, 'we ran to the nearest town and went to the police—'

'Hang on.' He held up a hand. 'What happened in the house?'

Suddenly, it seemed very quiet in the pub.

'It's obvious that you're frightened,' he said. 'But you have to tell me, Daniel. You can take your time—I've got all afternoon.'

I rotated my empty pint glass on the table, staring at the wet ring it created on the surface. I felt exactly as I would before getting up on stage in front of a thousand people. Sick and shaky. Could I do this, finally? Finally face the memories?

I pictured the Molotov cocktail as it was thrown into the office. Imagined a pair of hands trying to push Laura onto the Tube tracks. Saw the black dog leaping towards me.

I had to do this.

'OK. But let me get another drink first. And one for you.' I grabbed the glasses and stood. 'I think you're going to need it.'

Part Three

Romania
August 2013

Chapter Thirty-Four

I started by telling Edward what I'd already told Jake: the walk up the path to the house, going inside, looking around the entrance hall of the strange, secluded house. I told him how scared I felt, how I wanted to turn around, run.

The pub seemed to vanish around us as I told him my story.

The noise from upstairs.

It was an unmistakeable sound, even to non-parents like us. A noise that a mother or father is programmed to hear from a hundred feet, through stone walls and locked doors.

A baby. Crying.

That was it. From that moment, I knew that we wouldn't be able to leave this place until we had discovered the source of the crying, had seen for ourselves that the baby was well and safe. It was a primal instinct. Protect the young and the helpless. Perhaps this place wasn't bad after all. Maybe it was a family home, a woodcutter and his wife and kids. A happier scenario sprouted in my imagination. The woodcutter or hunter had been out in the forest checking traps and he had found the injured Alina—perhaps she had stumbled into one of his traps—and he had helped her, brought her back here to ask his wife to tend to her injuries. And all these goings-on had woken the baby. That made sense, was logical. I drew strength from it.

The cry came again, growing more urgent and frantic. Wherever the baby was, nobody had gone to comfort it.

Laura headed towards the staircase and I followed her. We trod as quietly as we could. The stairs were disintegrating in places, the floorboards loose and springy. I noticed something snagged on one of the steps and, looking closer, saw that it was a clump of hair.

There was a window halfway up the staircase, where it turned a corner. The view was of the back of the house and I saw, with surprise, that there was a narrow road that led through the trees into a backyard where a flatbed truck was parked. I had imagined that the house was only accessible through the forest. My spirits lifted a little further. We weren't completely isolated here. The road was a link to civilisation. The woodcutter/hunter scenario seemed increasingly plausible. We had simply approached from the wrong angle.

The baby was still crying, its sobs ebbing away before returning stronger and more urgent. Where was the mother?

We reached the next floor. Like downstairs, it was in darkness and I wondered about the source of the flickering candlelight we'd seen from outside.

'It's coming from further up,' Laura said in a hushed voice. The staircase continued to another floor and the crying was still coming from above us.

I took another deep breath and urged my legs to continue. I kept following Laura up the stairs, which were even more rickety here, creaking and protesting as we headed into deeper darkness. The walls around the staircase narrowed. As we climbed, the stench of mildew and rotting animals shifted, overpowered by other odours. Baby shit and human bodies. It stank like the part of a hospital where terminal patients spend their last days. Sickness and death, mixed with the smell of a dirty nursery. The more positive scenario I'd dreamed up receded with every step.

All I felt now was dread.

We reached the top of the staircase. Before us was another wooden door with a metal latch fixed across it, the type you just need to lift to open. A lock designed to make it easy for the person going in, but impossible for the person trying to get out.

The crying was coming from just behind this door.

I lifted the latch and, holding my breath against the stench and the fear of what we'd find, pushed the door open.

Chapter Thirty-Five

I raised my eyes to gauge Edward's reaction. He was staring at me, lips parted, enrapt.

'Go on,' he said.

I took another big gulp of my beer. It hurt to tell this part of the story. I thought about getting up, telling him I needed the toilet. Then I would slip out, run away like I had thought about doing back then. I hesitated for the final time, knowing how distraught Laura would be if she thought I was about to tell someone exactly what happened.

I would tell him what he needed to know.

On the far wall, against the windows, a number of fat white candles were lined up along the top of a pair of dark wood chests. Behind the chests, the windows were boarded up, so the light we'd seen couldn't have come from this room. I stared at the candles because they were the only thing here that made sense. Both Laura and I were paralysed by the scene in front of us, rocked by the smell in the air, the baby's screams echoing the sound that reverberated inside me.

There were four single beds and three wooden baby cots in the room. Two of the beds were empty, stripped back to reveal their thin mattresses. They looked like the beds you might see in war films—springs sagging, hard, like torture devices. The crying baby was in one of the cots, lying on its back, screaming, its face shining with tears. It waved its arms above it, clawing at the air, but was too small to roll over or sit up.

On the other two beds were a pair of women. The woman in the nearest bed was asleep or unconscious (*or dead?*), a filthy white sheet drawn up to her waist. She was wearing a thin pink gown that revealed how malnourished she was. Her arms were like pipe cleaners and her flat chest rose and fell jerkily as she breathed. Her head looked like a skull with stringy brown hair attached. Forcing myself to step closer, bracing myself against the acrid smell of urine and rot that emanated from her, I saw that her ankles were manacled to the foot of the bed.

Laura gripped my arm as I tried to step closer, holding me back. She raised her free arm slowly and pointed at the further occupied bed.

This woman was less skeletal than the first. She had blonde hair that was matted and stuck out at all angles. Her eyes were sunken, cheekbones like razors, arms skinny and weak. She was wearing a gown like the other woman, her sheet bunched up by her feet, which were also chained to the bed. Her skin was covered in bruises and tiny round scabs. Cigarette burns.

She was awake, her eyes screwed tight. Tears slid down her cheek, dampening her thin pillow.

Shaking, I approached the bed. As I did, the baby, who was in a cot close to this second bed, fell quiet, like it had run out of breath and tears. Laura walked over to the cot and leaned over it, her hand shaking as she brought it to her mouth, emitting a little sob. For a moment I thought there must be something wrong with the baby, but it was in a better state than the women. It was dressed in a pale blue sleep suit and wrapped in a wool blanket. A boy, I guessed. He had thick blond hair, a pink face, rosebud lips.

The blonde woman (his mother?) opened her eyes and saw me. Panic flared in her eyes, and I braced myself, sure she would start screaming. But she stayed silent, staring at me with wide eyes, then turning her head to look at Laura. She didn't move, or attempt to sit up.

She whispered something, the act of doing so seemingly causing her great pain.

Leaving Laura by the cot, I moved closer to the woman, crouching beside her.

'I'm sorry,' I said. 'I don't understand. I'm English.'

She gazed at me with the look of a prisoner who has been tortured, broken.

'Do you speak English?' I asked.

'Help,' she said. I held her hand, realising the reason she hadn't sat up was that she was too weak.

To my right, Laura had lifted the baby out of the cot, was holding him against her, his head resting in the crook of her neck, one hand stroking the baby's back through the blanket he was wrapped in. The woman in the bed looked towards the baby, a mixture of love and fear in her eyes. Then her gaze flicked towards the door.

'My baby,' the woman said. 'Help.'

'Who did this to you?' I asked in my softest voice.

She stared at me. Maybe she didn't understand. She whispered something else in what I assumed to be Romanian, then spoke in English again. 'Please. Baby. Help.'

A scream came from below us.

Both Laura and I froze. The woman in the bed looked towards the door again.

'Go. Baby,' she said.

I looked at the door, then at Laura. 'What shall we do?'

———————

Edward's mouth was ajar, his eyes wide. No one had ever listened to me more raptly. He was there with us, in that room.

'For God's sake, you can't stop now. What did you do?'

'I . . . Laura hugged the baby against her. I asked her again, "What shall we do?"'

I told him the rest of the story.

———————

The scream came again. My heart was banging so loudly that I was sure whoever was downstairs, whoever had done this to these women, would be able to hear it.

'We have to get out,' I said, answering my own question. 'We'll go to town, get help. Send the police.'

I turned to the woman in the bed.

'We'll send police,' I said. More tears fell from her eyes.

I turned back to Laura and reached out to take the baby, to put him back in his cot. But Laura backed away, hugging the baby against her.

'He's coming with us.'

'Laura . . . We have to leave him. We can't run through the forest with a baby. We have to get away.'

'No,' she snapped. She held the baby like he was her own, like I was threatening to take him and feed him to lions. 'I'm not leaving him.'

'Laura . . .'

'Look, Daniel. Look.' She pointed to the far side of the room, beyond the cots.

A small bench was positioned against the wall. Stacked on top of this bench were items you might find in a normal nursery: baby clothes, nappies, barrier cream, bottles, along with tubs of formula milk. There were a couple of small teddy bears too, lying askew. Their fur was stained with something dark that looked black in the candlelight.

There was something beside the bench. It was a tiny coffin, about two feet long. It looked like it had been built by an amateur, the angles not quite right. On top of the coffin lay a few flowers, the kind we had seen growing in the forest, along with another teddy bear.

I looked back at the unconscious woman. Was her baby in there? A small part of me wanted to look, to confirm the horror. But I tore my gaze away from the coffin, catching a glimpse of something else. It was a mind-snapping moment.

We both walked slowly to the wall, aware that we had to go, knowing the person or people responsible for all this could come in at any moment. Pinned to the wall were about two dozen Polaroid photos. Some of the photos were of women, staring at the camera lens with terror or surrender. One photo showed a woman on her back, naked, her mouth open in a scream. Beside her crouched a man, holding some kind of metal instrument which he held between her thighs.

The other photographs were of babies. Newborn babies. All of them lay on their backs. Some wore blue, but most were dressed in white. Some were crying, others placid. Some with eyes shut, some looking towards the photographer.

Each of the photos had a date inked on its white edge. The baby's date of birth, I wondered? And then I noticed: a few of the pictures had a second date added, with a large X beside it. The Polaroid in the bottom right corner had two dates. The first was 2.7.13. The second of July 2013. The second date read 13.8.13. The thirteenth of August. Just a few days ago.

I turned my head back towards the women on the beds. The blonde woman was weeping, the other still passed out. The baby in the coffin must be hers. It had been born here. And died here, in this squalid, stinking room.

From downstairs, the scream sounded again, a scream of pain that chilled my blood.

Breathing hard, I once again spoke to the blonde woman. 'We'll be back. OK? We'll make sure your baby's safe.'

She looked at me, then at the baby.

I realised I might need a weapon when we got downstairs, looked around for one. I blew out one of the candles and wrenched it free of its black metal candlestick. I weighed the candlestick in my hand. It was heavy, solid.

Laura was already opening the door, hesitating and peering down the stairs. I followed after her, passing the first bed.

A hand shot out and grabbed my leg.

I cried out, pulled away. The skeletal woman in the bed stared up at me with huge eyes, opening her mouth to reveal that most of her teeth were gone. The remaining teeth were white, healthy, suggesting that the missing teeth had been punched or pulled out. I accidentally kicked over a bedpan that sat by the bed, the foul-smelling, brownish urine slopping over the side and onto my shoe.

The woman smiled at me, insanity in her eyes, and I ran, pushing Laura through the door, letting it slam shut behind us.

Beneath us, the screaming had stopped. Instead, I could hear thumping. Someone coming up the stairs, very slowly.

Chapter Thirty-Six

'Let me go first,' I said.

I began to descend the stairs, slowly. I stumbled on a loose stair and almost tripped, falling against the wall and managing to stay upright.

We turned the corner onto the lower section of the stairwell, Laura one step behind me.

The man stood at the bottom of the stairs, looking up at us. He had a gun in his hand, a black pistol, the kind that would be used by a policeman or soldier, not a farmer or hunter. He had thinning dirty blond hair and looked to be in his thirties, short but powerful. Wiry.

Behind him, at the bottom of the staircase, a woman lay face down. Black jacket and jeans, black hair streaked with red.

Alina.

He lifted the gun towards us, made a beckoning motion with his free hand.

I didn't move, desperately trying to work out what to do. Go back up, look for another way out? He could shoot me as soon as I turned, and even if he didn't, what were the chances of finding another exit? And the thought of him hunting us through his own, dark house was even worse than facing him here.

I walked down the last few steps, aware that he was eyeing the candlestick. He took a couple of steps back, past the prone Alina, gesturing for us to come down into the entrance hall.

We stood before him, all three of us breathing heavily. It struck me: he was nervous too. Not as scared as Laura and me, of course. But there was definitely fear in his eyes.

He turned the gun on Laura and pointed his other hand at the baby. Behind her, I could see Alina's back rising and falling. She was alive.

'Mine,' the man said, his words jerking my attention away from Alina. I was surprised to find that he spoke any English. He gestured for Laura to hand the boy to him.

Laura didn't move. I stared at the gun, feeling the candlestick in my hand, trying to work out if I could strike him with it. At this moment, it wasn't worth the risk.

'Laura . . .' I began.

'No,' she said, moving towards the door.

The man gestured angrily at her, at the baby—then pointed the gun towards me.

'Give the baby to me,' he said.

Laura looked at the gun, then at me.

'Laura,' I said. 'Give it to him.'

It was her turn to look angry.

'Give me,' the man said again, his voice a little louder, his anger growing.

Laura took a step towards him, holding out the baby, and the man lowered the gun so he could take the boy. The baby started to scream, as if it knew, could sense, who, what, he was being handed over to. The man flinched and Laura thrust the baby towards me, yanked the candlestick from my grasp as I took hold of the boy, and swung it at the man. He backed away—but held on to the gun, pointing it at Laura, who stood panting, clutching the candlestick

211

Mark Edwards

tightly. I held the screaming baby, juggling it instinctively, its cries drilling into my skull.

'Put him down,' the man shouted above the noise. 'The baby. On the floor.'

Laura shouted, 'No!'

But what choice did I have? I stooped and laid the still-screaming infant on the floor at my feet. Laura started to cry, her whole body shaking.

As the man moved towards the baby, I ran for the door, grabbing Laura's arm and pulling her after me. She dropped the candlestick and I yanked open the door, convinced a bullet would fell me at any moment. But as I risked a glance back I saw why the shot hadn't come. Alina had got onto her hands and knees and crawled nearly to the candlestick. He was distracted by this, needed to stop her from reaching it.

I pulled Laura through the door and down onto the path.

She tried to struggle out of my grip. 'Let me go!' she shouted.

'No! Laura! For fuck's sake—let's go.'

'But the baby.' She was shaking and crying and desperate to get back to the tiny boy, but I couldn't let her.

'We have to get out of here. We'll get help. He'll be out here in a second!'

'No—'

A gunshot.

The baby stopped crying.

I could hear screaming and thought it was me or Laura—my senses were fucked up, muddled—but then I realised the screaming was coming from inside the house. It was Alina.

'Come on, please, please. Let's go.'

Another gunshot. And this time, Alina fell silent.

We ran down the path towards the edge of the clearing. There was no time to find the road that I'd seen through the window. My

212

heart was pounding. He was about to appear, he would shoot us both, bury us out here and we'd never be found. Two more travellers who go missing in a foreign land and are never seen again.

I looked back over my shoulder and saw the door of the house opening, the dark figure of the man appearing, and holding Laura's hand I ran faster than I'd ever run before, down the path, through the forest, back to the tracks. Out we came, bursting out of the trees, back onto the path, stumbling over the rail track, almost falling, one of us catching the other, stopping only to scoop up our backpacks from the edge of the forest.

We ran all the way into town.

We didn't talk.

We didn't look back.

Part Four

London
November 2013

Chapter Thirty-Seven

I finished my drink, immediately wishing I had another. I felt weak, drained. Telling the story, reliving it again . . .

'Daniel? Hello? Are you OK?'

I closed my eyes. When I opened them, he was still there, waiting. 'There's one more thing. As we reached the trees, we heard another shot, then another a few seconds later.'

Edward thought about it, then nodded. 'He went upstairs and shot the two women.'

'That's what I think. We'd seen them; he must have assumed we were going to tell the police. He wanted to remove the . . . the living evidence. Although the whole place would have been full of their blood and DNA. I don't know.'

'Maybe he decided he didn't have any use for them anymore.'

'Like I said, I don't know.'

'So why didn't you go to the police?' he asked, frowning deeply.

'We did. Well, we tried. We went to the local police station in Breva, after running into town.' I explained what had happened at the station, how we had ended up running from there, too.

Edward looked pale, even a little sick. He hadn't touched his pint since I'd started telling the story.

He got up from the table. 'I'm going to start by making some calls, doing a bit of research. I'll call you tomorrow morning, OK?'

'OK,' I said.

'You coming?' he asked.

I shook my head. I didn't want to leave the pub. I was going to stay here and get thoroughly fucking drunk.

I watched him go out through the double doors. He knew all of the story he needed to know to help me. I had done the right thing.

I don't remember getting home or going to bed. The next thing I knew it was light outside and my mobile was ringing. The display told me it was Edward. I realised I was fully dressed and the room smelled like a distillery. It was just after eleven in the morning and my head was throbbing. My throat felt like I'd chain-smoked forty cigarettes and as I moved, a horrible, wobbling nausea overcame me. The phone kept ringing and that's when it all came back to me. The Molotov cocktail. Telling Edward my story. Staying in the pub and getting blind drunk.

Oh Jesus.

Ignoring the phone, I went into the bathroom and threw up in the toilet. After that, I felt a little better. I called Edward back.

'I tried to ring you last night,' he said. 'Where were you?'

I groped for a reply, and he said, 'Never mind. I've got some stuff to tell you. I'll come to yours.'

I took a shower, drank two cups of strong coffee and checked my emails while I waited for Edward. There was a message from Rob.

Mate,

I know you're having a tough time at the moment but I'd really appreciate you not coming round here at midnight, banging on the door, chucking stones at Laura's window and waking Oscar up. It took two hours to get him back to sleep. Laura made it clear she doesn't want to see you. Personally, I think the two of you need your heads banging together, but if she says she doesn't want to be with you anymore and doesn't want any contact, you need to respect that. Next time, Erin will probably call the police.

And you might want to send Erin a note of grovelling apology if you want her to ever talk to you again.

I really think you need to lay off the booze for a while too.

Rob

I was mortified. What had I done when I left the pub? And why was Laura refusing to talk to me again, saying she didn't want me to contact her? I had a flash of memory that made my whole body cringe: me, standing in Erin and Rob's back garden, lobbing pebbles at the window and shouting Laura's name like some drunken, rejected Romeo.

I picked up my phone and checked my texts. Fuck, I'd sent Laura over twenty messages after midnight, telling her I loved her, that I wanted to see her, asking her to marry me. She had sent a single response:

Leave us alone.

I went into the kitchen and took every bottle of alcohol out of the fridge and the cupboards, uncorked the wine, the smell making me gag, popping the tops from the beer bottles, and poured everything down the sink. I dropped the empties into a bin bag and carried it outside, slung it into the recycling. When I looked up, Edward was walking towards me, hands in pockets, head down.

'Everything all right?' he asked when he saw me.

'I'm never drinking again,' I said.

'Get rat-arsed, did you, after I left?'

I nodded, leading him inside.

'I have to admit, I felt like getting pissed too after that story you told me. But instead, I spent the evening working. After dealing with the bloody insurance company, that is. Somebody needs to send them into a house of horror in the woods.'

Seeing my expression he said, 'Sorry. Shouldn't even joke about it. I had a nightmare last night, the first I've had in years. Firebombs and women chained to beds and babies crawling through the flames.' He shuddered. 'Then I had the police round first thing, asking lots of questions about who might want me dead.'

'What did you tell them?'

'I told them I have no idea. But they are going to want to talk to you.' He handed me a card. 'Here. This is the investigating officer's number.'

A great wave of exhaustion washed over me as I took the card. I was going to have to talk to the police. It was all going to come out, everything that had happened.

I set the card aside. 'I'll talk to them later. First, I need to know what you found out.'

'Make me a very strong coffee and I'll tell you.'

As I waited for the kettle to boil, Edward paced the room, running a finger along the spines of books, peeking through the curtains at the street, like he was looking out for someone.

I carried two coffees over and he sat on the sofa while I pulled up a chair.

'I have to say, Daniel, the story you told me sounded like just that—a story.'

'But it's the truth!'

He held up a palm. 'All right. I'm not saying I don't believe you. The thing is, from what I found out last night, it gets even weirder.'

I waited for him to continue, dreading what I was going to hear.

'So, after talking to you last night I went to see this guy who recently did some work for me. A translator. He speaks all the Eastern European languages, including Romanian. He's a bit of paranoid nutcase but he's useful. I got him to call the police in Breva, to act as an interpreter.'

I was horrified. 'You told this interpreter what had happened?'

'Daniel, please listen. If you keep interrupting . . .' He gave me a smile that was intended to be reassuring. 'I asked to speak to the policeman you told me you saw. Constantin. I wanted to check out what you told me.'

'What? But I was sure he was involved . . .'

'Daniel, for fuck's sake. I needed to check it out, that's all. It's standard practice. I'd be a pretty shit investigator if I took everything I heard as gospel. Because we need to find out if this Camelia person is connected to what you saw.'

'OK. Makes sense.' A fist clenched and unclenched in my stomach.

'So . . . I asked to speak to Constantin. Or rather, my interpreter did. The Breva police were really evasive at first. Wanted to know why we were calling them, where we were ringing from, etcetera. So I told them I was following up on a crime that had been reported back in August, and they eventually put me through—but not to Constantin, to another officer. He looked on the system, told me they had no record of an English couple coming in and reporting a crime.'

Edward's phone began to vibrate. He glanced at the screen and dismissed the call.

'Where was I? Oh yeah. This police officer told me they had no record of any such report, that they get very few English people coming to Breva, apart from the occasional loser looking for vampires or werewolves. Did you know Breva is famous for werewolf sightings? I looked it up on Google.'

I shook my head.

'Anyway, I asked again if I could speak directly to Constantin.'

'And? Did you get to talk to him?'

Edward looked at me over the rim of his coffee cup. 'No. Constantin has gone missing. Nobody has seen him for two weeks.'

'Have they got any idea what's happened to him?'

'They wouldn't tell me. But it didn't seem like it.'

'What else did you tell them?'

'I told them what you told me about the house and what you'd seen. An abbreviated version of it, anyway.'

I had no idea how to feel about this. 'What did they say?'

'To say they were sceptical would be an understatement. I mean, I was talking through an interpreter, and *he* was looking at me like I'd lost my mind.'

'So the interpreter *does* know . . .'

He tutted. 'But I eventually got them to promise to go and take a look in the forest. To find the house. I tried to put the idea in their heads that they might find Constantin there. Which, who knows, might actually be true.'

I stood up, strode across the room and back again. My legs were trembling.

'I haven't heard back yet,' he continued. 'I assume they were waiting till today, so they could go when it was light. I'm waiting for the Breva police to ring me back.'

Anxiety was coming off me in waves. Edward said, 'Listen, don't worry about the police in Romania. They'll find the house . . . Maybe there are women being held prisoner there right now. At the very least, there must be evidence of the crimes that took place. The guy who did this will finally be stopped.'

'You have a lot of faith in the police.'

He shrugged. 'Maybe. Anyway, while we're waiting to hear, I want to go through everything else you told me. OK?'

'OK.'

'Good. Got any paper? Or are you one of those people who only has screens?'

I grabbed a few sheets from my printer and he spread them out on the table between us.

'OK,' he said. 'We're going to write down all the questions, all the things that don't make sense, and then we're going to answer them as best we can, see if we can make this puzzle fit together.'

Between us, we spent the next twenty minutes writing out these questions in block capitals and sorting the sheets of paper into order. Apart from our voices, it was silent in the flat, so quiet you could hear the hum of the electrics, the creaking radiators, the occasional voice from the street below. It felt good to do this, better than tapping out the list of problems on my phone. I felt a growing sense of gratitude towards Edward, wished I'd found someone to help me like this earlier. I was able to push my anxiety—about my drunken visit to Laura and her messages, and what the police in Breva would find—to the back of my mind while we worked on this task. It reminded me of the nights when I would sit up working on my app, problem-solving, everything else in the world fading to grey while I concentrated on the puzzle before me. At one point, I heard the sound of tyres skidding on the road outside, the thump of a car door. But I was concentrating too hard on what I was doing to look out of the window.

After we'd filled each sheet with text, Edward sat back and surveyed them, rubbing a forefinger back and forth across his chin. 'Right,' he said. 'Let's see what we've got.'

The top left sheet of paper contained the words WHAT WAS CAMELIA LOOKING FOR?

'First of all,' Edward said, 'we don't know if Camelia is connected to the events near Breva. We assume she is because she's Romanian, but that could be a coincidence.'

'It can't be,' I said.

'But we can't assume.'

'If you say "When you assume you make an *ass* out of *u* and *me*" I'm going to fire you.'

'You definitely didn't meet or see her while you were over there?' he asked.

'No, definitely not. I'd recognise her. She's a very memorable girl.'

'Hmm. She certainly sounds it. Now . . . tell me exactly what Camelia said to you on both occasions you met.'

I recounted our conversations as well as I could remember them.

'So the first time you met her, she asked if you'd ever had a bad experience with Romanian women.'

'And when I said I hadn't, she asked if I was sure. Fuck.' I exhaled. 'And the second time, she kept asking me if I'd done anything illegal, broken the law. Over and over.'

'Trying to get you to confess to something you don't know about.'

'We did break the law,' I said, sitting up straight. 'Going into that sleeper carriage without a ticket. Maybe she was trying to get me tell her about that.'

'Daniel, that's hardly stealing the Crown Jewels, is it? It can't be that.' He thought about it. 'Let's assume that it definitely was Camelia on that CCTV video and that she was responsible for the burglary too. When she came into your flat, she ransacked the place the first time, didn't she? Like she was looking for something.'

'Yes.'

Edward went back to scrutinising the sheet of paper, as if the answer was hiding between the words. 'Let's think. We're pretty sure she's broken into your flat three times. Her and whoever she's working with. Once to ransack the place . . . and steal your laptop. Then to bring the laptop back. And then when they came back with the dog.' He rubbed his chin again. 'If they were searching for something, it makes sense that they turned your flat over. But why bring the laptop back? And why come back with a dog?'

'Because they wanted to hurt me. They thought the dog would kill me.' My whole body went cold as I said these words.

Edward went quiet for a few moments, then looked at me. 'Let's come back to that. I just need to . . .' He trailed off. 'How did Camelia get the key to your flat?'

'I have no idea. I haven't lost any keys.'

'What about Laura? Has she had any keys go missing?'

'I . . . hang on. Yes, when we got back to the UK, Laura didn't have her keys. We thought they'd probably gone missing at some point on our trip. But the thief who took our passports must have taken them.'

'That never crossed your mind before?'

'No. There was a lot going on in our heads when we got back. It didn't even cross our minds that the person who robbed us would take the keys to our flat.'

'Well, at least that explains how they got into your flat.'

'And makes it seem even more likely that Camelia is connected to what happened on the train, to the theft.'

'Well, maybe she was on the train. She, or her partner in crime. They took your keys so they could come over here and rob your flat.'

I shook my head. 'That seems a bit . . . unlikely. Travel all across Europe to rob a flat? And why wait three months? Plus it doesn't explain all the questions. And they brought the most valuable stolen item back anyway. Why?' I thumped my forehead. 'None of it makes sense. I need another coffee.'

I went into the kitchen and filled the kettle, made two more mugs of instant coffee. I'd bought Nescafé again. Jake would be looking down now, shaking his head and muttering about baby milk.

As I waited for the kettle to boil, Edward's mobile rang. He looked up at me. 'It's a call from Romania. The police.'

Chapter Thirty-Eight

Laura had paced the strip of carpet between the bed and window in her room at Erin and Rob's so many times now that she was surprised it hadn't worn away to reveal the floorboards. As she paced, she chewed the skin around her fingernails, sucking the blood from her thumb, pacing, chewing, sucking, pacing . . . She had a word stuck in her head: Putrescent. She didn't know why, or where it had come from, but it repeated over and over: *putrescent, putrescent, putrescent.* Pace, chew, suck, pace, back and forth, up and down, round and round and round.

She forced herself to stop, gulped down air, resisted her fingers as they called to her, urging her to bite them, shred them, make them bleed. She leaned her head against the cool glass of the window, imagined she could feel the rain that beat against it caressing her forehead, cooling her fevered brow, sure that she could smell her own rotting skin—

putrescent

—and aware of the *thump-thump-thump* of her heart. Last night, she had lain sweating beneath the sheets, like she often did just before she got her period, but this increased heartbeat, the shivering fear and unease that coursed through her, was worse than ever.

Worse than in the first nights after she'd seen the dying women at that house, before she'd heard the gunshots that killed them and Alina. Killed the baby, the poor innocent sweet big-eyed baby.

She took a deep, shuddering breath. She could hear little Oscar downstairs, crying, could hear the voices of Erin and Rob and the couple who were visiting them, a woman Erin worked with and her husband. This woman—Laura didn't know her name—was putrescent too . . . no, *pregnant* too—pregnant!—and Laura touched her own belly, wondering if she'd ever have a baby of her own. If she did, she would keep him or her sequestered away, give him or her the perfect life, unlike hers. The baby would be her clean slate, and she would keep her son or daughter safe from hands that meant harm, safe from ghosts, safe from the old man . . .

She had seen him again yesterday. She was sure he wasn't a ghost, too: he was real, all too real. He had been sitting in a shiny black car, parked across the road, watching the house. It was the kind of car the Devil drives in movies; the kind that pulls up at a crossroads on a highway in the middle of nowhere, inviting the hapless runaway to get in, offering a deal, a one-way ride to Hell. She knew, even if she was losing her mind, that she was letting her imagination run riot, that there was no devil who drove around in a black BMW offering rides to doomed mortals. But the old man was real. When he saw Laura approaching he fired up the engine and drove away, the car gliding silently up the street, slipping out of sight.

Laura had been stuck to the spot. Again, she was sure she had seen him before. Last night, when she'd finally entered a choppy, troubled sleep, the answer had come to her, shrouded by symbolism, and though she had grasped the meaning in the nightmare, when she woke up among cold, wet sheets she couldn't recall it.

She had told Alina about the old man, the devil, and the ghost had turned even paler, if such a thing was possible. Then she'd said *Don't worry. I'll deal with him when he comes.*

Alina had slipped away before Laura could ask what the dead woman meant.

Now, she opened her eyes and looked down at the spot where Daniel had stood last night, calling her name. She couldn't face him, couldn't bear to talk to him. It broke her heart to see him walk away. She wanted to run after him. More than that, she wanted to run so fast that she could stop time, turn the planet back, like Superman, and erase everything that had happened since last August. Change what had happened in that house. Then she and her Danny would still be together, still be happy.

She realised her face was wet, that she was crying.

Go and see him, a voice said. *Talk to him.*

She found a tissue and blew her nose, rubbed her eyes. Was there any chance they could make it work? Even now?

Downstairs, Oscar was crying, shrieking, and the sound penetrated Laura's skull, made it impossible to think straight. She needed to get out. She grabbed her coat and, scrutinising the garden once more to see if Alina was there, but not seeing her, headed out.

———

Now, thirty minutes later, she walked along the street where she'd lived not so long ago. The snow had been washed away by the rain, leaving a few patches of slush in the gutters, the odd frozen clump clinging to a hedge. Her legs had brought her here despite her head's protestations. All the way, she kept thinking, I'll stop soon. I'll go back. In a minute. But she couldn't stop walking, and now here she was. She had been happy here, had enjoyed such good times. Tears pricked her eyes again and she was almost overwhelmed by regret. If only . . .

As she approached the building where Daniel lived she heard a noise and turned—the devil?—but it was just a fox, padding away from her across the road. A pretty fox. It stopped in the middle of the road and turned its face towards her. At that moment, a silver car, old, battered, the opposite of the shining black vehicle driven by the old man, screeched around the corner and barrelled towards the fox. Laura gasped as the car skidded to a halt, closing her eyes, certain she would hear the impact of metal against bone.

When she opened them, the fox was gone. Under the wheels? She ran into the road, trying to see, ready to shout at the woman behind the wheel of the battered car, a woman who was staring at her, a smile on her face.

What was so funny?

The car door opened and a blonde woman with chunky silver rings on her fingers got out.

'Laura?' she said. She had the same accent as Alina.

'Yes? Who are you?'

'Get in the car.'

'What?'

The woman produced a knife from beneath her coat. 'Get in the car.'

Chapter Thirty-Nine

Edward murmured into the phone, facing away from me, so I couldn't really hear what he was saying. The police in Breva must have found someone who spoke English. As Constantin had been able to do. I was desperate to hear what Edward was saying, attempted to get in front of him, but he kept turning away from me, shooting me irritated looks until I gave up.

The call ended.

'Well?' I said. 'Have they been to the house? What did they find?'

He ran a finger across his eyebrow. 'Nothing.'

'For God's sake, tell me what they said.'

He held his hand out and waited for me to hand him his coffee. I was tempted to chuck it at him. 'They found the house, but said it was deserted.'

'What, you mean . . . like no one lived there?'

'Exactly. He said that the whole place was empty. No food in the cupboards, a single, rusty bed in what would have been the master bedroom, with a bare mattress. No plates in the kitchen—or mugs. Certainly no sign of Constantin.' He sipped his coffee and winced. 'One weird thing: one of the bedrooms on the top floor appeared to have been decorated recently. It still had that fresh paint smell. But it was completely empty. They found some furniture in one of the rooms—some chests, a dresser, a few ancient chairs—draped with sheets.'

'So he's gone. And covered up the evidence.' I swore under my breath, though to be honest I hadn't been expecting the police to find anything. In a way, I was pleased. I wanted that place, any traces of what I'd seen there, to be wiped from the face of the earth. Of course, I wanted justice for those women, for Alina, for the babies who had died, but the possibility of that seemed so remote . . . Part of me wanted to hear the place had been burned to the ground. It was a place of evil, and this world would be better without it.

Edward continued. 'I asked him if there was any record of who lived there. He said the last resident, according to their equivalent of the Land Registry, was a woman who died in 1991. The place has been empty for over twenty years.'

'Except it hasn't.'

'I want to talk to Laura,' he said.

'Why?'

'Because I want to see if she's been experiencing the same kind of things that you have. And . . . well, I want to check her version of events.'

I stared at him, the anger, which had drained from me in the kitchen, simmering again. 'You think I'm making the whole thing up?'

'No, don't be stupid. I want to see if Laura remembers anything that you don't. Like, maybe *she* saw Camelia on the train. Maybe Laura has had contact with Camelia too, in the last couple of weeks.'

'Oh my God. You're right.'

'What's Laura's address?'

I told him and he wrote it down in his notepad. I said, 'Maybe it was Camelia who tried to push Laura under the Tube train. Oh Jesus. I bet she killed Jake.'

'Camelia? But why would she do that?'

'Because she must have known I'd talked to him. And she went after him for information about whatever the hell it is she's looking for, thinking I might have told him, and . . . had to kill him so he wouldn't tell me she'd been to see him. Or maybe she murdered him because she was so angry with him because he didn't have the info she needed.' I paused. 'And the only reason she hasn't tried to kill me is that she thinks I'll still lead her to what she's after.'

'But she did try to kill you, didn't she? The dog.'

'Maybe she was just trying to scare me.'

'I don't know, Daniel. It doesn't make sense. Would a skinny, slight woman like Camelia be able to overpower Jake?'

'She would only have to catch him off-balance to be able to push him off that bridge. And we know she's not working alone. It was probably the man on the video. Both of them.'

'This is all even more reason to talk to Laura.'

'But she refuses to see me. I can't go anywhere near her.'

He gave me a wry smile.

'Who said anything about you coming too?'

Chapter Forty

The blonde woman didn't speak at all on the way to wherever it was they were going. She glanced at Laura in the rear-view mirror whenever they stopped at a traffic light. Laura had tried to open the door but the child locks were on.

When Laura tried to talk, to ask the woman who she was, what she was doing, she found that her voice box didn't work. Not just that, but all the words in her head had vanished. All but one.

putrescentputrescentputrescentputrescent

'Stop fucking doing that,' the woman snapped, shattering the silence.

Laura's eyes swivelled towards her.

'Biting your fingers. Stop it.'

putrescentputrescentputrescentputrescent

Laura sat on her hands.

The woman cursed. 'This traffic.'

Laura forced herself to get a grip, to start noticing things. She might need these details later. The driver was Eastern European, very pretty. She smelled of cigarettes. Her roots were poking through. She wore silver rings. She crunched the gears whenever she turned a corner and shifted down to second.

The urge to pull her hands out from beneath her and start chewing them again was almost overwhelming.

What else? The car was a Skoda, the type favoured by minicab drivers, and seemed pretty old, but not too old to have child locks. There was a rip in the upholstery beside her. And they were driving east, through Islington, up Essex Road and now they were in Hackney. Victoria Park wasn't far from here. They kept going, stopping and starting, got stuck behind a bus for a long time, skirted the edge of Hackney Marshes. Now they were in East London proper. Leyton, squatting dejectedly beneath the colourless winter sky. And soon they pulled up in a quiet back street outside a house beside a vacant shop. The house had a boarded-up door and a front garden that was so badly overgrown that it was spilling onto the street.

The blonde got out, came round and opened the passenger door, poking the knife towards Laura. 'Out.'

She led Laura round the back of the house, where the garden was even more jungle-like than at the front. The back door had several broken glass panes. The woman stuck her hand through the jagged hole and opened the door from the inside. Again, she jabbed the knife at Laura and told her to go inside.

Laura thought about running, trying to escape. But for the second time that day, her legs wouldn't obey her brain.

I'm going to die, she thought. And she found that she didn't feel scared. Death, she decided, would not be unjust.

It was dark inside the house. It smelled of something rotting—
putrescent
—and the light fittings were empty. The woman led her into a boxy living room. Black bin liners covered the windows, so it was pitch-dark inside.

'Where the fuck is he?' the woman muttered, and Laura's heart lurched. He? Who was *he*?

The devil, a voice whispered in her head.

Now she was scared.

Swearing under her breath, the blonde used her mobile to cast faint light into the room, searching through the drawer of a cabinet until she found what she was looking for. Two candles and a box of matches.

She's not holding the knife on me now, Laura realised. This would be the perfect time to run. But yet again, her legs wouldn't do what she wanted. She was too transfixed by her surroundings. This place, the smell, the candles, the old dark-wood furniture. It was like that house, the evil house . . .

The woman turned to her, wearing a cruel smile. 'Well, it looks like it's just you and me, Laura. Men. They are *so* fucking useless.' She laughed bitterly and pointed the knife at Laura, gesturing at a sofa that looked like it had been rescued from a rubbish dump. 'Sit.'

Laura managed to speak. 'Who are you? What do you want?'

'I just want to ask you a question,' the woman responded. There was a fake Prada bag on the floor, and the woman crouched and opened it, producing a pair of handcuffs. She yanked Laura's shoulder and pulled her around, then snapped the cuffs over her wrists.

'You won't be able to bite your fingers now,' she said.

She pointed the tip of the blade at Laura's face. 'Listen to me, and don't speak. I am going to ask you a question. You are going to tell me the truth. If you don't, I will hurt you, very badly.' She took hold of Laura's sweater and yanked it upwards, revealing her bra. 'I will slice off your nipples. I will cut out your eyes. I will fucking circumcise you.'

Laura was too terrified to speak. *You've seen worse*, she told herself. *You can get through this. Talk to her, reason with her. She's a woman. She'll let you go.* But just like her treacherous legs, her tongue wouldn't work.

'But if you answer,' the woman said, 'if you tell the truth, you can leave this place in one piece. OK?'

It was freezing in the room, but Laura could feel sweat running down her back, and something wet on her cheeks too. Tears. She was crying silently.

'OK. Here is the question. When you returned from Romania, you had two backpacks with you. Where are they? And what did you do with the contents?'

Laura stared at the woman, unsure if she had heard the question correctly. 'Backpacks?'

Sighing, the woman pulled Laura's sweater up again and stuck the knife down beneath her bra, between the cups, the flat edge cold against Laura's skin. She pulled and the knife sliced through the fabric. The bra fell open, exposing her breasts. She grabbed Laura's right breast and pinched the nipple, making Laura cry out.

'Where is it?'

'The backpacks? We left them behind. In the police station. In Breva.'

The woman stared at her. 'I don't believe you.' She pressed the tip of the blade against Laura's throat. 'You sold it, didn't you? Just tell me, and then this will all be over.'

'I don't . . . I don't know what you're talking about.'

'Liar!' The woman screeched in her face, spittle flying and spraying Laura's forehead. 'I'm going to kill you if you don't tell me the truth.'

'We left them in Breva. I swear. I don't understand— what . . . what are you looking for?'

The woman stared into her face, into her eyes, for several seconds, and then stepped back and, to Laura's astonishment, began to laugh hysterically. She doubled over, barely able to breathe. She looked up at Laura and, catching her breath, said, 'You're telling the truth?'

'I swear. I promise.'

As suddenly as it had appeared, the woman's smile vanished.

237

'After all this. You left it in Romania. And you don't even know what I'm talking about do you? My God.' She muttered something to herself in another language. Then she said, 'OK. I'm going to wait till he gets here and you can tell him yourself. He can decide what to do with you. I've had it with all of this shit.'

Bang bang bang.

The blonde turned towards the sound. 'That must be him. At last. Why doesn't the stupid asshole just let himself in?'

She left the room. Laura heard the back door opening, then a woman's cry, and a thump.

The man stepped into the room and, later, Laura would be amazed that she hadn't wet herself at that moment.

It was him.

The devil.

'Hello, Laura,' the old man said.

He held an iron bar in his hand. He stared at her naked breasts for a long moment, licking his lips, then pulled her sweater back down, covering her. 'The key,' he whispered, leaving the room and coming back a minute later to unlock the handcuffs.

'Come with me,' he said. 'I'll take you home.'

He grabbed hold of her wrist and pulled her up. He put an arm around her shoulders and walked her towards the door. She felt dizzy, sick, barely able to stand upright. She stared at her feet, trying not to fall. As they reached the threshold of the room she heard a soft thump, like someone dropping a heavy bag, and a voice that she had heard before said, 'Camelia?'

The old man sighed, took his arm away from Laura's shoulders and stooped to pick up the iron bar again.

'Wait here,' he said.

Chapter Forty-One

I paced the flat, watching the sky grow dark outside, puzzling over everything Edward and I had been talking about. Claudia Sauvage had told me that in order to recover from my PTSD I needed to be able to confront what had happened to me, to slowly peel back the protective layers I had built in my mind and deal with the reality of the events that had frightened me so much.

But that hadn't happened. Instead, those layers had been ripped away, burned as if they'd been struck by the Molotov cocktail chucked into Edward's office, and now I felt like that guy in *A Clockwork Orange*—strapped down, eyes clamped open, forced to stare at the most horrific scenes, the evidence of humanity's darkest heart. With no warning, the horror would flash into my real life, replacing it whole. When I looked at the framed photographs on the wall, I saw the Polaroids pinned up in that house. Walking into my bedroom, I found an emaciated woman with black spaces instead of teeth manacled to my bed, grinning at me. A neighbour's baby cried out and I imagined it locked in that tiny coffin, beating against the lid.

I prowled into the kitchen, desperate for a drink, but I had poured all the alcohol down the sink. I clawed at my own face, sucked in deep breaths, tried desperately to calm myself.

If I concentrated on the puzzle, maybe that would work. Camelia. What did she want? I grabbed a fresh piece of paper and tried to summarise what we knew, or at least what we thought we knew, so far.

Camelia and her partner had keys to my flat. They must have obtained these in Romania, which meant they had to be the thieves from the train.

They had broken into my flat, searched it, taken my laptop and brought it back again. I presumed they must have looked through it, but why return it? I had searched it for viruses and spyware when I got it back, and it was clean.

Then they had come back again with the dog.

Finally, on two occasions Camelia had tried to seduce me, succeeding the second time, but stopping when I was unable to give her the information she wanted.

What was that information?

Something illegal.

I closed my eyes and went back to that night in the train carriage. The thief—Camelia—had taken our passports, our money, tickets and keys. There were other valuables in our bags, like the camera. Why didn't they take that? My phone had been sitting on my chest and would have been easy to take, but they had left it.

Why?

Because . . . The answer was almost there. I forced myself to concentrate. Why take only the items that would most inconvenience us, forcing us to cut short our trip around Europe? The loss of our passports meant we had to fly home. Was that their intention, to get us to come back here? To leave Eastern Europe? It almost felt like a prank, an act of mischief, something the thieves barely benefited from.

I sat up. Did that mean the theft wasn't the point?

My mind flashed back to the CCTV video. The male intruder searching drawers and cupboards, the woman holding the dog on

its leash. Did they really bring the dog so it would attack me? Why
the roundabout method when they could just wait for their chance
out in the world to get me? Why the dog? I pictured it now on the
slightly grainy video clip. Straining at the leash, sniffing around.

'Fuck!' I shouted.

Sniffing around.

I had it.

⌣

The wait for Edward to return was agonising. Finally, I heard his car
pull up outside and a moment later he pressed the buzzer to be let in.
I had been over and over my logic in my head and was sure I was correct. I knew what Camelia was after. I knew what this was all about.

Drugs.

It was the only thing that made sense. Camelia and her partner,
whoever that was, had planted drugs in my and Laura's backpacks.
Then they took our passports, knowing this would mean we'd have
to go home. Two middle-class English people, respectable-looking,
normal, not acting shiftily because we were oblivious to what we
were carrying. The perfect drug mules. The plan must have been
to intercept us once we were back in London, to retrieve the drugs
before we found them.

They couldn't have known that we would be thrown off the
train. Or that we would leave our backpacks in a police station in
Romania. I laughed when I thought about this. I would love to have
seen their faces when they found this out. Then I thought about
what would have happened if Laura and I hadn't left the backpacks
behind, if we'd been caught at customs trying to bring illegal drugs
into the country, and my laughter died.

I went through it again. They had broken in, searched my flat,
then come back with a dog to see if it could sniff out the drugs.

I guessed they had left it here when it failed to find anything, probably in a fit of temper, wanting to punish me. Then Camelia had come back for another try, clearly believing that I must have sold the drugs: that was the illegal act she wanted me to admit to.

In my moment of triumph, having figured out the mystery, I didn't stop to think about the rest of it: how this connected to all the other strange and horrible stuff that had been going on. Like, what did they hope to achieve by firebombing Edward's office? Had they killed Jake? If so, why on earth had they? Why attempt to push Laura under a Tube rather than try to get information out of her? If I'd thought about it in any depth, I would have realised this violence just didn't fit. If I was a vicious drug dealer I wouldn't pussyfoot around. I would have waited here for me, grabbed me and tortured the information out of me.

But, sure I'd solved the puzzle, I didn't wonder about that. The main question that bugged me was why they had waited so long to try to retrieve the drugs. It had been three months. What was the explanation for that?

Edward came into the flat and before I could open my mouth to tell him about my Eureka moment, he said, 'You will never guess what I just saw.'

He ushered me into the living room, as if this was his own flat, and threw himself down on the sofa. I remained standing.

'So . . . I went to the address you gave me, where Laura's staying. When I parked I could see a woman standing by the gate. It was her.' He pointed at the picture of Laura on the wall.

Edward went on. 'I was about to get out of the car, call to her, but she went into the garden. She was acting . . . Well, I don't know her, don't know what she's normally like, but she was acting weird. Like she was in shock or something. As if she hardly knew where she was.

'I went up and looked through the gate. It was odd—I could hear a woman's voice coming from somewhere in the garden, but

I couldn't see anyone. I didn't want to scare her, because then I thought she'd never talk to me, but I wanted to see what she was doing. Was she talking to someone? I could hear only one voice. The voice sounded frightened, almost . . . on the verge of hysteria.'

'That's what she's been like recently,' I said.

He nodded. 'Anyway, I opened the gate as quietly as I could and went into the garden. I could see Laura clearly now. She was gesticulating, miming what looked like one person striking another. And then I realised she was talking to someone else.'

He paused dramatically, then said, 'Describe Alina to me.'

'Alina? She was quite tall, skinny, pale skin. Black hair with red streaks in it. She wore a black leather jacket and black jeans. Quite attractive if you're into that sort of thing. Why do you want to know that now?'

'Because I just saw Laura talking to her.'

'What? But—'

'Daniel, unless I've developed the ability to see ghosts too, Alina is very much alive.'

Part Five

Romania
August–November 2013

Chapter Forty-Two

Alina stopped as she stepped between the trees and looked up at the dark canopy of the forest, black branches knitted together against the sky, the faintest watery trace of moonlight seeping through. She was a city girl. She wouldn't hesitate to walk through a dark underpass, to cross one of Sibiu's roughest housing estates. Give her the darkest spaces of the city any day over this creepy, silent place.

Still, she was desperate for a piss and there was no way she was going to squat in front of the English couple, even if they promised to look away. She would find a spot here, close to the edge of the forest, not too far in, and then they could be on their way, so she could try to salvage this plan, make sure it worked despite what had happened.

The plan had been Ion's idea. Ion . . . She still couldn't decide if she really liked him or not. He was good-looking, confident and capable in bed, with no hang-ups, unlike some of the more sensitive writer and artist types she'd been with. When Ion had told Daniel that he was writing a book she'd had to work hard to keep her face straight. Ion had borrowed that line straight from Alina's ex, a guy whom Ion mocked on a regular basis. All that stuff about collaborating on a graphic novel was bullshit too. Ion had no interest in her artwork, though he liked it when she drew naked women, would urge her to give them bigger breasts, curvier butts. He was an idiot really. He wasn't even that tough, even though he talked the talk. He was a schemer and a dreamer. He wasn't a violent thug. She wouldn't have been with him if he was.

Anyway, once this was all over, when she had her cut of the money, she had decided she was going to leave him. She would use the money to buy herself enough time to finish her graphic novel. It was called *Mirela* and was the story of a girl who walks the earth after she is murdered by a cabal of serial killers, seeking revenge. Mirela finds everyone who is connected to her suffering and kills them in a variety of imaginative ways. Alina had already been working on it for two years, spending every spare minute, when she wasn't at her shitty waitressing job, immersed in this tale of blood and redemption.

She didn't think Ion would care too much when she left him. He would have his money, and Alina knew he had a thing for Camelia, who had moved to London last year, dreaming of making her fortune. The last Alina heard, Camelia was working as a fucking stripper or something. It suited her. Camelia had been showing everything to the boys at school in exchange for cash since she was fourteen. She traded on her beauty—a slutty, obvious kind of beauty—and Alina was pretty sure the girl would either end up married to a millionaire or murdered in an alley. Her fate lay in the hands of men.

Alina was different. She was going to make her own way, succeed or fail because of her own talents and luck. She accepted that, sometimes, other people would get hurt along the way. She felt guilty about wrecking the English couple's holiday, for example, but not *too* guilty. They already had money, they were privileged without realising it, soft and gullible. What was the worst that

could happen to them? As Ion had pointed out, people like that—
wholesome, middle-class English people—didn't get pulled aside at
airports. With their passports stolen, their grand tour would be cut
short. Oh, how her heart bled! They would go home, get married,
start having babies, and they would soon forget all about their truncated trip. Best of all, they would never know what they had carried
through customs. They would live on in blissful ignorance, while
Ion, Alina and, unfortunately, Camelia experienced for the first
time how it felt to have money.

It had all started with a stroke of luck. Ion knew a guy called
Kris who had ripped off a drug dealer in Sibiu and had given the
cocaine to Ion for safe keeping while Kris tried to convince the drug
dealer that he was innocent. Ion, who dreamed of being a gangster
but was too soft to do anything about it, had gone along with it,
thinking it would impress his friends. With grim inevitability, the
dealer and his gang had tortured and killed Kris. Ion, fearing he
would be next, had suggested to Alina that they go away for a while.
He sold it to her as a romantic adventure.

Then came the good fortune. They got as far as Hungary when
Ion heard that the dealers had been arrested and charged with Kris's
murder. They would be in prison for a long time. At which point,
Ion revealed to Alina that he had half a kilo of pure cocaine in his
suitcase.

She was furious. He had smuggled the drugs across the
Hungarian border. Was he so stupid that he didn't know what happened to people caught with such a large quantity of drugs? Life in
jail. For both of them.

But Ion had a plan, which he laid out to her over the next hour.
It involved Camelia, which immediately put Alina's back up. But
Ion had already spoken to the little slut and she'd assured him that
she knew someone through her pole-dancing club who would be
interested in buying the drugs. 'I can't sell them back home,' he said.

'It's much too risky. If the gang who originally owned the drugs found out, I'd be dead.' So they needed to get the coke to London.

Alina stared at him. Carrying the drugs into Hungary was stupid enough, but taking it through an airport, or on a boat, into the UK? That was insane. They argued for a while about Eurostar, and how risky it actually was, when Ion let slip that he would surely get searched at customs because of his previous conviction for possession, which Alina hadn't known about.

'But you could do it,' he said. 'If you love me . . .'

'Who said I love you?' she asked. 'I'm not doing it. I'm not risking going to jail.'

They fought some more until, eventually, Ion said, 'Then we'll have to find someone to take it for us.'

Before that, they decided to head back into Romania, to Sibiu. They would have to cross the border again, but on the train here the guards had been half-asleep. If they took the night train back, the guards would probably be comatose.

They spotted the English couple at Budapest Station. They didn't look like typical backpackers: they had a more well-to-do air about them; they looked cleaner, and the guy was carrying an expensive camera. Ion nudged Alina and whispered his plan to her. It was a crazy scheme.

'Why,' Alina asked, 'don't we go to the airport and find an English couple there?'

Ion shook his head. 'What opportunity do you think we'll get at an airport to put the drugs into somebody's bag? This is perfect.'

Yet again, they argued, until Ion eventually sighed and said, 'OK, let's see how it plays out.'

She agreed, almost certain that nothing would happen. That they would end up back home with the drugs.

Except . . . the opportunity did arise. Ion chatted them up, spinning a lie about how they were going to see her parents, who were actually both dead. Alina felt awkward and withdrawn at first, intimidated by this wealthy English couple, until she realised that she had no reason to feel like that, and she had decided to play along, to be friendly. She actually quite liked them, especially Laura, who was sweet and far less pretentious or stuck-up than Alina expected. She felt genuine sympathy for Laura when that creep stared at her. Daniel was OK too, even if he was typically eager to talk about himself. But she still didn't think they'd get the opportunity to put the cocaine into the couple's backpacks, unless one of them could lure the English couple to the buffet car, or hope they both went to the toilet at the same time, leaving their bags in their new friends' care.

Then Ion spotted the empty sleeper compartment and persuaded them to go for a nap, promising to keep an eye out for guards. After they went, Ion and Alina sat in tense silence for a while, before Ion said, 'Wait here', and carried his own bag out of their carriage. When he came back five minutes later he was sweating.

'Well?' she whispered.

'I did it,' he whispered back. 'They were sleeping like babies. Two hundred and fifty grams in each backpack. They each had a small bag of dirty laundry at the bottom of their packs. I put them in those.'

'In dirty laundry?'

'Yeah. Well, I figured they're not going to stop to wash their underwear on the way home. I took their passports, tickets and bank cards too. I got some keys too, in case Camelia needs them, and the girl's phone, a nice Samsung. Daniel just has a crappy, scratched-up iPhone 5 with a cracked screen so I didn't bother. Why don't people take care of their gadgets . . .'

Alina shook her head, wondering if she was dreaming. 'What are you talking about? What about the guards? When they come through to check passports, what will they do? Won't they arrest them?'

'What for? This is why I'm a genius. They'll tell them they need to leave Romania. That as soon as we get to the end of the line they'll have to head home. I imagine they'll escort them to the airport and put them on the plane back to England. Whatever, they'll be forced to go home.'

'A genius.' She laughed and he looked hurt.

'Why do you have to be such a bitch? You won't be complaining when you get your hands on the money.'

Feeling a little contrite, she said, 'I'm sorry.'

He harrumphed. 'Good. I'm starving. The buffet car will be open now. I'm going to get something to eat. Maybe while I'm gone you can think about why you have to be such a bitch to me.'

She watched him stomp off through the carriage, in the opposite direction to the sleeper carriages, contrition turning to anger. She was sick of being called a bitch. Maybe she should put him in her comic book, one of Mirela's misogynistic victims . . .

After Ion had been gone a few minutes, the door he'd left through opened and the border guards entered. They woke the few other people in the carriage and checked their passports. They spent a while talking in low voices to one passenger who was outside of Alina's line of vision.

She felt sweaty and tense. She didn't share Ion's confidence about what the guards would do when they discovered the English couple's passports were missing. What if they searched their bags? The plan would be over before it had begun, though she reminded herself there was nothing to link the drugs to her and Ion. Still, it would mean the loss of the money she was already counting on. She tried to relax but when the guards got to her she fumbled with her own passport, dropped it on the floor, making them snap at her to hurry up. For whatever reason, they were in a bad mood and highly alert. So much for them being semi-comatose. As she retrieved her passport, someone stepped past her, heading in the direction of the sleepers; she just caught a glimpse of a man's legs.

Eventually, after asking her a dozen questions that made her sweat, the guards left the carriage and headed towards the sleepers. Where was Ion? Chatting up the girl in the buffet, no doubt. She got up, went to the other end of the carriage and peered into the next one, but there was no sign of Ion. When she turned around she saw the old man whose bags she'd carried walking towards her through the carriage, presumably on his way back from the toilets, which were located just before the sleepers. She smiled at him and waited for him to take his seat then went towards the sleepers and peered through the greasy glass.

She could see the guards standing outside one of the compartments. Daniel and Laura's? Then a border guard broke away from the group and came rushing towards her, through the door, almost knocking her over, and hurried away out the door at the far end of the carriage. She returned to her seat and waited, wishing Ion would come back. What if Ion was wrong about what the guards would do? What if they arrested the English couple and searched their bags? She had a sudden attack of conscience. She liked them. They seemed nice, harmless. A happy couple with a bright future, planning to have a baby and get married. If the guards found the drugs, Daniel and Laura's lives would be destroyed. And, she thought selfishly, the money Ion had promised would vanish before she ever got her hands on it.

The border guard came back through the carriage, the ticket inspector following. Holding the door open, she could hear raised voices, Daniel protesting. What should she do? The passports and tickets were here, in Ion's bag, and she could grab them, tell Daniel and Laura that they must have dropped them on the seat.

If she could reason with the guards, persuade them that she had seen the English couple with their tickets and passports when the

Hungarian guards came through, that they were innocent victims of theft, that they were foolish foreigners who didn't understand that they shouldn't be in the sleeper carriage . . . It was her best option. She slipped through the door and went to join the party.

But it hadn't gone well, had it?

That was the fucking understatement of the century.

———

Treading her way into the forest, twigs cracking beneath her feet, her eye on a spot a few feet ahead where she could piss, she almost laughed. The guards had been hostile, called her a 'punk bitch', and she had got angry, lost her cool, called them 'fascist lapdogs'. That had been it. The next thing she knew they were being marched back to the carriage—Ion still AWOL—and the train was slowing to a halt and then they were thrown off. Her phone was left behind and she had no cash. She couldn't wait to get to a pay phone, to call Ion, to tell him what a fucking idiot he was and how this was all his fault.

She unbuttoned her jeans and pushed them down. The jeans were so tight it was impossible to squat without toppling backwards or getting urine on her clothes. This was ridiculous. She unlaced one boot and pulled it off before pulling one leg out of her jeans. OK, this would work. She was even more happy that no one was watching her.

As she crouched, she thought about how, despite this hiccup, the situation could still be redeemed. The plan could still work. The cocaine was still in the backpacks, undiscovered. Daniel and Laura had no passports or access to money. They would have to go home. When they reached town they would be able to hitch-hike, or sell that fancy camera to get some cash for train tickets. She would escort the English couple to Bucharest, encourage them to take a plane home and let Camelia know their flight number. It would be Camelia's job to intercept the couple, enlisting one of her dodgy friends: a pair of muggers with knives. Daniel and Laura wouldn't put up much resistance.

Yes, it would still work. And then she would have her share of the money. No harm done apart from a truncated holiday for the English couple.

She finished and stood, pulling up her knickers and slipping her leg back into her jeans. She reached out for her boot and heard a noise. Her heart paused.

Was someone there? She peered into the darkness, and heard more noises—a crunch, a rustle, something snapping—but before she could cry out there was a hand over her mouth and another on her throat, breath warm in her ear and a voice whispering that if she struggled or tried to scream, she would die.

Chapter Forty-Three

Where the fuck was Alina?

Back home in Sibiu, Ion couldn't do anything—couldn't eat, couldn't shit, couldn't sleep—without this question flashing in neon lights inside his head. It had been more than two days now since he saw her standing on the train platform, a figure that grew smaller and smaller as the train gathered pace. The two Brits stood beside her, the backpacks beside them on the ground. He focused on the bags, a knot growing in his stomach as the precious drugs, all that money in powdered form, vanished into the distance.

But, he had thought, sitting down before he attracted the attention of the guards, it would be fine. Alina was there. She would ensure the plan went ahead, that Daniel and Laura got on a plane home. Maybe it would take a while for them to get to Bucharest and onto a plane, if none of them had any money. But Alina was smart. Ion knew, despite his constant references to his own genius, that she was cleverer than him. He wished he'd been chucked off the train too, or had seen what was going on in time to jump off after them, but he'd been too busy chatting with a pretty girl in the buffet car. Still, at least the Brits hadn't been thrown off on their own. Left to their own devices they'd probably wander into the forest and be eaten by bears!

So Ion waited. He was tired out by all the excitement and slept a lot, like his pet cat. He made sure his phone was charged and beside him at all times. Needing to score some weed, he sold the British girl's Samsung and spent a happy few hours indulging his herbal side. He watched a lot of porn on his old computer. And he waited for Alina to call or knock on the door.

But she didn't do either.

So where the fuck was she?

Chapter Forty-Four

Alina woke up and instinctively tried to roll over, but her legs wouldn't move. Every morning started the same way: she would try again to move her legs and then jerk awake, remembering that her ankles were chained to the bed. And then, with daylight creeping through the narrow gaps between the wooden boards that covered the windows, all the other memories, the horror of her situation, would come rushing back.

When she got over the daily shock she always sat up—she was able to do that—and peer towards the cot, checking that little Luka was OK, waiting for the monster to come and take him from his crib and hand the baby to her. And she would cuddle him and kiss his head, that soft, fragile patch beneath his downy hair, and even when he cried she didn't mind. Despite everything—all the things the monster did to her, the terrible fear that her fate would be the same as Luka's mother's—while she had the baby to look after, she could endure.

She heard movement on the stairs and braced herself. Sometimes he would bring her breakfast—bread rolls, water, meat. Animals he'd trapped in the forest, she assumed. He would inspect the room, wandering about while she ate, browsing the display of

Polaroid pictures on the wall like a visitor to a ghastly exhibition. That first night, there had been a little coffin over there, but that was long gone.

The monster was shorter than her, like Ion, with a beak-like nose and stringy hair the colour of a sewer rat. The top of his head was bald and pocked with scars. He had the pallor of a man who never sees sunlight and his skin was always coated with grime. His teeth were yellow and gappy and his tongue was covered with a white layer.

Other times he would come in, ignore her and hand her Luka along with a bottle of milk before leaving the room. He would unchain her and lock the door, leave her to roam the room, to play with Luka. She tried not to look at the Polaroids, the babies and the women who had died here. She knew that Luka's photo was there. But hers hadn't been added yet even though the monster had flashed the camera in her face one morning. Perhaps he wouldn't add her to the wall until she was dead. Maybe that was how it worked.

The monster always left food for Luka, baby food in jars, along with shampoo and creams and nappies. He instructed her to ensure the baby was fed, clean, in good health. She realised very quickly that this was her role: an enslaved nanny. And this wouldn't have been so bad—terrible, but not the worst fate in the world—if it wasn't for the other role she had to play.

Because on the worst mornings, once or twice a week, he would pull the covers off her, tie her wrists to the rusting bed posts and, after squirting some kind of lube onto himself, he would climb on top and push himself into her. She would close her eyes and tried not to inhale his stinking breath, the stench of body odour that came off him. After he came and hoisted himself off her, she would be desperate to wash in the basin in the corner of the room, to use a little of the baby soap on herself. But he wouldn't let her. Instead, every time, he lifted her bottom and pushed a cushion beneath her, elevating her so his semen remained inside her. He always left her like that for an hour, naked and exposed, hands and feet chained to the bed, before returning and untying her. Sometimes, flies would land on her body, crawling about on her skin, and she would buck and thrash, unable to shift them as they sipped at her flesh.

Every time, she would lie and sob for hours, clutching little Luka to her, praying to God that the monster's seed would not find fertile ground. That her body would reject it.

Chapter Forty-Five

Ion stepped off the bus, wrapping his coat around him, and looked up and down the street at the prefabricated buildings, the grim-faced women pushing prams, the cars with ancient licence plates. He'd looked it up online: Breva used to be a prosperous gold-mining town, and there was even a museum of gold here. He laughed humourlessly at the thought of tourists visiting this place. Ha! He bet Daniel and Laura didn't have this ghost town on their fancy itinerary.

After a few days had passed and Alina still hadn't called, Ion began to get really worried. He called Camelia in London and asked her to check if Daniel and Laura were home. Rather bad-temperedly, she had agreed and called back to report that there were lights on in their flat, that she had seen people moving around inside. She hung about until someone matching Daniel's description came outside to put some trash out.

So they had gone home.

'I'll post you the keys,' Ion said to Camelia, 'and you can go inside, check their backpacks. They must have found the stuff by now—' He was paranoid about mentioning the drugs on the phone. 'Can you check the English news? Any reports of tourists finding, um, stuff in their backpacks?'

Camelia had laughed in a way that made his balls crawl up into his body. 'Ion, I can't believe you.'

'What? Why?'

'You really think your *girlfriend*—the word dripped with contempt—'would have followed your original plan? What would you do if you were her? You'd take the *stuff* and vanish. Sell it and keep all the money yourself.'

'I wouldn't.'

'Well, I would. And that's exactly what Alina would do. She'd take the money and use it to buy pens and pads so she could work on her stupid comic books. I bet you a thousand pounds—shit, I've been living here too long—that's what she's done. She wouldn't risk the English couple taking it through customs which, let's face it, was a ludicrous idea, probably the worst you've ever had, and that's saying something.'

'Hey. It was genius.'

Camelia laughed at that for a while. He amazed himself: even when she was mocking him, he found it impossible not to picture Camelia's lovely breasts, which she'd showed him once in exchange for an eighth of weed. 'Face it, Ion. The drugs—'

'What? Who is this?'

'The *stuff* is long gone. Your punk princess has taken it and you'll never see her again. And after you promised me a share of that money, I'm stuck here pole-dancing for limp-dicked perverts. Thanks a lot.'

She hung up.

The more he thought about it, the more he realised Camelia was right. Hell, Alina had probably planned to get herself, Daniel and Laura kicked off the train. Cause a big fight with the guards, make them so angry that they would feel compelled to stop and eject her and the Brits. Then she would sneak the stuff . . . the coke—it was safe, he reminded himself, if it was only in his head—out of their backpacks and find someone to buy it.

Furious, he went into the bedroom where Alina had left some of her artwork, the comic book she'd been working on for months, and tore it into shreds. He didn't feel any better so he punched the wall, but that hurt like hell. He yelled, making the cat shoot out of the room, and then looked around at the dump where he lived. He needed that money. He'd planned everything he was going to buy. The new TV, the gaming chair, the bearskin rug. He had been robbed.

She wasn't going to get away with it.

He found a small, cheap room in a Breva hotel that smelled of cabbage and cabbage-induced farts and threw his bag down on the bed. He felt like a bounty hunter, retracing Alina's steps.

He had already been to the station where Alina and the Brits had been kicked off the train. It was a spooky place, not a soul in sight, unless you counted the little pack of dogs that were hanging around. One of them growled at him and he chucked a stone at it, making it yelp and run away. He spotted a map pinned up inside the abandoned waiting room and kicked in the door so he could go inside and take a proper look.

Where would they have gone from here?

He wandered out to look at the abandoned village, the quiet road. It was possible they'd hitched a lift, but how much traffic would there be in the middle of the night? None. Surely they would have headed towards the nearest town, Breva. He imagined them sitting here, waiting for first light, then walking into town along the road. That's what he would have done.

So here he was, having trekked through the forest, lovely in the morning light. Alina had been here. He could sense it. He had a photograph of her and he took it around town, going into bars and shops, asking if anyone remembered her. No one did. They all looked at the photograph with blank eyes. The young people asked him what it was like in the big city and he told them about the great riches there, how it was a place where dreams came true. He took a local girl with haunted eyes back to his fart-stinking room and showed her his genius beneath the sheets until the guy in the next room banged on the wall. The next night there was another girl, and the night after that there were two. He had intended to stay in town for a few days, until he either found some useful information about Alina or failed. He ended up staying for over a month.

Back home he was a nobody. An ant in the colony. Here though, as the exotic stranger, the man from the big city, he was a somebody, and he liked it. Maybe he could stay here forever, sleep his way through all the girls in town, although that was risky. He'd already had to hide out for a few days after the boyfriend of one of the girls he'd slept with found out about them and came look-ing for the out-of-towner. Despite his pumped body, Ion was a yellow-bellied chicken when it came to violence; it was one of the reasons the gangs back home wouldn't let him join. And on top of the danger from jealous boyfriends, he was running out of money, and there were no jobs here even if he wanted one.

He needed the money he would get from selling the cocaine. And if Alina had already sold the coke and spent the cash, he would make do with revenge.

But he had no way of finding her, no leads. Until he met the policeman.

Chapter Forty-Six

Alina had been here for forty-nine days now. She had counted the sunsets. A couple of times she'd panicked, sure she'd forgotten the number, but then it had come back to her. Little Luka was almost crawling now, rolling over and smiling at her. He was going to be a big, strong boy. She felt pride swell in her belly.

Her period had arrived yesterday. When the monster saw the blood he hit her, punching her again when she laughed and mocked him, told him she would rather die than bear his child.

She watched Luka playing with the wooden rattle the monster had left in the cot and wondered what Ion was doing right now. What had he done after he got off the train? Was he waiting for her to call him? Had he worried when she didn't get in touch? Did he care? She knew he wouldn't have reported her absence to the police, because of the cocaine. He would be too scared of questions. But what about the plan? What did the English couple do next? Did they carry the drugs unwittingly to England? Did Camelia rob them as planned? She could picture Camelia and Ion now, having decided to split the proceeds in two, pleased that she had vanished. When the monster raped her she conjured up pictures of her former boyfriend and the hate consumed her, created a force field that protected her from the reality of what was happening. It had been *his* stupid fucking idea, *his* fucking stupid fault. She lay in her bed and imagined hurting him, a red rage enveloping her, and her fantasies flickered between smashing the monster's face with a brick and smashing Ion's face, until the two became interchangeable. When the monster hit her, it was as if Ion had hit her. When the monster parted her legs, she remembered how Ion had done the same, and she regretted every second she had given to him.

And what about Daniel and Laura? At first, she had been convinced they would seek help, go to the police. They had come here to look for her, had escaped—thanks to her!—and she was sure they would send people to rescue her. That night, the monster had shot the two women in this room, replacing them with her. She had watched as he dragged the bodies from the room.

On her first full day here, chained to the bed, trying to be brave, to be defiant, she had heard voices downstairs, and was convinced the police must be here, asking questions. She screamed until her throat felt like it was bleeding. But no one came, not for hours, and then it was just him, the monster, and that was the first time he'd beaten her, little Luka watching from between the bars of his cot. That night, she had woken and sensed someone standing over her. Two people, she was sure. But she felt too groggy from the beating to focus, and she soon slipped back into unconsciousness.

For days after that, she waited, but still no one came.

And with every day that passed, her hatred of the English couple grew.

———————

The light between the window boards told her the sun had been up for a couple of hours but the monster hadn't come to see her yet.

Luka was crying, hungry, reaching out for her from his cot. Her chest ached, seeing him like that, but at the same time she allowed hope to flare. Maybe the monster had gone away, or was dead. OK, so her ankles were chained to this bed, but if she had enough time she was sure she could free herself.

But then the door opened and, as always, she braced herself. Would he discover that her period had started? Beside her, Luka whimpered as someone came into the room and switched the light on.

It wasn't the monster. This man was older, with a bald head. Despite his age he looked fit, with broad shoulders and a body with more muscle than fat. She recognised him but her head was so muddled she couldn't remember where from.

She began babbling immediately. 'You have to help me, I'm being kept prisoner here, a man kidnapped me. Are you the police? Oh God, please God, have you come to save me?'

He ignored her, walking over to the cot and lifting the baby, stroking his head and making little noises to comfort him. Luka was a good boy and he soon fell quiet. The man turned him this way and that, inspecting him. Finally, he nodded and put him back in the cot, handed him a bottle of milk and watched as the baby lay drinking it.

He turned to her. He appeared to be amused. Where did she know him from? She thought she had it but the knowledge slipped away.

He sat down on the edge of the bed and stroked her face.

He spoke to her in their native language. 'You've done a good job, looking after the little baby. Well done.' He patted her hand.

'Luka,' she whispered.

'You gave him a name?' He smiled. 'I like it . . . but he'll have a new one soon.'

She blinked at him. She was so weak, hungry, sucked dry of life and energy. She was filthy and needed a hot bath and tampons and clean clothes. Tears crawled through the dirt on her cheeks.

'Are you here to save me?' she asked.

He stroked her face again, brushing away a teardrop then squinting disapprovingly at the grey smudge on his thumb. 'I'm afraid not,' he said. 'Not you. Not now. I'm here to take little Luka.'

She jerked upwards, trying to push herself up onto her elbows. 'No!'

The man shushed her. 'Don't worry about him.' He laid a hand on her bare belly. His palm was ice cold. 'Soon, if all goes well, you'll have a baby of your own to look after.'

He stood up, the mattress creaking, and walked back over to the cot, bent to lift Luka, who had drained the bottle, foamy milk streaking the plastic.

The man walked towards the door.

Alina cried out. 'Please, no, don't take him. He's mine. He's my baby. Luka!'

The man stopped, tipping his head to examine her tear-streaked face. The way he looked at her reminded Alina of a farmer appraising livestock. For a single wonderful moment she thought he would change his mind, let her keep the baby. Instead, he lifted Luka's little chubby arm and made the baby wave. 'Bye-bye, Mama,' the old man said in a shrill voice. As Alina sobbed, the old man laughed and carried the baby out of the room. She heard his heavy footsteps thumping down the steps.

———⏝———

Several days passed. She couldn't sleep without the soft, snuffling sounds the baby made. She cried as if she was his real mother. When she wasn't thinking about Luka she tried to remember where she'd seen the old man who'd taken the baby away, but the inside of her head was so cloudy that every time she thought she had the answer it slipped away.

Shortly after dawn on the third morning without Luka, she heard a knocking sound from below. Somebody was at the front door. She wanted to cry out but was afraid of incurring the monster's wrath. She stayed silent and could make out men's voices coming from below. Three of them, she was sure. That made sense: the monster, the old man and the newcomer.

They talked for a while, and then she heard footfalls on the stairs. At least two people coming up. She braced herself, pulling the wretched blanket over her body.

The old man came in first, switching the light on, followed by a fat man in a policeman's uniform. For a moment, hope surged inside her.

'She's pretty,' the fat policeman said. He stepped closer to the bed. He had large hands and broken veins on his nose. A drunk. Alina's father used to have veins like that.

'Isn't she?' said the old man. 'One of the best we've had.' He pulled the blanket off her. 'Alina, take off your gown.'

She shook her head.

'Do it,' he snapped, raising a fist. The policeman watched, wearing an inscrutable expression.

Arms shaking, she pulled the gown up over her head, exposing her naked body. It was freezing in the room and she hugged herself, shivering.

'You want a go with her?' asked the old man.

'No. It's OK. A little early in the day for me.' The policeman chuckled. 'These days, I mainly like to look.'

Too fat and weak to get it up, Alina thought.

The old man nodded in an understanding way. 'Well, now that you've seen, we can go downstairs where it's warm.'

'Oh, must we?' the policeman said, his dead eyes still touring Alina's body. 'We can chat here, yes?"

The old man laughed and waved a hand. 'Oh, yes. You're not going to tell anyone, are you, Alina?' He laughed again. 'Take your arms away from your chest, girl. Show us what you've got. That's it.'

The policeman made a low sound as though suckling the breasts his eyes were feasting upon.

The old man went to the door and bellowed down the stairs. 'Dragoş! Bring us a bottle of vodka and two glasses. Not too early for that, I trust, Constantin?'

'Oh, no. Never too early.'

The monster appeared—so his name was Dragoş—with the drink and glasses, like a butler in a black and white horror movie. He fetched two chairs too and, after Dragoş had left the room, the two other men sat down, adjusting their chairs to maintain a good view of her, and opened the bottle.

'How's business?' Constantin asked without moving his eyes from her. Good God, was he going to jerk off right here and now?

'Oh, not bad. Just did an excellent deal. But I could do with some fresh stock.'

'I'll let you know if anyone suitable crosses my path,' said Constantin.

'Yes. The demand for high-quality product is stronger than ever. Especially among Russians.'

'But right now, you only have this one sow?'

The old man nodded and Alina blinked. The policeman really had used the word for a female pig. She fought back the urge to spit at him. If she could free herself from these manacles, get her hands on a weapon . . . She zoned out, entertaining herself with bloody visions of what she could do to him with a sharpened stick and a small knife. *I like to look.* She'd pluck out his fucking eyes. No need to cut off his limp dick.

'So, tell me what's happening in town,' the old man said. 'That's what you came here to talk to me about, yes?'

Constantin nodded towards Alina. 'A young man has been going around Breva, looking for this one, asking questions.'

'Really? What does he look like?'

'Hmm. Gym body, about five foot seven or eight, in his twenties.'

Ion! Oh God, he was looking for her. He hadn't given up. She tried to keep her face neutral but the old man was grinning at her.

'That sounds like her boyfriend, from the train. How sweet. He's come to try to find her. To save her.'

The policeman glanced at Alina, who was still trying to keep her face from betraying her emotions. She didn't feel completely alone anymore. Ion actually cared about her. In an instant she felt stronger.

'But don't worry. I have dealt with the situation. I have sent him off, searching for oranges.'

Alina swallowed. This was an expression often used by the older generation, dating from the time when the fruit was impossible to find in the country's shops.

'Good,' said the old man. 'What about . . . an English couple? Any British visitors to Breva?'

The old man stooped to pick up the vodka bottle as he said this, so he didn't see the look that crossed Constantin's face as he said, 'No. Why do you ask?'

Sitting upright again now, refreshing his glass, the old man replied, 'Oh, just something I heard about.'

Constantin shook his head and smiled. 'We don't get many visitors from England in Breva. Some steam train enthusiasts a while back, maybe one or two visitors to the Gold Museum. Oh, and a guy who was obsessed with werewolves.'

'OK. Well, that's good.'

271

After the men left, drunk and slapping each other on the back, Constantin casting a final greedy but impotent look at her body, Alina pulled the dirty gown over her head and stretched out her arm for the blanket. She couldn't reach it. She wrapped her arms around herself, shivering.

Why had the policeman lied about Daniel and Laura? She had seen his expression. He had definitely encountered them. Had they tried to report what they'd seen? She could imagine them talking to Constantin, him promising to look into it, the naïve Brits trusting this corrupt policeman.

Perhaps they thought they had done enough. She clenched her fists, digging her nails into her palms. Pathetic. Because she was still here. They were home, safe and well. And she had no doubt she was going to die here, the sow, slaughtered in an abattoir.

Chapter Forty-Seven

I on sat on his bed back at home in Sibiu. The first thing he'd done when he returned, exhausted and dispirited, was call for his cat outside. But after two months, the creature had no doubt found someone else to feed it.

After meeting the helpful policeman, Constantin, he had gone to Bucharest to look for Alina. According to the cop, Alina had been in Breva shortly after the incident on the train. The cop, who seemed much nicer than the bastards back home, went and spoke to the guy in the ticket office at the station who remembered selling a ticket to Bucharest to a girl matching Alina's description.

So Ion had gone to Bucharest. By this point, seven weeks had passed. Progress in the city was slow. He trudged around bars and seedy nightclubs, showing Alina's photograph to club-goers and doormen. A week in, a heroin addict Ion met in a hostel said he was sure he had seen this girl dealing drugs, he wasn't sure what exactly, at a club called Sapphire in a district called Dristor. Ion wasted another week hanging out at this sleazy place, but there was no sign of her, and no one else had seen her. Ion realised the heroin addict had been lying.

Then something really shitty happened. He attracted the attention of a group of local gangsters, who wanted to know what he was doing, if he was trying to muscle in on their turf. They beat him up, put him in hospital for two weeks. As soon as he felt better, when he no longer needed painkillers every four hours, he came home.

Shattered and sick of the fruitless search, he spent the last of his money on a bag of industrial-strength skunk and holed up with his Xbox. He could have stayed like that until hunger forced him out to find a job, to get on with life.

And then Camelia had called him.

'So,' she said. 'Did you find her?'

He groaned into the phone. 'No. She's vanished from the face of the earth. A policeman in Breva—'

'Where?'

'It's this shithole in Transylvania. He told me that he'd seen her, that she went to Bucharest. But I might as well have been searching for a virgin on—' He named the housing estate where he and Camelia had grown up.

'Fuck.' She sighed, then switched into a tone of voice he knew well. The sweet, seductive Camelia. 'Can I ask you a favour? Can you lend me some money?'

He roared with laughter. 'I'm skint, Camelia. I have no money. An eviction notice came yesterday. I'm going to have to get a job. Luckily I know a lot of dealers but . . .'

She cut him off. 'I've got some money issues myself,' she said. 'You know I owe a lot of money to the guys who helped get me over here? I've been paying them off by working at the club. Now they're saying they want their money back faster. They want me to go on the game.'

'Right.'

'To become a prostitute, Ion.'

'That's . . . bad?'

'Fuck you,' she spat. She sounded like she was on the verge of tears. He waited while she gathered herself. 'So. Have you found any evidence that Alina sold the stuff? Or that she's been trying to sell it?'

'No. None.'

'Shit. Maybe I was wrong. Perhaps the English couple did bring it back here after all.'

'But you said . . .'

'Yes,' she snapped. 'I know what I said. I thought that was the most likely explanation . . . Hello, are you still there?'

'Yes. I'm just wondering. If Alina didn't take the stuff, what's happened to her? Where is she?'

'I don't fucking know. But I bet our English friends do. I thought you'd be able to find Alina, that she'd leave a trail like some kind of punk slug. But now . . . the Brits are all we have. Our last chance of getting that money. Do you agree?'

Ion nodded.

'Well?'

'Sorry, I was nodding yes.'

She made an exasperated sound. 'I'm desperate, Ion. If I can't get my hands on some cash quickly I'm going to have to run.' Now she began to cry, a sound Ion couldn't bear. 'I don't know what I'm going to do.'

'Come on, calm down.'

'You've got the keys to their place, haven't you? Send them to me. When they're out, I'll go in, take a look around. Even if I don't find the stuff they must have loads of things I could sell. The guy looks like the type who'd have a top-of-the-range computer. She's probably got jewellery. There might be cash lying around. Please, Ion.'

He agreed to call her back then looked around the room, at the filthy carpet, the crappy furniture, the eviction notice lying face-down on the side table. He thought about how he was going to have to start selling drugs for some jerk who would treat him like a slave. But could he scrape together the fare to England? Maybe if he went by train. It would take a lot longer, but if he sold his Xbox, the remainder of the weed, went to visit his aunt and helped himself to some of her jewellery . . .

He cursed the idea that he'd wasted the past three months. But Camelia was right. The Brits must know something. He went online and searched English news reports. There was nothing about a British pair returning from Europe and handing in a haul of cocaine, and he was sure that would have made the news. He knew they hadn't been arrested at customs. That meant there was still a chance they had the cocaine or, if they'd sold it, the money. It was better than sitting around here doing nothing. And at the end of it, there was a chance he'd be rich.

He'd always wanted to see England too.

'Hold off,' he said, when he called Camelia. 'I'm coming over. Your knight in shining armour.'

Chapter Forty-Eight

Today was the day she was going to do it. Put an end to it. She giggled at the thought of his face when he came into the room and found her lying in a puddle of her own blood. What would he do? Would he cry? The notion made her giggle again, the laughter bubbling through her like water surging through an unblocked pipe. For months, laughter had seemed like something she would never experience again—like beer and pizza and soft sheets and shopping and bus rides and hair dye and friends and beaches and TV and books and music and cuddles and happiness. But now, now she'd started, she couldn't stop. *Blood, blood, glorious blood*, she sang to herself, changing the words to an English song she'd heard when she was a little girl, and she stroked the veins on her wrists and wondered it if would hurt and whether she'd care. And as suddenly as it started, the giggling stopped.

She had lost count of how long she'd been here. After the old man came and took Luka away (little Luka—she couldn't remember what he smelled like anymore; could barely recall what he looked like), she'd stopped counting sunsets. All the days, the long-short days, blurred and warped and ran together like a painting in the rain. All she knew was that it had got colder and colder in the room, that even with all the blankets wrapped around her she still shivered. She was sure Christmas had come and gone. It was a new year now.

She spent every day lying on the bed, fantasising about revenge. The cop, Constantin—she would push him from a great height onto spiked railings; they would pierce his arsehole, disembowel him while she shook with laughter. Laura and Daniel, for their pathetic attempts to save her—she would make him watch while she slit Laura's throat and bathed in her blood, and then she would cut off his cock and make him eat it before hammering a nine-inch nail into his puny chest. The old man, whom she hadn't seen for ages—he had a very special punishment awaiting him. She whiled away the hours daydreaming about sulphuric acid and knives and vinegar and ropes and hammers and pliers. Sometimes, she became aware that she was speaking her fantasies aloud—and that the monster was listening, excited by what he heard, pulling off his clothes. Those were the worst times.

The monster climbed into her bed every two or three days, more frequently in the middle of the month. While he did his thing—it never took very long—she imagined them in Hell together. But he would be a condemned soul and she would be a fallen angel, one of Satan's army, and they would spend an eternity of torture and suffering together.

Every day she hoped he would kill her so she could go to Hell and wait for him.

Sometimes when he was on top of her, she would look over his shoulder and watch a crack appear in the centre of the dim room, a tear in the fabric of the world, throbbing at the edges, and she would imagine herself stepping through it, escaping this world. In these visions, she didn't go to Hell but back to her old life, the city, and she would run through the streets, dodging traffic, laughing, dazzled by the lights and drunk on lovely exhaust fumes. The monster couldn't follow her there. Sometimes the crack appeared when he wasn't around, during her daily forty-five minutes of freedom, but when she stepped towards it, it would seal, like it had been zipped shut, and vanish.

Her period had come again this morning. Dragoş hadn't seen it yet. He came into her room, as always, at first light, with her breakfast on a tray. Water and porridge. He unfastened the clamps that held her ankles in place and left the room, allowing her forty-five minutes to exercise and wash. She knew he would inspect her when he came back, to see if she was pregnant. The blood disgusted him. She, as a woman, disgusted him. She could see it on his face. That must be why he never stayed to watch her when she washed or used the toilet—lucky, because her bladder would have exploded by now.

For a while after Luka was taken she had thought that maybe she could make him like her, feel some affection for her. Maybe she could persuade him to let her go. But when she talked to him it was as if she was speaking a foreign language; he didn't react. She kept trying, telling him about herself, her family, trying to make herself more human, to create a bond. Until one morning as she was speaking he punched her in the mouth and split her lip. She didn't talk to him again after that. She hadn't spoken for weeks.

Alina washed and used the toilet in the corner of the room. How long did she have left before he came back and chained her up again? Not long. She needed to act now. She started giggling again when she pictured him finding her, but forced herself to stop. *Blood, blood, glorious blood* looped in her head and the crack hovered in the centre of the room, luring her with its fake promise. She ignored it. There was only one way out of here.

279

She crossed to the window and listened. The forest was still, the birds silent. The house was silent too. Usually around now she would hear a toilet flush somewhere in the house. The monster taking his morning dump.

The window was covered by three rough, vertical boards, each one nailed to the window frame at each corner. A sloppy job. The nails hadn't been driven all the way in. For weeks now, during this forty-five minute period, Alina had been working on the middle board, alternately tugging at its edges and gripping the heads of the nails securing it and pulling on them, ignoring the pain in her fingertips. For days, none of the nails had shifted at all. But, like the sea eroding a pebble, she worked at it repeatedly until, one morning, the first nail moved a fraction. Encouraged, she redoubled her efforts until another budged, and then another, and then the last. She had to go slowly, working at loosening each nail's hole so that it could not only be pulled out but pressed back into place with her aching thumbs so the monster wouldn't notice anything. With all of the nails loosened, her leverage on the board increased, and increased yet again when she could get her fingers behind it and properly work at it.

And then, yesterday morning, the board and all its nails came free in her bloodied hands.

She had kissed it, a tear rolling down her cheek.

Now, it was time.

She pulled the nails out and tugged the board away from the window. Just as it had when she had first glimpsed it yesterday, the beauty of the scene beyond brought tears to her eyes. The snow-tinged trees, the clouds, the sky. She had thought she would never see the world again. It hurt her eyes and a line from a poem came to her, tumbling out of her subconscious. *Beauty is nothing but the beginning of terror.* She stood transfixed for a moment then heard a toilet flush in the bowels of the house and was startled into action.

She went to the bed and pulled the filthy sheet from the mattress. It was easy to tear a strip off; she wrapped it around her hand and went back to the condensation-streaked window. She raised her fist and punched the glass between the remaining boards as hard as possible.

The window shook but didn't shatter.

Taking a deep breath, she tried again. This time the window broke, a crack snaking across its middle. Panting slightly, Alina pressed against the glass, both hands wrapped in the sheet now, until a section fell away, bouncing down the outside of the house. She caught her breath, certain he would hear, that he would come running and stop her. But the house was silent. With her fingers still inside the sheet, Alina tugged at the broken glass, pulling away a perfect shard.

With a final glance towards the door, and the empty cot, she counted to three, determined to do it before she lost courage. She couldn't stay here any longer, not one more single day, and she closed her eyes as she sliced the glass across her arm and watched the blood as it flowed from her and dripped on the floor, watched it like it was somebody's else's arm, somebody else's vein.

She crumpled to the ground.

Chapter Forty-Nine

She was still breathing when Dragoș entered the room. A click as the door opened, a long pause during which she imagined him taking in the scene: her motionless body lying half-concealed beneath the dirty sheet, the hole in the window behind her exposing the snow-capped trees beyond, her arm outstretched, the blood pumping from her slashed veins, pooling across the floorboards towards the empty cot. She hoped, as her lifeblood left her, as her exit drew closer, that he would cry out, give her the satisfaction of hearing his pain when he realised how stupid he'd been, leaving her here unchained, trusting that her fear would keep her from doing anything stupid.

But there was no cry, no sound of pain. Instead, after the pause, the only sound was that of his footsteps coming closer as he rushed across the room, pausing to stare down at her before stooping to take her slashed wrist in both hands, a moment of hesitation before he reached for the sheet, pulling it away to expose her other arm, the hand in which she held the shard of glass.

With a scream that made birds rise from the trees outside, with all the hatred and fury that boiled in her veins, Alina drove the jagged spike of glass into his neck.

Dragoş collapsed onto his side, making a terrible choking sound that seemed to come not through his mouth but through this new hole. His arms spasmed as he tried to grab at the glass, to pull it out, but there was too much blood, the slippery liquid making it impossible for him to get a grip. Alina jumped to her feet as he thrashed about, the blood pumping from his body ten times faster than it had from hers. The cuts on her arms were superficial; she had taken care not to slice the major artery in her arm. She snatched up the sheet now and tore off another thick strip, wrapping it tightly around her forearm to stem any more blood flow. Her arm stung but this pain was nothing, nothing. As she tied the sheet she looked down at the monster, his legs kicking out as he tried to get onto his knees, slipping on his own blood and landing on his belly.

She ran to the open door and hurried barefoot down the stairs until she reached the hall in which the English couple had left her when they deserted her, abandoning her to her fate. She ran over to the front door, pulled it open. A blast of icy air hit her. She gazed down at herself. She was wearing only a grimy, blood-stained cotton gown. If she went outside like this she would die of exposure.

She looked around, and heard a thump from upstairs, a roar of pain. The monster was still alive. She needed to hurry. A cry stuck in her throat. Why hadn't she finished him off? She froze for a moment. Clothes. She needed clothes and shoes. Anything would do.

She didn't want to go back up the stairs. Forcing herself to stay calm, she remembered the room where the monster had taken her that first night, before Daniel and Laura arrived. A door led off from the corner of the hallway and she ran over to it, her shadow bouncing behind her. The door was unlocked and led, as she remembered dimly, through the fog of the last three months, to a short stairway down to another room. She ran down these steps now, stumbling and jarring her ankle. She swore, then laughed, then swore again before entering the room.

It was dim and smelled of bad breath and rank meat. There were a dozen heavy crates stacked up along one wall. She lifted the lid of the top crate and was shocked to see her own clothes inside. Her jeans, T-shirt, leather jacket. Her underwear. Her boots were there too, the ones she'd left in the forest and on his front path; Daniel had carried one into the house with them, and the other the monster had wrenched off when she tried to kick him as he dragged her towards the house.

She took off the disgusting gown and got dressed. It felt strange, unreal, to wear proper clothes again after so long. The bra felt too big, the jeans loose on her hips. She wondered if there was a mirror nearby, but dreaded seeing her own reflection. *I bet I look like a dead woman*, she thought, and something about this made something in her brain pop, and she grinned.

She checked the back pocket of her jeans. Her passport was still there. She remembered that on the train, the border guards had come through and checked it; she'd slipped it into her pocket instead of putting it in her bag. This was all going better than expected.

She heard a bang from above.

The front door? Had she left it open? She looked around the room, opening more of the crates, searching for a weapon. In one crate she found a pile of paperwork. It looked like a list of transactions. She took a few sheets, folded them and shoved them into her pocket. In the other crate she found women's clothes: twelve sets. In the cold room she suddenly became aware of their spirits, a dozen dead, and heard them whispering to her.

For us.

She took the lid from another one of the crates. It was stout, made of three strips of wood running lengthways with a single, shorter strip holding them together. Dropping it to the floor, she put her boot across two of the strips and pulled at the third, the dead women urging her on. She grunted, felt blood ooze from her cut wrist, but the strip of wood broke free. She hefted it, and headed towards the stairs.

At the top of the staircase, she paused before the door. Was he there, on the other side, waiting for her? She turned the handle and pushed it open, holding the plank over her shoulder, ready to strike. He wasn't there. She entered the room, looking left and right.

And she saw him.

He was lying a short distance from the bottom of the central staircase, a trail of blood glistening behind him. He held his neck with one red hand. In the other hand, which trembled as he reached out towards her, he held his gun.

His face, despite everything, remained blank. She figured he would be able to get off one shot before she reached him. She walked towards him, remembering all the times he had raped her, the way he had chained her to the bed, treated her like a dog, a sow, a slave. She recalled the pain and the loneliness and how it had felt when little Luka was taken away. When she was halfway across the hall, he squeezed the trigger with his last ounce of strength and dropped the gun, and it was as if the bullet passed straight through her—a miracle. She heard the voices of the other women rise into a chorus—*for us, for us*—as she reached him and raised the thick strip of wood.

After he was dead, after she'd smashed his skull and his face was no longer recognisable, a pulp of blood and bone, she dropped the plank and turned to see the bullet hole in the wall. It was no miracle. He was a bad shot. That was all.

⌒

Alina didn't remember much about the next week, about her journey through the forest, about breaking into houses and stealing food and money, checking the internet in an empty café and finding out where she had to go. She barely recalled hitching rides with men who thought they might stand a chance with her until she gave them the look that made them go pale. The days when she hid and the nights when she travelled merged into one, and she began to see her life like a graphic novel in which she was a dark figure who drifted across the panels, no speech bubbles, crossing a series of borders: Ukraine, Poland, Germany, where she paid a truck driver to take her with him to France. He was small and silent and had yellow teeth like a rat. He told her she reminded him of his daughter, who had gone missing when she was nineteen, a dozen years ago. He had never given up hope, he said. One day, he was sure, he would receive a letter or a phone call, just to let him know she was OK. Alina listened, thinking the girl was probably dead, had most likely been murdered, probably by this man beside her, and as she thought this she felt another spirit join her band. So there were thirteen of them now, following her across Europe.

In France, the man with the rat's teeth dropped her off and gave her a hundred euros which she spent on a ticket to Calais. There she boarded a ferry which crossed the English Channel on a freezing February night.

She stood on the deck and watched the dark coastline approaching. She was calm. The sea churned beneath the ferry and she decided that when this was over this would be a good place to end it.

After she'd cleaned up.

Another line of poetry came to her. *All angels are terrifying.* She smiled to herself. *Oh yes,* she thought. *And I am the most terrifying of all, the Angel of Vengeance. I am Mirela,* she whispered, and around her the thirteen dead women whispered *Amen* back.

Part Six

London
November 2013

Chapter Fifty

It was fully dark by the time we pulled up outside Erin and Rob's house. I was still reeling from what Edward had said.

Alina was alive. The shot we'd heard from inside the house hadn't killed her. Did that mean the baby was alive too? And the women who'd been tied to the beds in the upstairs room, who had haunted my nightmares for months—what about them? I badly wanted to know, because I needed some good to cling to among the chaos, the revelations that had come thick and fast since I'd hired Edward. Chief among these was the shock of working out, assuming I was correct, that Camelia and her partner-in-crime were looking for drugs.

I explained my thinking in the car on the way to see Laura.

'The dog, brought to sniff out drugs. All the questions about doing something illegal. It's got to be drugs.'

Edward agreed it made sense. 'So the person with Camelia on your video . . . Could it be Alina?'

I shook my head. 'It was definitely a man. So I think . . . if Alina's actually alive, and here, then it must be Ion. The guy in the video is the right height and build.'

'And the three of them are in together.' It felt as if the fog was clearing around me, our words cutting through it. But lots of questions remained. 'Why wait so long to come for the drugs?'

'Because Alina was trapped in that house?' I still could hardly believe she was alive. 'How did she get out?'

Edward swung the car hard around a corner. 'We'll be able to ask her soon.' Darkness glinted in his eyes. 'This Ion seems like the most likely candidate for firebombing my office. Trying to stop you from talking to me.'

'It must have been him at Camden Lock, watching Laura. And I bet . . . I bet he pushed Jake off that bridge.' Anger burst inside me and I thumped the dashboard. 'That fucker. Him and Alina. We trusted them. There are still . . . still parts that don't make sense.'

Edward swung around another corner. We were close to our destination now. 'My guess is that Camelia was their contact in London who was going to retrieve the drugs when you got back. I think they must have taken your passports so you would have to fly home straight away to get new ones, bringing the drugs with you. But then something went wrong: you and Laura got kicked off the train, along with Alina . . . Unless the whole thing with the house was part of the set-up—but I can't for the life of me work out how that could be the case.

'Also, I can't figure out this whole thing with Alina and Laura,' Edward continued. 'She showed herself to Laura, made contact with her. Do you think Laura knows that Alina is real? Or does she really think she's a ghost?'

The question irritated me and I felt a surge of protectiveness towards Laura. 'She definitely thinks Alina is a ghost. Listen, Laura is not stupid. But she's been through an awful lot . . . She's extremely vulnerable.'

Edward nodded. 'We need to talk to them, but my guess is that Alina was following Laura, spying on her, trying to find out if *she* had the drugs, and Laura saw her. And, believing Alina was dead, and having a track record when it comes to this sort of thing—'

I finished the sentence. 'Laura assumes that she's being visited by Alina's spirit.'

I prayed that Alina was still at the house. Then, finally, we would get all the answers.

We turned into the road where Erin and Rob lived.

'Oh shit,' Edward said.

I looked up, following his gaze as we pulled up to the kerb.

There was a police car parked outside Erin and Rob's house. My mouth went dry. What now?

I tore off my seat belt and jumped out of the car, ran towards the house and began banging on the door. Rob opened it almost immediately, a look of hope on his face that vanished when he saw me. He held a photo of baby Oscar in his hand. Behind him, in the hallway, Erin stood with two uniformed police officers. She was crying.

'What is it?' I asked. 'What's happened?'

Rob swallowed before he spoke. 'It's Oscar,' he said. 'We can't . . . we can't find him.'

Chapter Fifty-One

I tried to imagine what Erin and Rob must be feeling. I couldn't. Panic, terror, desperation. They were only words. The look on Erin's face told the whole story.

She came over to the door. She held a small pink comforter, with the head of a teddy bear, which she gripped so hard her knuckles were white. She had dark circles around her eyes, as did Rob, and her hair stuck up at a hundred different angles. She wore a loose top with what I realised were milk stains on the front.

'Has she been in touch with you?' she demanded. 'Do you know where she is?'

'You mean Laura?'

'Yes!' She spat the name through clenched teeth. 'Who else? She's taken my baby. That . . . bitch has stolen my fucking baby.'

One of the police officers, a black woman with a round, kind face, stepped forward, laying a hand on Erin's shoulder. 'We don't know that Miss Mackenzie has done anything criminal.'

Erin turned on her, the comforter trembling in her hand. 'Nothing criminal? She was meant to be watching Oscar while Rob and I grabbed an hour's sleep. I knew we shouldn't have done it, should have taken him into bed with us.' Her voice cracked.

'But I'm so tired. So, so tired. I thought it would be OK for an hour.'

Rob tried to put an arm around his wife but she shrugged it off.

'What was I thinking, trusting that crazy bitch with my baby? She tried to kill herself last week. She talks to ghosts. She's insane.'

'Ghosts?' the policewoman said, confused.

'Yes, she—'

'Alina's not a ghost.'

Everyone turned to look at Edward, who had appeared in the doorway. He introduced himself.

'I think you'd better come in,' said the policewoman. 'I'm PC Elaine Davies.' She also introduced the male police officer, who nodded at us as Edward shuffled into the hallway and closed the front door behind him. An expensive-looking black pram sat beneath the coats that hung on the wall. Rob glanced at it then looked away like it stung his eyes.

'You're Laura Mackenzie's boyfriend, is that right?' Davies asked me, leading Edward and me out of the crowded hallway into the living room, while the other cop took the two stricken parents into the kitchen. I heard him say something about putting the kettle on in a falsely bright voice. The living room was messy, with muslin squares screwed up on the floor, teddy bears and cuddly rabbits lying around, DVDs spilling out of box sets. The room had a musty, sweet smell, a faint trace of baby poo.

'Yes. Well, ex-boyfriend. We came here to see her . . .' I trailed off. 'What happened?'

'As she said, Mr and Mrs Tranham asked Laura to keep an eye on Oscar so they could grab an hour's sleep. Oscar was asleep in his cot in the nursery upstairs. Do you have children yourself, Mr . . . ?'

'Sullivan. No, I don't.'

'I remember when my daughter was a newborn. All you think about is sleep. It becomes a kind of obsession. When she woke up, Mrs Tranham looked at the clock and saw that two hours had passed. She had asked Laura to wake her after an hour but assumed Laura was trying to be kind. She went into the nursery. Oscar wasn't there. He wasn't anywhere. And neither was Miss Mackenzie.'

'She's probably just taken him out for a walk,' I said, not really believing it.

'She didn't take the pram,' Edward said, and PC Davies nodded.

'That's right. And Mrs Tranham has a baby sling too, but that's hanging up in the nursery. As far as the Tranhams can tell, Laura hasn't taken anything with her. The bag they use to transport nappies in is still here. Mrs Tranham says that they had just used the last nappy from the packet and the new one hasn't been opened. And you saw the comforter. That was left in the cot.'

'Have you tried ringing her?'

I didn't blame PC Davies for the look she gave me. 'It's going straight to voicemail, immediately, like it's off. So you've had no contact from her?'

Edward spoke as I shook my head. 'I saw her a little earlier. That was at four-thirty. Two and a half hours ago.'

'Where was she?'

'Standing in the garden. She was talking to a young woman called Alina, a Romanian woman.'

Davies had her notepad out now. 'Alina? Do you have a surname?'

'No. Sorry.'

'And what's her relationship to Miss Mackenzie?'

I looked to Edward for help. He shrugged. 'It's complicated.'

'All right. Let's come back to that. You said something . . . about a *ghost*?'

'Yes. Laura has a history of imagining spirits. When she told Daniel that she'd seen Alina, he assumed that she was seeing another ghost. We believe Laura thought she was a ghost too. But she's very much alive. I saw her.'

The policewoman looked at both of us in turn, trying to work out if we were winding her up.

'So Laura Mackenzie has mental health issues?'

'No! I mean, she has been . . . acting strangely recently. But she's not crazy. And she would never harm a baby.'

'Or allow it to be harmed?' the policewoman asked.

'She drove Erin to the hospital, was there at the birth. Erin's her best friend. She would never allow anything to happen to her baby.'

Davies made more notes in her pad. I saw that she had written the words 'mental health' and wished I hadn't said anything about ghosts.

'So,' the policewoman began. 'This Alina was here at four-thirty as well?'

Edward nodded. 'That's right. In the garden.'

'Let's take a look, shall we?'

To reach the garden we had to go through the kitchen. Rob was in there with the male PC, holding a mug of tea close to his lips, not drinking it. I could hear something buzzing from upstairs.

'Erin had to go and express some milk,' Rob explained. 'She should be feeding Oscar right now.'

Davies made a sympathetic face. 'We're going to find him, Mr Tranham. I promise you.' He was clearly desperate to believe her. 'We need to take a look in your garden.'

Rob unlocked the back door and led us outside. It was dark, but the police officers had torches which they switched on, the twin beams crossing halfway down the lawn.

'We hardly come out here in the winter,' Rob said, as if he was apologising for the overgrown lawn, the mulchy leaves that swamped the flower beds.

297

'They were standing right here,' Edward said, indicating a spot parallel to the side gate. 'Laura was here, facing into the garden, while Alina was here, looking towards the house.'

'Alina?' asked Rob. 'Who the hell's that? When did you see them?'

'Could you hear what they were talking about?' Davies asked, addressing Edward but placing a hand on Rob's arm.

'No. Laura doesn't know me so I thought it was better to fetch Daniel, to get him to talk to her, confront her with the truth that Alina is real.'

Davies tutted loudly then walked off across the lawn towards the end of the garden, sweeping her torch beam left and right. I wasn't sure what she was looking for. Some evidence that Laura had brought Oscar out here?

Edward and I tried to follow her but she told us to stay back.

'Who the hell is this Alina woman?' Rob pressed us. 'What is going on?'

When I assured him it was all too much to go into now, pleaded with him to be patient a few minutes longer, he surprised me by acquiescing. I think he'd reached overload for the moment. He slumped against the house, chewing his fingernails.

Near the back wall was a little copse of apple trees and a shed where the lawnmower and gardening tools were stored. We could see Davies's torch flitting about in the darkness. There was a creak and a bang, which I assumed was the policewoman yanking the shed door open.

'Mr Tranham,' she called a moment later.

Rob walked past us towards her voice and Edward and I followed. When we reached the shed, Davies said, 'When was the last time you looked in here?'

'I don't know. I think I cleared it out just before Christmas.'

'Do you recognise these items?'

She shone the torch into the dark interior of the shed. I peered in, standing just behind Rob. There was a sleeping bag stretched out on the floor, and crisp packets and chocolate wrappers were scattered around it, along with several empty water bottles.

Rob's mouth dropped open. 'No. Well, the sleeping bag is ours, but it's usually hanging there, wrapped in its bag, next to the other one.' He pointed. 'The rubbish . . . that definitely wasn't here before. Oh my God.'

'Looks like someone's been living in your shed.'

'Alina,' I said. I guessed that she usually put the sleeping bag away during the day and took away the rubbish.

Davies rubbed her chin. 'This kind of thing happens quite a lot. We often get calls from people saying they've found a homeless person squatting in their shed.'

'Won't anyone tell me who the fuck Alina is?' asked Rob, looking at me, his fists clenching and unclenching like he was going to grab hold of me. 'Is that who's taken Oscar?'

'In a moment, Mr Tranham,' Davies said. 'Come on, let's go back to the house. Mr Sullivan, I need a full description of this Alina.'

She took her radio out and called in as we walked back towards the house, relaying my description of the Romanian woman we had left for dead in that house.

When we reached the kitchen, Erin had reappeared. She held a bottle of breast milk. Rob took it from her gently and put it in the fridge while Erin stared into space, seemingly lost. Capable, calm Erin was paralysed. She stared at her phone, as if it would give her the answer she so desperately needed. Where was her baby?

'There's another person we need to tell you about,' Edward said. 'Alina's boyfriend. His name is Ion. There's a third party too, called Camelia.'

Edward went on to tell the police officers about how he believed it was Ion who had thrown a Molotov cocktail into his office. He told them the bare, essential facts about everything else too. How Laura and I had met Alina and Ion. How we believed the Romanians had come looking for us, and why. I was glad he didn't mention the house in the forest because as he talked Davies looked more and more like a woman who was paddling out of her depth, while Erin and Rob stared at us incredulously. Davies scribbled notes in her pad.

I explained about the break-ins, the dog attack, how I'd reported most of it to the police already. I was going to mention Jake too but could see that this could be a distraction.

'The important thing,' I said, 'is that they think Laura is either holding or knows the whereabouts of the drugs they planted in our luggage. I bet they've got Laura and Oscar locked up somewhere now, and that they're threatening to harm the baby if Laura doesn't tell them what they want to know.'

'Harm the baby?' Erin shrieked at me and I flushed with shame.

'I'm sorry, I don't mean . . .' Rob was looking at me like he wanted to kill me. Like it was me who had taken his baby. 'They haven't done anything violent so far.'

'Apart from set a dog on you and chuck a fucking Molotov cocktail into this guy's office!' Rob's face was purple with anger, a vein throbbing in his forehead.

'Mate, calm down.'

'Don't fucking call me mate!'

'I'm certain Oscar will be fine,' I said, turning to Erin. She sank into a chair, covering her face with her hands, sobbing.

Rob pointed a finger at me. 'This is your fault, you and Laura. We knew something freaky had happened to you in Romania and now we know what. You got mixed up with drug dealers. And you brought them here. You put my family in danger.' His face twisted in fury as he jabbed his finger into my chest. 'Why didn't you warn us? If anything happens . . .'

There was nothing I could say. No way I could defend myself.

Davies stepped between us. 'This isn't helping. Mr Tranham, I need you to stay calm.'

Rob tried to get round Davies, to get to me, and the male police officer grabbed hold of Rob's arm, holding him back.

'Come on, sir.'

Rob shot me a look of contempt. 'Where are they? These drug dealers? If you don't help us find them, if anything happens to Oscar, I'm going to kill you.' And he started to cry, his chest heaving as Erin pulled him towards her and they embraced.

I stared at them, trying to imagine their pain, knowing that this was worse than anything I'd been through. And in that moment I vowed to help them. I was going to find Laura and Oscar. I was going to end this.

Chapter Fifty-Two

Davies asked me to give her full descriptions of Alina, Ion and Camelia. She left the room to make a phone call, and returned a few minutes later with an update.

'OK. Photos of Laura and Oscar are going straight into circulation along with descriptions of the three Romanians Mr Sullivan told us about.'

Erin made a whimpering sound.

'We don't know,' Davies went on, 'that this trio have anything to do with it. There's still a very strong chance that Miss Mackenzie has taken Oscar out for a walk and will come back through that door at any moment, wondering what all the fuss is about.'

'At which point, I'll throttle her,' Rob said.

We all knew that Laura hadn't simply taken the baby out for a stroll.

Davies took a deep breath. 'We've got more specialist officers on their way here now,' she said.

'Specialists in what?' Rob asked. 'Child abduction?'

Davies nodded hesitantly.

Right on cue, the doorbell rang. Rob rushed to answer it, and when he returned to the kitchen he had a man and woman with him, both wearing suits. The man was in his fifties, with five o'clock shadow and baggy eyes; the woman was British Asian, with sharp eyes that flicked across each of us in turn before resting on Edward. She nodded and I realised they knew each other.

'Well. Fancy seeing you here,' the male detective said. 'You wait all year for a case involving Edward Rooney, and then two come along at once.'

They introduced themselves to the rest of us as Detective Inspector Rita Desi and Detective Sergeant Simon Farrow. Davies took them into the living room to brief them.

'You're in good hands,' Edward said to Erin and Rob. 'My work brings me into contact with the police quite a lot, and Desi is one of the good ones.'

After five minutes that felt much longer, the detectives returned, Davies loitering behind them.

'This is quite a tale you've told,' Desi said, looking at Edward then me. 'I suspect there are a lot of missing details, though. Am I right?'

Edward met Desi's eye. 'I promise you, Detective, we've told you everything you need to know.'

'You should let us judge that.'

'It will take too long to explain it all,' I blurted. 'We shouldn't be standing around here chatting—we need to be out there, looking for them. It's got to be the Romanians. Once we find them, we'll find Oscar.'

Davies took Rob and Erin back into the kitchen, leaving Edward and me with the two detectives.

'Have you checked with Immigration?' Edward asked. 'We think Ion and Camelia only entered the country recently.'

'We're checking it now,' Desi said. 'It would help if you knew their surnames.'

Mark Edwards

'What about the Romanian community in London?' Edward asked. 'Have you got officers talking to community leaders? Going round the Romanian bars and cafés?'

'Please stop trying to tell us how to do our jobs.'

'I'm just saying what I was planning to do next.'

Desi pursed her lips, and I wondered if she and Edward had a history. I couldn't stand still. I wanted to be out there now, doing what Edward had suggested—racing around the places frequented by Romanians, describing Alina, Ion and Camelia.

I pulled Edward aside and spoke in a low voice. 'Let's go. We're not doing any good waiting here. We'll drive around. You can take me to all these places you were planning to visit. We might find someone who knows something before the police do.'

He looked over at the detectives. Desi's phone rang and she turned away to take the call, wandering into the hallway. Farrow had gone into the garden to look at the place where Alina had been sleeping.

'Come on then.'

We slipped out the front door and walked over to the car. This was better than being stuck in that house with Erin and Rob crawling the walls with anxiety, waiting around for the detectives to do something.

'You really shouldn't blame yourself,' Edward said. 'You didn't invite this chaos into your life. It found you.'

I didn't reply.

'I'm going to look up Romanian restaurants,' I said. As I tapped words into Google on my phone, Edward nudged me and I looked up. We watched as Desi and Farrow hurried out of the house to their car and, without hesitation, sped away, tyres screeching.

'Something's happened,' Edward said, and my stomach lurched. 'Let's find out what.'

I closed my eyes and prayed that they hadn't found a body, or maybe two, and all I could see was that tiny coffin in the house in the forest.

Edward pulled out into the traffic and began to follow the detectives' car.

Chapter Fifty-Three

The detectives attached their 'blues and twos' to the top of their car, the blue light flashing, siren wailing, and we followed in their wake as the heavy traffic pulled aside. Darkness clawed at the windows as we got stuck in an underpass before finally emerging onto the A12, which would give us a relatively clear run east. I gripped the seat, staring out at the flickering city lights, flinching as a taxi cut across lanes between us and the detectives' car. Edward hit the brake; the car shuddered.

'Arsehole,' Edward breathed, shifting gears.

'Do you know this area?' I asked.

'Not well. I had a client whose husband was cheating on her with a woman who lived near Valentines Park. It looks like we're heading in that direction.'

Please, I prayed silently. *Please let Laura and Oscar be there.*

It wasn't until after we'd pulled off the main road into a series of side streets that we lost the detectives' car. Edward swore, turning from one small, cramped road into another. Many of the houses had large satellite dishes for picking up foreign TV channels; others displayed England flags. We reached a dead end and Edward backed up, tried another street.

'There,' I said excitedly, pointing at two marked police cars parked outside a little house, along with the detectives' grey Passat. A small crowd had come out of their houses to watch. I jumped out as soon as Edward squeezed into a parking space and ran up to the front door. I banged on the door and a uniformed officer opened it.

'Are they here?' I blurted.

The female police officer's face was a worrying grey colour, like she'd just seen something sickening. She said, 'Sir, this is a crime scene; please step away from the house.'

Edward reached us just as Desi came to the front door. She looked just as ill as the first woman.

Sick with fear and desperate to see inside, I tried to push past them but the two women blocked my path. 'You can't come in here,' Desi said.

'What's going on?' Edward asked. 'We saw you run out of Erin and Rob's house . . .'

'And decided to follow. Typical. We got a call . . . A neighbour reported someone crying for help, broke in and called the police.'

There was a ball of ice in the pit of my stomach.

'Is the baby here? Laura?'

Desi stepped past the policewoman onto the overgrown front path. She rubbed her face.

'No, they're not here. But Ion is. And a woman.'

She sucked in freezing air and exhaled, her breath clouding the space between them. 'Ion has taken a hell of a beating but he's still alive. But the woman is dead. Beaten to death.'

I gawped at her. *Please, God, no . . .*

'What does the other woman look like?' Edward asked 'Red and black hair? Punky looking?'

'No. Nothing like that.'

307

I couldn't hold back. I ducked past DI Desi and ran into the house past the policewoman, whose back was turned. Desi shouted, 'Hey!' and I could hear her chasing me into the squat, but I was faster. I heard voices coming from a room up ahead and ran through the door, not caring that I was contaminating a crime scene. The police had their backs to me, looking at the body of the woman on the floor.

I couldn't see her face and, in the shadows, it was impossible to see if her hair was blonde like Camelia's or strawberry blonde like Laura's. I crept closer, holding my breath.

It was Camelia.

I gasped, and one of the police officers turned around and shouted at me.

Desi arrived, grabbed my arm and helped another officer drag me out of the house. She pushed me onto the lawn.

'You fucking idiot,' she barked at me.

'I needed to see, to check it wasn't Laura.' I turned to Edward. 'It was Camelia.'

Desi threw up her arms in exasperation then went back into the house, but not before snarling, 'Keep out.'

Edward put an arm around my shoulders and led me out of the garden to the pavement. At the same time, more police arrived and began to string up crime scene tape across the entrance to the house; two officers urged the growing crowd to keep back. Children ran about in the road, excited by the action, while their parents strained to see what was going on. Edward led me across the road, away from the mob.

I could hear a siren wailing, growing louder. An ambulance pulled up across the road. The siren cut out, and two paramedics got out and jogged into the house. Before long, they came back out and went in again, carrying a stretcher.

'Come on,' Edward said, leading Daniel to the rear of the ambulance.

After a few moments, the paramedics came back out of the house, bearing the stretcher with Ion on it. Detective Desi walked just behind them. Ion lay with his face towards us, eyes closed. Seeing him again sent a shudder through me and I put my hand on the ambulance to steady myself. Members of the crowd had raised their phones and were filming the scene; a woman shouted something about foreigners and filthy squatters.

As the stretcher reached the back of the ambulance, Ion opened his eyes and looked straight at me.

He smiled.

'Hello, Daniel,' he said.

The paramedics began to lift the stretcher but Desi held up an arm. 'Wait.'

'We need to get this man to hospital now,' one attendant said.

'Just a moment.'

Ion continued to stare at me, the faint smile still on his lips. He winced with pain as he forced out a few words. 'I just. Wanted. To make. A little money.'

I wanted to grab hold of him, to hurt him for what he'd done, what he'd put us through. For what we were still going through. Edward saw the anger on my face and held me back.

'Nothing personal.' Ion squeezed his eyes shut.

'Where's Alina?' Edward asked.

Ion opened his eyes again, still looking at me. 'Alina?' He tried to laugh, the act sending a new spasm of pain through him. The paramedics rocked from foot to foot, tried to move the stretcher, but Desi urged them to wait a moment.

'Yes. Where is she? Please tell us.'

'I wish I knew,' he said.

'We have to get him to hospital now,' the paramedic said again, and in a blur of movement they lifted the stretcher into the back of the ambulance, slammed the doors shut and drove away, siren blaring.

Edward turned to Desi. 'What did he tell you? Who did this?'

The detective inspector addressed me instead. 'Mr Sullivan, do you know anything about an old man? In his sixties or seventies. Bald head. Blue eyes. Romanian. Does that mean anything to you?'

I stared at her, bewildered.

'Ion told us this is who attacked him. An old man, speaking Romanian.'

'Did this old man say anything to him?'

'He said, "Do you remember me?" But Ion didn't. He swears he's never seen him before.'

'And you asked Ion about Oscar?' Edward said.

'Of course I did. It was the first thing we asked him. He didn't know anything about it. And I believe him. He's been lying there for hours. None of these three can have anything to do with Oscar Tranham's disappearance.'

'Except—'

Desi cut him off. 'Go home, both of you. Leave it to the professionals.' She pointed a finger at me. 'And you—stay home, don't go anywhere. It seems like everyone in this fucked-up case is connected to you. I'm going to want to talk to you later.'

She marched off towards the house, a dozen camera phones flashing around her.

Chapter Fifty-Four

*P*utrescent putrescent putrescent putrescent . . .
Laura sat in the back of the devil's car, baby Oscar asleep in her lap, his little head resting against her chest. Alina sat beside her, staring out the window at the cars passing on the motorway. The devil was driving, his eyes—those cold, hooded eyes—glancing at them every so often in the rear-view mirror. Alina was, Laura noticed, wearing her seat belt. Which was surely strange behaviour for a ghost. Had this devil given Alina human form, granted her a new body in which to walk the Earth again? Laura wanted to reach out and touch the Romanian woman, to see if she was warm or cold, but was too afraid.

. . . *putrescent putrescent putrescent . . .*

She thought back to earlier, replaying what had happened. She found it hard to connect to any of it. It was like she was watching herself on a movie screen from a great distance. Playing it back, it was easy to believe that she was an actress, playing a part in a strange, scary movie. But then Oscar would squirm against her and she would remember: this was real. And she couldn't withdraw into herself, pretend it wasn't happening. Because she had her best friend's baby with her. As if reading her mind, Oscar opened his eyes and focused on her, oblivious, trusting. Innocent. She had to keep it together. Not for herself, but for him.

At about half-past four, the devil had dropped her back at Erin and Rob's house after rescuing her from the crazed Romanian woman. In the garden, she had spoken to Alina, telling her what had happened. Alina had asked a lot of questions about the woman and the old man. Especially the old man. Laura wasn't certain, but Alina appeared scared.

Could a ghost feel fear?

Then Laura had heard Erin calling her and gone inside. She realised now that she had neglected to lock the back door. Erin told Laura that she and Rob were about to die of tiredness and could Laura watch Oscar for an hour while they took a nap? Of course she agreed. Her friends went to their room and she watched Oscar sleeping in his cot for a while, sitting in the chair by his side, trying not to think about what had happened earlier, trying to decide if she should call Daniel. She knew she should, but he thought she was crazy. He wouldn't believe her when she told him the devil had saved her. She imagined him calling her parents, and her mum turning up with a doctor. A doctor who would take her away to a hospital and give her pills and put her to sleep.

She would rather take her chances here, with the devil and the ghost of a murdered woman outside, than go to a hospital.

What happened next? She had smelt something sweet. Oscar had filled his nappy. She wanted to help her friends, to allow them more than an hour's sleep. If she could change Oscar's nappy without waking him . . . She had seen Erin do it, knew what to do. But the nappies and wipes were in the living room. With a last look at the deeply sleeping baby, she crept out of the nursery to the living room.

When she got back, he wasn't in the cot.

She tried not to panic. Erin or Rob must have come to get him. She ran down to the kitchen, expecting to find one of her friends there with their baby. Instead, she found the back door standing open. And just outside stood the devil, with Alina beside him.

The devil was holding little Oscar. Laura looked from him to Alina. The ghost was immobile, no expression in her eyes. So ghosts *could* feel fear. It made sense: a ghost would be afraid of the devil. Laura could hear her own heartbeat, *ba-boom ba-boom ba-boom.*

The devil spoke in his soft but deep voice. 'Come with me.'

Laura opened her mouth.

'If you scream, or make any noise at all, I will kill the baby. He wouldn't be the first.'

He walked off towards the gate, holding Oscar in one arm, his other hand gripping Alina's wrist, pulling her along. Laura followed, realising she was still holding the nappies and baby wipes. Once they were in the car, the devil said, 'Just so we are clear: any attempt to get away, and I *will* kill the baby.'

A little while later, he pulled over and watched Laura while she changed Oscar on the back seat. Oscar woke up, and made that little bleating noise he made when he was tired or hungry. The newborn baby poo smelled sweet, like sugary milk, and the devil told her to pass him the dirty nappy.

He got out of the car for a minute, to put the nappy in the boot. Laura whispered to Alina: 'What's he going to do with us? With Oscar?'

Alina trembled. Her eyes were wide open but, Laura was sure, she wasn't seeing Laura or the interior of the car. What could she see? The inside of the house where she'd died? Had she met the devil there?

'I've been watching all of you,' he said, getting back into the driver's seat. 'It's been most entertaining. You know, I love young people. So sure you know best, certain that you know how the world works. Looking with pity, or indifference, at people my age.'

Laura was confused. These were strange words for the devil to speak.

'You still have so much to learn.' He grinned again. 'So very much.'

At one point, on the motorway, Oscar, who had fallen asleep as they left London and entered Essex, had woken up and cried out, rubbing his head against Laura's chest, searching futilely for her nipple. He cried out and Laura shushed him, wished she had something for him to drink.

'He's hungry,' she said.

The devil laughed. 'There's milk at the house. We'll be there soon. In the meantime, keep him quiet.' He looked at her in the mirror again, then at Alina.

'I only need one of you. You would do well to remember that. I only need one of you to start again.'

Beside her, Alina began to cry. Laura was startled. Alina? Crying?

She reached out instinctively to comfort the dead woman and was shocked to find her hand making contact with warm flesh.

Chapter Fifty-Five

We got back into Edward's car and sat in silence for a moment. I felt curiously calm. Many times in my working life I have encountered a nasty problem—a piece of code, an element of design or user-friendliness—and worried myself into a frenzy of stress, only for a tranquil sensation to come over me. There is always a solution that can be found through logic and clear thought.

The police didn't know Laura. I did. Surely this placed me in a better position than them to find her and Oscar. I was also the only person, apart from Edward, who knew the whole story. I explained this to Edward.

He raised both eyebrows. 'Except we don't know the whole story, do we? Who is the old man?'

'I don't know. Let me think.' I tapped my forehead, speaking aloud to aid my thought process. 'We thought Ion and Camelia had taken Laura and the baby so they could blackmail us into telling them what we'd done with the drugs. But we now know that isn't the case.' A pause. 'Ion said he didn't know where Alina is. Maybe he was telling the truth.'

Edward hung his head from what I assumed to be exhaustion. I didn't feel tired at all. My body hummed with adrenalin. I hadn't felt like this for a long time. Since emerging from the forest that night three months ago, I had been confused, anxious, unable to think straight. A week ago, faced by this situation, my impulse would have been to hit the bottle, hide away and hope for the best. But I felt absolute certainty: this fucked-up situation, this mess, this horror story, had started with me, with a single unwitting mistake I'd made back then, choosing not to buy the more expensive sleeper tickets. That decision had set everything else in motion. Now I had a chance to redeem myself.

Something had been germinating at the back of my mind since Edward had discovered Alina was alive and in London. I had never considered the possibility that the man from the house would try to find Laura or me. But now that I knew that Ion had followed and found us, it made me think. Had someone else followed us too? Or maybe . . . Alina was here. She had seemingly escaped. And—my mind whirred through the problem—her abductor had followed her. Killing Constantin en route? The timing of the man's disappearance was too perfect for me to believe anything else. I had believed from the very beginning that Constantin was corrupt, that he already knew about the house, which was why we'd fled Breva. Constantin had gone missing at the same time all the weird stuff had started to happen here. But what had occurred over in Romania? Did Constantin try to save Alina? Had Alina killed the policeman? Whatever the answer, the fact that Constantin had vanished just before Alina appeared in London made me think it couldn't be a coincidence.

And when she escaped, the man holding her prisoner had come after her. And today, everything was coming to a head. He had killed Camelia, left Ion for dead, then grabbed Laura and, I presumed, Alina, taking Oscar too.

Edward started to ask me something but I held up my hand. I needed to think.

There was one problem with this theory: the man we'd seen in the house had not been old, according to Ion's description. He'd been in his thirties. But perhaps he had an accomplice. Someone who already lived here? Or someone he had sent over?

'Call your police contact in Romania,' I said. 'I think I know why the house is empty now.'

I explained my theory.

'I don't know . . .'

'Do it, Edward.' He looked surprised by my new assertiveness. 'We need to know who lived in that house.'

As the private investigator called the number I watched the squat, though it was difficult to see much thanks to the crowd of rubberneckers outside. Another ambulance had arrived and I watched them carry out Camelia's body. An image flashed in my head: Camelia on top of me on my sofa, blood streaking her half-naked body, the top of her skull caved in. I shuddered and closed my eyes, forcing the image away.

I listened as Edward spoke to the English-speaking police officer in Breva, impatient to know what was being said at the other end of the line. Edward made a note on a piece of paper, said, 'OK,' a few times, then ended the call.

'Well?'

'He wanted to know why we are asking so I told him your idea, that this abductor and murderer—who the police over there don't even believe exists—had come to London.'

'And what did he say?'

'He said that they'd managed to find out who owns the house. Or rather, who owned it.' He held up the sheet of paper on which he'd jotted the name. *Nicolae Gabor.*

'You said owned? He's dead?'

'Disappeared, presumed dead. Apparently, he was a policeman during the years of Communist rule. My new friend in Breva said Gabor had something of a reputation . . . When I asked him for more details he told me to look him up on Google. But they are going on the assumption that Gabor owned the house but never lived there, and when he disappeared it was just left to rot. An abandoned house in the forest.'

I had already taken out my phone and typed Nicolae Gabor into Google. I quickly found his name on a page called 'Villains of Communist Romania'. The page, which contained a long list of 'crimes against the people,' was in Romanian so I pasted the web address into Google Translate.

'According to this he was a member of the Securitate, the secret police.' I read aloud, amending the slightly garbled translation as I went along. '*Like many of his comrades, Gabor was vicious and corrupt, using his high rank and the . . . terror he induced in ordinary people to amass a personal fortune. Following the Revolution, a number of women came forward to claim that Gabor had raped and abused them, that he ordered his underlings to use the fear of rape as a tool to intimidate whole families.*'

'A real charmer,' Edward deadpanned.

I carried on reading aloud. '*After abortion was made illegal after 1966, many of the children fathered by Gabor and his squad of rapists were sent to the country's terrible orphanages where they suffered appalling cruelty.*'

There was a link to a page about Romanian orphanages during the Communist era. I had read about these places before, just a paragraph in my Eastern Europe guidebook. I had tried to read the section aloud to Laura—the terrible facts about children tied to the bars of their cots, the systematic abuse and neglect—but after a few lines she had tears rolling down her cheeks, and I had to stop reading. It was too awful to think about.

But it echoed what we had seen in that house, with a sickening twist. This time the mothers were chained up, emaciated, the babies relatively healthy and well-looked-after. The baby we had seen, anyway. We had no idea what had happened to the others, like the poor soul in that tiny coffin.

'*After the Revolution, Gabor disappeared. He is assumed to have been murdered by one of his former victims seeking revenge. But no body was ever found.*'

I lifted my eyes from the screen. 'But he didn't die. He moved to that house and carried on raping women, getting them pregnant.'

'Except he's not the man you saw there, is he? He's too old.'

According to the web page, Gabor would be seventy now. I shook my head. 'The man we saw must have been an accomplice.'

'Is there a photo of Gabor?' Edward asked.

There was no photo on the page I'd been looking at, so I went back to Google and submitted the search again. There was nothing immediately obvious.

'I'm going to head over to see Sophie, check how she is,' Edward said. 'I'll drop you at home on the way.'

'But I don't want to go home. I need to be out here—looking.'

He ignored me and started the engine. 'There's nothing more we can do at the moment, Daniel. We need to leave it to the police.'

'No. I want to go to the hospital, to talk to Ion. I need to know more about this old man. He asked Ion if he remembered him. Maybe I can jog his memory with this information about Gabor. Maybe Ion knows where to find him.'

'But there's no way the police will let you see him. We don't even know if he's still alive.'

'I don't care. I'm still paying you, aren't I?'

As we were arguing, I continued to flick through results pages on the search engine. Another result caught my eye. *In pictures: The men of the Securitate.* I clicked on the link and waited for the page to load, then scrolled down. There were numerous photos of men wearing secret police uniforms, frowning at the camera. Halfway down the page was a shot of Nicolae Gabor taken in the late eighties, shortly before the Velvet Revolution. He was quite handsome, with a strong jawline. He glared at the camera, clearly unhappy to have his photo taken.

As he stared out of the photo, I stared back. It felt like he was looking right at me. Into me. And as I stared at the photo, I recognised him. I'd seen him before.

Chapter Fifty-Six

We pulled into the hospital car park twenty minutes later. I asked Edward to let me lead and he nodded his agreement. At the back of my mind I knew I was heading for an adrenalin crash, that soon my body would notice that I hadn't eaten anything all day. But for now I was riding that chemical wave.

I wasn't entirely sure how we were going to locate Ion but as we entered the lobby I spotted the female police officer who'd been at the squat. I followed her at a discreet distance as she walked towards the lift, Edward a few steps behind me. The lift arrived and as she got in I hurried closer, saw her press the button for the fourth floor.

The stairwell was located beside the lifts, so I ran up the stairs to the fourth floor without waiting for the private investigator. I didn't feel at all out of breath when I reached the top, just in time to see the policewoman press another button just down the hall and wait to be buzzed in through a set of double doors.

I followed, pressing the red button and waiting to be admitted. An Asian nurse let me through but then stepped in front of me.

'Visiting hours finished an hour ago,' she said.

'I'm police,' I replied, using my authoritative voice. There is no great trick to getting people to believe a lie. You simply have to sound convincing. In this case, it also helps if you act like you are going to be aggressive towards anyone who gets in your way. 'I'm here to see Ion . . .' I trailed off, realising that I still didn't know his second name. 'The stabbing victim. It's urgent.'

'Oh, yes . . .' She hesitated. Shit. She was about to ask to see my badge. So much for fooling her with my authoritative air. But then another nurse appeared and called her, used the word urgent, and the Asian nurse hurried after her.

'Nurse, which bed?' I called.

'Forty,' she replied as she vanished around the corner.

Edward's face appeared at the door and I buzzed him through. 'Bed forty,' I said. 'If anyone asks, we're police.'

'What? Oh, I see.'

We walked through the ward, searching for bed forty. It wasn't hard to spot. The ward was divided into several distinct areas. Bed twelve was in the furthest of these, easily identifiable because of the policewoman sitting on a chair beside it, flicking through a magazine. Ion appeared to be asleep, or unconscious. He was hooked up to a drip, along with a machine that monitored his heartbeat. I guessed he'd lost a lot of blood.

'We need to distract her,' I said.

Edward chewed his lip. 'All right. Wait here. You'll only have five minutes, OK?'

I backed away, hiding behind a large laundry bin on wheels, aware of a couple of other patients watching me suspiciously, while Edward hurried up to the policewoman and began to wave his arms about. He gestured frantically for her to follow him. She hesitated, looked at Ion, then made her mind up and followed Edward towards the exit of the ward. As soon as they'd gone past me I approached the bed. I wanted to pull the curtain around for privacy but feared this would attract attention, plus I wouldn't be able to see anyone coming.

Ion's torso was wrapped in bandages and his breathing was ragged, his face pale and sweaty. There was a vicious purple bruise around one eye and more bandages on his head. Looking down at him I experienced a surge of hatred. But I was glad he was still alive. There had been so much death, so much blood. Ion, by some miracle, had survived. And now he had a chance to make amends.

I put my hand on his shoulder—it was cold and damp—and shook him. He stirred, wincing as he came out of sleep. But he didn't open his eyes. I tried again and, leaning close to his ear, whispered his name. I was aware of time ticking away. Either the policewoman or a nurse or doctor could appear at any moment.

'Ion,' I whispered again, and he opened one eye. It took him a moment to focus. I guessed he would have been given heavy pain-killers but they couldn't completely eradicate the soreness from the beating he'd received.

'I'm lucky,' he said. I had to lean closer to hear him. 'I have a hard head.' He laughed, which brought on another coughing fit. He screwed up his face in agony. 'My ribs.'

'I need you to concentrate,' I said. 'Laura and a baby, a completely innocent baby, are missing. I need you to answer some questions.'

He looked at me through half-closed eyes, a small smile on his lips. Perhaps the painkillers made him feel high. Or maybe he found this whole situation amusing.

'The old man who attacked you—was this him?'

I held up my phone to show him the photo of Nicolae Gabor.

Ion nodded almost imperceptibly. So that confirmed it. Gabor was here. *Everything* was connected to what we'd seen in that house.

'Was he part of your gang? Were you working for him?'

He laughed, making a hissing noise, pain shooting across his face. 'The old man? I never saw him before.'

'Don't lie, Ion.'

He frowned with confusion.

'He was there, on the train. He was the old guy that Alina helped with his luggage.'

'Helped with his . . .' Realisation dawned on Ion's face. 'Oh my God. I didn't recognise him. I didn't remember.'

I believed him. Unless Ion was lying about the old man asking if Ion remembered him, it had to be the truth. My mind raced, trying to make sense of it all. Gabor had been on the train. We had been kicked off close to his house. That couldn't be a coincidence. He must have arranged it in some way.

I would work it out later. Right now, there were things I needed confirmed. 'What happened on the train, Ion? You planted drugs in my and Laura's backpacks?'

Pain flickered across his face. 'You found it? The cocaine?'

I ignored this. 'And then you sent Camelia to try to find out what happened to the cocaine?'

'Yes. You know—' He coughed. 'It would have been a lot easier if we'd done what Camelia wanted to do after we checked your bank account. There were no big deposits, so we were sure you either still had the coke or the cash from selling it. Camelia was all for us crashing into your place then and there—tie you up, stick a knife in your face, force you to tell us where the coke was, what you'd done with it.' He shook his head. 'But I'm not a violent man, Daniel.' He tapped the side of his head, and winced. 'I use my wits, not my fists.'

'We never had the cocaine, Ion. I didn't even know for certain that I was right until you just confirmed it. We left our backpacks in Romania—with the cocaine still inside, I assume—at the police station. With a cop called Constantin.'

Ion's eyes widened. 'That *bastard*.'

I heard a noise at the other end of the ward. A middle-aged man calling for a nurse. I didn't have long. I needed to get to the point.

'Ion—do you know where they are?'

'Who?'

'Laura and the baby. And Alina.'

Confusion flickered on his face again.

'Did Gabor say anything about them?'

'No.' He coughed. 'He was too busy beating me with an iron bar to stop for a chat.'

'He didn't say anything about taking Laura and Alina?'

'Why do you keep talking about Alina?'

'Because . . . What do you mean, why do I keep asking?'

'I haven't seen Alina since that night.' He rolled his head and stared at me, his eyes opening a fraction more.

My mouth gaped open. 'You didn't know she was here?' If he hadn't seen her since the train, he wouldn't know what had happened to her. And right now, I didn't have time to tell him.

'What happened after you were thrown off the train?' he asked. 'You came home, but where did Alina go?'

I didn't reply. I was too busy thinking. I still didn't know who had taken Laura and Oscar. A sickening thought hit me. What if Alina had taken them? Alina, seeking revenge because Laura and I had left her in that house? Or maybe Alina knew Gabor was after them, and they were hiding. But why take the baby?

Edward and the policewoman were still absent, but a nurse had come into view. She was standing with her back to me, but could turn round at any moment. If she saw me, she would throw me out.

'I have to go,' I said. This visit had been a waste of time, even though Ion had confirmed my theory about the drugs. I still couldn't remember where I'd seen Gabor and Ion was no help.

There was a question that had been bugging me for ages. I decided to ask Ion before I went. 'Why did you and Camelia return my laptop?' I asked.

'Huh? We didn't. I bought myself a nice new one with your card, but Camelia had your old one.'

'So she returned it?'

'No. She sold it.'

'But . . . it ended up back in my flat. It's the same computer.'

Ion gave me a blank look.

'Who did she sell it to?' I asked quickly. The nurse had turned around and was walking towards us, a stern expression on her face.

Ion thought about it for an agonisingly long moment. The nurse was almost at the bed. 'Some old guy she met at the pole-dancing club. She sold your PS4 and iPad to him too. She was laughing about the idea of this old guy playing *Call of Duty*—'

I interrupted him. 'The old man she sold my laptop to—was it Gabor?'

'I don't know. I never saw him. But he was Romanian, like us. That's all I know.'

'Excuse me, you're not allowed to be here.'

The nurse folded her arms across her chest, tapped her foot.

'One moment.' I grabbed Ion's arm. His skin felt cool, clammy. The nurse moved towards me. 'Are you sure?'

'Yes. I remember now. She said she sold it to a man who had been harassing her at work. She said it was a weird coincidence: the day after we . . . came to your flat, he asked her if she knew anyone with a laptop for sale, because he needed one.'

No such thing as coincidences, I thought.

'It must be Gabor. He must have been watching her . . . Saw her come out of my flat . . .'

'I really must ask you to leave,' the nurse said. 'I'm about to call security.'

I looked up at her, so stunned by what Ion had said about the laptop that I could hardly see her. But I became aware of another person walking towards us. The policewoman. And behind her, Edward, gesturing for me to come.

I jumped up from the plastic chair, ducked past the nurse, swerved around the policewoman before she could challenge me and grabbed Edward's arm, thumping the door release button with my palm and pulling him out into the corridor. We ran down the steps, our footsteps echoing dully behind us.

'What did you tell the policewoman?' I asked.

He waved a hand. 'Oh, that I'd just seen someone steal an old lady's bag. I led her on a wild goose chase through the hospital. I am going to be in so much shit if they find out what we were up to. You know I rely on the police in my work?'

'Do you want to know what Ion told me?'

We reached the bottom of the stairs and headed through the lobby.

'My laptop. Camelia didn't return it to my flat—she sold it to Gabor.'

He stopped walking. 'What?'

'*He* must have returned it. How did he get a key to my flat? Jesus, it's like every-fucking-body had a key. Half of fucking Romania was waltzing in and out!'

'Why would he return it?' Edward asked as we exited the hospital. 'You checked it for spyware, didn't you? When it first reappeared?'

'Yes. But . . . Oh shit.'

'What?'

I broke into a run towards the car.

Chapter Fifty-Seven

Laura stared out at the motorway. Since leaving London they had driven in what was pretty much a straight line, through Essex, the devil sticking to the fast lane whenever he could, the speedometer nudging 100 mph. Then they hit traffic and the devil hissed and cursed, rhythmically rapping the steering wheel with his knuckles as the car crawled forward.

Oscar, thank God, was asleep, his face against her chest, occasionally making a little snuffling noise that broke her heart. He had cried himself to sleep as they left London, the devil growing increasingly irritated. Laura had rocked and shushed the baby, telling the devil the baby needed milk, that he was hungry.

'There'll be milk when we get there,' he said.

'He's breast-fed,' she dared to say. 'He won't drink formula.'

The devil snorted. 'He'll soon drink it if he's hungry.' He turned and looked through the gap in the seats, staring blatantly at her chest, making her skin creep. 'He wouldn't get much of a meal from those. Good hips though. Healthy, physically at least. Your tits will grow when the time comes.'

Alina sat in silence through all of this, staring straight ahead. Like she really was a ghost, an apparition. Laura could smell her though.

Stale sweat. The stink of fear coming from her pores. Not a ghost. Real. And if Alina was real flesh and blood, it followed that the old man driving the car was not a supernatural being either. He was just a man.

They were stuck in traffic for a long time, the old man's impatience growing every minute. At one point, Laura thought he was going to get out and punch the car in front. Finally, they started moving again. Laura counted the cat's eyes in the road to calm herself down. When she was a child she would play a game where she would count white cars and red cars on family trips. If red cars outnumbered white, something bad would happen: she would fall ill, one of the girls who bullied her at school would be extra vicious. If white won, something good would occur: her mum would leave her alone for a day, Beatrice would visit her.

There was no point counting cars today. The worst had happened. She had resigned herself to it. Her only hope now was that she could protect Oscar. If she could somehow persuade this old man to return him to Erin and Rob, she would do whatever the devil asked. She would accept her punishment.

———

They turned off the M11 and skirted past Bishop Stortford, heading further east. Laura saw a sign for Hatfield Forest and soon they were turning onto a quieter road, then another, lined by jagged trees. The beam of the headlights illuminated them as they reached out towards the car with bare, spindly branches. Beyond the headlights' beam lay the deepest, blackest night.

They headed further into the forest. Laura clamped her eyes shut, held Oscar against her. She could hardly breathe. The car slowed and she opened an eye, saw that they were approaching a large house half-concealed by ancient trees. Oscar squealed and she realised she had squeezed him.

Beside her, Alina looked equally stricken. The ghost of a ghost.

The car drew to a halt outside the house and the devil killed the engine, leaving the headlights shining.

Laura could hear Alina breathing. Strangely, witnessing the Romanian woman's fear made her feel braver, forced her to assume the role of the strong one. The car's lights revealed a period house with white painted walls, a house that had stood here for such a long time that it felt like an organic part of the forest. It appeared to be in some disrepair, cracks in the window, the roof sagging in places. There were no other houses in sight.

'Just like home,' the old man said. He grinned at Laura, then turned his attention to Alina. Although his accent was thick, he spoke perfect English, like someone who had been studying it for a long time. 'You thought you'd escaped me, didn't you?'

Alina refused to look at him.

'Remember when I came to take little—what did you call him?—Luka away? We should have killed you then. Dragoş was growing weak, as was his seed. Unless it's you who are barren.' His smile was cruel. 'We shall soon see. I'm going to do the job myself now.' He rubbed his groin. 'Still life in this old dog.'

Laura thought she might vomit. She struggled to make sense of what the man was saying. But it was clear he was connected to the house, that terrible place.

The man shifted his gaze to Oscar, forcing Laura to focus on the present moment.

'This one will fetch an excellent price. I already know a couple who will be interested. A Russian couple, old acquaintances, who've moved to London. Too old to have a baby themselves now.'

Laura heard Alina whimper. Or had she made the noise herself? She wrapped her arms protectively around the baby. 'What are you talking about?'

It was cold in the car now the engine was off, and the man's breath plumed as he spoke. There was a gleam in his eyes that chilled Laura more than his words. He had the air of someone who believes himself to be invincible.

'Your friend here killed my son. A bastard, but still, my son. She ruined everything. You know how long we lived in that house, happily running our business? Twenty-four years. Since I was forced to flee my job because of the fucking revolution.'

Alina looked up at that point, her mouth slightly open, revealing the gap in her front teeth.

'Before that, it was a good time to be a policeman. A powerful position. So many women.' He said this wistfully, and went on, entranced by his own story. 'Most of the babies that I fathered went to the orphanages but when Dragoş's mother became pregnant I was starting to think about my legacy. When the baby turned out to be a boy I decided to keep him. The mother was . . . a bigmouth, never knowing when to shut this.' He pointed at his own thin lips. 'So, after she . . . died, I bought the old house in Hunedoara and sent Dragoş to live there with *my* mother, God rest her soul. She raised him. And then, years later, at the same time Dragoş came of age, the revolution happened. And I disappeared.'

His eyes shone in the darkness. Laura was reminded, in a perverse way, of her granddad, who never passed up the chance to reminisce. 'It was boring at first. So dull, after all the excitement of my job. But then one day, when Dragoş was a teenager, something wonderful happened. Can you guess?'

He looked from Laura to Alina and back, then gave a disgusted grunt. 'No imagination! A pair of hikers appeared at our house. A young man and woman, lost in the forest, like Hansel and Gretel. They came to the door, asking for directions. So I strangled him and then Dragoş and I had fun with the girl. It was about time Dragoş lost his virginity.' He paused. 'Hmm. I can't remember if we made

Hansel watch while we screwed Gretel. But anyway. I decided to keep her, so we finally had something to entertain us. It was fun.'

Laura swallowed hard. Oscar wriggled again on her lap.

'And then,' he said, as if he was growing tired of the story, 'Gretel became pregnant. Maybe my baby, maybe Dragoş's. I was going to kill her but then had an idea. A stroke of genius. We were running out of money. And I was so bored, even with a nice young girl to fuck. I went back to some old contacts, people who had clung to their wealth. And the rest, as the saying goes, is history.'

Alina spoke up, making Laura jump. 'You're a monster too. Like your son.'

He laughed. 'She speaks! No. I am a businessman. There is a demand, so I supply it.'

Laura reached out and took Alina's hand, squeezing it gently. After a moment's hesitation, Alina squeezed back.

'You have spirit, I'll give you that,' he said to Alina. 'I knew you would come here, to England. Because you wanted *revenge*, didn't you?' He pointed at Laura. 'She wanted revenge against you, for going without her. For leaving her to rot. Isn't that right, Alina?'

The Romanian women cast her eyes downwards. She didn't reply.

'Constantin, that fuck, lied to me. You witnessed it, Alina. He blatantly lied, because he didn't want me to know about the drugs he'd found in your backpack, Laura. He paid the price for that. I buried him in the forest. The last thing he said, thinking the information would save him, was your and your boyfriend's names.'

He reached out and stroked Oscar's downy hair. 'This little one wasn't part of my plan. He's a bonus. Another sign from God.' He stroked the baby's head again and Laura fought the urge to snatch Oscar away, to cover him with her body. 'I was excited to find the baby in your care, Laura, his parents asleep in their bed.'

Laura hugged Oscar against her. She had been trying to work out why the old man had taken her back to Erin and Rob's after finding her in that squat. She had thought it must be because he was targeting the baby, but if he now spoke of Oscar as a bonus . . .

'Why?' she asked. 'Why take me back if you weren't planning to snatch Oscar?'

The old man grinned and pointed a finger at Alina. 'Because this naughty girl has been hiding from me. I've been waiting for her to show herself.'

Laura understood. When she'd told Alina about the devil rescuing her from Ion and the other Romanian girl, Alina had finally come out from her hiding place—revealing herself to the man who was hunting her.

She snapped out of her reverie as she heard the old man speak again.

'Alina, you destroyed what I had in Romania. But it's fine.' He smiled like a wolf. 'I can start again. Here in England. And I already have my first little piglet to take to market.'

Chapter Fifty-Eight

I asked Edward to make coffee while I booted up the laptop. While I waited, I grabbed a sheet of printer paper and attempted to draw a Venn diagram, with stick figures representing the players in this drama. In one circle, the Romanian would-be drug dealers, Ion and Alina and Camelia. In another circle, Gabor and his unnamed accomplice, the man at the house. On the periphery, unwittingly drawn into the drama, Erin and Rob and Oscar. The policeman, Constantin, was there too, as was Edward. And in the centre, where all these circles intersected, were Laura and me.

Camelia had sold the laptop to Gabor. It had to be him. There were no other old Romanian men in the picture. I knew how Ion's group had gained access to my flat: they had the set of keys they took from Laura's backpack. I didn't know how Gabor got a key. Maybe he'd picked the lock. For now, it didn't matter.

'What are you doing?' Edward asked, sitting down beside me.

'Checking my spyware.'

'But you already did that, didn't you?'

'I know. But only when the laptop was first returned. I didn't tell you about another weird thing that happened.' I told him about the photographs from the train that had vanished before my eyes.

'For God's sake, Daniel, why didn't you tell me about that before?'

'I was afraid that I'd imagined it. That I was losing my mind.' If I wasn't crazy, there was only one possible explanation for the way the pictures had vanished. In the hospital car park, trying to work out Gabor's motive for returning the computer, I had remembered what had happened immediately before I saw the photos that vanished: I'd received the email with the kitten picture from Laura. Except I was willing to bet that it hadn't really been from Laura. If I'd looked closer at the time I would no doubt have seen that it had come from an email address set up in Laura's name. And the picture of the kittens had contained what I was now looking for. Gabor must have guessed I'd check my laptop for viruses when it was mysteriously returned—so he'd delivered the virus later.

I explained this to Edward as we waited for my virus-checking software to scan my machine.

Then it stopped. An alert flashed up on the screen.

I put my face in my hands. 'Fuck.'

'What just happened?' Edward asked.

I tapped the laptop screen. 'There it is. Spyware.' I turned my head to look up at him. A piece of software on my laptop that gave someone else remote access to the computer. They could see everything I typed. They could add and delete files.

'Can they see what you're doing now?' Edward asked.

I returned to the keyboard. A minute later I said, 'OK. I've blocked the connection. But they'll be able to see that I've blocked it. If they're looking right now, they'll know I'm onto them.'

'And can you trace them? Find the other person's computer?'

'Let's see.'

While I worked, Edward called Rob and Erin's house and spoke to PC Davies, asking how the couple were doing.

'What did she say?' I asked after he'd hung up, not looking up from the screen. I was getting close. Gabor's computer was still trying to connect to mine and I was trying to find the IP address of that computer.

'Erin's gone to sit in the nursery, staring at Oscar's cot. Rob's gone out to search. Apparently, he couldn't bear to stay in the house doing nothing. The police have already gone door to door to talk to all the neighbours . . .'

'Did any of them see anything?'

'She wouldn't tell me much. But Rob's got most of these neighbours out of their houses, and they're going round the adjoining streets . . .'

I continued to type into the Command box, edging closer to finding that IP address.

'Davies said they've shown Laura's photo on the news. It's all over the web. People on Twitter are going crazy, calling her a baby snatcher, sharing her picture . . . The whole country is looking for her.'

I winced. 'That's so *wrong*. She wouldn't have taken him.'

I returned to the screen, tapping commands into the box, edging closer. Gabor appeared to be using some out-of-the-box hacking software, not particularly sophisticated. He'd probably bought it off some kid on the dark web.

'Got it,' I hissed.

'It?' Edward asked, sitting up straight.

'The IP address. Right . . .'

I went onto the web and pasted the IP address, a string of numbers, into a specialist website. The result came back within seconds, giving me the region along with the longitude and latitude.

'It doesn't give me the exact address, but . . .'

I opened Google Maps and brought up the area in which the IP address was located. My eyes met Edward's.

'Back to the forest,' I said, and a chill rippled across my skin.

Chapter Fifty-Nine

The old man led them up the crooked path. First Laura, holding onto Oscar, her arms wrapped around the baby to guard against the bitter cold, then Alina, trailing behind, her chin dipped. Laura's legs were stiff and she felt like there was a swarm of flies buzzing inside her gut.

'Come on,' the old man urged, unlocking the front door and grabbing Laura's elbow, pulling her inside. He was strong, and Laura suppressed a shudder at the thought of his hands on her flesh. He grabbed Alina too and shoved her, sending her staggering ahead of them into an entrance hall. The air smelled of dust and it was even colder, if that was possible, inside the house than out among the trees. Laura tried to catch Alina's eye but the Romanian woman had withdrawn again. Laura knew how terrifying this must be for her. Laura could only imagine what was going to happen, what it would feel like. Alina had been here before, in another house, another forest. And Laura wasn't scared for herself. All she cared about was protecting Oscar.

The baby was quiet and motionless in her arms and she hugged him against her, worried that the cold was making him weak and listless. Cold and hunger. Could a baby his age go into shock? He needed his mum, he needed milk, warmth, familiar comforts. Her body pulsed with hatred for the man who had brought them here. Yes, just a man. And men could be hurt.

The old man made a sweeping motion towards the stairs and swore at them when they held back.

'Do you want me to hurt the baby?' he asked, reaching out, and Laura snatched Oscar away, which made the man laugh. Then his face grew stern and impatient. 'Get up there.'

Laura went first, then Alina, the old man following. They went up one floor and he flapped his arms, telling them to climb to the next. Just as in the other house, there was a closed door at the top of the stairs. The old man reached past them and turned the handle. The door swung inwards and they stepped inside.

Alina stiffened. Laura reached out to touch her arm.

It was a replica of the room in Romania, but smaller with fewer beds and cots. No Polaroids on the wall. Yet. The two beds had white sheets and blankets, metal frames. Two sets of cuffs were attached to the frames at each end of both beds. Laura could hear Alina's breathing grow heavier. She tried to stay calm, to take in the rest of the room. Next to the second bed was a white wooden cot. Piled up in the cot were several wool blankets, and Laura hurried over and snatched them up, wrapping them around Oscar. The old man watched her do this and blew on his hands.

'Good girl,' he said.

She turned to him. 'You can't believe you'll get away with this, do you? The police will find us.'

He smiled. 'You might want to feed him.' He nodded towards the far wall, where a table contained numerous items, the kind of things you would find in the home of anyone with a small baby. Plastic bottles, tubs of formula milk, nappies and wipes, barrier cream and a packet of dummies.

The windows were boarded up, planks of wood nailed across the panes.

'Can't have a repeat of what happened to Dragoş, can we?' the old man said to Alina. He nodded at Laura. 'Why don't you make the baby a drink?'

Laura hesitated, not sure what to do with Oscar.

'I'll take him,' the man said.

Laura thrust Oscar at Alina. The Romanian woman blanched.

'Take him,' Laura urged, and Alina acquiesced, holding him as if he was made of crystal, like he might shatter in her arms.

There was cold water in a jug. Laura poured some into a bottle and added three flat scoops of formula powder.

He had never had formula milk before. Would he take it, especially cold like this? Would it make him sick? She took him back from Alina, sat down and gently pressed the teat against his lips. After a few moments, he took it and began to drink, obviously starving. She felt him relax, and he looked up at her with his big blue eyes.

The old man watched.

'I knew you'd be a good mother,' he said. 'The first time I saw you. I have a sixth sense for it now, after all these years. When you went into that sleeper carriage without the correct tickets—'

Laura's eyed widened with surprise.

He laughed. 'Yes, I heard you all chatting about it. I was watching you, thinking how wonderful it would be to have you at my house. The beautiful, valuable babies you'd have. I watched this little bitch's boyfriend sneak into your carriage and come back, the two of them whispering together.'

Laura glanced over at Alina, who hung her head.

'And I was still watching as the train started to near my house and the border guards appeared. That's when I realised: I could make this happen!'

Laura stared at the old man as Oscar continued to drink from the bottle.

'I had a nice little chat with the border guards, told them about the arrogant English couple travelling in the sleeper without a ticket. That I'd heard you boasting about it, saying there was no way these Romanian morons would throw you off the train in the middle of nowhere.' He was talking faster and faster now, his breathing growing heavier, excited by his own tale. He pointed at Alina. 'It worked out even better than I hoped. I wasn't expecting this one to get thrown off the train too.'

'You're going to die,' Alina said.

He laughed. 'I'm starting to think I should only have brought the English woman. I only need her.' He reached inside his jacket and took out a knife.

'Get on the bed,' he said to Alina.

Laura watched as Alina obeyed, lying flat on her back upon the empty single bed, her arms crossed over her chest, no emotion on her face. The old man snapped a cuff over one ankle, then the other. He did the same to her wrists. He pressed the sharp edge of the blade against Alina's throat and put his face close to hers.

'You killed my son,' he said.

'It felt great.'

Alina continued speaking, switching to Romanian. Her voice was low, a sneer on her face as she spoke. The old man responded, also talking in his mother tongue. Although she couldn't understand the words, it was clear to Laura that Alina was taunting him, and that it was making him angry. His face grew pink as Alina spat harsh words at him, then laughed. Then she said something that made him stand straight and look at Laura, surprise in his eyes.

He stared at her for a long moment, as Oscar finished his bottle, and then he laughed again. He was about to speak to her when Oscar opened his eyes and began to cry, a sudden wailing that made the old man clasp his hands over his ears. On the bed, Alina laughed, and the old man pointed the knife first at her and then at Oscar.

'Shut him up,' he said.

Laura tried to shush the baby, rocking him in her arms. 'He's still hungry,' she said.

'I don't give a fuck. Shut him up now.'

He approached Alina again, the knife outstretched. The baby continued to scream, louder and louder, resistant to all attempts to quieten him. Alina's laughter grew increasingly hysterical, tears rolling from the corners of her eyes.

'Shut up!' the old man yelled. 'Shut the fuck up!'

Something banged far below them. For a moment, Laura didn't think the old man had heard it above the infant wailing and the laughter. But then he stopped moving, cocked his head.

'Do anything while I'm gone and I kill this bitch *and* the baby,' he said. He left the room and Laura heard the click of a key turning and a lock snapping into place. And as soon as he'd gone, Oscar fell silent, as if it was the evil old man's presence that had been making him scream.

Alina stopped laughing and rolled her head towards Laura.

'Do *exactly* as I say,' she said.

Chapter Sixty

We drove into the forest and stopped a hundred metres from the house we were looking for. As Edward killed the engine we were plunged into silence, as sudden as switching off a radio. I opened the door and got out, staggering like a newborn foal. The sight of the trees in the darkness made me cling to the car, my instincts screaming at me to get back in, get out of here, back to the city and lights and people.

Here we are again.

I felt like a man who is scared of heights standing on a cliff edge. I could hear the trees murmuring, stretching out their bare branches and whispering my name. Somewhere in the dense foliage, something shifted and darted away.

This time you won't get away.

'Are you all right?' Edward asked, joining me.

I licked my dry lips. 'I thought . . . I was going to be OK. But it's just like . . .' I swallowed, though there was no spit in my mouth. 'It's just like last time.'

'You want me to go alone?' he asked, placing a hand on my shoulder. 'You can wait here.'

'No. No! I have to do this. They're just trees. It's just a forest. And the place we're going—it's just a house.'

And the man we're looking for—he's just a monster.

'We don't know for certain this is the right place,' Edward said.

'It is. I can feel it.'

He didn't respond to that. We had stopped briefly in the village on the edge of Hatfield Forest and gone into the pub, asked the barmaid if she knew of any houses in the forest that had been sold or rented recently. A large, secluded house, probably. I felt certain that Gabor would look for something familiar. And if he had been planning to take Laura and Oscar, he would need somewhere without close neighbours.

'The old witch's house,' said a man at the bar with pock-marked skin.

I whirled to face him. 'What?' I was thrown back to the night in the forest, standing at the door, a little boy's voice in my head telling me a witch lived here.

'It's not actually a witch's house,' laughed the barmaid, who was in her mid-forties, with twinkling eyes. 'People just call it that because the local kids all said the woman who lived there ate children. She died, ooh, five years ago now.'

'I heard someone had bought it,' said the man with the acne scars.

They drew us a map showing us how to get there, not asking us why we were looking for it.

'I still think we should have called the police,' Edward said now, looking along the dark path that led in the direction shown on the map. 'We should have left it to them. This fucker firebombed my office, almost killed Sophie—and me.'

We had figured out that Gabor must have seen me submitting the online contact form to Edward and felt compelled to act. I guessed that was his main reason for spying on me. To see if I had told anyone about what I'd seen in Romania. I tried to follow his reasoning. It would be much riskier for him if he killed me or Laura. There would be an investigation, a manhunt. It was much harder to get away with murdering a middle-class couple in the middle of London than in remote Romania. He must have been out of his criminal comfort zone, a spider straying from his web. So he'd decided to watch. To see if we did anything that necessitated the risk.

'We've been over this,' I said.

I knew if we went back to the police we would have to go through the whole story, the details of how we'd traced Gabor, in great detail. It would take time—time we didn't have while Laura and Oscar were in danger. And there was another reason: I wanted to do this myself. I wanted this chance to make things right.

We had a single torch between us, just as Laura and I had had when we walked through the forest looking for Alina. This path was wider—was in fact an unmade road—but everything else felt the same. I had come full circle: back to the beginning of a journey I hadn't wanted to go on. Tonight, one way or another, that journey would end.

The torchlight traced patterns in the trees. I saw faces there: not animals or monsters or witches, but people. Women and children, their mouths twisted into screams. Black eyes focused on me. I thought I could see dead babies hanging from the branches. Imagined children peering from between the trees, whispering.

Go back. Go home.

I stopped, paralysed by fear, my legs refusing to do what I told them. I heard another noise that sounded like a growl. It faded to a whisper, and that was worse.

Edward put his hand on my shoulder.

I cried out.

'Daniel, calm down. It's OK. We're fine. You can do this.'

I nodded. I could. I *could* do this.

We continued along the path. It curved to the right and as we rounded the bend, Edward said, 'There it is.'

The house loomed up out of the darkness, glowing faintly in the moonlight that bathed the clearing now we were free of the trees. Once again I was thrown back to the events of last year. The big difference was that this time I had come prepared. I had a kitchen knife in the inside pocket of my coat, which I hadn't told Edward about, sure he would try to stop me. I had my phone too, fully charged, though when I looked at it I saw that the signal here was extremely weak, just one half-bar, and no 3G.

We walked between two crumbling brick walls into the court-yard of the house, where a black car was parked.

'Can you hear that?' I asked.

He nodded. From high above came the faint sound of a crying baby.

I peered through the car's window and quickly called Edward over.

'That's Laura's,' I whispered. There was a hair scrunchie lying on the back seat. Laura's poppy scrunchie.

'Are you sure?'

'I'm certain. I was with her when she bought it. She wears it all the time.'

The baby stopped crying.

'I think we should call the police.'

'No. We don't have time.'

He took a deep breath. 'OK. Right. We can't just go up and knock on the door. Let's go round the side, see if we can find a way in.'

We crept along the edge of the house and found a pile of firewood logs stacked up on an apron of concrete along the wall. Above them was a small window with a rotten frame.

'Let me take a look,' Edward said. He climbed onto the woodpile and grabbed the windowsill, straining to peer through the window, to shine the torch into the dark interior. I put my hand on my chest. I couldn't believe my heart could beat so hard or so fast.

'I can't see any—'

His words were cut off as the log on top of the pile wobbled and suddenly the whole stack toppled from beneath him. I jumped out of the way and Edward clung to the sill, his legs dangling two feet from the ground. The logs rolled to the concrete with a series of loud bangs. Edward held on for a few seconds, then dropped, falling onto his side before pushing himself up and inspecting his fingers. The torch rolled away towards the grass and blinked off, leaving us in the pale moonlight.

Edward shook his head. 'I'm going to call the police. This is ridiculous.'

He took out his phone and began to dial.

Distracted by this, I didn't see the man appear around the corner from the front of the house. By the time I noticed him, and realised it was Gabor, he was raising the shotgun he held and pointing it at us.

'Edward!' I shouted.

He looked up from his phone just as Gabor fired his weapon.

Edward twisted as he fell to the ground. He didn't make a sound. I froze for a second, watched Gabor point the shotgun towards me, and somehow managed to make my legs work. I dived to the right, away from the house, the second blast of the shotgun reverberating in my ears. I lay in the mud, a few feet from where Edward lay. He wasn't moving. I saw Gabor walk towards us, reloading the shotgun as he came, a grim expression on his face. I scrambled to my feet and ran towards the back of the house, certain that I would at any second hear another blast, feel the lead in my back.

I turned the corner of the house and saw a small coal shed on the edge of the lawn. I ran towards it and ducked behind it, crouching in the overgrown grass, peeking out towards the house as Gabor came around the corner, looking left and right.

'I can see you,' he said. 'Come out. I won't kill you.'

How fucking gullible did he think I was? I scrabbled in my pocket for my phone and, using my body to conceal the light from the screen, checked if I had any signal. Still half a bar. My hands were shaking so much I could hardly hit the numbers on the screen. Nine. Nine.

'Drop the phone.'

I looked up. Gabor stood over me, the shotgun barrel a few inches from my face. My thumb hovered over the final nine.

'Drop the phone *now*,' he barked, jabbing the gun at me. 'Now!'

I did what he said. He stamped on it, cracking the screen.

'Stand up. Hands in the air.'

Again, I did what he told me. The knife was in my inner pocket but even if I was fast enough to grab it without getting shot, what could I do with it? My kitchen knife against his shotgun. I might as well have been carrying a teaspoon.

He smiled now. 'I'm actually glad you found me. You're the final loose end. The last one who knows anything about my son and our business.'

I stared at him.

'Except you don't know all the details, do you?' He shrugged. 'Sorry. You'll have to die without knowing the full story.'

He pointed the shotgun at my face.

I held up a hand, as if I could stop a shotgun blast.

'Where's Laura? What have you done with her? And baby Oscar?'

He grinned, if you could call it that. It was the grin of a crocodile looking at a wildebeest.

'Don't worry about them.'

He steadied the shotgun again. I cringed, waited for the blast. But he hesitated, as if he were savouring the moment. Could I extend that moment, keep him talking, get to the knife in my pocket and surprise him?

'Please,' I said. 'Just answer one question.'

He nodded, the shotgun barrel still trained on my face.

I sucked in a breath. 'The photos. Was that you? When did you take them?' My hand crept towards my pocket.

Another nod. 'While Alina was having her passport checked. I snuck in, saw you were snoring like pigs and took a couple of snaps with my phone. I sent them to my son so he'd know who exactly he was looking for.'

'But why show me those photos?'

He shrugged with one shoulder. 'I was trying to flush out Alina. I thought you would tell your girlfriend about it, that the two of you would figure out that Alina was back. Help lead me to her.'

My fingers brushed the edge of my pocket.

'Why did you delete the photos?'

'Because it amused me, Daniel.'

I pulled out the knife and lunged at his leg. He dodged it easily, stepping aside and kicking at my hand and sending the knife skittering away. He laughed.

'It's a shame we can't talk for longer,' he said. 'I've seen and heard about some things I'd love to tell you about.'

He pointed the barrel of the shotgun at my face.

I closed my eyes. I was going to die. Worse, I had failed to save Laura and Oscar.

I deserved this.

Chapter Sixty-One

P ull my boot off,' Alina said as soon as they heard the old man's footsteps recede down the staircase. 'The left one.'

Laura laid the now-sleeping Oscar gently in the cot and did as Alina asked. It slid off easily and Laura was thrown back to a moment in the past, finding this very boot lying on the path among the trees.

'Now pull out the . . . the inside part.'

'The insole?'

She nodded as well as she could. Laura hooked her fingers around the edges of the insole. It was still warm and emitted a faint, unpleasant odour. It made a ripping noise as she pulled it out. Behind her, Oscar stirred in the cot but remained asleep.

'Be careful,' Alina said. 'Under the insole should be a small piece of metal.'

Laura tipped the boot up gently and felt something drop into her palm, then bounce from her grasp and drop to the floor.

'Fuck!'

'Please, Laura, you have to find it.'

Laura dropped to her hands and knees, peering under the bed. She spotted the piece of metal straight away. Her heart thumped as she reached beneath the bed to retrieve it, gripping it firmly between forefinger and thumb. 'I got it.'

Alina exhaled.

'What is it?' Laura asked, standing up. The object was the shape and size of a small key, but without teeth, just an oval head and a long flat stem.

'It's called . . . I don't know the English word. A *șaibă*. You need to unlock my hands first. Hold the round part and slide it into the cuff, where the teeth are.'

Laura knelt on the edge of the bed and leaned over Alina. She took the cuff in her hand and inserted the *șaibă* into the space between the teeth and ratchet.

'Now, push down on the teeth as if you are tightening the cuffs, and push the *șaibă* in at the same time.'

Laura did this and, to her amazement, heard a click.

'Now, undo it.'

She pulled the cuff open, freeing Alina's left arm.

'You came prepared,' Laura said, as she moved around the bed to work on the other handcuff.

'It is the first thing I bought when I came here. I spent months chained to a bed. I was never going to risk that happening again.'

'I'm so sorry,' Laura said, her voice cracking. 'I . . . we thought he shot you as soon as we left. We tried to report it but . . .'

'I know.'

'The old man . . .'

'His name is Nicolae Gabor. I found his name on some papers in the house. Along with the names of all his victims. All the women he and his son raped and murdered in that place. They are here now, with us. Urging me on.' Her eyes glinted.

Laura looked at the air around Alina. She nodded. 'I can feel them.'

'I have the names of all the babies too, the families they sold them to. It's in my back pocket. Take it.'

She lifted her bottom and Laura plucked a crumpled sheet of paper from the back pocket of Alina's jeans.

'Look after it, Laura. It's the only chance those children have for justice. Promise me.'

'I promise.' She hesitated. 'I'm so sorry. That we left you there, in that house. With *him*.'

Alina shrugged. 'His son was worse.'

Laura shook her head, continuing to work on the cuffs. This one was awkward, refusing to open.

'I'm glad I went to that house,' Alina said.

Laura gaped at her.

'They'd have gone on doing it if I hadn't.'

Laura saw it then. Yes. They had been meant to go to that house. She went back to work on the cuffs.

'When I think about how close we came to *not* going there.' Alina shook her head. 'Gabor gave Dragoş hell about almost screwing it up. I heard them.

'We made the first part of it easier for them. Dragoş was meant to intercept us at the station, pretend to be a helpful stranger or force us to go with him at gunpoint, I don't know. But he was slow. By the time he got going, we were already walking along the tracks towards him.'

The second cuff clicked open and Alina rubbed her wrists. Laura handed her the *şaibă* so Alina could work on her ankle cuffs herself.

While Alina worked, she said, 'If I hadn't gone into the woods, I guess he would have intercepted us on the tracks, at the closest point to the house. That's when it started to go wrong. He grabbed me, took me back . . . Gabor was furious that Dragoş didn't just leave me there, tie me up and go straight back to you. But he was over-excited, started tugging at my clothes, telling me all the things he was going to do to me. He was never that talkative again.'

The third cuff clicked open and she moved on to the final one.

'He was so busy taunting me that he didn't hear you and Daniel enter the house. You know what happened next. But he didn't tell his dad that you were ever there, that you escaped. Too ashamed. Gabor believed that you must have thought I'd run off, and that you didn't know the house existed. When Dragoş eventually told him the truth Gabor went crazy. I heard him beating Dragoş. He was screaming at him, saying you and Daniel could have gone to the international police. But you didn't, did you?'

Laura closed her eyes, shame washing over her.

'Because you'd been and gone and weeks had passed by the time Dragoş told him, Gabor assumed they were safe.'

'I have poison,' Alina said, looking Laura in the eye. 'Cyanide tablets.'

'What, like a suicide pill?'

'Or murder.' Alina paused and looked at Laura intently. 'I planned to give them to you and Daniel.'

Laura stared at her. Alina continued to work on the final cuff.

'Gabor was right. I wanted to punish you for leaving me behind, for not going to the police. The real police, I mean. Not that shit, Constantin. And also . . . I couldn't bear the shame. You knew what had happened to me. I didn't want anyone to know about it. I thought if I removed everyone who knew of my ordeal, I would be free. I could start . . . fresh. Be born again. You understand that, don't you?'

The two women locked eyes.

'My plan was to kill you and Daniel, then go back to find Gabor.'

'So why didn't you do it?' Laura asked, her voice shaky, as Alina unlocked the final cuff, then reached for her boot and pulled it back on.

'I was going to. But then I saw Gabor. At the hospital.'

'What?'

'He was looking for you. He got your name from Constantin, didn't he? I think he must have been following you, hoping you would lead him to me.'

Laura shook her head. Of course, she had known Gabor—the devil, as she called him then—had been watching her. She remembered the day she had almost fallen under the Tube train, sensing somebody watching her on the street. Had he pushed her? Or was that Alina? She was too frightened to ask.

'We were all watching, all circling each other,' Alina said, reading Laura's mind. 'When I saw Gabor, I became fixated on killing him. I thought if he kept watching you, if he stayed around, an opportunity would arise for me to get him. But then Camelia fucked everything up.'

Because, Laura thought, when that woman had kidnapped her, tried to get information out of her, she had forced Gabor to act. And when he took Laura back home, he finally drew Alina out of hiding, as he must've known he would, and grabbed the opportunity to take them both. With the baby as a bonus.

She was about to speak when she heard another bang in the distance. A gunshot.

Alina jumped off the bed and ran to the door, trying the handle even though she knew it was locked. She dashed over to the window, tugged at the planks that were nailed to the window. They didn't budge. These had been nailed tight.

'It might be the police, come to save us,' Laura said, aware that her voice was shaking.

Alina ignored her. 'We have to get out of here. Maybe we can start a fire and burn the planks away.'

'What? Are you insane?'

Alina turned to her. 'Yes. We both are, aren't we?'

Laura didn't know what to say to that. To her relief, Alina quickly gave up on the idea of starting a fire and moved over to the door. She stood facing it for a moment, then lifted her right leg and slammed the sole of her boot against the door handle. The door shuddered in its frame.

'Hold onto me,' Alina said. 'From behind, so I don't fall.'

Laura hooked her arms beneath Alina's armpits and put one leg behind her to make herself more steady. Alina lifted her foot high and again kicked at the door. The force almost made the two of them topple backwards. Laura leaned forward against Alina's back, providing more support. 'Try again,' she said.

Alina lifted her foot again and slammed it with all her strength into the door.

Chapter Sixty-Two

Gabor stood over me, his finger twitching on the trigger, relishing the terror in my eyes. This was it. I was dead. Behind Gabor, Edward lay motionless on the ground. I closed my eyes, wished I believed in God and Heaven and that I was about to go somewhere better.

A crashing sound came from the house. Gabor looked over his shoulder and I opened my eyes, grabbing the opportunity to roll away. He turned back and fired, but only kicked up a great gouge of earth beside me. He swore and opened the shotgun, feeling in his pocket for more shells.

I threw myself at his legs, rugby-tackling him to the ground. He still held on to the gun but it hung open, the shells falling to the grass. He kicked me on the underside of my chin, then kicked again, connecting with the side of my head. I fell flat in the dirt, pain exploding in my skull, and Gabor pushed himself to his feet, then bent over to grab the dropped shells. He muttered to himself in Romanian.

I lifted my head and saw a black-clad figure run around the corner of the house, barely visible in the moonlight, heading towards us. I blinked, unsure if I was hallucinating, if the blow to the head had damaged my brain. It was Alina. She dipped to pick something up as she ran and trod on a stray twig, which cracked. Gabor, who had finished loading the shotgun and snapped it shut, whirled around just as Alina reached us, but Alina was already swinging the rock in her hand with all her weight behind it. The sound it made as it connected with the side of Gabor's head was dull and wet.

He bent over, staggered but did not fall, and then Alina brought the rock down again, using both hands. I heard his skull crack, a loud, splintering sound. He fell forward onto his belly and Alina used her foot to roll him over. He was still alive. He tried to speak, but made a whimpering sound instead.

Alina held out the rock to me. 'You want to do it?'

From behind her, I watched as Laura came around the corner, walking slowly, a bundle of blankets in her arms. The bundle made a noise and I realised it was Oscar.

'Daniel?' Alina asked. 'You want to?'

I shook my head.

'Your choice.'

She held the rock in both hands and slammed it down on Gabor's face.

'For us,' she said.

She brought the rock down again.

'*For us.*'

And again.

I looked away, trying to tune out the sickening crunching noises. I focused on Laura coming towards me, and I had tears in my eyes, tears of relief. She was alive, the baby was alive. And so was I. Laura stood beside the coal shed and stared at me. I couldn't read her expression but could see tears shining in her eyes.

Beside me, Alina dropped to her knees besides Gabor's body. She reached over and took the shotgun from his limp hands. She held it out to me and, still kneeling, looked up, her face glowing white in the moonlight.

'I killed your friend,' she said to me.

'My friend? For God's sake, he wasn't my—'

'Jake. I killed your friend Jake.'

I gave my head a shake, unable to take in what she'd said.

She offered me the shotgun again and, without thinking, I took it.

'I pushed him from that bridge. I knew you had told him about the forest, about what happened to me. I was watching you. I was going to kill you next. Gabor, then you, then Laura. You left me in that place, left me to die. I came here for revenge. I am Mirela.'

I couldn't speak. Mirela? What the fuck was she talking about? I didn't even care that she said she'd come here to seek vengeance against Laura and me. All I could think about was that she had killed Jake.

'But you two don't deserve to die. You're good people.'

Behind her, Laura took a couple of steps closer. She said Alina's name but the Romanian woman ignored her.

'I hated you for leaving me in that house. But I understand why you did it, and I don't blame you anymore. You did what you had to do. And now you have to do one more thing.' She gestured towards the gun in my hands. 'I want you to kill me.'

Laura said, 'No.'

'I killed Jake,' Alina said. 'I waited for him on the bridge, pretended I was going to jump. He climbed up onto the railing to pull me down. He offered me his phone, said I could call somebody, that I just needed someone to talk to. And as soon as he gave me his phone, I pushed him. I watched him fall, and I ran away, left his broken body lying there. Sent a text to the last person who'd texted him.' She looked into my eyes. 'So now you have to kill me. I deserve to die.'

'Daniel, don't,' Laura said. She was shaking now.

I could picture what Alina had described. Could see Jake, good-hearted Jake, trying to help this distressed stranger. He would have had no idea who she was. I could see his body on the road below. My best friend. A young man on the cusp of achieving everything he'd ever wanted. His future stolen away by this woman.

Hands trembling, heart thumping, I pointed the gun at her.

'Do it,' she said. She smiled and stretched her arms wide. 'I am ready to join my sisters.'

'Daniel,' Laura said. 'Don't. Don't do it.'

My finger trembled as I caressed the trigger. Tears splashed down the front of my shirt. Beside me, I was aware of Gabor's body, his face a bloody mess of smashed bone. Alina closed her eyes, a peaceful smile on her face, as if she were facing the sun. In the distance I could hear police sirens. Somebody must have heard the gunshots and called them. The sirens grew louder, closer. I steadied the barrel of the gun. Alina had not only killed Jake and Claudia, she was responsible for Edward's death too.

And I understood her motivation. When she was dead, there would be no one left who knew about that night in the forest, who had witnessed what Laura and I had done—and hadn't done. Only Laura and I would remain. Everyone I'd told was dead and Ion didn't know what had happened after we were thrown off the train. Alina was the last one. With her gone, we could go back to normal, pretend none of it had happened. The earth would be scorched, the forest burned to the ground.

As if from a great distance, I heard Laura say my name. The sirens were very close now.

'Do it,' Alina said.

I squeezed the trigger.

Part Seven

London
January 2014

Chapter Sixty-Three

I rang the bell and waited to be buzzed in. It had been raining since Christmas and I stood here now during a rare lull in the downpour, watching ominous black clouds heave into view like battleships.

I didn't care about the rain. I had my life back.

As soon as I entered the office, Sophie gave me a hug.

'You've had the decorators in.' The last time I had seen this office it was ablaze.

'Yeah. The skinflint in there has even promised to let me buy some art for the walls.' She stepped back and looked at me. 'So, how are you doing?'

'I'm OK,' I said.

'Great. And . . . how about Erin and Rob? I saw them the other day, actually, wheeling Oscar in his pram around the park. I recognised them from the newspapers.'

'They're all right, I think. Still shaken by what happened, but obviously massively relieved.' Sophie handed me a glass of water. 'They're not really talking to me. But I've got to go round there later, help Laura move her stuff out.'

'Oh?'

It was my turn to smile. 'She's moving back in with me.'

Sophie clapped her hands together. 'Thank fuck for that.'

'Yeah, we've decided . . . well, she's decided to give it another go. I never wanted us to be apart in the first place. But Laura and I have got so much history together, and we never stopped loving each other.' I paused. 'We're seeing a therapist together now. He says we have to accept that what happened to us is part of our history. That it's something we went through together. And now it's over, we should be able to move on. Though I think if he says "closure" one more time I'm going to jump over his desk and thump him.'

She laughed.

'So,' I said. 'How is he?'

Sophie didn't get a chance to answer.

'I'm fine. No thanks to you.'

Edward stood in the doorway of his office. I was relieved to see a small smile on his lips. He moved towards me, still moving tentatively. The shotgun blast had struck the left side of his chest but missed his heart, damaging the ligaments in his upper arm. He had stirred moments after I had shot the already-dead body of Nicolae Gabor and dropped the shotgun, having refused to grant Alina's wish. I couldn't kill her.

Then the police had arrived, two cars screeching into the courtyard, officers jumping out and trying to process the scene before them. The ambulances arrived minutes later. It was blurry in my memory: the journey to the hospital to be checked over, the questions from the police, seeing my own name flash on the TV screen in the ward as reporters tried to make sense of what had happened.

Over the coming days, the papers and news websites had been full of the story. Profiles of Nicolae Gabor, history lessons about 'Romania's dark past', stories about Eastern European drug dealers on the streets of London, babies for sale, a heroic private detective who had uncovered what was going on and who was now recovering in hospital from a shotgun wound, the boyfriend of the kidnapped woman who had disregarded his own safety to save her and the missing baby . . . There was an operation going on in Romania right now, too: the police were excavating the grounds around Gabor's house, digging up the bodies of women and babies. Plus they were trying to track down the babies who had been sold, using the list Alina had given Laura; a debate raged in the media, both local and international, about what to do. Some of these children were grown up now, and all of the natural mothers were dead. But the couples who'd bought them had broken the law . . . It was a mess.

But the police and the media didn't know the whole story.

They didn't know about Alina, who had slipped away into the forest as the police sirens grew near.

When we were questioned, Laura told the police that she had taken Oscar out for some fresh air and Gabor had grabbed them both. She told them what he had planned to do to her and the baby, how he planned the re-start his baby-farming operation here in England. And I took the 'credit' for killing Gabor, said that I had picked up the rock and struck him with it when he had pointed his shotgun at me. That I had hit him again, and again, and then picked up the shotgun and shot him, just to make sure he was dead.

I hired a lawyer and there was talk of criminal charges, arguments about whether I had used reasonable force with the rock, about what should be done about the wildly gratuitous shotgun blast. In the end, I think the Crown Prosecution Service took public opinion into account. It would be a waste of taxpayers' money to charge me for the murder of a baby-abductor and mass rapist.

The police knew about Alina's camp in Erin and Rob's garden but Laura denied that Alina had been with her that night, said that she hadn't seen her for days. I had been worried that the police might analyse the interior of Gabor's car, or the room in which he'd chained Alina to the bed. But with the old man dead, with Oscar recovered, and with Laura sticking to her story, they had no real reason to dig deeper. The case was closed.

'The phone's been ringing off the hook since I came back to work,' Edward said.

'Well, you're a hero.'

'I don't know about that.' He gestured for me to join him in his office. I sat opposite him.

The clouds I'd seen outside drifted across the sun, dimming the room.

'Have you heard what happened to Ion?' I asked.

'He's gone home. Deported.'

I nodded slowly. 'Good.'

'He and I were in the same hospital. A different ward, but . . . he came to see me. He'd seen the reports on TV, wanted to talk to me about it. He's either a great actor or he was genuinely regretful about what happened. He said it was just about money, about trying to create a better life. I think he comes from a pretty impoverished background. And he's not the brightest spark.'

I made a noise in my throat. I found it very hard to be forgiving, poor upbringing or not.

'Anyway, he did tell me one interesting thing. He said that he's pretty sure Camelia was in league with Gabor. He thinks the old man persuaded her that he would be able to find the drugs.'

'And she gave him the keys to my flat?'

'That's what Ion thinks. And it makes sense.' He stared at the surface of his desk. 'And then Gabor killed her.' He looked towards the window. 'Alina's still out there somewhere, isn't she?'

'Maybe.'

He gave me a curious look. 'Do you think she's gone home too?'

I had thought about this a lot. There was part of me that thought she was still in England, could feel someone watching me sometimes. But when I turned around, there was no one there. Then I imagined her going back home, to work on her graphic novel, to try to live a normal life again. Or maybe she had gone travelling, had reinvented herself. After all, she was free to start again. Nobody knew about her involvement, nobody knew where she was.

When Alina had handed me the gun and ordered me to kill her, I had pictured Jake's face, had felt the anger and hatred fill me up. I'd almost pulled the trigger.

But there had been so much death already. And, despite what she'd done, even though I hated her for killing my best friend, Alina had suffered more than most of us could imagine. And she'd just saved my life. So I'd aimed the gun at the person who truly deserved to die. In the moment I pulled the trigger, I imagined he was still alive, begging for mercy. And I had unloaded the shotgun in his face.

Why did I let Alina vanish afterwards? Why not tell the police about her? Because of Laura. She begged me not to tell the police about Alina. She said she didn't want her to be punished. But it was also because Alina knew exactly what had happened in that house. If Alina was questioned by the police, there was a chance it would all come out, become public knowledge. Neither of us wanted that. So even though I wanted Alina to be punished for stealing Jake's life, I acquiesced. But I made it clear to Laura that if Alina ever turned up again, I would have to tell the police. There could be no more secrets, no more lies.

'I really don't know where Alina's gone,' I said, answering Edward's question.

We sat in contemplative silence for a minute.

'So you and Laura, eh?' he said eventually. 'That's great news.'

'Thanks.'

'You're lucky, Daniel. But make sure you look after her, all right? Here's my advice: She wants to travel first class, pay for first class.'

I laughed. 'Don't worry.'

He laughed too and winced, holding his upper chest. 'God, it still hurts.'

'You need a holiday.' I checked my watch. 'I'd better get going. It's been great to see you. I still . . . You need to let me know how much I owe you.'

'A million pounds.'

'Well, if I sell this new app I've started working on . . .'

He smiled. 'Honestly, you don't owe me anything. Buy Laura a present or something.'

'Thanks, Edward.'

I could tell he had something on his mind, something else he wanted to say.

'What is it?'

'Just . . . This whole thing with Gabor, what he did. You know, I used to think when people talked about evil, about how some human beings have that inside them, that it couldn't be true. That it was just a way of describing behaviour most of us don't want to analyse too hard. You know, it's kind of an easy way of explaining things. He's evil. She's evil. Like that nurse who's been in all the papers, the one who was convicted of killing all those old people, who's been released because of a mix-up with the DNA. I used to roll my eyes when the media said she did it because she was evil. But now . . .'

'You believe some people are born that way.'

He grimaced. 'I don't know. But it's keeping me awake at night.'

We shook hands and I went out into the rain.

Chapter Sixty-Four

I walked to Erin and Rob's, oblivious to the weather, thinking about what lay ahead. I knew it wasn't going to be easy and straightforward with Laura. We weren't going to skip into the future, holding hands with a Disney soundtrack swelling around us. We were going to have to work at rebuilding our relationship, to get back to a point where What Had Happened didn't sit in the room with us like a snarling demon. I knew people whose relationships had been rocked by an affair and they had never been able to get over it fully. The cheater tried too hard; the cheated couldn't forget. We couldn't be like that.

Rob greeted me at the door and nodded tersely.

'How's Laura?' he asked.

'She's OK, thanks. Her dad seems to be making a swift recovery.'

'That's good.'

We stood awkwardly in the hallway. Last time I'd been here, this space had been full of bodies and fear.

'Where's Erin?' I asked.

'Taken Oscar out to the shops. She's still . . . affected deeply by what happened. She won't let Oscar out of her sight for a second.

He sleeps with us in our bed now, and she wakes up four times a night to check he's still there.'

'I'm sorry, Rob . . .'

'But I suppose I should thank you for finding him. And the police told us Laura looked after him, kept him warm.'

'She did.'

He sighed. 'We don't hate you, Dan. It's just . . .'

I put a hand on his arm. 'It's all right, mate. You don't need to say it.'

He cleared his throat. 'Right. Well, you know where Laura's room is. How are you going to get the stuff home? Do you need a lift?'

'No, I'm going to call a cab. There's not much.'

'I'll leave you to it, then.'

I went up the stairs and into Laura's room. The bed was unmade because Laura had left in a hurry yesterday after hearing that her dad had suffered a heart attack on the golf course. It was a minor cardiac arrest, but Laura had immediately decided that she needed to go and see him.

'They're still my parents,' she said. 'And maybe it's not too late to try to make them understand how badly they treat me, the way it makes me feel. Plus I'm going to quite enjoy lecturing him about changing his bad habits, eating better, giving up the cigars and taking up proper exercise.'

As she was leaving for the train, I told her that I would come here and pack up her stuff. 'So you'll be moved in when you get back.'

'You can't . . . You don't have to do that.'

'I want to.'

'But I'm not sure I want you going through all my stuff.'

'What do you mean?'

'You know, like my underwear and everything. And you're really bad at packing . . . It will be totally disorganised and messy.'

I kissed her. 'I'm not that bad! I promise not to rifle through your undies. I'll just chuck everything in bags and you can sort it out when you get back. OK?'

She still looked worried, but her train was due in an hour and she didn't have time to argue any more. As she was leaving, she put her arms around me.

'I love you,' she said. 'And . . . thank you.'

'What for?'

'For not telling Edward the truth about what happened at that house.'

I pulled her against me. 'You don't need to thank me, Laura. Anyone would have done the same.'

She touched me face. 'They wouldn't. And that's why I love you.'

'Your secrets are safe with me, Laura,' I said. 'All of them.'

She frowned and pulled away, leaving me a little confused. But I had let it go.

There wasn't that much stuff to pack up, mostly clothes and cosmetics, a few books, a hair dryer and her iPad and its charger. There were a couple of bottles of wine which I decided to leave behind. I wasn't drinking at the moment, was giving my liver a chance to recover after all the abuse it had suffered. It was proving to be easier than I'd thought.

Laura had brought everything here in holdalls, which were folded up under the bed. I took them out, placed them on the bed and began to fill them, putting the heavy items in first, then the clothes. I found a photo of the two of us Blu-tacked onto the back of the wardrobe, which made me smile. We had our cheeks pressed together and were squinting a little at the sun. I untacked it from the wood and set it aside and sat on the bed for a moment, remembering our drunken encounter in this room.

We had first slept together again after Jake's funeral, back at my flat—which would soon, again, be our flat—the kind of sex in which you cling to each other, the room shaking from the release of emotion and stress and pain. Intense, powerful sex that lasted all night, the kind we'd had when we first met and fell in love.

The cremation had been, in one way, wonderful. Full of people who loved Jake, music playing, a huge turnout. A celebration of his life. At the same time, though, it was terrible, one of the worst experiences of my life. I sobbed as his body slid beyond those velvet curtains while Laura sat white-faced beside me. Since then it had been announced that Universal were going to release an album of tracks he'd already recorded. 'It's what he would have wanted,' everyone said. But that was bullshit. What he'd wanted was to be alive, to sing those songs to audiences, to feel the applause. What was the point in posthumous glory? But I didn't say this. I kept quiet.

I forced myself to stop thinking about Jake. Today was meant to be a happy day. A day for positive thoughts.

I emptied the chest of drawers from the bottom up: T-shirts and vests, then tights and leggings and jeans. Finally, I came to her underwear drawer. I laughed at the thought of her saying she didn't want me to rifle through it. It wasn't as if I hadn't seen it all before. Still, Laura was a private person. She wasn't the kind of person who sits on the toilet while her partner is in the room.

I scooped up an armful of bras and knickers and, as I carried it over to the bed, something dropped to the floor. It thudded on the carpet and bounced under the chest of drawers. I stooped to pick it up. It was an iPhone.

That was weird. Laura had never had an iPhone. She didn't like Apple products, had lectured me about how their treatment of workers in China was abhorrent. Why did she have one?

I put the phone into a holdall and carried on packing up. Half-way through, Laura called me to tell me she was heading home early, that she was already on the train. Her dad was fine. And she wanted to be at home, with me.

I was about to ask her about the phone when we got cut off. I guessed her train had gone into a tunnel. I shrugged. It wasn't a big issue. I would ask her about it when she got home.

I smiled to myself. Home. Our home.

The very best place to be.

Epilogue

Laura sat on the lid of the toilet, trying not to think about a different train journey. She held the white plastic stick between forefinger and thumb, hardly daring to look. It could be stress that had made her period so late. Stress and worry and the fear that she lived with now. Or maybe she would be lucky.

Maybe here was the good fortune she didn't deserve.

After Jake's funeral, she and Daniel had gone back to his flat together. They had ended up in bed. She could hardly remember the details of the night, except that she had cried after they'd made love, and Daniel had held her and told her this was their second chance. That had made her cry more. And then he'd told her he had lied for her.

'What do you mean?' she asked, her voice loud against the silence of the night.

'When I told Edward what had happened at the house, I changed the details.'

She sat up, staring down at him, pulling the quilt over her chest. 'But . . . why?'

'Because I wanted to protect you, Laura. I didn't want him to think badly of you. I don't want you to think badly of yourself. We were out of our heads. Another day, it could have gone as I told him it did. And in the end, we both ran anyway.

'What did you tell him?'

'I told him it was you who grabbed the baby. I said it was you who insisted on taking the child from that room.'

As he talked, it all came rushing back for Laura.

Daniel descended the staircase with the baby under one arm and the candlestick in the other, Laura behind him, barely able to make her legs work, only able to continue because he urged her on.

She begged Daniel to hand the baby over to Dragoş, to do what this terrifying man with the gun said. But Daniel thrust the baby into Laura's arms so he could strike at the monster with the candlestick.

'I told Edward and Jake that Dragoş grabbed you, that I was forced to choose between you and the child.'

'But that never happened!'

She closed her eyes, saw it all. How, even though she was the one who had insisted that they go into the house, as soon as she was confronted by the horrors of that upstairs room, her courage had evaporated. Daniel became the brave one.

While the two men squared up to each other, Laura panicked. She pushed the baby into Dragoş's arms. And she ran. Out the door. She fled for her life, and Daniel had no choice but to follow her, to leave Alina and the baby behind.

And then came the gunshots.

It was all her fault. She had abandoned them. She was the coward.

Afterwards, the shame had driven her mad. She, Laura, the woman who had dedicated her working life to helping children, who'd had such a terrible childhood herself, had failed the test. In those moments, her own self-image had been destroyed. Her confidence, her belief in herself—ruined. Consumed by guilt and shame, she had been unable to live with Daniel, because now he knew who she really was. He was kind, said it didn't matter, that she had just been scared. That most people would have done the same thing. But his words had no impact. She had failed herself, failed Alina, failed that poor baby and the women upstairs.

She had begged Daniel not to pursue it with the police afterwards. Daniel had wanted to follow it up later, despite being convinced that Constantin was corrupt. Laura had persuaded him not to. He told her that it didn't matter, that no one would judge her, but he didn't get it. He didn't understand. She judged herself. And she didn't want anyone to know what she'd done.

When she found out that Daniel had been speaking to his therapist about their experience, she was mortified. What if he told her everything?

But then the therapist's house had burned down. It was like the gods were protecting Laura.

For a short while, Laura thought the problem had gone away— until Daniel texted her to say he'd spoken to Jake. Laura was horrified, panic-stricken. Mad, frankly. There was no denying it. She imagined Daniel telling Jake everything, what she'd done. Now, not only did Jake know about her failings, know that she was a coward, a murderer by proxy, but he was the worst possible person for Daniel to tell. Jake was a gossip, never able to keep anything juicy to himself. Oh Jesus, what if he wrote a song about it? Or spoke about it in an interview?

The whole world would know who Laura really was.

That night, after Jake's funeral, Laura lay in Daniel's arms and told him she was shivering because of the cold and the emotion. He was so happy that night, ecstatic to have her back. And he was convinced she would be pleased with him, grateful that he'd changed the story when he spoke to Edward.

'What about Jake?' she asked, not daring to look at Daniel as she spoke.

'Oh. I only got a little way into telling him, up to the point where we heard the baby crying, and he rushed off. He . . . he was dead before I could tell him anything else. But I would have told him the same version I told Edward. I hope you weren't worried about it.'

She wanted to scream at him. Why hadn't he told her that at the time? Why leave her to think he'd told Jake everything? But she couldn't scream, couldn't say anything at all.

Because Daniel could never know what she'd done.

⌣

Shortly after receiving the message from Daniel telling her he was going to talk to Jake, Laura went out into Erin and Rob's garden. Alina glimmered between the two apple trees, camouflaged by shadows. Not a ghost, Laura knew that now. Just a woman. A woman who had come here to avenge what she and Daniel had done.

'Something has happened,' Laura said.

She told Alina about the message she'd just received from Daniel.

'You need to go and see him,' Alina said. 'Talk to Jake. Beg him to keep it secret.'

So she had set off straight away. She was hurrying towards his flat when she saw him ahead of her, on Thornberry Bridge, heading home. She caught up with him, called his name. He stopped. It was late and there was no one around.

'Laura? What are you doing here?'

'Hi Jake.'

He swayed a little and she realised he was drunk. He laughed. 'Oops, a bit tipsy. We had champagne. Lots of champagne! I think they're going to sign me, Laura. After all these years, I'm finally going to make it.' He moved to hug her but she backed away.

'How can you bear to hug me?' she asked.

'What?'

'Daniel told you what happened in Romania.'

He was so drunk he could barely stand up. 'Yeah. Romania. Fuck, Laura.' He stared at her. 'You know what I think? That whatever happened, you shouldn't have run off. He's a broken man, Laura.'

This came like a slap in the face, but he was right. There was no end to the damage she had done, the damage she would go on doing. Before Jake could react, she climbed up onto the railing, staring down at the traffic below, wondering how long it would take to hit the asphalt below.

'What the fuck are you doing?' Jake asked, climbing unsteadily onto the railing beside her. 'Whoa!' he said, looking down at the road below. He sat down on the thick ledge that ran along the top of the railing, his back to the road. Laura sat beside him.

'You can't ever tell anyone,' she said. 'I need you to promise me that you'll never tell.'

He stared at her. He looked ill. Oh God, it was because she made him sick. A blast of cold air hit them and they both swayed. Cars rushed beneath them, almost drowning out his words. 'We need to get down, Laura.'

She didn't move.

'Please, Laura.'

'Promise me!'

'Yeah, of course, my lips are sealed. Scout's honour.'

But his eyes shifted, the way someone's eyes shift when they say 'I love you' and don't mean it. And she knew in that instant that the secret, her shame, was not safe with him.

He took out his phone saying he was going to call Daniel, and she snatched it from him. That was the last thing that could happen. More pain, more hurt and confusion for Daniel. No.

There was a temporary lull in the traffic; the lights must be red further along the road.

'Swear on your niece's life. You will never tell.'

'Laura, that's ghoulish. That's terrible. No, I'm not going to swear on Cleo's life—'

She pushed him.

She looked at her own hands. Looked over the edge of the bridge, saw his body lying on the road. Not hers. Too cowardly to join him, and unable to bear the sight of what she'd done, she turned and jumped down from the ledge onto the pavement.

She was a killer. A coward, a liar, and now a murderer.

The skin that had grown back was not the old skin. This was her new body and there was no wall of silk to hide behind.

And he'll never tell, she thought. *Nobody will ever know the real you.*

Hands shaking, looking left and right to check there was nobody coming, she quickly typed out a message to Jake's sister:

I've decided I can't go on anymore. Everything is hollow and not worth fighting for. I'm sorry. I hope you don't think I'm a coward. Please give Cleo a big cuddle from me. I love you. Jake xxx

She sent it and hurried home, tucking the phone into her pocket. She needed to get rid of it because, if she was found with it, everyone would know she'd been there when Jake died. She couldn't throw it away now though. It would have her fingerprints all over it. She would dispose of it later. For the time being, she needed to hide it.

Now, of course, she knew that when Jake said 'You shouldn't have run off' he meant that she shouldn't have split up with Daniel. But how was she supposed to have known that at the time? Why couldn't he have been clearer? When he had looked ill, it was because he was drunk, not because she made him sick.

She stared at the pregnancy test, still waiting for it to develop, and tried to remember what she'd done with the phone. The days following Jake's death were so blurry. She had lost her mind for a while, until the night Gabor abducted her and Oscar.

Somebody banged on the door of the toilet just as the result appeared on the test. She stared at it, hardly able to breathe.

I don't deserve to have a baby, she thought. *I don't deserve happiness. A coward, a liar, a murderer. What kind of mother would I be?*

'Are you coming out of there?' The woman's voice was shrill, desperate.

'Yes, hang on.'

She flushed the toilet and opened the door, trying to ignore the way the woman tutted at her as they passed. In her pocket was the pregnancy test, complete with two lines, a positive result, and as she walked back to her seat she made a decision.

She was going to be a mother now. She had to put this behind her. She could never let Daniel find out what she had done. When Alina had lied to Daniel about killing Jake, she had gifted Laura the freedom to go on. Laura could learn from that, and from the way Daniel had lied for her too.

It was time to shed her skin again. To shed the killer's skin and start afresh.

There would be no more cowardice, no more lies, no more fear. As soon as she got home she was going to tell Daniel the good news about the baby. Their baby! What they had wanted right back at the start of all this. He would be so happy. They were going to be a family. And she made a vow to herself. She would never confess. Daniel could never know what she'd done.

She found her way back to her seat, saw the inspector coming towards her and took the ticket out of her purse, smiling sweetly as he stamped it, trying to ignore the way the air shimmered behind him, the crack she'd tried so hard to seal splitting open again, evil pushing through into the world. She closed her eyes, counted to three and forced herself to open one eye. The crack was gone.

For now.

She had one other secret, hidden here in her bag. It had arrived in the post a couple of days ago, with a French postmark. It was issue two of a comic book called *Mirela*, drawn by hand, just thirty-two pages long. But those thirty-two pages told a familiar story: two couples meeting on a train, a black-clad girl being taken captive and subjected to unspeakable things, then her escape and, finally, vengeance. Laura had raced through the pages until she found the scene in which a young man falls from a bridge. The reader doesn't see the hands that push him, just the terrible look on his face: the shock, the realisation.

In another frame, Alina had drawn the heroine cradling a baby, both of them staring defiantly at the reader. Laura took the comic out now and turned to this illustration, looked at the baby, ran her finger over it.

She laid her hands on her belly and a tear trickled down her cheek, attracting the attention of the woman opposite, who offered Laura a tissue. Struck by this gesture, by the kindness of strangers, Laura began to cry, then sob, then howl, until everyone in the carriage was either staring at her or huddled around her, trying to comfort her. The train moved on through the oblivious countryside, gliding into a dark tunnel. Laura braced herself, eyes shut tight, waiting to re-emerge into light, and at that moment she remembered, with a sickening lurch that had nothing to do with the motion of the train, what she'd done with Jake's phone.

THE END

Letter from the Author

Dear Reader

Thank you for reading *Follow You Home*. I love hearing from readers and can be contacted in a variety of ways:

Email me at markcity@me.com;
Find me on Facebook.com/vossandedwards;
Follow me on Twitter with the username @mredwards.

Please note, the rest of this letter may contain spoilers, so please don't read it until you've finished the book.

Like my previous novels, *The Magpies* and *Because She Loves Me,* this novel was inspired by something that happened to me when I was younger, an experience that I took and turned into something much scarier in order to entertain my readers.

When I was nineteen, my then-girlfriend and I scraped together our pennies so we could go Interrailing around Europe. We spent months planning our itinerary, intending to enjoy a whistle-stop tour of the Continent that would last the entire summer. The budget was tight but we were going to have the time of our lives.

Three days into the trip we took a night train south to Avignon. We went into a private compartment and shut the door. Exhausted after a day trudging around Paris and a sleepless night on a noisy campsite, we fell asleep. When we woke up, the pouches we wore around our necks, which contained our Interrail tickets, passports and money, had been stolen. We ran up and down the train but, of course, the thieves were long gone. The reality of the situation sank in as we arrived in Avignon at dawn. Interrail tickets are not replaceable. Our Grand Tour was over before it had begun.

We hitch-hiked to Marseille to obtain documents that would allow us to travel back to the UK, arriving late in the evening. We spent the night lying on the floor of the train station, drinking water from the taps in the public toilets, with no food . . . (I hope you have your violins out.) At one point, a shifty man approached and asked us if we would like him to buy us a hot meal . . . We refused and hid.

Deciding to make the best of the situation, we hitch-hiked home, Marseilles to Calais, 663 miles. It took two weeks. And apart from the nights spent lying beside the autoroute, the rides with men who fortunately didn't turn out to be serial killers, and an unfortunate incident with a packet of laxatives on a campsite near Dijon, we had a great time.

When we got home, the English papers were full of stories about French bandits gassing tourists on night trains, sending them to sleep so they could steal the passengers' possessions at their leisure. Though this may have been typical British paranoia about the French.

I do hope that this book does not put anyone off visiting the beautiful, historic country where it is partly set. The bad guys in this novel are as fictional as the vampires of legend. Or to put it another way, monsters don't only live in faraway forests. They are just as likely to live next door.

But please, if you find yourself in a train carriage far from home, whatever you do, don't fall asleep. And if you ever happen upon a creepy house in a dark forest, take my advice.

Run.

Thanks again for reading.

Best wishes,
Mark Edwards

Acknowledgements

I am extremely lucky to be surrounded by a small but perfectly formed support team who help me write and edit my books and get them into the world.

Chief among these is my beautiful wife, Sara, who yet again did all the really hard work (taking care of our three kids) so I could hide away and write this book, allowing me to get away with saying 'I can't help—my brain is in a forest in Romania' when she called me with news of the mayhem at home. Sara also read this novel before anyone else and made numerous astute suggestions as always.

This is my fourth solo book with Amazon Publishing in the UK and I am grateful as always to the tireless and enthusiastic team there, including Emilie, Sana and Neil. Thanks too to David Downing, my editor, for his insight, honesty and wit.

Thanks to my agent, Sam Copeland. Somebody should buy him the PlayStation 4 he craves. He's worth it.

To Louise Voss for patiently waiting for me to finish working on this book while we were meant to be writing our new one together.

To the author Helen Fitzgerald for her extremely helpful advice that rang in my ears as I was writing this book.

Two characters in this book were named after readers who won this dubious privilege in competitions on Facebook: Sophie Carpenter and Alina Ghinescu. Alina also helped me by reading the manuscript and checking the Romanian sections for accuracy.

Thank you to Jonathan Hill who answered my pharmaceutical questions.

Thanks to everyone at Latuske's café in Wolverhampton for providing me with fuel for my writing: the best scrambled eggs and coffee in the West Midlands (and possibly the world).

Last, but most importantly, thank you to the many readers who have contacted me over the last couple of years, via email, Twitter and Facebook. Your kind words kept me going when I thought I would never get myself or my characters out of that dark forest . . .

About the Author

Mark writes psychological thrillers. He loves stories in which scary things happen to ordinary people and is inspired by writers such as Stephen King, Ira Levin, Ruth Rendell, Ian McEwan, Val McDermid and Donna Tartt.

Mark is now a full-time writer. Before that, he once picked broad beans, answered complaint calls for a rail company, taught English in Japan and worked as a marketing director.

Mark co-published a series of crime novels with Louise Voss. *The Magpies* was his first solo venture and topped the UK Kindle charts for three months when it was first released. Since its success, the novel has been re-edited and published by Thomas & Mercer on 26 November 2013. *Because She Loves Me* is his second spine-tingling thriller.

He lives in England with his wife, their three children and a ginger cat.

He can be contacted at: markandlouise@me.com
Twitter: @mredwards
Facebook: www.facebook.com/vossandedwards

Download a Free Story by Mark Edwards

Consenting Adults

A new short story featuring private detective Edward Rooney from *Follow You Home*.

Set shortly before the events of *Follow You Home*, Edward Rooney is hired to find a missing Belarusian woman who was working illegally at a hotel in London.

Has she run away with her boyfriend—or has something far more sinister happened to her?

Download now at www.markedwardsauthor.com/free